Of Earth and Sky

We Are Gods
Book One

Lee Nash

DEDICATION

To all those who believe, when some of us can't.

Other books by this author

We Are Gods

Of Time and Space
Of Might and Magic

ACKNOWLEDGEMENTS

These things are never easy, and never done alone. I would sincerely like to thank all those who helped along the way. Sibel, first and foremost, for always encouraging me to just get it out there, and giving me a great first edit. Also, to Erich and Meegs, for the valuable input that helped me to rethink some small aspects of the story. Every bit makes a difference. Thank you.

Part
One

~ Origin ~

Chapter One

Deidra had been on Io Station for four years now, and the navigation of the corridors came as second nature. It left her mind free to wander. *Conspiracies around every damned corner.*

At twenty-four she'd graduated from Harvard with a PHD in Astrophysics and a degree in Quantum Tech. She'd then gone on to MIT where she'd obtained degrees in computer programming and Quantum mechanics. By thirty she'd been scouted by the Allied Terran Forces Technology and Defence Division, and by thirty-one she was head of their quantum research facilities, working with all kinds of physicists to come up with new and improved ways of employing quantum tech.

Five years ago, Heinrich Faets, working under her in the Paris Institute, had come up with an extraordinary equation. He'd never liked her much, and the feeling was mutual, but she admired his brain.

It was all about the frequency generation, he'd told her. They'd just have to learn how to control it. If she would only take his proposal to the board.

She had. And, after reading the hypothesis, had requested to be a part of the project. It was exciting and impressive with so much potential, and she truly believed it was something they could achieve. But she hadn't expected them to make Heinrich the man in charge. No one who had actually met the man would see him as a leader.

She stopped in the dooryard to Lab One, just shy of the Comms Room.

Heinrich stood over the primary console, fingers tapping on his tablet. She wasn't sure whether to back out slowly or move to the secondary console.

"I take it you are here to go over the calculations?" Heinrich's question settled it; she moved to the console.

"Beats lazing about with Dee and Dum," she answered as she retrieved her own tablet from her coat pocket.

He made a couple of adjustments to his console. Her suspicious mind wanted to double check his work.

"I take it you are doing the recalc?"

"Yes, I too loathe the life of the lazy."

"Any foreseeable problems for stage six?"

He looked up at her. His light grey eyes pierced through a veil of messy, grey-streaked, dark blonde hair. For a moment, she didn't think he was going to answer. But then, he snapped his gaze away, and the words he spoke had the sound of a speech well-rehearsed. "While I feel little concern about the Tachyon Frequency Generation, I am somewhat baffled by the readings on the light-speed propulsion device."

Deidra frowned. She'd designed and built the chip for that device herself. Had built the whole damned system! If there had been an error in the calculations, she'd have known before now. Her eyes narrowed. "What's the reading?"

"One quarter over."

Her eyes bulged. Her growing suspicions temporarily overcome by alarm. "One quarter over! That could be a disaster!" She moved toward the glassed off section of the lab, heart a lump in her throat. But Heinrich caught one of her sleeves.

She turned.

"It can't hurt," he said.

She looked up, into his eyes, searching for something that would make her believe he genuinely meant it. While inside, her mind screamed that it most certainly would not be alright. The power requirement was already higher than she was comfortable with. Twenty-five percent over that? She choked back a shudder.

Deidra yanked her coat sleeve from his light grip. She spared a single glance for the room beyond the glass, but the unspoken threat that loomed within the older scientist made her move toward the corridor. She turned right into the hall, then left into the first doorway.

If she was right, it would not be long before he made his report to the Earth Base. He disliked having others around when he spoke to the Board, and so she had planned to eavesdrop. Heinrich had always given her an uneasy feeling, and the closer they got to stage six testing, the more suspicious she became.

Like the rest of the station, the comms room was devoid of anything that resembled beauty. No pictures, no ornaments, no vases with flowers, or posters with motivational support. Just unrelieved white walls, white tiles, grey benches and consoles, with black, unpadded swivel chairs that had been bolted into floor. Anything that could undermine the uniformity at the station had to be relegated to personal quarters. One of the many nonsensical rules that Heinrich enforced.

The main comms console was at the rear of the room.

Deidra searched for inspiration. There wasn't enough space

under the desks for her to hide and she wasn't about to crawl into the vents. That left only the storage closet. *Not exactly the most original place to hide, but at least I'll have a good view of the screen.*

With determination she opened the door to the tiny room and squeezed inside. It was uncomfortable, cramped, and smelled as sterile as a hospital. The minimal light that filtered through the small vents in the door showed the shelves to be empty.

She momentarily questioned her own sanity. Was she simply being paranoid? Was her time on the station without sunlight and greenery having an effect on her mental well-being? She knew it was entirely too possible, but she pushed the thought away, certain that Heinrich was hiding *something* from her.

As she'd predicted, not long after she'd settled in, Heinrich entered the room. His demeanour screamed arrogance, even when he was alone. Tall, lean but muscular, aged but not elderly, with a stride that projected confidence.

Deidra scowled from her hiding place as he took his seat at the console. *I know you're up to something, old man, and I am going to find out what it is.*

She made her breathing silent, became still as a statue, and watched the man make his weekly call through the vent of the storage room door.

A military man popped up on the screen. Deidra frowned. The ATF Research Division was meant to be wholly civilian.

"Dr Faets," the man said. "What is it?"

Heinrich made a single sharp tap on the console. "I was expecting the General." There was a painfully long pause while they waited on the initial lag adjustment.

"He's a little busy. You got me. Make it quick."

"We're almost ready for stage six testing," Heinrich told him.

Like fucking hell we are! She thought in alarm, fighting the urge to burst out of the closet and contradict the scientist.

"Hold off on that. Orders from the General."

"We are running fine. All tests are confirmed," Heinrich assured. "Why would we put a halt to things now?"

The Colonel glared through the screen. Evidently, he did not like Heinrich, either. "Because you were told to," he replied. Heinrich remained silent. "Not good enough for you?" The Colonel looked somewhere off screen and gave a nod.

"Very well," the Colonel continued. "We have a fleet arriving in orbit around Io as we speak. They're there to combat the Ganymede Incursion, so no, they cannot go elsewhere. Your base is safe ground. You need to cease all testing until after they leave."

"If I must," Heinrich grated out.

"You must." The Colonel's tone held a note of finality. There was a moment of silence between them, then the Colonel cut the line.

"*Scheiße!*" Heinrich hammered the console with a fist, hard enough to shake the screen. "*Du Scheiße! Du verdammter Hühnerleber, gelben Bauch, Arsch Fett Scheiße!*"

Deidra couldn't understand a word — German had never been a language she'd studied — but she could tell he wasn't happy about the delay. *What's the rush old man?*

He visibly calmed himself before he made his way out of the room.

She waited until he'd been gone for a full five minutes before she came out of the closet.

The orders to wait made sense, and not just because they had a fleet arriving — though that was a surprise. But also, more than half the station had gone home on leave, and they were running on a skeleton crew. She wasn't sure how well appraised of the situation the Colonel was, but there would be some serious dangers involved in a stage six test when they were so severely understaffed. They barely had enough to keep things from falling apart. Most of the maintenance crew, all of the soldiers and airman, and half the scientists had shipped off to Ganymede two days ago. If they started stage six now…

You can wait ten more days, can't you, Heinrich? She wasn't sure he could.

~

Their ships were no bigger than Captain Harvey's. Bulbous things, they looked like logs covered in barnacles. Wherever they'd come from, he'd not seen their like before.

"We're now in range," their Navigator, Xavier, informed them. "Controls over to Lance."

"Got it," the Pilot replied.

"Shields up?" Harvey asked.

"Yes, sir."

Annabelle Kristin raised her head from the comms desk. "We have incoming on four channels — MM216, 228, 272 and 274 all requesting permission to engage."

Weiz smiled. "Permission granted."

Kristin pushed down several buttons and scrolled across the screen. "Following on query — all permissions granted. Engage at will."

Harvey kept his eyes up front.

They'd been assigned this mission because they were the closest fleet to Jupiter when the Ganymede Incursion began, less than twenty-four hours ago. An unknown alien force had descended on the moon en masse, destroying two stations and a civilian habitat. A Docker from Earth would have taken eighty days to come out this far. *And so, a six-month mission turns into eight.*

Lance ran his hands over the controls as they made their final approach. The tattooed eyes on the back of his bald head twitched with expression. "We're almost in it," he told them.

Xavier locked off their heading for the return and stepped back from his controls to watch the screen.

Kristin looked back at them. "MM274 reporting; Shields holding, small rounds effective."

Weiz nodded. "Good to know. Relay the message on all frequencies."

Harvey cocked his head slightly to look at the Commander while he kept the forward screen in view. She was short, slim, hair so blonde it was almost white, and crystal blue eyes that looked out of a pale face with intensity. There was a history between them he hoped to revive, though their respective ranks would make that difficult.

"Weiz, I am glad to have you on board for this."

She arched an eyebrow at him. "A rare sentiment, Captain. I am essentially stealing your command."

"It's the company, Commander. And the advantage of hearing orders directly from you." She squeezed his arm. A moment of familiarity.

"You're getting soppy, Captain," Xavier told him.

"You're stealing my lines," Lance said.

"You took too long."

"I was concentrating."

"On what? We haven't engaged yet."

At that exact moment, something struck the ship on the starboard side and Harvey had to dance a step to avoid a collision with Weiz. The lights flickered once, then everything normalised.

Lance flipped a switch and the main screen immediately split into eight. He needed to see where the shot had come from.

"What was that?" Weiz questioned.

Dames' voice cut in over the internal speakers. "I thought you said they were using lasers? The sodding fucktards are using Mini-A's. Couple more hits, the powers out and we're screwed. You better keep us from getting hit, Viatri."

"Thank you, Dames," Harvey said between clenched teeth. He

really did not appreciate the man's language at times. But, he and Walt were the best Gunners in the fleet.

"You know I am good for it, Dames," Lance told the Gunner. "I swing, you hit, that's the deal."

It was Walt who replied. "Always the deal. Keep all your cams on, Eye-Tye, these fuckers move fast."

Lance did not reply to the barb, he just took the controls firmly in hand, and began swift manoeuvring.

Kristin turned in her chair, dark eyes wide. "Mini-A's?" It was easy to forget that she was a new recruit, the way she fit so flawlessly into the team.

"Atomisers," Xavier answered for him with some awe. "Designed specifically to disintegrate the molecular structure of dense materials, tearing them apart, atom by atom. It's completely theoretical on Earth."

"Goes right through the shield, too," Lance said as he pulled sharp to the right, giving Walt and Dames a good shot at two of the alien craft.

Seconds later, the crafts blew apart, a single lick of orange from each the only evidence of explosion, before the void of space doused the flame.

Walt and Dames whooped loudly over the internal speakers. Harvey closed his eyes for a moment.

Weiz breathed in deep. "Relay the message, Kristin."

"On it."

They were in it now. Xavier kept an eye on the secondary screens in case an enemy ship came up on a blind spot. Kristin relayed messages, and Harvey stood back and watched as the battle unfurled.

The alien craft zipped easily from side to side like a feather in a downdraught. They avoided shots with a grace that would have embarrassed a ballet dancer, despite their distasteful appearance. In one section of Lance's view screen, he saw an MM class ship attempt to out-manoeuvre and gun one down, but the sprightly thing stayed doggedly on the ships tail, blasting the ship with lasers until —

The power went out, then came back on. The ship jolted sharply and rattled alarmingly.

Lance swore and thumped his control lever in frustration.

The ship Harvey had been watching was no longer in view.

"MM262 is out," Kristin informed.

There was no time to mourn, however, as five enemy craft pulled into formation on their tail. Lance gave them a good run, but they stayed glued.

"Call for nearest assist!" Harvey barked.

Kristin put the call out with immediate reply. After all, the Commander was on this ship, and that loaned them priority.

Two MM ships came in behind and sprayed the logs with small shells. They each did a small loop, then came in at the sides. Lance pulled up on his controls, hit the rear thrusters, and managed to get in on top of the one in lead position. Walt and Dames got a few shots off before it peeled off and slunk away.

The two ships that had come to their aid peeled off. Harvey lost sight of them, but they had other fish to fry.

A very large, very intimidating, bullet shaped *thing*, was headed directly for them. It fired the biggest laser shots Harvey had ever seen.

Lance dodged them with room to spare.

Harvey pushed down the internal com button on his right cuff. "Walt! Dames! Give me everything you got on that thing. I want it gone. *Now!*"

The Gunners did not bother to reply. As soon as Lance was in a good position the enemy ship was raked by large shells and laser fire. Everything that hit did damage. In moments, the ship came apart. *Far easier than the smaller ships.*

As far as typical Space battles went, this wasn't far off the mark. The enemy was nimble, but they lacked Shields. They had mini-As, but their aim wasn't very good. Like most, a balance of weakness and strength.

The screen was now filled with scenes of space battle. The squat, almost plain looking MM ships versus the barnacled logs. The debris of exploded ships, shell casings, shield flares, laser fire, all hove into view with the destruction of that ship.

Harvey didn't panic. He became calm. Here is where it was. That moment when everything in the universe suddenly became clear. That moment that he lived for and hoped to die in. That moment that always passed far too quickly.

"Take us right into it, Lance."

Weiz and Harvey exchanged looks. She understood that moment, better than anyone he'd ever known. In fact, she'd been the one to explain it to him in words, over twenty years ago when they'd both been pilots.

"Would you like to take the reins, Commander?"

"I'll leave it to you, John." Her use of his first name sent a shiver down his spine.

She hasn't forgotten. He couldn't help but smile.

Harvey returned his attention to the screens. A small wing of MM ships were in a tight circle, nose-to-tail, while they each sprayed the enemy with small weapons fire every time they approached. Other groups had adopted this same strategy, though some, like Harvey, were out on their own.

Lance took them toward one of the tight groups. A pass over to rid them of the vessels that lurked above their position before they came into range.

"This should be over quickly, if things keep going as they are," Weiz commented. "I haven't even had to give orders."

"Don't say that!" Kristin whispered and gave herself a sharp double-tap on the head.

Viatri gave her a quick sideways glance before adding, "This *is* what we're trained for. If you had to tell us to fly, to shoot, to get out of the way, there would be little hope for us all, don't you think?" A tattooed brow arched in their direction.

"How *do* you do that?" Weiz asked with obvious humour.

"If he ain't flying, he's practising those expressions in a mirror," Xavier answered drily.

"Oh, ha ha," the pilot replied, but it was clear his attention was on the battle.

As time wore on, and the battle grew thicker, it was evident the aliens had more up their sleeves than the start had indicated. No matter how many they removed from the fight, more kept coming. If the fleet zigged, the aliens zagged. And they were taking more than a few loses of their own.

"Kristin! Get everyone left standing to reform. I want a wall that starts with us," Weiz commanded.

Kristin relayed the message, and in minutes, those who were not under direct fire, were forming the wall.

"Push forward and sweep," the Commander said.

The MM ships swept forward, at least a hundred of them, filed ten over ten. As they moved, those above came down in front of the row below it until they formed a blanket over the field. Those in range of the enemy took their shots, then ranked up again, and repeated the procedure. Moving fast, they rolled over the enemy with brutal force.

The strategy didn't come without losses, and their own ship was hit more than once. With lasers, thankfully. But as long as it continued to work, they continued to do it.

For the next hour, the battle raged on, tactics relayed and discarded as the aliens came back again and again. Harvey wondered just how many ships they had to throw away. And where they were coming from. He was certain that if the aliens had thrown everything at them from the start, they would not have stood a chance.

The freaking logs just keep coming. He sighed in his mind, but kept his expression neutral. He looked at Weiz. *What do we do?*

"I hope the ground forces are doing better on the Ganymede surface," she told him, just low enough for him to hear.

He resisted the temptation to rub at his eyes. "We can hope."

They now looked upon an entire fleet that outnumbered them three to one. They'd used almost every strategy and tactic at their disposal, and the damage they'd caused the aliens should have routed them. One on one, they weren't much of a match.

In the middle of a reprieve, no one fired. They awaited the order of Commander Weiz.

The logs formed a stationary wall, directly across from their own. Just under eighty ships facing close to three hundred. For the first time in this battle, Harvey wasn't sure how to proceed.

"We can't withdraw," Harvey said.

"No," Weiz agreed. "We can't."

"Orders, ma'am?" Kristin asked. She, at least, did not seem at all concerned about their current situation.

Xavier watched them. Tall, muscular, with dark hair, blue eyes and tanned skin. *The very reason we call him Superman.* Though why he was thinking of it now, he could not say. *Mind on the task, man.*

Weiz took a deep breath. "Last gambit," she said.

Kristin's face drained of colour, and for a moment it looked as if she'd question the order. But she just turned and relayed the order.

Harvey glanced sideways at his superior. *You're sure about this?*

She gave a nod. It wasn't that she could *actually* read his mind, but they'd always had a knack of communicating without words.

When he looked back to the forward screen, Harvey saw that

squads of eight ships were forming into tight circles, much as they had early on in the battle. This time, though, it was not a defence tactic. They were going to rush those alien ships.

Lance fell into formation with the closest group. It was hard to keep an exact eye on things as they stood when one was moving in constant circles, but it was something that all pilots had been trained for, and they knew what they were doing.

"Now," Weiz said.

As soon as Kristin relayed the message, they moved forward as one, each group an eight-pointed shuriken headed straight for the enemy with speed. Each forward pointed ship sprayed a bout of small shells fire, the next ship on point followed with lasers, then large shells, in round.

The barnacled logs dodged and twisted, zig-zagged, swirled, twirled and danced around the fire, but they had to break formation to do it, and once they had, the MM ship formations broke apart, singling out their own targets in groups of two.

Walt and Dames fired on four consecutive targets, while another ship guarded their rear. Each of the alien ships avoided any real damage from the two Gunners, but they'd managed to manoeuvre them into positions where they were easily obliterated by other ships.

While it looked as if things were going well, the truth was becoming evident as ship after ship was lost to a bombardment of Mini-A's. The enemy had used them so sparingly, Harvey had thought they had few to use. Here and now, he was being disabused of that notion.

Another shock was the sudden appearance of a giant ship that now took up most of the view screen, and hid Jupiter behind its massive girth.

Things are not getting better here. "Where the hell did that come from?" he queried no one in particular.

"Your guess is as good as mine, Captain," Lance said. His tattooed eyes were squeezed shut.

He prepared to send a prayer out to the universe, for surely there had come an end. But instead of the annihilation he was expecting, the smaller ships they'd been fighting retreated into the huge spacecraft.

His jaw hung open. The larger ship did not fire. He turned to Weiz to see a similar look of confusion. Then a thought occurred to her.

"Retreat!" she yelled.

Kristin opened the comms and relayed the order.

Harvey took hold of Weiz's hand. She held on. *Son, forgive me for not coming home.*

"The Docker is at Ganymede. They've won the ground," Kristin told them.

"We're for Io, they can swing back and pick us up there." *Not that we're likely to make it.*

Only Xavier eyed them with some understanding, before he turned to his Nav station and settled in the coordinates for the autopilot once they were clear.

They raced beneath the giant ship on a course for Io. Jets of steam pushed out from the ship, and slowly at first, it began to move away from them. Then, with a concussive shock that shook their ship, the giant monstrosity was gone.

Harvey didn't realise that his heart had been hammering a hole in his chest until it began to slow. "Miracles," he murmured beneath his breath.

Weiz disengaged her hand, but shot him a small smile that told him she'd appreciated it. He almost laughed.

"She's on auto," Xavier said. Lance released his controls with a loud exhalation. Io was not far.

"That was —" his sentence was cut short by a wave of *something* hitting the ship. The instruments flickered, died, came back to life; did it all again.

"What the..." Another wave, this one stronger, shook the ship and Harvey fell in a sprawl. Weiz landed on top of him, drove the wind from his lungs and crushed his hip. He let out a sharp yelp.

This time the instruments stayed dead; the emergency lights came on. They drifted.

"Kristin, open the comms," Weiz demanded as she righted herself. "I want to hear what's going on."

Kristin worked over the console at a furious pace. Nothing came through the speakers but an eerie silence.

Harvey sat up with a grunt. He pressed the internal comms button on his cuff, "Walt, Dames, status?"

The speakers crackled, cutting in and out with static. "We're fine," Dames replied. "No screens, and no idea what the fuck is going on, but we're not bleeding or dead."

"We'll count that a win, then, sirs." He turned his body and pain lanced through his left hip. "Kristin, general sweep status enquiry. If that ship comes back, I want to know where it is."

"All ships, status updates. Do we have eyes on? Repeat. Do we have eyes on?" The line remained silent, and after a moment, she repeated the query.

Xavier lurched forward to stand beside Lance. "You need to open her up. I can't direct you without knowing exactly where we are."

"I can direct myself, thank you." But he flipped the switch that would raise the screen visor to give them a direct view. It moved slowly, like the roof of a sporting arena.

Anticipation welled in Harvey's chest as he levered himself to his feet with a wince. He wanted to know what had hit the ship. Why the instruments weren't working.

His eyes stayed on the visor, now three quarters retracted. Xavier turned to them. "This doesn't make any sense." He looked back at the screen. "I don't recognise these stars."

"What do you..." The question stopped in his throat as he saw what was coming up in the lower left corner of the screen. "Lance, give us a south-east tilt, I want to see what that is."

Lance adjusted their heading. The engines were sluggish, but slowly, they came around.

"Uh... I'm not the only one seeing this, right?" he asked.

Weiz looked to him. "I don't think so."

"No, no, you're not the only one," Lance told them. "So long as it's a very earth-like-but-not-earth planet you're seeing, that is."

"That's the one," Harvey murmured.

The speakers blared on.

Chapter Two

Deidra was still trying to decide what to do when Alex walked into the lab. Though Heinrich had not returned since his call, she was still too anxious to make her move. In her imagination, every time she walked into that glassed off section, Heinrich grabbed her from behind. *Because my mind has to go to those places. It's all those B grade horror movies. I should stop watching them.* They were ridiculous, but she found them amusing.

Alex stepped forward, which reminded her of his presence. He looked uncomfortable, grey eyes darting from her to the door and back again. Either he'd picked up on her own anxiety, or he had some problems of his own.

You are not completely powerless, she told herself. *You can change it later. You have time.*

"You've been here all day?" Alex asked, finally.

Deidra cocked an eyebrow. "I don't imagine where else you would think I'd be. It really is very cold outside."

Alex frowned. "That's not what I meant." He looked around the lab again. "Care to take a walk with me?"

Deidra indicated that he should lead the way. She wasn't getting anywhere in the lab, anyway. She kept getting the same readings, and Heinrich had locked off his console, so she couldn't make secondary changes to the calculations without his Security key.

The corridors were empty. Steel grey walls, white doors, mottled white ceilings with large air vents every few feet. Light grey, almost white, metre square tiles covered the floor.

The heel of her boots clicked loud in the deserted hall.

"So, you're conversing with the enemy?" Alex asked after a while.

Deidra blinked. "He's not the enemy, Alex. This entire project is his, so he gets to run the station. That doesn't make him the bad guy." *Even if I have my suspicions. Or... was he even talking about Heinrich?*

"Fine. He's not the enemy, but he's not one of us, either." He stopped walking and faced her. His grey eyes intent on her own chocolate brown.

"And who are *we* that we need a dividing line?" She took a step back.

"Look. There's the authority — Heinrich — and the Citz — us. The Citz don't like authority. It's been that way since the dawn." He shot out a pale hand to take hold of her own, but she sidestepped to avoid it.

Really, she could not understand the point of this exchange, but she'd been baited, and she couldn't back down. "You realise that I am second in command? That by your logic, you do not like me?" She wasn't hurt or angry. In fact, she was sure he was attempting to flirt with her.

"It's not the same," Alex tried to explain.

"It *is* the same, whether you like it or not. Now, enough of this. Why did you ask me to walk with you?"

"I enjoy your company. And I thought that you enjoyed mine."

"You realise that I am engaged?" She had been since the day before her first tour on Io. Dane had wanted a commitment, knowing that long distance rarely worked. She hadn't seen him in eighteen months, but they spoke as often as possible, and he was due to join her on station in ten days with the rest of the replacement crew.

"Does that mean we can't hang out anymore?" Alex looked genuinely confused. Obviously, she had misread what he meant. He turned and began walking again.

She followed him on unsteady feet, a little embarrassed by her assumption. He was a handsome man, average height, lean and trim, blonde and tanned. Not at all her type. He was one of the only other Americans on the Station, and they spent a lot of down time together, so why she thought he was suddenly flirting... She shook her head.

Alex's voice cut through her thoughts. "I don't think you can make the changes. Dr. Faets... I'm not sure you'll be safe."

Deidra was dumbfounded, and this time it was she who stopped. Alex walked on a few paces before he noticed, then came back.

"You know about that?" she queried. "Were you there to rescue your damsel in distress? Did you think it would win you some points?"

He threw his hands into the air. "I didn't mean it like that!"

Why do I keep pushing? "Then how did you mean it?"

"There is no winning with you, is there?"

"That wasn't an answer."

Alex grabbed at his face in frustration and turned his back. He took a few deep breaths before facing her again. "I try understanding, I try humour," he said, quiet but passionate. "I try honesty. But you are determined to take everything I say and twist it into something else. I'm not out to get you. I'm not trying to sabotage you. I am trying to help!"

Deidra took a deep breath then looked to the ground as she expelled it slowly. "I know. I am sorry. I just have a lot on my mind. I think I might be losing it."

"We're all physicists. We understand the theory," Alex assured.

"And you know that the read is a quarter over?"

Alex nodded. "I know. And we can tell the others when they get here. We can tell them and do something about it then."

"It could be dangerous. *Catastrophic!*" She had to let it out. "To have it just point one percent out would shift the calculations monumentally, and without adjustments the results would be unpredictable. But twenty-five percent over? Twenty-five percent! *Anything could happen.*"

"Of this I am aware."

Deidra looked up then, and realised, *He's on my side.* She didn't need to explain. He wasn't trying to stop her. "I'm sorry."

"You said that already." He smiled.

She was about to say something when the ground shook beneath her and she fell into him. She almost laughed as she pushed herself away, an apologetic look in her eyes. But before she could right herself, the place shook again, and they both sprawled to the ground.

Tremors caused by the tidal flux of the moon's crust were not uncommon. The magnetic fields of Jupiter and Io competed at times, but rather than oceanic waves, the entire crust expanded and shrank, rivers of molten lava flowed, and volcanic activity kicked up a notch. But the continuous shake of the station around her felt different. It had been built to withstand the expansions and contractions, the outer walls somehow absorbing the movements.

When Deidra got to her feet, she had to spread her arms to keep from falling once again. Alex rose beside her, his stance a little more graceful.

"We should check this out," he said.

With a nod of agreement, she followed him as they made their way, fast as they could, toward Hangar Bay One. Through the corridors that now constantly shook. That threatened to drive them from their feet at every turn.

There were four geothermal power domes surrounding the Station, and they always needed to be monitored closely. That was done in the offices above the hangar.

Alarm klaxons started to sound. A whooping that drove through the ears and settled in behind the eyes. She was sweating. Her heart beat in her chest like a rapid-fire gun, her breathing became laboured, and Alex steadily pulled ahead. She was not fit, had hardly made time for the gym. She probably could have stood to lose a few, but Dane had never minded.

Why am I thinking of this now? she wondered, and shook her head to clear it of fog and panic.

There was no way to keep up with Alex, but she kept him in view. She grabbed hold of the wall to her left and leaned hard against it to stop her from falling as she moved forward.

The lights flickered. The whoosh of the ventilation system was overridden by sounds like distant thunder, and a deep grinding rumble that made Deidra swallow in fear.

They were close to the hangar now. "Alex!" she shouted over the cacophony. "Alex!" He didn't hear her.

She tried to quicken her pace. To catch up. But her body defied her. She took a step forward and twisted her ankle as the ground moved beneath her. She collapsed into an undignified heap with a yelp that was drowned out by the klaxons.

When she looked up again, Alex was running back toward her, horror on his face as a flow of lava chased him down the corridor. Her mouth moved, a silent prayer. *Dear God, let him make it. Dear God, let him make it.*

The quake intensified, Alex tripped, hopped on a few paces, looked like he would right himself, but instead fell forward, and slid sideways into a wall. He didn't even pause; he climbed to his feet and resumed his headlong run.

It took her some time to realise, as she sat there, numbed of emotion, that if she didn't move, she would be covered in that lava flow in seconds.

Strangely, it didn't frighten her. Rather, the whole scene came at her in slow motion. The creep of the orange glow that streamed ahead of the lava. Alex, as he rose and continued. The explosion that rocked the corridor and bought a ton or more of rubble down on his head. The way he fell forward, onto his side, left arm stretched outward as if it grasped for something to hold to. The complete refusal to give up.

Then, the twenty-inch-thick titanium blast door came down with a sharp *clang*, right in front of her, and it was like the spell broke.

She inhaled a ragged breath. The tip of her left foot was millimetres from the edge of that door. If she'd been one step further along — one step! — she'd have been killed under the weight of it.

"Alex," she gasped. "Alex?" She stretched out a hand toward the door. She knew there was nothing she could do. Knew, as sure as she breathed, that Alex was dead. But a part of her continued to deny it. *"Alex!"*

She had to do something. Logic warred with the denial that swarmed within her. There was no way past this door, and even if she managed to get through, the lava... The rubble would slow the lava, but it wouldn't stop it. The door should. It would be reckless to attempt opening it.

She collapsed against the door, her cheek sliding down the smooth cold surface. *Alex. Alex.*

Hands grabbed her under the armpits from behind and she shrieked. They pulled her upward and she struggled against them. Reached for the door, though there was nothing to hold onto. She kicked out with her twisted ankle and screamed at the pain that shot up her leg. The hands held tight, however, and she was drawn backward into a tight embrace.

A mouth moved down close to her ear. "Calm down, Deidra! It's me, Heinrich. Calm down."

She stilled in his grip. Breathed a few fast shallow breaths then pushed herself away from him. But he held tight and would not let her go.

"There's nothing you can do for him!" he said to her. "You have to let him go, girl."

He continued to hold her to his chest until she'd stilled for a good few minutes. It took that long, at least, before she realised the klaxons were no longer ringing. That the ground was no longer moving.

She looked up behind her at Heinrich. It amazed her that he was capable of acting like a human being, though she did not know why. He certainly scared her, always had, but it didn't mean he wasn't as human as anyone else. And the way that he looked right back at her with honest concern, made her relax. He let her go.

"Are you alright?" he asked.

"I think so." She brushed down her lab coat, covered in dust from the fallen masonry. "What happened?"

Heinrich shook his head. "I'm not sure, exactly. But we can find out in the Storage Two offices. Provided, of course, that wasn't also compromised."

She nodded. The shock had her shaking, but her head was clearing. Storage Two held the backups for the monitoring station. She took a step, and fell to the ground. She laughed. She'd forgotten about her ankle.

Heinrich was by her in a flash. He helped her to her feet. "You'd best lean on me. I'm sure the med labs have been compromised, but there should be packs in the rec."

"If that hasn't been closed off too," Deidra replied.

Deidra leaned into Heinrich's side, while he in turn wrapped an arm around her back and held her upper arms. Nothing in the slightest bit inappropriate. The very thought of it made her shudder a little. If Heinrich noticed, he said nothing.

"You were going to check on the monitors in the hangar?" she asked to keep her mind in the present.

He nodded. "I was. Good thing, too, it seems, or I'd not have come across you." He squeezed her arms gently.

The rest of their short trip through the halls of the station was made in silence. Deidra limped along, a wince for every second step.

When they reached the lift to the Storage Two offices, Heinrich propped her up against the rails and pressed the button marked three, then swiped his card through the slot.

The doors closed quietly. The lift rose without the sensation of movement.

Heinrich had his back to her now, and she grimaced at it. Without provocation, she found she was angry with him. Found herself wishing that it had been *him* who the rubble had fallen on. *Him* who had been trapped in the corridor with the lava flowing inexorably toward him.

The doors flew open, and Heinrich turned to help her. She put a hand on his shoulder and limped forward with a tight smile.

The whole room before them looked like a bomb had hit it. Equipment, broken and shattered, littered the floor of the large office. The red light of the warning system flashed in its circle over the room, illuminating the devastation.

Heinrich stepped out of the elevator, reached to the left and flipped the light switch.

Halogen lights flicked — once, twice — and then remained on with a steady hum. The ventilation whined as fresh air was pushed into the room through crumpled vents.

They both glanced over the scene. Deidra blinked, not sure what to do next. "Well," she breathed.

"Well." Heinrich nodded. He spared her a glance. "At least the chairs are bolted to the floor. I'll take you to one and then I'll see what can be done."

She didn't trust herself to answer.

He settled her into a chair, then turned and surveyed the damage. With a nod, he moved to the wall opposite her, and began picking through the mess on the floor. When his hands were full, he deposited his find onto the bench bolted to the wall, then bent back to the task.

"Where were you when this happened?" she wondered aloud, curious.

Heinrich stopped, turned his eyes toward her, then continued what he'd been doing. "I was in Lab Four," he answered.

She squinted down at him. He was lying. *It doesn't mean anything,* she told herself. *Get your suspicious mind under control, woman. He helped you, didn't he? He's come to see what happened, hasn't he?* Even so, Deidra could not help but be sceptical of her co-workers' motivations.

Heinrich grunted as he sifted through the equipment on the ground. It seemed he'd found an undamaged monitor. "Now let's see what's going on."

He put the monitor down on the bench, took a box from the pile next to it, and swiped his card through it. He punched in a sequence of numbers, and spoke his name. The screen came to life.

Outside, the mostly grey landscape of dried and cooled lava crust that she was accustomed to seeing, was almost completely drowned in a fresh flow of red-orange lava. The screens flicked steadily from one camera to the next as Heinrich pushed a button on the box. A few showed nothing but static. Eventually, they came to a camera that showed them a geyser of lava erupting from a corner section of the geothermal dome closest to Hangar One.

"Will the liquid nitrogen release be sufficient enough to stem the flow?" The alternative was hard to contemplate. She'd spent too long on this project to just have to give it away to nature.

Heinrich, on the other hand, appeared very calm for someone whose life work was in danger of being utterly destroyed. "I should think so," he replied, but kept his eyes on the screen as he flicked through the cameras. "Every corridor released a load of crushed concrete and stone before the blast doors closed. Then, the liquid nitrogen was released through a sprinkler system. The Station was built to withstand something like this. They knew a breach was possible. Even likely, eventually."

"So... you're not worried?"

He looked at her then. "I didn't say that. There just comes a point where you know there's nothing you can do."

"We should probably notify Earth Base."

"We should, yes."

He flicked through a few more images before they got back to the first camera. He put the box down next to the monitor.

After he'd collected her, they made their way to the Comms Room as swiftly as they were able.

She noted as they moved through the abandoned halls, that there was very little damage in this section of the station, and for that she was grateful. She hoped that the others had been at work, as she knew without a doubt that the Scientist Quarters were now behind the impenetrable blast doors. They'd have to do a sweep once her ankle had been wrapped and she had some crutches.

The Comms Room itself was blessedly untouched, and looked exactly as it had that morning when she'd spied on Heinrich. *Was it only this morning? God, Alex.* Her lip trembled and she choked back a lump in her throat. Tears welled in her eyes, and she fought them off. Now was not the time.

A cold flush passed through her, and she felt the sudden need to urinate, which she ignored.

Heinrich sat her down on the chair in front of the primary console. "You make the call. I'll go and find a med pack."

He looked down on her until she nodded.

She flipped on the screen and dialled in the extension for Earth Base on the touch pad.

Nothing happened.

She tried again. Still nothing.

Thinking perhaps the screen was not working, she brought the desk mic to her mouth. "Earth Base, this is Deidra Ward of Io Station, do you read?" She waited a moment, then repeated the query.

Nothing happened.

She traced her hand over the dialling pad and pressed auto. She wasn't supposed to know that there was a Docker in orbit, but if she sent out a general hail...

"This is Deidra Ward of Io Station, does anyone read?"

There was a slight crackle over the speakers attached to the screen, but the monitor did not light up. She was about to try again when a woman's face popped up on the screen. She wore the navy-blue coverall uniform of the ATF AF, with a badge on her left shoulder that showed her to be a Commander, and a badge on her right shoulder that said she was a Colonel in the Luftwaffe.

"This is Commander Weiz," she said in only slightly accented English. "Please report."

"We've had an incident here. The Station is compromised, and we cannot get a connection with Earth Base." She could barely keep the relief out of her voice.

"I'd be surprised if you could," the Commander told her sternly. "Do you have any idea where we are?"

"What do you mean?"

"Have you looked out a window lately, Scientist?" Her words were laced with a contempt that got Deidra's back up. She straightened in her chair.

"There are no windows on this Station, Commander. I suggest you speak plainly."

A man with sandy blonde hair and hazel eyes edged his way into the picture. He had an angry look on his chiselled features, but his voice came out clear and controlled.

"Look, I'm Captain Harvey of Ship MM294. I don't know what you lot are experimenting on, and believe me, I couldn't care less, except that we're clearly not where we're meant to be, and I have to assume that's because of you. So kindly, whatever you *did*, undo it."

A look of dumbfounded surprise flitted across her face as she jerked her head sharply toward the screen. "Excuse me?"

"You don't know what's going on?" He looked to the Commander, who shook her head.

"There was an eruption..." she started but was interrupted by the Captain as he moved his communication device, so it faced the forward section of his bridge.

"Look!" he intoned. "Does that look like Earth to you? Cause it sure as shit doesn't look like it to me." He left the camera in place to make sure she got a good look. She was glad, as at first, she wasn't sure what she was looking at. By the time he brought the camera back to his face her mouth opened and closed soundlessly. She had no idea what had happened...

"*Dear God,*" she exclaimed, breathless. *But even... no. Not possible. It defies physics. Unless — unpredictable. Did Heinrich do this?* Every suspicion, every screaming instinct had told her he was up to something, and here she might be looking at the evidence of it.

The Commander took the camera back after a short, mumbled conversation with the Captain. "Since our Docker is not with us, we're going to need a place to land while you figure this out. We're running low on fuel, and we don't exactly carry rations on these ships. So, prepare for an intrusion, Scientist."

"Doctor," she corrected, absently.

"Doctor, then."

"How many ships?" Her head was swimming, and that need to pee came to the fore with a vengeance that made her squirm in her seat. *Take it for nerves if you like.*

"Current count is thirty-eight." She didn't sound happy about that. "But we're expecting as much as fifteen or twenty more. Not everyone's comms have come back online."

"We..." Deidra cleared her throat. "We — uh — don't have room for that many in the hangar. The main hangar is — well, it's gone."

The Captain took the camera back. "Well how much room do you have?" he shouted at her.

"Enough for five, maybe six. The secondary Hangar is a lot smaller."

"Fine, we'll send in that many. Maybe a crew or two can help you lot get us back to where we're meant to be."

The communication cut out.

Deidra dropped the mic on the desk in front of her and looked around the room sightlessly.

CHAPTER THREE

Harvey rubbed at his eyes as Weiz assigned five crews for Io. The rest were silent over the speakers. Like Harvey, they waited.

"We could land on the surface," Xavier offered.

Harvey turned his head slowly toward the man. "We don't even know what's down there," he said.

"Superman has a point though, Captain," Lance interjected. Xavier scowled at the name, but inclined his head.

"And what is that?" Harvey was getting a headache.

"We have no idea how long those twats on the station are going to take to get things right. And that's assuming they're the ones who even got us here."

"If not them, who? The aliens we were just fighting?"

Lance nodded. "Entirely possible we were swept up in the wake of their retreat. But beside the point." He put his hands up to prevent anyone else from interrupting.

"And you might have been trying to bluff somewhat on the fuel point, but we *are* running low. And that little chickadee didn't seem to have much of a clue as to what's going on. If we can't all go to the station, we need to go somewhere, and we'll have to do it soon or we may not have enough fuel to break atmosphere."

"We don't know what we'd be walking into down there," Kristin piped in. "We don't know if the atmosphere is breathable. If the water is drinkable, the vegetation edible or the locals hospitable. We don't *know* anything. What if it is the alien home-world?"

The pilot shrugged. "Way I see it, we have to take our chances. Damn well looks enough like Earth that I am willing to take the wager on the atmosphere. And the aliens? I'd rather die in a fight, than floating in space twiddling my thumbs."

"Me too," Xavier added with an emphatic nod.

"Settles it then, I suppose," Harvey grumbled. "Hell must be freezing over right now, you two agreeing on something. Weiz?"

The woman next to him nodded slowly. "They have a good point. We'll have the fuel to break orbit if we siphon from other ships, get the crews to co-bed it, so to speak."

Harvey grunted. There were going to be a few pissed off Captains, and a very angry ATF AF General. "And if we stay up here?"

"A day, maybe, before the fuel is out, just making sure we don't drift. Life support could sustain another thirty or so days, but without even basic amenities..." The pilot shrugged. "These ships were never meant for long term engagements. You know that, Captain."

"We'll have to send a scout," Weiz said. "Volunteers?"

He'd forgotten that the Comms were open and on speaker. A hail of replies broke through, each the equivalent of a hand raised.

Weiz seemed to be able to separate the voices, as she called out, "Greenway, you're it. Take your team down and report back A-SAP."

"Yes, Ma'am. We're on it."

They waited.

Captain John Harvey looked at his crew. Xavier Rouse, Navigator, born and raised in Las Angeles, California. Ranked Captain in the US Air Force. Lance Viatri, Pilot, born in Italy, moved to England in his early teens where he spent his formative years before going back to Italy and joining the Air Force as a combat pilot; rank, Lieutenant. Annabelle Kristin, Comms Officer, born and raised in Sydney Australia, unlike most, though, she was a soldier, not an airman. Army rank, Lieutenant.

His gaze shifted to the Commander. They'd known each other for more than twenty years. Had served in the ATF together before they'd had the technology to mount such sophisticated space battles. She was a legend in her own right. She'd been the key figure of a tactical defence that stemmed the tide of the first Alien Incursion of 2421. Had been the Captain of the Series 3 Space craft that had dropped a devastating Imploder Missile on the Alien Mother Ship of 2424. She was instrumental in obtaining an undamaged alien craft during a skirmish in Earth orbit in 2425 that had allowed the ATF RD to backwards engineer the MM craft they used today. And most importantly, to him, at least, she was the love of his life.

Time for introspection always left him thinking of her, and by extension, his wife. He knew that it should have been the other way around, but it had always been so. He'd been married for mere months when he'd met Weiz on their first mission in 2418. They'd known then that what they felt could come to nothing. But now, his wife dead only a year, and he couldn't help but wonder. The guilt of it couldn't stop his mind from planning it all out.

He'd have to resign his commission, but he didn't mind. He wanted to spend more time with his son, anyway. He'd be thirteen in a couple of months, and it was important to give him a father who'd be around. He would not have come on this outer system tour if he hadn't already been contracted before his wife's death. It had been sudden, and he knew, if he'd seen it coming, he would have made different choices.

"You're staring," the Commander told him.

"Thinking," he replied, and pulled his gaze away. She gave him a look that said she understood. "Have they reached the surface yet?"

Weiz shook her head. "They'll call in when they have news."

James Walt and Joseph Dames, American and Canadian respectively. Both ranked Sergeant. Very few people had ever seen Dames, though he had a stellar reputation. He was actually retired from the Air Force, though the ATF decided he could stay on. He'd been wheelchair bound for two years, and adjustments had been made to this ship. Though he no longer needed the chair, the ship had been marked as his. Whoever inherited this ship, inherited that man, and only the Captain would ever see him. Of course, that meant that Walt would come with the ship too. Harvey didn't think he would leave Dames. They were close knit, like best friends, or brothers.

"This is Greenway." The speakers blared, and Harvey jumped before he could stop himself. "Atmosphere is a little thin, but breathable. Gotta tell you guys, it looks a hell of a lot like Earth from down here too. We got trees, grass, blue sky, and a clean water source. Drinkable."

"Send us a heading, Captain." Weiz smiled.

Kristin's console beeped, and she worked her magic on the touch screen. "Navigators, be advised, heading is being forwarded direct to your stations."

Xavier turned to his desk and bent over it. "Ten minutes, at most."

The news was welcome.

"I must say," Weiz breathed, loud enough so only he could hear. "You and your crew are taking all of this damned well. I mean, what if we don't get back? You saw the look on that woman's face when she called in, she had no idea what had happened. Do you think it's likely they'll have a quick fix, there? The equipment could have been destroyed, for all we know, if what she said about an eruption is true."

"I don't know why it wouldn't be," he replied. "And if I am to be completely honest, I really hadn't thought of any of that. And I kind of wish you'd not bought it up." He gave her a wistful look. One that said, *don't worry, I don't blame you and won't hold it against you.*

"Do you think it's occurred to them?" She gestured toward the others with a flick of her head.

"Probably not. Let's hope it takes a while to sink in."

We do have too much faith in those scientists, he thought. *If she was the only one left on the station, we may never get out of here.* The image of his son, the last time he saw him before the launch of the Docker, flashed through his mind like a guilty reminder. *We* have *to get out of this.*

There was some minor turbulence as they entered the atmosphere. The visor, still drawn back, showed a burning aura that encased the ship. The speakers were silent.

When they came in view of the plain, Xavier tapped at his console. "Lance, she's all yours. Heading, straight ahead ten kilometres."

"Thanks, C.K." The Pilot took up his controls, the tattooed eyes doing a dance on the back of his head. They looked toward Harvey.

"Lance..." he warned.

The Pilot laughed. "Sorry sir, I forgot how much you hate it."

"Damned demon eyes," he growled.

It didn't take long before they saw Greenway's ship, parked on the grass of a vast plain, a forest to their left, and a river directly behind them.

Lance eased them in, slow. As he approached the other ship, he banked slightly to the right, did a one-eighty and settled in beside it. "Ladies and Gents, we're about to hit ground level. Please prepare yourselves for a thud." He flipped off the engines.

Harvey nearly had a fit. But then realised, there was no movement. *Oh, Ha. Ha ha.* He was not in a good mood.

"*That,*" Kristin said, "was some smooth landing, Viatri." Her fat lips pursed together, unsure if she should be impressed or angry.

"Ah! Wasn't it though?" Lance shot her a self-impressed grin, to which she replied with a finger. The Pilot put a hand to his heart, a look of mock hurt on his angular face.

"That," Weiz breathed, "had to be the singular softest landing I have ever had the pleasure of experiencing." She looked to Harvey. "Do you have a crew of savants, Harvey? Is there something I should know?"

He gazed at her. She was playing with him. "Would you like to get off this ship?" he enquired.

"Right." The Commander turned to Kristin. "The Comms are still open?"

"Yes, Ma'am."

"Well, then, you all heard that. We're getting off this ship, so if you have anything to say it'll have to wait until after you land." No one replied.

"Let's go!" Harvey ordered, and suited his own words by heading for the outer hatch.

The seriousness of their situation was momentarily drowned out by the excitement of setting foot on an alien planet. Questions of how and when they may get home, pushed aside in favour of the prospect of exploring the unknown.

The air, when he first took a breath, was like that halfway up a mountain. Just a little too much oxygen, it made the head swim slightly, and the eyes water, but it was enough.

Thin. That's what Greenway had said. He hadn't fully

comprehended what that had meant until now.

Behind him, he heard similar in-drawn breaths, as he stepped out onto the grass of the plain.

The ground was oddly firm, the grass itself a mere few inches in length. The gravity seemed a little light. Not as bad as that of Mars, but certainly not as heavy as Earth. Perhaps somewhere between.

"Might make you Superman for real, Xavier," Lance jibed.

"The guy was Kryptonian. He got his powers from our sun, not from gravity," the Navigator rebutted. "And stop calling me that."

Harvey walked behind the back of his ship, the silver-grey hull gleaming in the early morning sunlight of a cloudless blue sky. He looked up. It really was a lot like Earth.

Greenway and his crew were waiting by their own ship, looking directly at them. Or rather, at the Commander. *It's a new situation, and they need to know what to do. They need someone to give them answers, to guide them by the hand. So glad it isn't me.*

He'd been offered Commander by the ATF AF many years ago, several times. But he knocked it back, again and again, and eventually they'd given up on the idea. He was a Captain, and that was as far as he wanted to go. Besides, when they got back, he was going to hand in his resignation.

They approached the waiting party. Grass crunched underfoot, unheard over the landing of other ships.

Greenway was a tall man, matching Xavier for height. Slim, almost to the point of gaunt. His cold yellow-brown eyes looked out of a long face that looked like it belonged to a corpse. Close cropped grey hair stood on end. For all of his appearance, though, he was one of the few captains that Harvey liked and respected.

He nodded his head toward the man as he stopped before him. "Captain," he said.

"Captain," Greenway nodded back. "Commander!" He saluted, as did the rest of his crew.

Weiz saluted, and their hands fell to their sides. "So, I am going to say something rather scary right now. You all know as much as I do."

Everyone looked at her, then at each other and back. For a career soldier, or airmen, it didn't matter if the commanding officer knew more than you or not, it mattered only that they told you what to do.

She sighed. "I'll wait 'til everyone is down and assembled before I start handing out orders."

To suit her own words, she started marching further out across the plain, away from the ships.

"It won't take them long," Harvey said.

"No, I know," the Commander replied.

Lance, Xavier and Kristin had a short conversation too low to hear, before they sat themselves down.

For a misfit bunch, they were very relaxed around authority figures. He'd let their attitudes ride too often, he knew, unchecked and undisciplined. *They do what needs doing when it matters,* he thought. *And they're very good at what they do. Weiz doesn't seem to mind.* But, appearances were everything. If one crew wasn't on top of the game, then others would soon follow their example, and while he knew that his people could get away with it, he didn't know others well enough to judge it.

"Crew," he said, in a low voice. "Were you given permission to sit?"

They looked up at him with surprised faces, then at each other. But it was Lance who replied, ever the spokesman. "Since when do we need permission?"

"Since always, Lieutenant," he glanced at Weiz who looked at him with a straight face. "Now, stand up. All of you. We're not the only ones in this place, or in this mess, and we have to show those other crews that we can follow orders as good as anyone else." They looked at each other again, but the look of understanding crossed Kristin's face first, and she was the one who answered.

"Oh, right, I get it." She stood quickly and motioned for the others to do the same. "At your command, sir!" She snapped a smart salute. He couldn't tell if she was being serious or not.

Technically, Xavier should have been leading these two, as he outranked them, but natural leadership was hard to ignore.

Harvey saluted and Kristin's arm fell to her side. They stood at ease, eyes forward, feet planted, hands clasped behind their backs. He nodded at them. "When we can be seen, we follow rules. You got me?"

"Yes, sir!" They answered him as if he were a Drill Sergeant.

Weiz was amused. He winked at her. She put on a stern face, and he almost laughed, but bit it back.

It was a ludicrous situation. On an unknown planet, in an unknown solar system, with no idea how they'd got there, or how they'd get back. Each of them attempted to be professional and calm, when all they wanted to do was laugh. He could see it in the eyes that faced him.

There was a part of him that understood they were all probably going through the stages of shock. That it might be a while before reality truly began to sink in.

The whine and drone of ships engines still filled his ears, and he knew that behind him the last of the ships were landing. He didn't need to see it. The sound of boots on the grass alerted him to the arrival of another team, and he spun to face them.

Greenway took a single step forward, then motioned for his crew to join Harvey's. They'd file in ranks, it seemed.

"Where are your Gunners, Harvey?" Greenway enquired.

"Still in the ship."

"Didn't think they should make the landing with everyone else?"

Harvey arched an eyebrow at the man. "They did make the

landing. They just didn't get out."

"Point." Greenway smiled, a row of perfectly straight white teeth behind thin lips. "But why are they not joining us, is my question."

"That, my friend, is a question you'll have to ask them."

Greenway barked a laugh. "They're strange ability to remain unseen has become legendary. We've all begun to wonder if they even exist."

Harvey shrugged. "They're real enough. Just shy."

"Shy, is it?" But he left it at that.

Harvey looked over to his crew to see the barely contained amusement on their faces. They had seen Walt and Dames, gamed with them aboard the Docker before the engagement above Jupiter. They understood that it was a game for those two, after Dames had gotten out of the chair.

The sound of engines suddenly died, and Harvey knew with certainty that all the ships that would land had done so. More airmen were coming up behind them, and he saw Weiz rise to her feet.

In all, he could see thirty-six ships. In total, that would be two-hundred and seventeen souls. Not as many as he'd hoped to see, even knowing that five had been called off to help on Io Station. Best case scenario, those that had survived the battle, were still around Jupiter somewhere, likely soon to be picked up by the Docker. *Be glad. They, at least, will get home.* But part of him thought that whatever had happened to get them where they were, those other ships that were no longer with them, had been destroyed, torn apart by the forces that had rattled his own ship.

The procession that marched toward them across the plain had the look of ghosts coming home from war, not yet aware that they had died. Their eyes searched for loved ones, their expressions showed bewilderment and relief, grief and sadness. Absurdly, Harvey played the music of a funeral dirge in his mind as they walked over.

In your mind, they are already dead, Captain. How did that happen? He could not answer himself, and so let the matter drop.

Thirty-four ship captains filed in behind him and Greenway, their crews falling in behind his. All eyes were on Weiz, and the silence deafened. There was an unanswerable plea there that could not be ignored. How do we get home?

"Shock," Weiz began, "is a powerful thing. And I think I speak for everyone here when I say *shock* is what we felt upon realising we were not where we were meant to be. The hows, the whys, whens and wheres, and the what-do-we-do-nows. Except for the last, these are not things I have answers for."

She paused to look over them. All of those people under her command, and therefore, her responsibility. Her face did not change, but Harvey knew her well enough to know what she was thinking. *I have no idea how I am going to get you all home, but I will do my best to keep you alive. And that is a promise.*

"Airmen, these are your orders." Ears pricked up. "I want three teams to stay here with me." She pointed to the back of the captains line. "You, you and you. Gather your crew and meet me back at the ships."

With salutes, the singled-out captains gathered their crews and set out back toward their vessels at a trot.

"Right, I want the next three teams, — captains from the back of the row, as before — to head out north-northwest and get us a lay of the land. If you find food, report back immediately. Go." The teams gathered and headed off at a trot.

She rattled off this order, changing only directions — northwest, west-northwest, west etc. She left out from northeast to east, as in those directions, all that could clearly be seen, was more of the grassy plain. But each team, along with two others, were all assigned.

Captain Harvey was with Greenway, and a short, stocky woman

with dark hair and eyes that matched her complexion who introduced herself as Captain Harley Walters.

They set out toward the forest on an east-southeast approach. The only weapons they had were the small, standard issue, fifteen round semi-automatic nine millimetre, strapped to their thighs. There were a few pulse rifles and laser shooters aboard their ships, but only if the captains had bothered to check that they were stocked. Often as not, they weren't. *We're flight crew, not soldiers.* The thought made him look to Kristin.

"Did we stock any large weapons?" he asked the Comms Officer. She smiled at him. "A few."

Forest creatures beware. We have an Aussie in our midst. This was going to be a long day.

~

Foliage crunched under boot as they entered the forest. The sweet smell of honeysuckle pervaded her senses and made her want to hold her breath. She'd never imagined that she would still be around when other planets were discovered, much less be walking their surface. But what amazed her most, was its similarity to Earth. So much of the flora looked the same, the sky was blue, the sun yellow, and from what she'd seen, had a single moon. What were the odds that some freak accident had delivered them to this place? One in a billion? A trillion? More?

A cough and a sniffle from Lance as he trudged alongside her broke her from her reverie.

"Coming down with something?" she asked.

"Hay fever," the Pilot replied, an unhappy scowl on his face.

Harvey and Greenway marched silently ahead of them. The other captain and her crew had peeled off to the left and paralleled them.

"What are the chances, do you think, of us finding enough to survive on?" Kristin was interested.

Lance opened his mouth to answer and sneezed instead. He was wracked by a string of sneezes that bought him up short for a moment. "God fuck it!" He stamped a boot hard into the ground as he moved forward.

"Think maybe you should head back?"

Lance glanced sideways at her and gave her a cheeky grin. "And be without your fine company, dear Belle?"

She punched him in the shoulder. "I told you not to flirt with me, Viatri."

"Was I flirting?" He put a hand to his mouth, his eyes showed mock dismay.

She hit him again. He laughed.

"I'm trying to think of this as a 'company picnic'." Xavier said behind them. "A chance to get to know the people you're working with outside of the regular environment."

"And that works for you?" Said Lance.

"Not sure yet." He shrugged. "You guys are the only ones talking. Half the others have gone off on flanking trails."

Harvey looked back on them all but kept moving forward. "You know why everyone else is quiet, Nav Man?"

"No, sir."

"Because noise scares potential prey into hiding!" he hissed. "Kristin, take point. Xavier, go to the right and join up with Greenway's crew. Send one of them back here. And the lot of you — shut up."

Annabelle Kristin gave the Captain's back a sloppy salute and stuck her tongue out at Lance as she retrieved her pistol from the thigh holster and moved forward at a trot to take the lead.

This was her first mission with the ATF. She'd worked toward it for most of her adult life. A good way to earn money, get away from her abusive parents, and attempt to give her little brother, Mitch, opportunities she'd never had growing up. When she'd gone to their

Sydney office on her nineteenth birthday, seven years ago, they'd enrolled her in Officer training with the Australian Army and advised her to pick a speciality. She'd chosen communications, and had never looked back.

But this first mission could be your last, she told herself. *What are the damned odds, eh?* She shook her head.

Laid out before her was a forest much like any other. She could have been taking a stroll through the Blue Mountains, or Wollemi National Park. She kept her eyes open, sweeping along the underbrush for signs of game, snakes, scorpions and other venomous creatures. They scanned tree trunks for tusk rubbing or claw marks, and glanced up to make sure they didn't run into spiders or drooping branches.

Her boots hit the ground in almost silent steps as she ranged out further and further ahead. She was ready to prove herself to the Captain. She wasn't just a comms officer. She wasn't just a soldier. She was also a hunter.

~

Harvey watched the girl disappear beyond the trees in front of him and shook his head. First timers always felt like they had something to prove. Some invisible barrier to pass, some imagined competition to win. They held close their feelings of inadequacy, dispensed with their disbelief, and if their superior told them to do something, they went about it with such seriousness and narrow focus that if they failed, they'd never forgive themselves. Some had even been known to throw their lives away in suicidal missions in order to rebalance the scales. Fortunately, that was not a fate he thought Kristin would face.

Gunner Brian was the man Xavier sent as his replacement, and Greenway indicated he should take up position with Lance in the rear, not a word between them.

They walked on in silence for some time. Harvey had to figure that so long as he didn't hear Kristin scream, yell, or see her pop her head up from wherever she was, that the path was clear. The woman hadn't left any tracks!

"Woman's a ghost, Captain," Greenway told him, low enough so that only he could hear, and then, barely.

"So it would seem," he replied in kind.

"It occurs to me, John, that you may have understood our situation better than most. Am I wrong in this?"

He looked at the man from the corner of his eye. People called him Harvey so often that even he had begun to think of it as his name, so it always took him aback when anyone bar Weiz used his first name. When she did it, it just made his heart race.

"Oh, I understand, Aiden."

The Captain nodded and spat off to the side. "Now, for me, I don't know that I mind so much, you know? I haven't quite decided on that yet. God knows I've nothing to go back to on Earth except an empty apartment and bills for things I use maybe three weeks a year." He paused. "But my crew, they got people."

"They got people," Harvey agreed. He knew where this was going. Not one of the captains in this fleet would neglect to think of such things.

"Aye. They got people." His Nova Scotian accent thickened with the build-up of emotion in his voice. "But all my people are here. You get me? The only reason I want to go home is 'cause they want to go home, but I wonder if that is enough for me to pull them through."

Harvey put a gentle hand on the man's shoulder. "I can't say I'm of two minds as you are, Aiden. I have a son to go home to, and that is that. But I'd offer you this; we need food, and we need water. Before any other concerns are these. Concentrate on one thing at a time."

"One foot in front of the other."

And one life at a time. He let his hand drop off the Captain's shoulder. The man's earnest words had made him think of Weiz. She, too, had no one at home. Had such thoughts run through her mind? Was there a part of her that wanted to stay and explore this world? Become a part of it? What would he do if she did? It was not something he cared to consider. *Would my needs pull you through? Will my desire give you strength?* He could only hope so.

Ahead, he saw that Kristin had stopped. She stood in a crouch, facing them as they approached.

"You'll want to see this," she said.

CHAPTER FOUR

Deidra stayed at the console after her conversation with the Commander. She waited for Heinrich to come back.

Her hands shook and she thought she might wet herself if she didn't get to the bathroom *soon*. The news had been a shock. Just one more in a day of them. She couldn't believe that it had only been four hours since she'd walked into the lab that morning and Heinrich had told her of the anomaly.

She drummed manicured fingernails on the desk and squeezed her legs together as she bit her bottom lip. Her eyes watered.

That was it. There was no way she could wait for Heinrich to come back. She had to go now.

She levered herself up and used the chairs as guide rails. As soon as she stood, however, she almost let go, and if she could have, she would have danced on the spot until the feeling passed.

Deidra had made it only a few steps before Heinrich waltzed into the room. When he saw her, he ran to her side.

"Where are you going?"

"I really need to pee," she told him. Despite the urgency, she felt embarrassed at the statement.

He didn't so much as lift a brow. He just took her around the waist, planted one arm across his shoulders, and near carried her down the corridor to the bathroom. He elbowed the door open, found the nearest cubicle and deposited her on the seat.

"I trust you can take care of the rest." He walked away without an answer.

She closed the door.

Somewhat mortified, but oh so sweetly relieved, she breathed a sigh as she finished.

When she was done, she opened the door and hopped to the sink to wash her hands.

Her reflection in the mirror showed a dark oval face with full lips, and frizzled hair coming undone from the tight bun she'd woven it in that morning. She took a moment to plaster the offending hairs down with damp hands. She knew it wouldn't hold, but the illusion was enough.

She found Heinrich resting against the wall as she emerged from the bathroom. His arms were crossed, his head tilted back. He looked weary, and Deidra felt a pang of sympathy run through her.

He's just a man, she told herself. *An old grumpy man, but still just a man.*

When she approached, his eyes shot open. He reached for her then, and as before, just about carried her back to the Comms Room where he'd left the packs that he'd found.

"Nothing grand," he said. "Just a first aid kit and some rations. I won't be able to tell you if it's broken, and couldn't fix it if it was." He looked up with a fatherly smile. "But we have bandages and cream."

He raised her right foot in gentle hands and removed her shoe, a simple black runner that she'd found more comfortable than most others. He placed it to the side, removed her sock, then began wrapping the ankle in a brown pressure bandage.

"What did Earth Base have to say?" he asked as he tended to her.

She'd forgotten that he didn't know. In a rush, she explained what the Commander had intimated. The expression on Heinrich's face was controlled. He didn't give away what he might have felt at the news.

Ankle wrapped, he rested it on the bench beside them and looked her in the eye. "If it is as they say, then we're going to have more than low rations to worry about."

"How do you mean?"

"There's a planet down there."

When it dawned on her, exactly what that statement meant, she clapped a hand to her mouth, her eyes went wide.

Heinrich looked down on her with a wry smile. "We're not there yet."

"No." She swallowed. "Not yet. But how long?"

"We'll have to find out. I need to get you a crutch." He wandered off, and moments later, returned with a broom. He measured it against her height, then handed it to her.

"Not ideal, I know. But it's better than nothing."

She nodded, took hold of the broom, propped the head of it under her arm and stood. The tip hit the ground and she took a few experimental steps. It was adequate for the moment. Enough to get her from A to B throughout the day without having to rely on Heinrich to haul her around, or attempting to hop around on one foot.

"Thank you, Heinrich." It was hard for her to say those words, but not as hard as it would have been that morning.

He gave her a brief nod. "Well. You had best go to the hangar and direct those airmen to where they can best help. Then you can meet me in the labs, and we can work this out." He turned awkwardly, and strode out the door.

Deidra breathed deep. She had to remember her suspicions. She couldn't let his humanity stop her from doing what was right. And the way that he'd looked at her when she told him what was going on with the fleet... *He wasn't surprised. He didn't even blink.* He'd known that something happened. But how could he have known unless he was a part of it?

She made for Hangar Two. It wasn't far, — just across the hall and up five levels to the control room — but she took her time. It struck her as odd that she had yet to see any of the other scientists. True, they were running on a skeleton crew, but the thought that seven other people may have perished in the eruption...

The elevator doors opened with a ping. She blinked into the darkness and stepped forward. The doors closed behind her. She stretched out an arm to her left and felt along the wall until she found the switch. The lights came on.

After the devastation they'd found in Storage Two she wasn't sure what to expect, so when she saw the place was undamaged, save for a single fallen mug — which should not have been there — her lips twitched in a smile. The damage must have been restricted to the area directly surrounding the geothermal dome.

When they were on full complement, all of the offices were manned. Rarely did a thought need to be spared for the way things worked, as there would be *someone* around who could do it, or fix it. So, when Deidra sat down in front of the massive console, and looked down into the dark hangar, her brain froze.

"Uhm..." She looked down at the console, its numerous buttons, levers and sliders. It was stupid to assume that there would be a singular on switch that would take care of everything. No. She would need to test everything, one at a time.

"Lights," she murmured to herself. She swept her gaze over the console, back and forth, before she found a row of yellow buttons each marked with a number. If she were a designer of such things, that would be the colour she'd use for lights. She pressed one.

The floor lights on the furthest end of the hangar came on. A dull orange glow that would have been barely enough to see a hand in front of one's face. But, they were there so the pilots knew where to land. She pressed the buttons consecutively, without removing her hand from the board. All the lights came to life, like the stroke of a painter's brush.

That done, she had to think for a moment. The roof was closed. But, she knew that there would have to be some kind of atmospheric re-pressurisation, and that would not be done in the hangar. So, was that automatic? Or would she need to do something?

"I'd give my left hand for some hangar techs right now." No matter how hard and long she looked over this console, unless some magic instruction appeared, she had no idea how she was going to manage.

"Hangar Two," speakers blared around the room and startled Deidra enough that she almost fell backwards off her chair. She placed a hand to her chest and felt her heart race. *Jesus.* "This is MM238, on approach with four friendlies. We'll be coming in slow, within the minute."

Deidra looked around the room. Directly behind her was a comms station, mic upright in front of a monitor. The screen was not on, so she assumed the communication was audio only. For that, she was glad, she wasn't sure she could live down the embarrassment had the airmen witnessed her scare. She leaned over and retrieved the mic.

"MM238, we have a problem, please advise." She waited.

"What's the problem, Ma'am?" This man's voice was different to the first.

"Well, I don't know how to operate the controls," she said. "We were on skeleton crew when the eruption occurred, and I've no idea where any of the techs are, the buttons and levers aren't marked, and

I don't know where to find a manual. So, I pray that you, or someone out there, knows how to use one of these things and can tell me what to do."

There was silence over the speakers for such a long time that she worried no one would answer. But then, another voice, female this time, came through.

"What does the console look like?" She described it. "Right. Do exactly as I say, when I say it, and do not deviate. At least you got the lights on."

Deidra settled in.

The whole affair took less than ten minutes. A lever on the upper right corner opened and closed the hatch above the Hangar, and one at a time, each ship entered. The hatch was re-pressurised, automatically, and it was the lever next to the other that opened the Hangar roof and allowed the ship to land. After she'd repeated the procedure five times, Deidra felt she could do it whenever the need arose. The last instruction, before she left the console, was to "turn the damned upper lights on so we can see." This done, she moved to the elevator to meet the newcomers on the ground floor.

~

A woman named Captain Jewel Royce was the spokesperson for the ATF crews. She'd also been the one to help Deidra. As they walked the halls of the Station, Deidra explained the layout and what had happened, told them what kind of repairs had to be effected in order to get things up and running again.

"We don't, as yet, know the full extent of the damage," Deidra said. "So, the first thing that we'll need to do is assess what we have, what we can reach, and what we can do with it."

The twenty-nine other crew members shuffled along behind, talking amongst themselves. The corridors, being clear of anything but very minor damage, had them all looking around as if to call her a liar.

Captain Royce either looked ahead, or at Deidra. A Russian woman with dark hair, pale skin and blue eyes, a severe caste to her features and a confidence in her stride. She was almost as tall as Deidra, though she was slighter of frame. Never-the-less, the Physicist found herself intimidated.

"What's the situation on food?" Deidra sensed there was hunger behind that question.

She looked back on the others. *Probably haven't had anything to eat in hours. For that matter, neither have I.* She returned her attention to the Captain. "I'm not sure." She shrugged, and indicated the broom she was using as a crutch. "We really haven't had a chance to find out. Most of the food supplies are usually stretched out between the Mess and Storage Three. It's even odds as to whether the Mess made it through since it's right next to Hangar One."

"And the Storage?"

"We're headed there now."

The Captain gave a sharp nod. "And you don't know how we got —" she made a general all-round gesture with her right hand, "— wherever we are."

Their work was secret. They'd signed contracts that stated the disclosure of any and all information pertaining to the research and testing of the tachyon frequency generation and light speed propulsion devices was punishable by incarceration and hefty fines. So, while she would like to say that she had no idea, she did indeed have some, and she was afraid that showed on her face.

"Not for a certainty," was the answer she gave.

"But a clue?"

She shot the woman a wry smile. "Minimal. And that is honest. But we will work it out, and reverse it if possible. The eruption could have wreaked complete havoc with the instruments. Doctor Heinrich is checking on these things now." They rounded the last corner and were a few strides from entrance to Storage Three.

"This is it?" Royce asked when Deidra stopped.

"Assuming you want to get into the warehouse section and not the offices," she replied. She pointed down the hall to her left. "Elevator is over there, but you'll need a card."

Royce made a gesture with her hand and two of the airmen came forward. Another gesture and they opened the door. Before them was an empty locker room. Nothing was damaged or broken that Deidra could see, mostly because there was nothing in there that wasn't bolted to the floor or walls. Small, numbered cubicles, wooden slat benches to sit on, a fire extinguisher. There was a door to the right of the room clearly marked as toilets, and straight ahead, a door into the Storage itself.

"Are you coming with us?" The Captain queried.

Deidra looked at her makeshift crutch. It had begun to bruise her armpit. If she could sit for a short while, give her arm and ankle a rest, she'd feel much better. But, she knew she should continue on with them. "I've never been in the Storage warehouses," she told the woman. "So, I think I should. You might need my card for something, or a validation code."

"You could just give me your card, tell me the code," she offered.

Deidra gave her a tight smile but did not answer. Instead, she moved forward into the room ahead of the airmen, and was startled by a hand that reached out for her leg from behind the door. She jumped back with a yelp, landed on her twisted ankle, and fell on her arse.

Great. Just fucking great. This is how everyone's day should always *go.*

The airmen who'd opened the door rushed in and grabbed the owner of the hand, while Royce aided her to her feet.

Between them they held a young man in his pyjamas. They were soaked through with sweat, and possibly urine. He wore glasses, and dishevelled blonde hair fell in front of his face.

"Doctor Hans!" Deidra immediately recognised him. "What are you doing in here?"

The young man looked to each of his guards, and then out to the hall at the ATF Airmen. "It seemed like a safe enough place," he breathed, obviously shaken.

"What happened? Where were you? Have you seen anyone else?" Deidra's heart raced, her breath became shallow. She had to know. Their current mission completely left her mind in her urgency to find out about the others.

The Physicist shook his head, mouth opening and closing without sound. His blue eyes stared through the strands of his hair as if looking back on a memory that haunted.

"If he's yours," Royce stated, "then you can take care of him. We'll take our chances without you. If we need a code or a card at any point, I'll send a runner out to you. Is this agreeable?"

Deidra nodded dumbly, still not sure what to make of the man before her.

"Good," the Captain continued. "Where will we be able to find you?"

"The lab across from Hangar Two," she said absently.

Royce made a gesture and the airmen let Hans go. The doctor fell to his knees, but seemed otherwise fine. It was probably just shock. *And haven't we all had our share of that today?*

She made her way to the man and knelt down beside him. The ATF crews filed in around her, and made their way into the warehouse through the door opposite.

"Can you walk?" she asked him.

He looked up at her. "It's over then?"

She nodded. "For the moment, Ulrich." She gripped one of his hands. "Now, you'll have to help me to my feet."

He looked at her broom, then at her wrapped ankle, then up at her face once more. She saw life and understanding return to his shock fogged brain. He rose to his feet in a swift and graceful motion, effortlessly bringing her with him.

Most physicists were in their thirties before they got a job with the ATF RD. Multiple degrees and years in university to become masters in their field, and even then, it required genius. But Ulrich Hans was a Swiss prodigy. Barely twenty-two, he none-the-less had all the necessary qualifications to rival Deidra's own achievements.

"Where are we going?" Clarity and control had returned to his voice.

"You should probably get cleaned up."

He shook his head. "I ran from the quarters. They're not there anymore."

"Perhaps not your own clothes, then. But I am sure there will be crew uniforms somewhere around here. That should do."

Ulrich nodded his acquiescence, and they moved off.

~

Heinrich had his head down over the primary console in the lab, tablet in hand. He muttered to himself in low tones and did not look up when Deidra walked in. She sat herself down in front of her own console and placed the broken broom in a corner.

From her lab coat she dragged her own tablet, to find that the screen was shattered, and the most she was going to get from it was dull light. In frustration, she threw it at the window to the room holding the light speed propulsion device. Heinrich looked around then.

"That will not help anything," he told her.

"I know that!" she yelled, then sobered herself. "It's just one of those days."

He grunted and turned back to his work. "We're still in tachyon frequency," he informed her.

"Excuse me?"

"We're still —"

"I heard you the first time!" She thought she could no longer be shocked. *The read is one quarter over. Don't change it. Oh, I'll make a call to an ATF General and bypass Earth Base regulation. But wait, no, Io wants to explode, destroy half the station and kill some of the crew. Still not enough? Well guess what, there's more!* She grimaced.

"No need to get snappy," the old man said. "We're in tachyon frequency. So is the moon, and the ships that made the trip with us."

"Fan-fucking-tastic," she breathed. Most of the time she deliberately moderated her language, but the more that piled on, the less she cared. "And the light speed propulsion device?" she asked evenly.

"Triggered only for a brief moment."

"A brief moment?"

"Less than a second."

"And we are... Where exactly?"

He turned from his console and looked her directly in the eye. "I don't know exactly. I could guess, but I'd need a Navigator to know for sure."

Deidra squinted at the old man and pursed her lips. Every time he lied to her, he looked her directly in the eyes. As if that would stop her from suspecting something. He was looking her in the eyes.

"I dare say the ATF crews will have one available. How long do we have until we fall into orbit?"

He turned back to the console. "At most, I figure, three days at our current rate of approach. As little as two, if the gravitational pull is further out than we expect. No more or less than that."

Deidra looked around the room. "Do we have any more tablets? Mine was broken."

"And if it hadn't been already, you definitely finished the job." He glanced sideways at her. "I believe there may be a few in the comms room. Filing Cabinet on the right as you walk in. Top drawer."

She made herself get up and retrieve one. When she sat down again, she turned her console on and synced the new device to it.

Readings came through on her tablet screen in a drawl of calculations that she did not completely understand at first. But as she read through it, she saw what Heinrich had been talking about.

Suspicions rose again, but she tried to push them away so she could simply focus on the work at hand. *Why would the man do this to himself? We're stuck out in the middle of nowhere on a moon that could explode.* But still, that little nugget persisted.

"In order to work out how to get back, we need to first work out how we got here." Sometimes she needed to speak out loud while she worked out a theory. "Tachyon frequency was initiated, and the light speed propulsion device triggered for less than a second at quarter over readings. But the time it took for us to get from A to B, was only as long as the light speed was on." She chewed on her bottom lip as she continued to scroll through the readings.

"It may have been longer."

Deidra faced Heinrich, or rather, his back. "How do you mean?"

"While the effect was somewhat like instantaneous travel to us, it does not mean that it *was* instantaneous. Merely that it seemed so." He turned his head toward her. "Even going at light speed, assuming relativity, a trip to the nearest star would take twenty-six years. A known and quantifiable fact, yes?"

Despite the fact his voice had taken on a lecturing tone, she found herself responding as a fellow scientist. "Of course. But would we have not felt that time pass?"

"Not necessarily. Not if the frequency generation caused us, while in movement, to become no more than singular atomic particles. Not rearranged or changed in any notable way, except that they each acted of their own accord, rather than as a conjoined force."

"Or as a complete and defined conjoined force. All of us, who came with the moon and the ships. So, there was no thought of individuality."

"Just so."

"But what if it was instantaneous?" She was curious on the line of reasoning. *He's all too calm about this. I can see it in the way he pours over his work. He's* excited*! He isn't worried about getting home, which means he knows how...* That was the first time she'd had that thought, and it was alarming. She was very glad that he was not looking at her right then.

"Faster than even wormhole travel? Which, by the by, I might add, has yet to be experimented on."

Nah duh! She disliked the way he spoke to her as if she were a child, at times. She had been his superior before this project. *But that does not count, does it?* "Faster," she agreed.

"Impossible," he said with a snort.

"Why?"

"It is *physically* impossible."

"According to math as we know it."

"And according to you?"

"Wormhole."

The man gave her his complete attention. "Do go on," he drawled.

"Well, if our frequency was matched to tachyon, every atom vibrating at faster than light speeds without surcease, it would create perfect conditions for such an event to take place..." *Assuming someone knew how to trigger the event.* She paused as the thought entered her mind. She quickly took up her tablet as if she were looking for something, then put it down before she started up again. "Sorry, where was I?"

"Perfect conditions," he obliged.

"Yes. Right. It would create perfect conditions for such an event to take place, as we'd then be in the quantum world."

Heinrich snorted and turned back to his work. "Such a supposition then requires that every atom thus effected was capable of unanimous movement, through who knows how much space. The theory is flawed."

Deidra shook her head. She was onto something; she could feel it. *And you, Heinrich, know more than you are telling.* But she could not say it. The image of him looking down at her when she'd offered to fix the calculations on the propulsion device played through her mind. The way he'd held her arm, so contrary to the gentleness he'd displayed when tending her ankle.

She wished for the comfort of her fiancé. For the whispered words of encouragement, and the protection of his arms. He would not step down from the man before her. He would voice his objections, suspicions and speculations. He'd not be cowed by the scientist's height and demeanour as she was.

But the truth, hard as it was to swallow, was that she needed Heinrich. More than he needed her. Even if he knew nothing of what happened — of which she was not convinced — he understood the experiment on a more basic level, as it was his creation, even if she did help to make it.

Visions of home swept through her mind. The face of her father, proud and full of joy on her graduation from Harvard. Her mother, on a Sunday afternoon, baking sweet cakes for the children after church. The dry heat of summer spent swimming in her neighbour's pool, and the bitter cold of winters, holed up in her campus dorm studying like a freak with no life, the heater at her feet, a blanket around her shoulders.

She loved her family. Missed them when she spent six months at a time, working here on this station. But now, with the thought that she may not return to them, tears welled up in her eyes.

She grabbed the broom from its perch, levered herself away from the console and departed the room. If she was ever to have a hope of seeing them again, then she needed to find out exactly what Heinrich had done.

It was you, you old bastard. I know it. And I am going to find out how.

CHAPTER FIVE

The trees ended abruptly a few paces in front of them. Beyond them, was a wide expanse of tilled earth that reached into the distance, where a small shambling village of huts lay. Tendrils of smoke that rose from chimneys clawed their way toward the sky in steady streams through the still, humid air. A large bonfire was being built by the inhabitants on the outskirts, tables laden, presumably with food, lined the outer houses.

Kristin looked back at Harvey. "Do we go down?"

Harvey scratched at his jaw and glanced at the man beside him. Greenway had a measuring look in his eyes, like he weighed what could be provided to them by these villagers without cost to themselves. It was a natural reaction for a Captain to have. Had they been on Earth.

Despite his own encounters with alien races, he'd yet to see what a single one of them looked like. He knew that there were some on Earth who'd rummaged through the wreckage of their craft and found what the creatures truly looked like, but he never had. He wasn't sure what to expect.

He found his mind was pulling away from the idea of alien. They walked upright, they were clothed, and they seemed roughly the same height as an average human. They built things, knew of fire, and were organised to some extent or another. Also, judging by the tilled ground, they planted crops. It was this that finally decided him.

He pushed down the comms button on his cuff and hoped that the Commander had set up station on their ship. He was not disappointed.

"This is Harvey, reporting in," he said.

"Good to hear your voice, Captain," Weiz replied, her voice coming through weak over the tiny speaker on his lapel. "What have you?"

"We've found a settlement, Ma'am." He drew his brows down and ran a tongue across his bottom lip. "Permission to approach and assess."

"A settlement?"

"Aye!" Greenway interrupted, louder than he need have been. "Huts, people, that kind of thing. Though we're not close enough to know if they're human."

"Would it avail you if you were?" The Commander paused.

"Ma'am?" Harvey enquired.

He heard her sigh. "A question of language barriers, Captain, nought more. Go, do what you must. Assess. If they seem approachable, establish contact. Report back with your findings."

"Yes, Ma'am." He took his hand off the button.

Kristin looked to him now with hope in her eyes. *Or am I imagining that?* Greenway appeared to be in his own world. A quick glance to the rear showed Lance's tattooed eyes, and Brian's left ear. He didn't ask.

"We're forward, then. As before. Caution always, but they'll see us coming well before we get there, if we don't find a way around."

"Sir." Kristin saluted, but she hesitated before moving forward.

"What is it, Lieutenant?" He wasn't meant to address them by their army or air force ranks, but he almost always did.

"Well, sir, the Commander has a point. How are we going to ask them for what we need? Assuming they speak at all, and they don't communicate telepathically or something. Never mind, my head just goes there." She gazed upward a moment as if arranging her thoughts before she continued. "What I mean to say is, how are we going to ask for what we need and know — I do mean *know* — with utter certainty that it has been granted? And another scenario, that you might not have considered, sir. What if we can't eat it? We don't even know what they plant here. What have they got for sustenance? What if they say yes, and by some miracle we understand that acquiescence, but when they open their storeroom door what falls out is sand? Can't eat sand sir." She trailed off, muttering to herself.

Harvey blinked at her. That had to be, by far, the single longest string of words he'd ever heard the woman put together. Was she nervous? She didn't look it. Her stance portrayed confidence, her dark eyes intent. But that rambling...

"Did you just want to stand here, then?" he asked her. She shot him a look of hurt disbelief. *Are you kidding me? That's what she wants to say and won't.* "We can mime, Kristin. Pretty sure that's a universal language."

"So's art," Kristin mumbled as she took a step forward. "But that doesn't mean everyone understands it."

Harvey didn't think he was meant to hear that, so he let it go.

"She's got a point," Lance said behind him.

"As with the Commander," Harvey told him. "But we've been cleared, so we go down. This isn't a democracy, I give orders, you follow them. I don't know when you all forgot that, but you'll start remembering now, or I'll have you on latrine duty for the length of our stay here."

Kristin in front, Greenway by his side, Lance and Brian behind them, they all skirted the edge of the forest, eyeing the village. It wasn't long before they realised, they would have to take the open path.

The soft soil squelched beneath their boots, the smell more of flowers than manure. But as they drew closer, the stench of burning offal overrode all else.

No one looked up as they approached. But the closer they came, the more human these people appeared. *Two eyes, one nose, one mouth. Hands, feet, arms, legs. They don't look much different to us.* And yet they seemed indifferent to a troop of strangers waltzing through their village. Not something he could ever accuse an Earth human of being. *Indifference. The curse of the dying.* That made him halt short of the village.

Kristin kept going, but he bought her over with a hiss. She squelched back to him and waited.

"Smell offal?" he asked everyone. There were nods all round. "Notice they don't seem to mind us being here?" Again, with the nods. "In fact, not a one of them has stirred their attention toward us. Like they're ghosts or something."

Greenway raised a brow at that. "You assume *they* are the ghosts."

Lance came into the circle. "You think we're *dead*?"

Greenway shrugged. "Could be, if you think about it. Alien mother ship just disappears? Think that likely? The equipment stops working, but we get a Hail Mary pass from Io Station? And now we're here, and those people down there don't notice us. It's purgatory, or something like it."

"You're religious?" Harvey was actually shocked by that.

"Not so as you'd notice," the man replied. "But I have my beliefs."

Harvey shook himself. "I was thinking they maybe had the

plague," he told them, and eyes widened. "They have the indifference of the dying. I hadn't considered ghosts."

"Well, I damn well feel alive," Lance said. "Got hay fever to prove it."

"Doesn't prove anything," Greenway stated. He locked gazes with the Italian Pilot.

"Enough of this," Kristin interjected. "Are we going down or not?"

The Captain gave the inhabitants of the village a final look over before he waved for Kristin to move on. They didn't look sick, or ghostly. Nor was there any sign of bodies being burned or interred. But he couldn't shake the feeling that something was wrong.

They stopped at the first table they reached. Women with aprons on were kneading dough, all along the row. Preparing for a feast.

"Excuse me," Harvey said. The point was not to be understood, merely heard; noticed. But not one of those women looked up from their task, glanced his way. He coughed. "Excuse me." Again, nothing.

"Ghosts," Greenway murmured beside him.

"Not ghosts," Harvey asserted.

"But they're human. Or near enough. How else would you explain that?"

"Not ghosts!" he growled. "We'll just move on."

But every person they spoke to, whether tending to some duty, or merely lazing about, appeared not to hear them. Or see them. It was as if they did not exist.

Eventually, irritated by the mocking silence, Harvey raked an arm over a table full of food. He'd expected it all to go flying, but instead, his arm passed through it with something akin to the resistance of water.

"Believe it yet, Captain?" If Greenway kept baiting him, he thought he was going to smack him in the nose, no matter how much he usually liked the guy.

"Something's not right," he acquiesced. "But we're not dead."

"How do you know?"

"Cause my afterlife sure as shit would not involve trudging around some freakishly earth-like planet looking for food!" *And my son needs me. He* needs *me. I cannot be dead. I refuse to be dead.*

He stalked off back toward the forest and left the others to catch up as they would. He called in a report back to Weiz. After she'd heard it all, she said, "I'll put in a communication to Io station as soon as I can. Maybe they have an idea what this is all about."

"But you don't think we're dead?"

"No, Captain. I don't."

"You have great faith." He felt himself smile despite his foul mood.

A snort came over the comms. "I could eat a horse just about now," Weiz said, "and I've gone to the bathroom. As far as I am aware, ghosts, apparitions and other such things do not require sustenance, nor perform vital bodily functions as a consequence."

"Quite eloquently put."

"I've always had a way with words."

"And a clear way of seeing things."

There was a tension filled pause between them. He didn't want to flirt where someone else might hear, though his heart cried out for the comfort of her words. His gut clenched, a lump came into his throat. He waited.

The seconds felt like hours in his mind. "Get back to the mission at hand," she told him. "If you can grab anything from that village, do so. If they don't see you taking it, there will be no trouble."

"Can't take something that will fall straight through my fingers," he rebutted.

"Point taken. But try anyway. Weiz out." Harvey took his hand from the comms and turned to see his team in a semi-circle behind him.

"You heard?"

"We heard." Kristin nodded.

"So, let's see if we can steal anything."

~

The rampage through the village had been a waste of time, as far as Kristin was concerned. They raided the tables for food, but could not get a hold of any of it. They ransacked the huts of good-wives and hunters, but the sacks of potatoes and flour refused to be moved. All they'd managed to squander were a few fruits that resembled apples and pears from an unoccupied hut on the outer edges of the village. Which they all now ate. There would be none to share with the other crews back at camp.

Kristin let Harvey take the lead this time. He had a bug up his butt about something, and she was not going to ask him about it. She had a feeling she knew what it was. She wasn't getting in the middle of *that*.

Lance sidled up beside her, gave her a nudge. Juice from her pear-like fruit — which oddly tasted like an orange — slipped down her chin. She glared at him as she wiped it away. "Watch where you're going, you hairless ape."

"I'll have you know, I am actually quite hairy." He hid his head as if he couldn't believe he'd just said that.

"Vanity, is it?" She had to stop herself from laughing. "What? Wax? Shave?"

He rolled his shoulders, clearly uncomfortable. "Should've just kept my mouth shut," he said.

"You're only just now figuring this out?"

They entered the forest. Harvey had waited for them. He stood now beneath a tree, facing east-southeast at the opposite edge of the village.

"It's like they gouged a hole in the middle of the forest."

Greenway uttered.

"Or found a clearing and never left," Harvey opined. "If they've been logging the area, they're pulling the stumps."

"Then what are they burning?" It was the first time she'd heard Brian speak. His voice was a deep bass rumble.

Harvey shrugged and ran a hand over his chin. He did not like to go without a shave, that man, the way he kept feeling at it. "Easy enough to gather dried wood. Or maybe they log deeper in. Since we can't ask them, we may never know."

But Kristin had noticed something. Tracks, leading right into the forest, a few paces to their right. "Sir, game trail?" She pointed to it.

"Might be," Greenway acceded.

"Only one way to find out," Harvey told them. "Kristin, you take the lead. You seem to know what you're looking for."

You're damn right I do. You bloody airmen can't track worth a shit. They just weren't trained for it, she knew. Not the way soldiers were. They spent their lives on the ground, had to know what was poisonous and how to treat it if you got bit or stung. What tracks to follow and what tracks to stay away from. What you could eat if your air lift didn't come, and you ran out of rations.

The trail was not oft used, she could tell. What footprints there were had been buried beneath layers of foliage, but still, she could see the hard packed dirt beneath.

Rather than step directly on it and crunch the dry leaves underfoot, she stayed close to the trees, where the ground was mulched, the roots covered in lichen and moss. They absorbed her impact better, and though it would leave a clear trail, most would not notice it, or mistake it for a small animals scratching.

She paused in a crouch, looked down at the pear core in her hand — *I shall henceforth call you O pear,* she thought with a smile, entirely too impressed with her bad joke — and placed it gently on the ground beside her.

The Captain and the others were not far behind, she could hear them coming up the trail, no thought for the noise they were making. She needed to stay far enough ahead of them that if food came along, she'd be able to kill it before they got there, lest it bolt.

She scanned the ground in front of her. The trail led through the forest on a winding course that would either lead to a hunter's patch, or an outlook. She had a feeling it would be the latter but followed it anyway.

Kristin saw signs of animal life as she moved on, but as yet, no animals. Whatever they were, they were small. From the indentations they left on the ground, and the spore they left behind, she'd guess they were rabbits. Or something very like them. She spied a few birds too, looking down curiously at the humans who wandered through their domain, while they sat, heads bobbing on the highest branches. One shot, and they'd all fly off, so there wasn't much point. A small gun was not a hunter's weapon. A sling would be better, but she was not as proficient with those as she was with a bow.

If wishes were horses. To her left there was a sound in the underbrush, and she halted. She used her peripheral vision to see that a small cónifer was moving. From under its lowest leaves poked a grey haired, whiskered snout, two large teeth protruding from the upper jaw. It sniffed at the air. Beady, black eyes followed a long head and squat body covered in snake-like scales. It sat on hind legs, rubbed its paws together, and looked right at her.

The sound of the others coming up along the trail got louder, and the curious beast twitched its whiskered nose. It was as big as a dog, and except for the teeth, did not look dangerous.

It darted at her, and she stood her ground, eyes on the tail that stretched out behind it. *Snake-rat?* She felt some distaste, but she'd eaten snake before.

They closed on each other, the giant snake-rat clearly thinking she was food. She grabbed it by the throat and yanked hard to keep the teeth away from her. Saliva spilled on her arm. She shot it through the head.

"Hadn't wanted to do that, you dumb bastard," she muttered to the creature as she looked down on it with some disgust.

The steps behind her were now running, and less than a minute passed before the others joined her.

"What happened?" Harvey asked.

They all looked at the giant snake-rat with a mix of disgust and confusion. "Caught us dinner."

Lanced laughed. She looked at him. His face dropped. "You're serious." The colour drained from his cheeks.

"You want to eat, right?" She shook her head.

"Are there more of these... things?" The Captain asked her. He too looked a little pale, but for the most part he held up alright.

"Looks like there's a burrow under that bush." She indicated where she'd seen the thing emerge from. "But not knowing how many are in there, or if this was mum, dad or babe, I suggest we leave it. Let them come to us."

"And you think they'll do that?" It was Greenway this time.

Kristin shrugged. "We're not on earth, Captain. I wouldn't have a clue. But we'll assume, given the actions of this one, that they're predators of some kind. And that means, we wait."

"Does it not strike you as odd," Harvey said. "That they could see you?"

"I hadn't considered that, sir."

"Demons." Greenway nodded to himself.

She jerked her head back at the assertion and shot the man a derisive look. "First ghosts, now demons. You still think we're dead?"

"It would be the greatest of all vanities to assume we're the only creatures to suffer purgatory." He didn't look insane. But he darn well sounded it.

"Leave off, Greenway," Harvey said with a frown. "You can keep your opinions to yourself."

The other captain shrugged and turned away to face the forest on the other side of the trail. He walked a little distance away, brushing fingertips against the bark of trees.

Kristin kept her eyes on him as she spoke quietly with Harvey. "He's already given up, sir. We haven't been here more than a couple of hours, and he's already given up."

Harvey was also watching the man. "I've never known him to be so fatalistic before. Might just be his way of coping with the situation."

"Could be he's just insane," Lance offered.

Brian stepped forward then. It was his captain they were talking about. "He's been like this for months," he told them, sadness in his eyes. "We all thought that he was just having a rough patch, but he keeps putting us in situations that we shouldn't be able to get out of. We do, of course, else we wouldn't be here, but... I think he's suicidal."

"And he thinks he finally managed to get himself killed. Why didn't you report him?" Harvey looked saddened.

The Gunner shrugged. "He's our Captain." As if that was enough.

If you got like that on me, Harvey, I'd call it in. No way would I be doing a death run for anyone.

Harvey looked up at the sky. It was near to dusk, the twilight settling the forest into gloom. Though they could see well enough for now, it would not last long.

"We should start heading back," he told them.

They'd all taken their eyes from Greenway, let him wander off into the bush. And now, as they scanned the woods, about to call out to him, shots were fired. There was a strange echo, as if from a distance. Greenway hadn't gone far, and he came running now, a look of abject horror on his gaunt face.

"Run," he said simply, and led the way.

Kristin stood stock still. She was a hunter. You run, they chase, those were the rules. *Man's got a death wish, he can deal with it by himself.*

But then she saw it. A giant man like figure, fully ten feet tall or more, completely black and unclothed, androgynous in form. It walked through the forest trailing wisps of black smoke. Its attention was drawn to the rest of her team as they ran back down the trail toward the village. Its ruby eyes rested on her a moment. Then it evaporated in a swirl of black tendrils.

Her heart raced. Sweat slicked the back of her neck. "Holy fuck," she breathed.

Before she knew what she was doing, she was running down the path to join Harvey and Greenway. Her long-legged stride caught her up fast, and she gained on Lance and Brian by the second.

But the team was coming to a skidding halt. The monstrosity, silent and unyielding, strode toward them from the direction of the village. Its movements were slow and measured, in no hurry to catch its quarry.

The others turned to bolt, and she was only a step behind.

In the lead, now, she moved up the trail, taking the turns at a lean to keep up her pace. She didn't know how they were going to outrun something that shifted the way that thing did. *It's going to try and herd us.* She thought, frantic. *We're as boar to this thing.*

Sure enough, as she came shooting round an uphill bend, the creature appeared before her. Its steady regard for her was one of curiosity and intent. She could imagine the malicious thoughts that swam through its brain.

She did not stop moving. She veered to the left, into the scrub. Dodged branches and overhanging leaves. Small animals skittered out of her path. She didn't look back at the thing, or to see if the others had followed. She could hear them. They were close enough.

Gun shots sounded a staccato rhythm in the distance. They came from different directions. Some of them were rapid, and she had to assume the camp was under attack. No one else had fully automatic weapons.

In front of her began to appear boulders, partially covered in moss, thick layers of foliage at their bases, and condensed into the cracks between them. She could have clambered over them, but the footing would be dangerous and slippery. Instead, she shot right.

She followed their trail, as far as she could, right up to a short cliff face that strung out in front of her. Which, in all fairness, was not far. But her forward momentum had been stunted, and she was faced with a decision. Left or right? Did it matter? Right should lead back to the trail. Left, further into the forest, which appeared to thicken in that direction.

Kristin no longer heard gunshots in the background. But she did hear the team coming up behind her. She looked back.

Harvey was in the lead, Greenway only a step behind. Lance lagged, he carried Gunner Brian by waist and arm. Kristin was stunned to see the man bleeding from a large wound in his thigh. There was no sign of the *thing*.

"Where now?" Harvey asked her. Despite the exertion, he was not out of breath.

"Did you see that thing?" she wanted to know.

"Demons, I'm telling you," Greenway said.

"Greenway, shut it," Harvey growled.

"And you heard the gunshots. We weren't the only ones to run into something hostile," Kristin continued.

"And we don't know that we've lost it just yet," Lance put in. "So can I suggest we get moving until we find a place to hole up for a while. I need to put this bastard down before I throw my back out."

Brian looked at her with sober eyes. "Sorry 'bout the inconvenience."

Maybe one of them should have said something. A word of encouragement, or an assurance that it wasn't his fault. Though it could have been, Kristin hadn't been there to see why his leg was in its current condition, but even so. As it was, though, all he got was a grunt from the Captain.

"Cliff base like this, I'd say there's a cave somewhere in it," he noted.

Kristin nodded agreement. "But if it's got an occupant, we could be worse off. If that — *thing* — has gone its own way, we should just head back to camp."

Greenway looked up at the sky. The light had rapidly faded during the chase. Long shadows grew under the canopy of trees. "We might make it back if we double time it and don't run into any more trouble."

"Which we won't do with Brian's leg like that." The Captain chewed on a cheek. "We'll head back toward the trail along this cliff face," he told them. "If we find a cave we'll hole up for the night."

The decision made, they started off.

Something made Kristin look up. On top of the cliff face, five metres above them, stood the giant. And he had a friend.

~

Weiz leaned back in the chair. She'd been keeping tabs on the teams out looking for food through use of the comms console on MM294. The crews that she'd had stay with her were outside, either manning the perimeter or setting up a camp. One of the first things she'd had them do was dig a latrine pit. No way was she going to go squat in the bushes.

She hadn't heard from Harvey in some time. The sun was on its last hour of full light, and she'd expected to hear from him earlier. Worry filled her mind and clenched her jaw.

The sound of gun fire bought her up from her seat in a flash. She ran to the hatch and dropped down onto the grass. Gunfire still blared nearby. It came from the direction of the woods.

From the holster on her thigh, she pulled her own gun. Whatever was trying to breach the perimeter was in for a fight.

It took her only seconds to reach the first ring. Five Gunners with machine guns, facing toward a black sheathed giant with red eyes. In its massive hands it held a still screaming airmen which it threw, with little effort, at the crew she was now standing with.

As soon as the giant let go of its catch, the crew stepped forward, took a knee, and began shooting in short, controlled bursts. The bullets ripped through the black torso, without effect. No blood spilled, no guts splattered. It walked on, relentless, its feet a few inches from the ground. The dispensed airman fell to the ground some metres behind her with the crunch and snap of bones breaking.

The crew backed up in a crouch, weapons still aimed at the creature.

To left and right along the tree line, she saw that the other crews faced similar threat. Heard the roar of gunfire. Not just from them, but from beyond the tree line. There was a smell in the air, as of burned grass and the tang of iron.

The enemy that advanced toward them disappeared mid stride in a waft of smoke as the crew took another step back. They looked to each other, and then towards the other crews who still dealt with their own giants. Both crews were retreating back toward the rows of ships stretched out on the grass plain.

There must have been some unseen line. A point which the giants either refused to cross, or could not pass. But as each crew got close to the ships, the creatures that faced them just vanished.

The crews remained vigilant. They scanned the horizon with eyes not ready to believe that something so dreadful could just stop.

That their weapons were ineffective, and their strength no match, only confused them the more. An enemy of such efficacy would not just retreat without first achieving its goal. *Unless it did achieve it.*

A thought occurred to her. It was insane, but worth a shot.

"Captain," she said.

The crew looked up at her, at each other, then back up again. The one to her far left, a South African flag on her shoulder, was the one who spoke. "That was our Captain, Ma'am," she said, pointing to the mangled corpse behind them.

Weiz had not realised, until that moment, that the man was dead, his neck twisted at an unnatural angle. His dark blue eyes open, glazed, and staring sightless toward the sky. Not the way an airmen preferred to go.

"So, you're next in line?"

"Pilot Alison Fields, Ma'am." She was young, with a round face, light mocha skin, dark hair and hazel eyes.

"Send your men two steps forward." They complied with only a nod of the Pilot's head.

As soon as they took that second step, the giant reappeared, its gaze held directly on her own. The eyes seemed to bore straight into her soul, to see everything she had witnessed. It pulled to the surface memories — of happiness, sadness, guilt, atrocities and emotions she had no name for — and discarded them as if they were worth less than nothing.

"Step back," she ordered. Her voice cracked, she felt the blood drain from her face. Her heart skipped a beat.

As she had suspected, as soon as the airmen stepped back, the figure evaporated once more.

"We were in their territory," she heard herself say. "We'll need to warn the Captains."

"What are they?" Fields asked her.

"That, I do not know. And I am not sure I want to find out."

She glanced at the other two crews. "Pull in and maintain perimeter. Don't take a step over the line you now stand on. It could be worth your lives."

There was no salute, no answer to that. But understanding shone in their eyes. It was enough for her.

She turned to the body of the Captain. "And we should bury him," she told them. "One of you, get him aboard his ship, we'll afford him all the respect we can."

That done, she took herself back to her own ship. She had calls to make. Those damned scientists had a lot to answer for.

Chapter Six

Dust and debris covered the hall a good few metres in front of the blast door Deidra now faced. She closed her eyes and took a few deep breaths to stop agitation from overriding her good sense.

Beyond those blast doors was the entrance to the crew quarters. Completely inaccessible now. She'd planned on going through Heinrich's room while he was busy in the lab. She'd hoped to find some evidence of her suspicions hidden therein. A notebook, a tablet, a freaking scrap of paper. Something! She was more and more convinced that he knew *exactly* what was happening.

Anger seethed within her, barely held in check. Her left fist connected with the titanium door before she'd even realised she'd thrown a punch. It came away bleeding, though it strangely did not hurt.

I'll have to find it somewhere else, she told herself.

The sound of numerous sets of boots echoed in the hall as she began on her way back toward the comms room. She'd contact the Commander, let her know about the tachyon frequency. There would be no way for them to know, or even understand, what that meant.

As she rounded a corner, she almost collided with Royce, who pulled up short, her whole team stopping behind her.

"Just the person I wanted to see," the Captain said.

"What can I help you with?" She hoped her anger did not show.

The woman looked down at her knuckles, red and bleeding. She arched an eyebrow but said nothing of it. "Your Storage is practically empty. It would serve twenty for ten days, maybe twelve, on short rations." She looked meaningfully back at those behind her. Thirty of them. Then there was her, Heinrich, and Ulrich. Perhaps others who had yet to find their way out of the nooks and crannies they'd thrown themselves into during the eruption. At this point she knew it was unlikely, but held to hope none-the-less.

"What would you have me do?"

"Is there anywhere else that may have what we require?"

Deidra shook her head. "What you've found will suffice."

"You expect we'll be returning soon, then?" There was a glint in her eye. A glimmer of hope.

"Soon," she agreed. "We've only got a couple of days to make it happen. Beyond that, and it will not matter."

"I see."

"Look." She pulled the Captain aside with the flick of her head. "I know this probably sounds insane, but I don't believe this was an accident."

"No? But didn't most of your scientists die in this disaster?" Her face did not suit her words. She was not surprised.

"Don't play dumb." *I've had enough of people lying to me.* "Heinrich — he's the man in charge here." She gave the Captain the whole story, beginning to end as she saw it. "You got me?" She finished.

"I got you."

"So, do you mind maybe keeping an eye on him? If he does

something fishy, goes somewhere he's not meant to be…"

"We'll let you know."

"Thank you, Captain."

The woman grunted and strode back to the rest of her crew. Deidra watched her a moment before heading toward the comms room. Then she had a thought, and deviated from her path.

The power relay station, where the geothermal domes were monitored and controlled, was at the far end of Storage Two. She knew that the offices were a disaster, and the warehouse itself was likely no better, but she had a feeling. If she could prove it…

The eruption occurring beneath Dome One could have been purely coincidental. But something about that sat wrong with her. There were calculated measurements in play that should have stopped such a thing from happening. A kind of filter, built into the structure and the programming.

The halls around her became a blur, each limping step taken without limbs consulting brain.

When she reached Storage Two, instead of taking the elevator, she moved a little further down the hall and entered the locker room. It, like the one of Storage Three, was empty. Though the lights were on. Someone had been through here recently.

Her uneasy feeling grew, the further she went along. Her steps now slowed, she pushed open the door into the warehouse.

Inside, racks, fully loaded with lab equipment, had toppled sideways and leaned precariously, one against the other, all the way to the far right wall. There was shattered glass and broken boxes with half their contents strewn across the floor. There was no telling how much of it was salvageable. To her left, the damage was less evident.

Deidra moved now with purpose. She held to the wall, cautious of what lay underfoot.

At the far end of the warehouse, an elevator led up one level to the office of the substation. She swiped her card, input the appropriate numbers, and made her way in.

The place was perfectly untouched. One black chair, bolted to the floor, and a singular massive console. The screen in front of it was on. A window, looking down on the wires and junction boxes, took up most of the wall. A door led out onto a set of steel steps.

She moved to the screen.

It showed the energy output levels in megawatt hours, on a histogram of the last three days. She synced her tablet to the device, and extrapolated the data. She wanted precise times.

And there it was. Right there. *Got you now, you bastard.*

Around eleven-thirty that morning, Heinrich had adjusted the power output of all the domes, seeking to use more than forty times the usual wattage. It was before the eruption. This was evidence. Everything that was done that had the ability to compromise the efficiency of Io Station had to be carded and recorded. They could not be erased, and Heinrich would not want to destroy the station.

Then something else occurred to her. Heinrich hadn't meant for the eruption to happen. He had not factored it in to his equations. *He still has to figure out how to get us back without the same happening again, or worse! But he can't tell me he already knows everything. He has to make it look like it's as much of a surprise to him.* Too bad he'd already failed on that front.

On the heels of that thought came another, slightly more disturbing. *The experiment and testing doesn't require even a fraction of the amount of power that Heinrich drew on. Was this even connected to it?* And yet it had to be. The coincidence was too great, the destination too precise, the planet too convenient. And he'd only done it after the fleet had come close.

Was there another experiment? Another theory he'd wanted to test? Did it have anything at all to do with the frequency generation, or had that been accidental? Clearly, the light speed propulsion device had been instrumental, else he'd have let her fix the calculations. But what was the game? What did he hope to gain out of this *disaster*?

Deidra realised she was staring at the tablet in her hand, wasting precious moments while the day ticked away. It was getting to early evening now, her watch showed five-thirty-six.

She saved the file onto her tablet, and departed. She needed to speak with the Commander now. She didn't yet know if she'd share her evidence with the woman. Soldiers and Airmen had a tendency toward shoot first and ask questions later, and she still needed Heinrich to complete the calculations that would take them back to where they belonged. She couldn't afford the chance that she'd give the order. Royce, she felt sure, would not act before they returned home. Unless Commander Weiz gave the order.

The corridors, as before, were empty, save for the muted sound of scuffing boots when an airman passed nearby.

When she reached the comms room, she was surprised to see Royce, sitting at the primary console, having a conversation with the woman she'd been just about to call.

"Oh, Doctor Ward." She waved her over. "Just the person the Commander wanted to speak to."

Deidra closed the hall door. She did not want Heinrich to walk in on this.

She shot the other woman a look that asked if she'd said anything about their private conversation. As she stepped away from the screen, she gave a small shake of her head. Deidra was relieved.

She sat down at the console and put the broom to one side. "Commander," she intoned.

"We have a situation unfolding down here," Weiz informed. "This planet is occupied. Humans, and other — *things*."

"Humans?" she queried. Then shook her head. "Never mind. I've news. You might notice that things are not as firm down there as they should be. Then again, perhaps not, it's never been tested on humans before."

The woman's face took on the quality of stone. "What, exactly, do you mean by that?"

Deidra attempted to explain the use of tachyon frequency. The Commander seemed to understand, for which she was thankful. "So, the consequences are unknown. But the technicality of it, faster than light speeds vibration, means that there is no singular cohesion. They should pass right through dense matter. But everything that came with us would match our frequency, and therefore be unaffected. People and other such things should not be able to see you. Or your ships."

"There was an event, such as you describe. One of my Captains came upon a village, but could grasp nothing of use to us," she nodded. "But, alas, while they do not seem to see us, other beings of this world do."

"That should not be possible." She saw Royce from the corner of her eye. She took a seat at a bench against the wall and made herself comfortable.

"I assure you it is. It must be. We were attacked." The Commander elaborated on the situation. At length.

Deidra drummed her nails on the desk. A habit most found annoying, but it calmed her. The wound in her knuckle stretched and welled with blood, the surrounding tissue had swollen and begun to discolour. She ignored it.

"The simple observation of an atom," Deidra murmured when Weiz had finished.

"Explain?"

"The nature of atoms is not exactly something that can be explained in moments, but I'll endeavour. The simple observation of an atom can change its very nature. While it appears to move when seen from the corner of an eye, when faced directly it becomes inert. Or, it disappears. Changes location. Vibrates at a frequency that the human eye cannot track. There are a variety of behaviours that one might consider to be defence mechanisms. You understand?"

"So, you think because humans stood witness, is the reason why my Captain could not interact with the environment."

"Precisely."

"But these Giants see us well enough," Weiz told her. "Well enough to have killed five of my men. That I know about. There are others out there that are scouting the lay of the land, that I've yet to get a report from. The sun's almost down, and they should have returned by now. But I have over a hundred men still unaccounted for." Her concern was writ in her voice.

It should not have been possible, but, "Has anyone seen these Giants, as you call them, near the Villagers?"

"Not that I am aware of."

"They may be in the same frequency."

"They disappear at will, too," the Commander added wryly. Almost an afterthought.

"At any rate, this is hardly what I came here to discuss."

"No?"

Deidra shook her head, suddenly incredibly tired. "We're on a tight schedule. Whether you're starving to death or find a catch to last you a month, we'll need you back up here, in proximity of Io in less than two days."

"You've worked out how to get us back?"

"Not yet."

"I understand."

"Get them ready, then, Commander. I'll keep you updated as much as possible."

"Weiz out." The screen went blank.

Deidra looked up at Royce. "What were you talking about? You didn't tell her about the deadline?"

"Didn't have a chance to tell her anything. You walked in before I could."

"You knew she wanted to speak to me."

"It was the first things she said," the Captain replied.

Her mind was too filled with suspicion, she knew. Because of the events of the day. Because of Heinrich.

She sighed and ran a hand through her hair. "I feel as if I have been awake too long, walking in a haze."

"Have you had anything to eat today?" the other woman asked.

Deidra thought about that. "Porridge, for breakfast," she nodded.

"You're injured." Royce came closer, put a hand on her arm. "And you've been on your feet, almost all day. You require rest to heal, Doctor." She gave her arm a squeeze, then let go. "Rest, and food. I'll grab you a ration pack."

"There should be one on the desk near the door." It was where Heinrich had so gently tended to her. Where his genuine concern had almost fooled her into believing he had no malign intent. A bitter thought. Perhaps he had none. He expressed no desire to hurt anyone. But the science was everything. The experiment was life. Or so it went.

Royce retrieved the pack and threw it to her. "Eat. Take a break. Stay in here in case Weiz calls back in. I was going to send one of my airmen, but you should do it, there are answers only you have." She opened the door.

"As much as I'd like to agree, I do have work to do if we want to get back in one piece."

Royce nodded slowly. "True. But rest a little anyway." She took a final assessing look at Deidra, then departed, closing the door softly behind her.

Deidra dipped her hand in the bag and came up with a nutri-bar.

Grain covered in chocolate, which had it actually been chocolate might have been nice. But it wasn't. Deidra chewed mechanically.

She needed to work out the next step. She'd suspected, and now she had evidence. But what was she to do with it? Who did she give it to and when? What was the purpose of this, according to Heinrich? And was it even what he'd had in mind when he triggered it? Was he malicious in his intent? Or did he feel guilty, or indifferent about the deaths he may have caused? Did he even realise?

And so I ever circle my own mind. She'd always been like that. Always an over-thinker, over-analyser. She'd mull over things to the point of distraction. But when she finally made her decision, she knew that it was right one. She had no regrets for past decisions made.

Heinrich, you have me on this one. How could you have done what you did? Did you know what would happen? Even suspect? So many questions to be contemplated, and so far, no answers. No one she could ask an opinion of, or trust. Ulrich would be useless, and the Captain was military. Alex was gone. Her mind stuttered at that point, replayed the image of him walking with her, then with tons of concrete on him, arm outstretched.

She was half tempted to give in to depression. To just lay there, at the console, and sleep until the whole thing was over. No responsibility. No danger to her life, or to others. Just, sweet, relaxing, sleep.

Deidra shot up out of the chair, felt her ankle buckle at the weight, and sat back down. "Dear God, woman," she told herself. "You've not the time for such self-pity, so snap the fuck out of it!" She shook her head vigorously. "The day is not yet done."

~

Heinrich Faets, physicist of world renown, man of many faces, had made a mistake. Oh, the relocation of the moon and the partial fleet

— though he'd hoped for all of them — was exactly what he'd wanted. They'd even ended up exactly where he'd planned. He'd had a clue that the planet might be habitable, but he couldn't have known for sure until the ATF checked it all out. No, the mistake he'd made wasn't in any kind of calculation — they'd been precise. It was in helping Deidra.

She suspected him. He could feel it in the way she looked at him. Her dark eyes searching his brain for the smallest secrets. And now he had ATF crew watching him, everywhere he went, and they weren't subtle about it either.

He walked now from Lab One to Lab Two, the smallest of distances between them. He'd been working on the propulsion device, and all seemed to be in order, as far as he could tell. Now it was time for the frequency generation. Tachyon frequency, a marvel of modern science. Speculated upon for centuries, but *he* was the first to work out how to harness it. To use the knowledge for the betterment of mankind.

The eruption had been an unfortunate by-product of the required power. It now complicated matters because they'd need as much again to get back, and the Station could ill afford to go through that again. It would undoubtedly collapse. Time constraints, and power constraints. Dome One was gone. The power he needed would have to come from the remaining three. But that meant substantially less power if he wanted to avoid another eruption.

If he diminished the size of the field that the frequency and propulsion covered, he'd be able to manage the hop back. But, he'd then in turn need to leave the fleet, because the moon was too large as it was, unless they landed on the surface, which was inadvisable. Even then, though, the risk of another eruption was great.

Heinrich set down his tablet next to the workstation, and took his seat. His biggest problem, beyond the science, was that he liked

Deidra. She had been the first to listen to him concerning his projects, and had seen merit enough in them to request assignment on the Station with him. When he'd shown her the calculations of his theory it hadn't been the first time he'd taken them to a superior. He knew it was her weight behind his work that had got it off the ground at all. Something for which he would always be grateful.

Alas, there was always such restrictions on testing. Stage six, which would have involved a small two manned space shuttle — incidentally in Hangar One at the time of the eruption — should have been enough for him. But the thought of an entire moon? How could he refuse the challenge?

He shook his head, took up the tablet, synced it to the device behind the glass to take a reading. Anybody looking in on him would think he was hard at work, attempting to fix the little conundrum they now found themselves in. But, he was just taking measure of the effectiveness of the experiment. He hadn't done it all for nought.

He scrolled through his screen.

ERROR:/ LINE NOT FOUND
ERROR:/ SYNC TWO-SIX INCOMPATIBLE
ERROR:/ MEMORY ACCESS VIOLATION
ERROR:/ SYSTEM FAILURE

His face paled. System failure. He was going to need Deidra for this. It was not something he cared to admit out loud, but she was smarter than him. She seemed to have an instinctual grasp on things that he'd had to work hard on.

"*Scheiße*," he murmured.

Well, the woman had practically built the damned thing, so she should have no trouble getting it up and running again. He'd have to go find her.

~

Deidra's eyes flashed open as she half fell out of her seat. A firm hand gripped the desk as she righted herself. She didn't remember falling asleep, but now she was awake, she wondered what woke her. She could have sworn it was a tremor.

Her mouth felt thick with saliva, and her breath felt cold in her chest. Her vision blurred and cleared in round for seconds at a time before it finally resolved itself after rapid blinking. She was *tired*. More-so for having fallen asleep, she suspected.

It was unlikely a tremor had woken her. Probably just some residual anxiety from that afternoon, manifesting itself in her dreams. But she couldn't shake the sense of reality from it.

She glanced at her watch. Seven-twenty. She'd been asleep for perhaps an hour, no more.

A touching of the floor with the toes of her right foot revealed that the pain had substantially subsided. While it may have been a bad idea to walk on it just yet, she decided she would rather do away with the broom. She was going to have a massive bruise under her arm as it was.

Deidra limped over to the desk where the ration pack had been and looked around on the floor. She spotted her sock and shoe, and hurriedly put them on.

When she left the Comms Room, she had no location in mind. Left to Hangar Two, right to the bulk of the Station, just across the hall to the Labs. She went right. Heinrich was probably in the Lab, and she didn't feel like dealing with him just yet.

It was hard to believe it had been less than eight hours since she had spied on Heinrich. It felt like days. She was certainly tired enough.

The halls were eerily empty. They'd been empty for two days, but now, they *felt* empty. There was no echo of footsteps, no doors being opened or closed, no hum from the vents. Her eyes widened in sudden alert wakefulness. There would be only one of three reasons the air wasn't moving. Either the Mains Switch in the Substation had been flipped, there was a damaged vent or pipe, and the air was simply not getting through to a particular section, or there was a problem with the life support system.

Though she limped, she limped fast. Her flight toward Storage Two was uninterrupted. She saw not a sign of a soul in sight. This, more than anything disturbed her. Sure, it was a big station, lots of places to be, plenty of places to hide, but that ATF crew had not struck her as idlers.

When she arrived at the Storage Two elevator, she looked down the hall toward Storage One. There, she saw twenty odd, teary-eyed airmen, facing a titanium blast door in complete silence.

Deidra drew her brows down in thought. She was sure that Storage One had been accessible, though likely much worse off than Storage Two. If the tremor she'd felt had been a rubble explosion, and the blast door had come down, then that meant; *the lava is seeping through.*

She approached the crew. "What's happened?" she asked.

A clear-eyed crew member turned, shock evident on his dark face. "It came down on them," the man said with a thick French accent. "We were going to search through this warehouse. We weren't far behind. We saw..." He looked back to the titanium door.

"How many?" She found she had a lump in her own throat.

The man shook his head. "Six," he answered. "Captain Royce..."

Coincidence? The woman she'd told of her suspicions, who'd then asked her crew to keep an eye on Heinrich? Why did everything lead back to that man?

"The ventilation is off," she stated.

The airman looked at her, but the relevance of her statement obviously did not penetrate. "They're dead," he said.

"The ventilation system is off," she repeated.

Another crew member looked around. His eyes were red from tears. His pale face pinched and gaunt, bags under his blue eyes. He had a British flag on his right shoulder. "The ventilation's off?" He, at least, seemed to understand what she was saying.

"I need you to check the vents and see if any of them are visibly crushed," she told him. "I'm going to the substation to check the Main. If we cannot fix this, we are going to have bigger problems."

"We'll run out of air."

"We will."

He shrugged as if it made no difference. "Bates, Allen, Rich, Zim," the man called off. "You're with me. Groups of four or five, lads." He turned from the door, and those named followed after him as he moved down the hall to an access point. She noted that the first man she'd spoken to was one of them.

Deidra looked to the rest, but left them as they were. There was nothing she could do for them, or they in turn for her. If death was the price of the knowledge she held, then she would keep it to herself. Of course, she had no proof that Heinrich had collapsed the section, but the airman had mentioned nothing of lava.

You are becoming paranoid, woman, she told herself as she hurried for the substation. *A conspiracy around every corner. But not everything is a conspiracy. You may have been right about some things, but for God's sake, not* every *thought need be right. It may have been a lava flow. It* could *have been coincidence.* But as much as she tried to convince herself, she could not believe it.

The Substation was exactly as she'd left it. The screen on the same page. Nothing looked out of order or tampered with. She glanced out the window, but realised it was pointless. She was not an electrician. She didn't know what to look for.

She moved to the screen and pulled out her tablet. It was still synced with this console, so she updated the content, scrolled through the menu until she found Life Support, and clicked on it.

The readings came through clear. She ran a diagnostic.

A map of the Station came up on her screen. A sweep scan began, starting with Dome One, which was at the furthest point of the map. A progression bar showed at the bottom right. Compromised vent shafts began to show up in red — which was all of them — as the first five percent moved its way across the progress bar. Some began to show up in green and orange as the next five percent rolled along. The next ninety percent flashed onto the screen within seconds.

All along the map, the lines showed green, the squares where the fan hubs were, orange. Some squares flashed red beyond the destroyed part of the station. Deidra tapped on one of those flashing squares and read the report out loud to herself. "Air quality compromised. Cleansing measures taken." She didn't know exactly what that meant, but she had an idea of what had gone wrong. Sulphur had gotten into the vents, and they were no longer pushing that air through. But it *was* trying to fix itself. So that was something. But backup scrubbers should have been taking care of this.

She took her tablet back to the map and tapped on an orange square. *Flow suspended. Why would they stop in this part of the Station?* She flipped through a few more orange squares to read the same. *Flow suspended.*

Technically, it was all working just fine, it was just trying to rid itself of poison air. This, then forced her to find where the Main Hub for life support was situated. She scrolled back and forth across the map until she found the largest square. It was red, and next to Hangar One.

There were space suits in the Hangar, she knew, but it would avail them nothing if Hangar One was filled with lava. She found it hard to believe that there was no back up life support. Or that no alert had been sounded by the klaxons.

"There should be back up. Everything else has backup," she murmured to herself. *Shit, we even have two hangars, one on either end of the station.* Granted, though, the second was a great deal smaller, but it had been meant for evacuation.

She shuffled back to the main menu and looked for secondary or backup. She found neither. *Maybe they're not powered by the Mains,* she thought.

Deidra turned the screen off on her tablet and deposited it in her coat pocket.

It was time for her to find out what she could do to get them home. It was the only way they could get out of this mess without more casualties. Maybe.

CHAPTER SEVEN

The way the Shadowmen had looked down on them from that ridge left Harvey with chills all up and down his spine. All they'd done was watch while they stood there, until Kristin made for the right. Then, one jumped down in front of her. He noted, somewhere in the back of his mind, that it did not actually hit the ground. There was no sound, no tremor or thud to announce its landing.

They backed up a step. It followed. They backed up another step. It cocked its head to the side.

Harvey turned his attention to where they were going, and saw the other one behind them.

He took a shot at it with his pistol, but the bullets went straight through without slowing. He emptied the clip. Nothing.

He holstered his weapon and ran. There was no dignity in it, but better that and alive, than not. He'd probably pissed the damned thing off, and he'd exhausted his only weapon.

Harvey didn't have to look back to know that the others had followed his lead. They were being rounded up, for certain. Forced away from the trail and a direct line back to camp. He didn't know what they were or what they wanted.

The forest was dark now. They hid behind a large oak tree. A light rain drizzled through the canopy, large drops formed on leaves and fell to the ground in steady drips. *Clear day, rainy night, fields just planted. Must be spring here.* The smell of wet mulch slowly began to overtake everything else. There was no sign of the Shadowmen and had not been for some time. But, Harvey dared not move. Barely dared breathe.

"We should call in, Captain," Kristin whispered beside him.

He turned to see the rest of them. They were all mostly dry, though that wouldn't be the case for long. Lance leaned back against a cedar, his usual humorous demeanour nowhere in evidence as his eyes continuously scanned the forest around him. Brian, propped up next to Lance, his leg still bleeding in a slow trickle, looked deathly pale, and was in need of immediate medical attention. Greenway was to his left, hunched in a crouch, gun in hand, eyes wide. Kristin, damp, dark hair flipped over a shoulder to be tied in a braid. Bright brown eyes looking to him, steady, unwavering.

"How long has it been?" he asked the Comms Officer.

"Since we last saw them? Or since we stopped?"

"Either. Both." His sense of time was confused, though he knew it shouldn't be. He'd never seen anything like those Giants before. He hoped to never see their like again.

"Half an hour, I'd say, for the first. A couple of minutes, here, for the second."

He nodded. "Get Lance to treat Brian's leg. Do whatever he can."

"Sir." She moved off.

Harvey put a hand down on Greenway's shoulder. "You still with me?"

"I'm still with you," he growled. It was enough.

They were lost. No compass, no map, no sun and no shadows. At some point in his headlong flight, the twists and turns had stopped being counted, as time and again those Shadowmen loomed before them. Every now and then, one of them would ineffectually shoot at them. Lance had even thrown a rather large rock at one of them, but the creature had just moved to the side as it sailed past.

He pushed down the button on his cuff. "Weiz, you there?"

"Harvey!" It came through immediately. "You have no idea how good it is to hear your voice. I —" She stopped herself there. "There's been an incident back here at camp. And among the other crews I sent out."

"Let me guess," he sighed. "Black Giants."

"So, you've run into them too? Any casualties?"

He scratched at his stubble. "Well, that's the darnedest thing, isn't it? So far, those things haven't attacked. But they have been rounding us up quite nicely. Only I don't know where we're supposed to be going, and I've no idea where we are."

"But you're all alive?" Weiz sounded strangled. He had a feeling she had some bad news.

"Yeah. Brian's got a busted leg — snagged it on a branch while we were running — but he's kept up. He needs attention soon, but for now, we're all alive."

There was something of hysteria in the relieved laughter that came over the com on his lapel. "Captain, you are, as of this moment, the *only* crew to have suffered no loses."

Harvey had to let that sink in. There were thirty-six crews. That was at *least* thirty-six fatalities. "How many?" he asked simply.

"Ninety-three."

"And the injured?"

"Forty."

"Including Brian?"

"No"

Harvey closed his eyes and breathed deep. He looked back at the dishevelled crew behind him and thanked the universe that they were alright. *The only crew to suffer no loses. But Walt and Dames aren't here. Neither is Xavier.*

He was definitely regretting his decision to land on this forsaken planet.

"Do you have word...?" he asked, but couldn't bring himself to finish.

As always, Weiz knew instinctively what he was thinking. "He came back not long ago with Walters. The rest of her crew, unfortunately, did not make it. With the exception of Brian, of course."

He looked back at the wounded man to see if he'd heard. Lance had pulled a sleeve off his own coveralls to bind the wound, and it looked as if the man were asleep. Possibly passed out.

"And my crew?" Greenway asked over his own com.

"As yet unknown, Captain," Weiz told him.

Harvey thought a few moments before his next question. "Orders?"

"Get back alive."

He didn't have it in him to crack a joke at that, so he let it fall unsaid. "Harvey out." He released the button.

"Still think we're dead, Greenway?" he asked.

"No, Captain," he replied sadly. "I do not."

With a nod, he squeezed the other man's shoulder, then let go. "Do you think we should move? Or stay here?"

"Well, they haven't appeared since we got to this spot," Greenway offered.

"There is that. But if we stay here and that drizzle becomes a downpour, we've nothing here to take cover under."

"But if we move, and they come after us, your argument could be invalid."

They searched each other's eyes. Despite his religious paranoia of earlier, Harvey trusted Greenway.

"They haven't been violent toward us so far," he said after a while.

Greenway shrugged. "We haven't exactly tried to stand and fight. Besides, we couldn't, now. We're all out of ammo."

"So, they've no reason to harm us, then."

"Unless we go the wrong way, and be damned if I know the right one. Do you?" His tone was not angry, despite his choice of words. It was an honest question.

"We're all lost out here, my friend." He moved over to the others.

"Captain," Lance said at his approach.

He nodded toward Brian. "Will he make it through the night?"

"Hard to say, I wouldn't have thought he'd make it this far." The Pilot rubbed a hand over his bald pate. "He's asleep now, sir, and he needs it. Lost a lot of blood. My sleeve will only do him so good if we can't get some stitches in it soon. It might be infected."

Kristin sat silent next to Lance, a soft hand on his thigh. He didn't comment on it. "We should find some cover."

"All due respect, sir, and all the niceties and whatnot we're supposed to address you with when around other crews, but — fuck no."

Kristin poked the man in the ribs, and he pushed her off with a snarl. "You afraid, Sinatra?"

"Get off it, woman," he grated at her. "Where did you even hear that name? And I ain't afraid, I'm just not blind rotten stupid. We're lost as is, but if we wait for the sun to come up we might have some idea of how to get back. And I am fucking tired. I'll run if one of those things come along, but I ain't moving an inch unless." He folded his arms about his chest and glared a challenge at the Captain.

"Have it your way, Lieutenant." He shook his head. He couldn't blame the man — he was tired too. "Look then," he told them in a soft voice. "I'll scout out for a bit. If I find us somewhere out of the rain and wind to hole up for the night, I'll come and back and get you all. Sound fair?"

Greenway threw a twig at the ground, and broke another already in his hands. "If you feel the need to go do something," the man said.

"I'll come with you." Kristin stepped forward.

Lance looked up at her with disappointment, but stubbornly said nothing.

"Good. Let's go, then." He moved out at a steady trot, his eyes making swift scans of their surrounds.

He was glad that Kristin had chosen to take scout duty with him, as she was the best he'd seen when it came to ground work. In the Air Force, they were still trained as ground units, but not in the same way as a Marine or, as in Kristin's case, SAS.

They followed no particular path, though they stuck as close to protruding boulders as they dared. If they were going to find some cover, it would be among the rocks.

"So," he breathed after a while. "You and Lance?"

She looked back at him, a half-smile on her face. "Nothing happening, Captain."

"You looked a little... cosy."

"I was just trying to cheer him up, sir." She turned her attention back to what lay ahead.

They walked in silence.

A good time later, they came upon a boulder, twice his height and about ten metres long, that appeared too straight. It had an entrance that looked as though it may have been an archway, half buried in soil, and surrounded by smaller rocks.

The light of the moon bathed the stone in a blue glow, but they could not see inside. He leant down and squinted into the gloom alongside Kristin. He couldn't make anything out.

Kristin put a hand inside the archway and scribed a circle in the air. When she bought it out, she studied the arm. "No webs," she said. "Either they don't have spiders on this world, or they're just somewhere else on it."

Strange to think he, afraid of spiders, had never even thought about it. *A world without spiders. I can definitely deal with that.* "What's the significance of that?"

She shrugged. "Just an observation. They do tend to congregate around man-made structures. Especially if it's dark and dank."

"So, we're thinking this is man-made?"

"I'd say, by the way it's been cut. And this is only the top of it."

He glanced along its length both ways, then back at the soldier. "I wouldn't have thought those people with their mud huts could have built something this large."

"Didn't say it was them who built it." She took a few shuffling steps into the doorway in a crouch, arm outstretched. "Just that it was man-made. We have similar mysteries back on Earth, do we not, Captain?"

Harvey snorted. "So, you're not just a soldier, you're an archaeologist too, are you?"

If she took offence, she hid it well. "Too right! And somewhat of a physicist in my spare time, too."

She disappeared completely into the darkness. "Can you see anything in there?"

"Not a thing, Captain. But the space is large. I am following a wall. High enough for us to stand, too."

"Well, should I come in, then?" He hated to stand around and do nothing. One of the reasons they were here in the first place.

"No, I'm good. You can go get the others. This is sturdy enough. And dry."

He nodded, realised she couldn't see him, then said. "Right then.

I'll be back soon."

"Take your time."

Harvey grimaced, then shot a laugh. "You know, you're going to make a great Captain one day," he told her, then turned and began his march back to the others.

~

Clothed in darkness, finger tips pressed to a wall, feet scuffing through dirt, Kristin flinched at the comment. A Captain, sure. One day. If they ever got off this planet, which was looking less and less likely as time wore on. More than half of their number were dead or injured, and she guessed some fatally so. Brian would need stitches soon, before he lost too much blood, and he could very well be next on the list.

For a moment, she felt guilty for not giving more thought to the fallen, but the more practical side pushed it away. They could mourn when they were safe.

The Giant that had come out of the woods at them could have easily killed her, had she stood her ground. Too easily. And that was the problem. She saw no way to fight those things, and they were clearly trying to cut them off from the camp. But why weren't they trying to kill them, as they were so obviously doing to the other crews? That was what did not make sense to her.

After what she guessed to be around five minutes, she found herself back at the entrance. She estimated the place to be entirely hollow. Ten metres by four. Shuffling along in the dark took some doing, if you didn't want to fall on your face or get impaled on something.

She moved back outside and sat at the entrance, in case the Captain got lost on his way back, she wanted to be able to hear him clearly.

He's a smart one. He'll do just fine. This was her first mission. The six-month Docker flight out to Ganymede allowed her to get to know many of the people she was now stuck on this world with. She still couldn't believe it. She felt like she'd been with this crew her entire life. Even before they'd been stranded on this rock. And the way they all treated her? Well, she had to assume they all felt the same about her. *Captain's old enough to be my father, and I am starting to treat him like a pet. Here! Fetch!* She chuckled at the image of the Captain running all fours, chasing a stick. It wasn't that she didn't respect him — she did, but you can respect a dog too — it was just how things had fallen.

She glanced into the forest, but could hardly see anything bar the shadowed protrusions of trees and their branches by the bluish light of the very small moon. Not more than a few metres ahead, and that ground was clear. The interior of that building may have been dry, and she didn't see one of those shadowmen squeezing through the entrance, but they'd need some light.

Kristin pushed herself upright and moved to the tree line to scan the undergrowth with her eyes. There was plenty of hard and soft wood here, but she had to find pieces that weren't too wet. And enough to keep the fire going for a while.

Her stomach rumbled. She looked down at it. "Shut up," she told it. But it gave her another loud rumble to let her know who was boss, before it calmed.

She went back to searching the underbrush.

By the time she'd finished scrounging up kindling, and a couple of fallen logs, the Captain was back with the rest of the team. Lance had had to carry Brian, and he was not looking good.

Kristin deposited her arm load of wood in a pile at the entrance, then turned to watch Lance. "Has he woken?" she queried.

The Pilot shook his head.

Harvey and Greenway stopped at the entrance, and Lance relieved himself of his burden so he could squat and squint into the darkness beyond.

"Not much smaller inside, than outside, Captain," she said. "I'll led us in. Get a fire going so you can see."

Harvey nodded. "I'll get us some more wood."

Kristin glanced down at the pile at her feet, but didn't reply. If he wanted to be useful, then she'd let him be useful.

If he wanted to be useful, he could damn well find us something to eat. She thought, but didn't voice it. They were all likely as hungry as she, but they weren't close to starving yet.

She took up some wood once more, checked to see if it was mostly soft wood, then moved into the darkness.

It didn't take long for the fire to get going, and once it had, the others filed in. Harvey carried an arm load of wood, which he deposited next to Kristin with a tight smile. Lance propped Brian up against the wall, leg extended toward the fire, while he sat next to the man and hugged his knees. Greenway dropped unceremoniously into the dirt in a cross-legged position and stared into the flame.

"We weren't prepared for this." She wasn't speaking to anyone in particular, but they listened. "No rations, no canteens, hardly a weapon." She looked down at the gun in its holster. A knife would have been more useful.

She didn't think anyone was going to answer, and she didn't mind. After all, she hadn't asked a question. But Harvey said, "Why would they stock a space attack vessel? Usually, if we find ourselves in some trouble, we're open to the dangers of the void. They weren't designed to be landed. That's what the carrier ships are for."

Kristin nodded. "Well, maybe if we make it back, we should encourage a change in that policy."

A whistling sound from outside grabbed their attention, and they all swung their eyes to the entrance. They waited, but it didn't repeat, and the crackle and hiss of the wood as it burned, was all they could hear.

They had to find a way back to camp.

~

"I am so tired, right now," Weiz told the man next to her as she rubbed at itching eyes. "But it all has to be done, doesn't it?"

The man remained stoically silent as he gazed up at her from the corner of an eye. She wondered what he was seeing, or if he was thinking of a reply that wouldn't get him in trouble. That was the curse of leadership, of course, that people saw you as something more. If you won with minimal losses, then you were a good at your job. If you led them to slaughter, you were bad at it. The former accorded respect, the latter disdain, but neither held room for friendship.

She let out a sigh.

They stood on a rise in the plain. Below them, some thirty airmen worked to dig up ninety-three graves. *And let's hope that number does not grow.* Not all of them had been brought back to camp, but every one of them would have a space to be remembered. Those who had been, lay in rows of five to the side of the makeshift cemetery.

The crews she'd left on the perimeter still stood where she'd left them, hours ago. The Giants had not shown their faces again.

Weiz judged the hour to be close to ten-thirty, but she'd not been in the ship to check. The latitude they'd chosen to land at corresponded closely to Greenwich Mean, but it would take a good amount of observation to know how well.

After her call with Harvey, she'd left it to a Comms Officer to take the incoming. She had a feeling that they would not hear from those who'd not checked in yet. Another list of names to add to the fallen.

She had some faith in these scientists. They'd got them here, they could get them back. But she had a feeling, too, that Doctor Ward had been holding something back from her. Something important. She tried not to let it gnaw at her, but it worked its way from the edges of her thoughts to the forefront, again and again.

"To be buried on an alien world," she mused. "Would they have wanted to return to their loved ones? Or are they fine here? Did they, in the depths of their hearts, find they were explorers?"

She wasn't expecting a response, so when the man beside her spoke, she almost jumped. "Their souls will travel home with us, Ma'am. In here." He tapped at his temple. "But we can ill afford to cart them all back, and I think they'll forgive us for it."

Weiz nodded. She hoped he was right.

She watched, as one after another, the bodies were lowered into the ground, dirt heaped atop them, in unmarked graves. She'd have done more, if she knew how, but exhaustion and fear warred within all her airmen, and she knew it was as much as she could ask of them.

Everything had taken on a kind surreal haze. On the one hand, she knew it all to be real, but a part of her mind tried to deny it. Tried to tell her that it would be alright, if she just opened her eyes, if she just woke up. But she was awake. Her eyes were staring, red rimmed and bleary toward a nightmare. Of more than two hundred ships in her command, now only twenty-six remained. Perhaps less.

A heavy sigh escaped her lips. She cracked her jaw to utter something, a nonsense to fill the silence, when the airmen spoke again.

"Fyord is running over here," he told her. "Looks like it could be important."

She turned her head to view the running Comms officer, waving his hands to grab their attention. She moved swiftly to meet him.

"What news?" she asked.

"I have Io Station. Doctor Ward. She wants to speak with you directly, Ma'am." The man turned and began jogging back toward the ship. Weiz kept pace.

"Did she say what it was about?"

Fyord shook his head. "Just said it had to be you she spoke to."

They reached the ship in no time, the intervening space shot by in a blur as her mind raced.

"Doctor Ward," she said in greeting as she sat down at the console.

"Commander. I have some... sad news." The woman looked almost as exhausted as Weiz felt.

Weiz closed her eyes and forced herself to breathe. "What is it?"

"Two things..." She trailed off with a grimace, visibly braced herself before she continued. "First, I regret to inform you that during a ceiling collapse, six of your team were killed. Captain Royce and her crew, I was informed by the others."

Another six, dead, just like that. We've been away from the Docker less than twenty-four hours, and we're being systematically annihilated. If I can't get them home, if I can't keep them together... She let the thought go unfinished. That line would lead to self-pity, and she would not allow it. "What else?" she asked.

"We'll need you all back up here by this time tomorrow at the very latest," the scientist informed. "You'll probably have to get close to the surface, though it's going to be hot and tumultuous. If all goes well, then you'll not have to stay long."

"This time tomorrow?"

"Yes, Commander." A slight pause. "Our life support is down. I don't think we can get it up and running again without full maintenance and a complete evacuation of the station. So, we'll be dead before the moon drops into orbit, if we don't get us back."

Still, things were being left unsaid. "We'll do what we can," she told the woman. "But I have some airmen trapped out in the woods right now. I don't know how many of them are alive, or if they'll make it back. But I'd rather not leave without them, you understand me?"

Ward nodded. "I understand you, Commander. But, please understand this. We cannot wait. If you are not here when the time comes, we will leave without you." While her look was stern, it was also filled with sympathy. She did not envy this woman.

"Understood, Doctor Ward."

"I'd help, if I could. Wait, if I were able."

Weiz gave Ward a smile. Barely there, and sad, but a smile none-the-less. "I've no doubt. But, we have to do what we have to do. Don't we?"

A nod. "I'll update you in the morning." Then she turned off the screen.

The Commander leaned back in the chair and turned her head toward Fyord. "Do we tell them now? Or later?"

Fyord shrugged. "That's up to you, Ma'am."

"An opinion, Airman, that is all I'm asking for," she said, irritated.

"Let them have the night, Commander. We all need time to grieve."

"You think it was a mistake coming down here?"

Fyord shrugged again. Weiz wondered if it was habit or circumstance. "If we'd stayed, we'd already be out of fuel. Floating in space to a slow death isn't much better."

"You're the last of your crew, aren't you?"

"Yes Ma'am."

"Would you rather go pay your respects, then?"

The airman shook his head. "I'd like to keep busy, if it's all the same to you."

She nodded and stood up from the chair. She put a hand on his shoulder as he took her place. "Do as you will, Airman." Then she left.

Outside once more, she moved toward the perimeter. It was time for those airmen to get some rest.

Pilot Fields was exactly, to the inch, where Weiz had left her, hours before. Her dark eyes searched the horizon, wide in their wakefulness.

"Come," Weiz said as she reached them. "It is time for another to take your place. You need rest."

Fields looked back at her as if she had not understood the words. The others didn't even bother with that much. They just crouched in their positions, eyes on the forest ahead of them, hands twitched on pistols and machine guns, waiting for a chance to pull the trigger.

Weiz found that her own eyes scanned the forest. The memory of the Giant as it threw the Captain without effort, all too fresh in her mind.

A light drizzle began to fall, and she gazed upward. The face of the moon was small, a bright beacon in the night sky with its unfamiliar stars, its light a halo that touched the edges of the gathered clouds that raced toward it. Soon, the spotlights from the ships in the front rows, would be all they had to see by. It was not enough to break the gloom of the forest.

We already have water, you blind gods. She didn't really believe in any gods, but she felt the need to blame someone. *We need to get home.*

She glanced once again at the Pilot. The woman's gaze was still on her. Their eyes locked. "Go," she said. "Now. I'll send another team to relieve you."

This time the words seemed to penetrate as Fields nodded. Silent, she gave a signal to her crew, and they turned with Weiz, to come face to face with a Giant.

~

It was well after midnight, he was sure. Maybe only a couple of hours until dawn, maybe even less. From outside the cave mouth, a pair of ruby eyes stared in on them. He was exhausted, hungry, and the edges of his eyes burned with the need for sleep. But he watched on. Matched that stare with his own steady gaze.

Come for me, you bastard! Come for me and get this farce over with. WHAT DO YOU WANT? He crawled along the edges of insanity with his every thought. *I can see your eyes demon. Can you see mine?*

Greenway bit his lip to keep a chuckle from slipping through. He didn't want to wake the others. *Let them sleep. Let them dream of better times, better places. But you and I, Demon, we know better, don't we?*

If there had been a stone to throw at the thing he'd have done so. The fire had long since gone out, it's embers now ash in the fire pit. Viatri and Brian were up against the outer wall, Kristin and Harvey had lain down back-to-back as they slept, but he wondered if they were now face to face.

"One fine day, in the middle of the night, two dead men got up to fight," he recited in a whisper. "Back-to-back they faced each other, drew their swords and shot each other." His eyes never wavered from those red coals.

A movement behind him, he dismissed as either Harvey or Kristin rolling over in their sleep. *Sweet dreams. Sweet dreams.* Then a hand slapped down on his shoulder, and his heart hammered hard in his chest as he clamped teeth into his lower lip and drew blood. He licked it away. He'd not waste a glare on darkness.

"Taking up guard duty, Greenway?" It was Harvey.

"I'm waiting for it to come inside." *Inside, yes. Inside. Take me now, demon, I am ready for hell. Take me to our master.*

"Waiting for what to come inside?" There was concern in his voice.

"Can you not see it? The Giant's eyes?" He gestured toward the entrance.

There was a palpable pause. "There's nothing there, Greenway. Just the trees."

No. He denied without words. *It's there. Right there. I can see it. It waits.*

~

She rolled over. Unable to sleep, her mind wandered in circles. The scene played over and over. She couldn't escape it. Couldn't forget.

Something in her broke. It was like a rush of all the emotion that she'd not been able to let out, all condensed into one solid punch. When her fist connected with the Giant's torso, she thought it might break. It didn't seem to hurt the thing, at least not very much, but it was enough of a surprise that it gave them all time to run past it and into the line of ships.

Weiz held her right fist in her left hand and looked back with a wince. She could not believe that she'd just done that. Damned bullets fly right through the thing, and I punch it. Only that contact was solid... *She breathed in through her teeth, as the pain travelled up her arm.*

Fields stood beside her, breath shallow, eyes wide.

The Giant didn't move from the spot where she'd hit it.

The crew were lined up behind her. Some who'd been watching from afar now gathered in, so close to the ships their backs almost touched the cool, wet metal.

Still, the Giant did not move.

"You hit it," Fields said.

Weiz nodded, as shocked as Fields. "Yes."

"With your fist."

"Yes."

"Did you hurt it?" The woman's eyes turned on her then, intent. The rest of the crew watched her as well.

"Does it look like it's hurt? And I think I broke my hand."

Disappointment. Clearly writ on the faces of those around her. They just want some revenge. Hell, I do too.

The other crews that had maintained the perimeter were with them as well. In all, four Giants stood facing them, stretched out across the plain.

Something — a scream, a cry for help — broke out in the night. The ground trembled. The ships shook. Airmen balanced on the balls of their feet; arms outstretched to keep from falling. Then the movement ceased.

A rumble like thunder. The Giant she'd punched roared in their direction, unmoved from its position. A warning to keep their distance.

She rolled over again. A groan escaped her lips as pressure fell onto her right hand. She didn't want to relive this part. Didn't want to again witness the horror. But her mind defied her.

There was a moment of tense silence. Then, of a sudden, in a roar that challenged the Giant, those who had arrayed behind her, charged. Weiz looked to Fields and her crew, who understood better than most the futility of such a gesture, and so had stayed. She could see there, reflected in the woman's face, shock and horror.

"No!" she screamed at them. "Get back here! That's an ORDER!" She strained her voice with the last word. But barely half stopped to look back at her, much less turned and retreated.

And so, they converged on the Giant, their arms their only weapons. Across the field, three other Shadowmen turned their attention to the sound, but did not move.

Impossibly, it seemed that the Giant would be overwhelmed, as those who'd charged battered it with fists and knees, elbows and feet, while it stood like a tree. Unmoving.

They're playing with us, *she realised.* All we have to do is stay in our camp, and they'll leave us be. *But why had they shown up again? Were they checking on them? Had they been elsewhere? Answers she did not have. Nothing about this made any sense.*

When the Giant moved, it was like lightening. A heave, and those it touched flew in all directions. One airman, who'd been flung in the direction of the forest, was caught by another Giant who appeared out of thin air. That Giant tore the man in half, flung him back at the camp in two pieces, and disappeared once more.

Those who had stopped at her order, fled back toward the ships.

The others, who'd attacked the first Giant, in some kind of silent agreement, charged once more. Their thrown companions either lay unmoving on the ground where they'd landed, crawled or slithered their way slowly back to the ships.

Weiz found she was yelling for them to come back, to disengage. But no one was listening.

Now, as each airman came in contact with the thing, it simply grabbed their head and twisted. Each sharp pop announced the death of yet another crew member.

Weiz buried her face in the crook of her left arm. Hot, salty tears bathed her face. Even if all the crew who'd not called in since she'd sent them out, came back alive on the morrow, she'd have no more than seventy airmen. Enough for only fourteen or fifteen ships at the most. Fifteen of thirty-six.

On the floor of the bridge on MM294, Weiz cried until she had no tears left. Until they dried on her cheeks and left her eyes swollen and bruised. What madness had taken them? Her heart ached around the question.

Harvey, you fool. Come back to me.

Come back to me.

When sleep finally came, it was restless and filled with nightmares.

CHAPTER EIGHT

Deidra hadn't slept at all. At least, not since the nap she'd had in the Comms Room. And she didn't think she would again, unless she got them home by the end of the day.

The time now approached six-twenty in the morning as she read through the calculations in Lab Two, head drooping over her tablet, held steady by her left palm. She had not seen Heinrich since their discussion in Lab One, and she wasn't sure she wanted to. If he didn't offer up his knowledge freely, then it was likely she might be on the list of the slain. Though she had no evidence, she was still sure it was him who had caused the ceiling collapse.

She'd found that there was nothing she could do about the failure of the life support system. The air was hot, humid and getting harder to breathe. Her lab coat and shirt had been dispensed with, as had shoes and socks. Sweat fell in runnels down her cheeks, the nape of her neck, under her breasts and beneath her thighs. Were she in the comfort of her own home, she'd have removed the pants too. It had to be at least forty degrees Celsius, and she felt as if she were burning up.

All she kept getting from the frequency generator was error after error. She had a suspicion that they'd need to build another chip for it, which she had neither the time nor the tools for. So she persevered, tried to find a back door, a way around the problem. But it was getting harder and harder to think.

Footsteps echoed in the corridor and filtered through the gap beneath the door. It was not uncommon for the ATF crew members to ask her for things to do. But she'd run out of places to send them. Anything they did would be for nought if she didn't get them home, and it didn't seem as if Heinrich had much interest in doing that.

She pulled a nutri-bar from the pack beside her and took a sip of coffee. *At least we have that.* Coffee was a major staple in her diet. If she'd have had to go without it, she didn't think she'd make it through. It was a struggle as it was.

The door opened behind her, but she didn't bother to turn. "I've nothing left for you to do," she said around a mouthful of chocolate covered grains.

"Perhaps not," Heinrich answered, making her spin in her seat. "But I have something for you."

"Where have you been?" She shot him such an accusing glare that had it weight, he'd have fallen.

His clothes were clean. Not at all sweat soaked. He still wore his lab coat. His face was clean shaven, his dark blonde hair combed through. He raised an eyebrow at her. "Unlike you, dear, I am no longer young. I may not sleep as much as I once did, but those hours are all the more important these days."

"The next sleep you manage will be permanent, if we don't figure this out." She turned back to the screen, rubbed at aching temples with her palms.

"Yes. I'd planned on telling you about this problem." He moved to the console beside her, took a seat facing her.

"Oh?" She wasn't really listening any more.

"Indeed. Yesterday. I looked for you, but you seemed to be moving around a lot. I got tired. I took a nap."

"So are you just going to sit there, or are you going to help me?"

"I don't fix things, I just use them," he replied tersely. "I'll leave this to you. The figures on the propulsion device are fine. Well, at least what they were at yesterday morning. A quarter over, not a jot more." He paused. "There was a spike in the power output yesterday, so we'll need to adjust for that too."

She glanced up at him then, caught his eyes. That, she realised, had been a mistake. She was too tired to act surprised, and her words came out in a sigh. "We could easily blow the station if we used that much power."

He smiled at her then. A sad, thin twitch of the lips. "I thought so," he said, and raised himself from the seat. As he moved toward the door, his gait that of a man filled with confidence, he continued. "You, my dear, shall remain here. I'll take care of the rest. Don't you worry yourself about it."

There was a hard click as he closed the door, and the sound of arcing electricity, then a thud. He'd locked her in.

She turned back to her work. Too drained to do anything about it, too tried to care. He'd left her alive, and for the moment, that was all she needed. All the strength she had left in her was dedicated to getting them home. In her mind, the image of her fiancé, awaiting her arrival on the Docker that was still bound for Io Station nine days away. She wondered whether they'd been turned back. If anyone on Earth knew what had happened.

The tablet in front of her beeped and squawked at her as results from the last diagnostic flashed up on the screen.

Error.

Error.

~

Well, he'd hadn't wanted to do that, but it was done. The woman had evidence, so he'd have to do something about it. Only, he needed her to fix the Frequency Generator. Without it, they'd be stuck, and dead before long.

He strode across the hall to the Comms Room, and poked his head around inside to check if anyone was there. It was clear. He moved on.

If she had told any of the airmen, he wasn't sure what he would do. He'd planned every detail until this point, but there was so much he had not accounted for. So much that he had no way to take into consideration.

He was most certainly guilty of deliberately moving the moon. He would admit that, to himself, at least. But he could brush it off as a happy accident once they returned. A new mode of travel. They may forgive his "accident" for the benefits it would produce.

But if they had proof, somehow, of what he'd done... his life was over. If it wasn't the death penalty, it might well be a life sentence in a mining colony, or exile on titan. He hadn't really let himself think too much on it, before, but he was thinking of it all now.

Heinrich walked the halls with a purpose. He had more than twenty airmen to take care of, and he had to do it quickly. But how?

A heart felt sigh cracked passed his lips and came out as a hiss.

In 2402, while he'd been at university in Switzerland, a sickness had swept through Munich, killing thousands. His entire family — mother, father, brothers, sister, uncles, aunties, cousins — had died, in what came to be known as the Gauson Plague. Gauson had been an American IDC agent in Munich for a seminar with some colleagues. Somehow, he'd gotten hold of a contaminate and, for unknown reasons, had unleashed it at that seminar. The city had been quarantined for months. Supplies had been air-dropped to rushing mobs, where more than a few of the listed fatalities occurred, as riots took place in the streets, and those left fought for every scrap they could get their hands on.

What he had done, he realised, was much as Gauson had done. Only, he hadn't *planned* to kill anyone. And he hadn't planned to drag the ATF fleet along, either. If everything had gone as it should have, then they'd have been back where they were meant to be by now, and no one would have been hurt. They should hardly have noticed.

He shook his head. He wasn't going to get down on himself now. He just had to do what needed to be done. This project was not going to be swept under the rug as so many other before it.

Storage Three loomed up in his sights and he quickened his pace. He didn't know where the crews were, but he knew they'd come here for their rations, eventually.

What rations packs that had been found were lined up in a row along a bench in the locker room. Four had been discarded in a heap at the end of it. He eyed them, deep with thought.

Deciding he had more pressing matters at the moment, he moved on to the power substation. He couldn't raise the output until the frequency generator was online, but he had to figure out how much power he could draw, and do some calculations on how far the fields would extend. He had a baseline to work with, now, and he knew they could do it with less.

Tomorrow, he told himself. We can deal with them all tomorrow.

~

Something collided with the door. A loud bang that startled Deidra from her work. She spun in her chair to see through the glass portal. It was the French airman she'd spoken to after the ceiling collapse. Odd, though, that she hadn't heard him arrive.

She saw him take two steps back, then *throw* himself, shoulder first, into the door. The glass cracked, but held together with the metal mesh inside it. The door itself did not budge.

"While I thank you for your efforts," she said, loud enough that he should be able to hear her. "It's really not necessary."

The man looked like he might brace himself for another lunge, but then shrugged. "That man, he has trapped you in here, no? Do you not wish to come out?"

Deidra couldn't help a faint smile. "Trapped or not, this is where I need to be. The door being locked makes little difference, excepting the need for me to visit the bathroom."

The airman frowned then, looked down at his boots, then back at her. "The other scientist. Royce, she told us all to look out for him." It wasn't a question, but still he waited until she nodded before he continued. "He went to the Storage with the food. He goes now to the power place."

Deidra pinched at the bridge of her nose. "Fine. Get me Dr Hans if you please."

"The blonde man who wet himself?"

"Yes, that would be the one."

By the time the airman had taken his second step down the hall, Deidra was already furiously inputting calculations. Errors seemed to breed like rabbits in her programming. Every time she fixed one, two would arrive. Either the chips had malfunctioned, the core drive itself was corrupt, or the command lines were being overwritten for those sections as soon as she finished with the last.

Her head came up. An idea formed. She pursed her lips together in a pout, scrolled the screen down to the end and went back to the main page. If what she suspected now was right, then it could be a simple fix, though temporary. Or, it could prove impossible.

On the menu she selected the diagnostic tool, then before it had a chance begin, she typed in a command line that would make it deny all corrupt sectors. It would mean that she had to do some of her other calculations over again, but it was better than the alternative.

She watched the screen, eyes on the progression bar.

Footsteps outside. She glanced up.

Ulrich came into view first, his hair a mess, glasses askew, sweat dripping down his face. "Deidra, how can I help?" he asked.

She gestured to the lock. "You have a proficiency with electronics? Unlock the door."

The scientist looked to the airman, who shrugged. Ulrich dipped below her view through the glass of the door.

"Where did you find him?" Deidra wanted to know. She hadn't seen him since the warehouse.

"He was in the Hangar," he replied simply. "What would you have me do, now? The others, they watch and wait."

"What is your name, Airman?" she wanted to know.

"Richard Zim, Ma'am."

"Well, Richard — may I call you Richard?" He nodded his acquiescence. "Richard, I'd like you to stay with Doctor Hans, get him whatever he needs."

"You have decided to come out then. I am pleased." He smiled, white teeth flashing.

Deidra gave him a tight smile in return. *Don't be,* she thought as she glanced at her now empty coffee mug.

The tablet pinged. She looked down on it, and saw that her command had been registered and been employed. She might just get this done in time.

She got back to work.

~

He looked hard at the screen that now showed in the substation. A diagnostic map of the life support system. His eyebrows climbed. He'd known that the air regulator was off, but he'd figured that it was just one more error. To see it was in fact a life support issue —

Heinrich shrugged, shook his head, and moved to the main menu. *It makes little difference. Twelve more hours was all we'd have had.* He flicked through until he came to the power output controls, then sat himself down.

The screen before him now showed readings by the second on a line graph. It reminded him of brain waves, the peaks and troughs so close together with only the occasional spike. Each major system had its own line, and he was startled to see half of them did not move from zero on the graph. The Station was on its last legs, and likely would not survive the return. He had greatly overestimated the amount of energy this station was capable of outputting.

First, then, he would adjust the output parameters, set it to a time that should coincide with Deidra finishing her work. *Perhaps being inside a ship will be enough.* He hoped so.

That done, he found a red warning flashed on the screen.

WARNING! SET PARAMETERS WILL RESULT IN CATASTROPHIC FAILURE. PLEASE INPUT NEW COMMAND. WARNING!

Heinrich slammed his fist down on the edge of the console. Why hadn't it given him this warning last time? Obviously, it should have. But he could not reduce the amount of power required, he'd already adjusted his calculations to the assumption that the field would envelope only the moon.

He let out a growl of frustration. As he watched, another line on the graph turned red and fell to zero, where it stayed. The warning disappeared from the screen.

His brows lifted, hopeful. *Just another error, perhaps?* Either way, it was done. In ten hours, they would be home.

Now, he just had to check on Deidra's progress.

~

The lock clicked with a sharp hiss. Ulrich turned the handle, and the door swung inward with ease. Deidra nodded.

"Thank you," she intoned, with feeling.

A shy smile graced his lips. "You're welcome, Deidra."

There was an awkward moment then, when Ulrich and Richard

stood at the door unmoving, while Deidra remained where she was, tablet in hand.

"Should we come in, then?" the airman asked.

"Oh, please do. Yes." She waved them to other chairs along the bench. "Make yourself comfortable."

They shuffled in, Ulrich first, and sat down, one on either side of her. Ulrich squinted at her tablet, while Richard moved his head from side to side and glanced around the room.

"So, it is as you said," Richard said.

"As I said? What did I -?" *Oh, of course.*

"That you needed to be here. Trapped or not." He smiled at her, his dark eyes twinkled.

She bit her bottom lip. "Indeed. I have to finish these command lines before we can get back home, and I don't have much time to do it."

"The generator is almost fried," Ulrich mumbled beside her. "We'll maybe get one more use out of it, if you manage to get the corrupt sectors working. But it'll not work again."

She turned to face him, but his attention was on the tablet. "How do you know it's fried?"

He pointed toward the glassed off section of Lab Two without raising his head. "Scorch marks."

She handed the man the tablet, which he took without a word. She got up and moved toward the glass. Richard followed her.

Along the lower left quadrant of the massive device, electricity arced over the metallic surface. Dull soot covered the small section beneath it, and small tendrils of smoke curled up toward the ceiling.

"I'd not noticed that before," she said quietly. "In fact, I could swear it wasn't there." Her head swivelled in Ulrich's direction.

"Probably a by-product of what you were doing," he told her absently. His hands danced over the screen as he made adjustments to her command lines.

"Oh?" She wasn't sure if she should be offended by the other scientist taking over her work. In truth, she needed the help, but a part of her was too proud to admit it. Another part of her knew that Ulrich was probably the best person to do it.

"It could not be helped," he glanced up then, pushed his glasses to the bridge of his nose. "It will do the same as we continue." He looked back down, his hands resuming their intricate ballet.

"Why?" Richard asked.

Deidra looked at the airman, then back to the scientist. "Yes. Why?"

Ulrich shrugged. "It was damaged by the power increase. It was not designed to use that much power and the dampeners were fried."

"You can tell all that just by looking at it?"

"That, and the command lines that need to be re-written."

Before she had a chance to say another word, Heinrich walked in. His head shot back in surprise when he saw Ulrich with the tablet.

"So, you've told them, then?" The man sighed. He turned to Ulrich. "I had thought you perished with the others."

"No."

"Clearly." He returned his attention to Deidra, a steady cold, gaze that made her shiver despite the heat.

"I've told them nothing," she said. *Old man, you've much to answer for.*

"Neither here, nor there, really." He resumed his walk into the room, eyed the airman. "Are you a pilot?"

Richard glanced at her. She nodded. "I am."

Heinrich clapped his hands and rubbed them together. A smile bloomed on his weathered face. "Good. Good. We'll require your services when this is done."

Deidra frowned. "Why?"

"Why? Because the station is going to blow, that's why."

Ulrich stopped what he was doing then and glared intensely at the older scientist. Deidra and Richard exchanged glances, then focused on Heinrich.

"There is something that you are not saying, *homme mort.*" Richard stated.

"*Bien sûr, vous êtes sous-développé.*" Heinrich countered. "Don't imagine for a moment that I will not understand what you say, Frenchman. It is not I who is dead."

For hundreds of years there had been an abiding dislike between Germany and its neighbouring countries. If it all could have been condensed into two individuals, Deidra believed she witnessed it now in these men.

"Enough," she growled, surprising herself with the venom that emerged in the word. "It is done. It is all done. Ulrich will assist me with this, and you can go fuck yourself for all I care at this point, Heinrich. If you've nothing to offer here, then get out." She pointed toward the door.

The man looked stunned and confused. She was tired of his threats. She knew what awaited her once she'd finished, and she'd as soon not think about it. His presence looming over her as she worked — well, she'd just not have it.

"You make a mistake, Deidra," he intoned through clenched teeth.

"Did she?" The airmen smiled at him.

Heinrich snorted, "You think yourself bigger than you are."

Richard lifted his head a fraction, and Deidra's gaze swept past Heinrich to the men who now entered the room. She tried to keep her face neutral, but she could not help the grin that appeared. It was done.

The men each grabbed one of Heinrich's arms and lifted him from the floor. Heinrich glanced at each in quick succession, spluttering an oath. "You'll not have me long," he vowed as the airmen pulled him backward from the room. "You'll not have me long."

"Where are they taking him?" Deidra asked once the man's empty threats had stopped echoing down the corridor.

"One of the ships," he told her. "We've not seen a cell, here. We want him confined."

"Royce told you everything then?" He nodded. "And you believe he was responsible for her death?"

"We've no proof. But we assume." As she had no proof of it either, it was likely he would not be charged for that. Truthfully, she didn't have much proof of anything, except that one reading from the mains.

Ulrich peered up at them over the rim of his glasses. "What was that all about?"

Deidra shook her head. She'd forgotten he knew nothing of the events of the last twenty-four hours. She explained to him what Heinrich had done.

"His actions here were proof enough of his intent," Richard finished for her. "So, we confine him. He will be brought to trial on Earth when we return."

The young scientist shook his head and mumbled something she did not understand under his breath.

"Perhaps better to kill him, in case he finds a means of escape," Zim offered.

"We may yet need him," Deidra intoned. "And besides, regardless of what he has done, we are not murderers."

Ulrich rolled his shoulders backwards a few times, clearly uncomfortable with that idea. "We should get back to work. This will not do itself, and it may take the rest of the day."

Deidra moved to take a seat beside the man so they could look over the tablet together, then glanced back over at Richard. "You can go back to your team now."

"I'll stay," the airman stated with certainty.

Inwardly, Deidra smiled to herself. For the first time since the station had begun to crumble around her, she felt something other than dread.

Chapter Nine

The morning came with a burst of wind that rattled trees and whistled through cracks and crevices. The sky was still overcast, the mulch soft and damp, and a misty haze had settled over the brush in the woods.

Harvey hawked and spat off to the side. His lungs felt heavy from the humid air, and he couldn't quite clear the feeling of mucous from his throat. No doubt he was getting sick.

The others were still inside the building, which now, by the hazy twilight just after dawn, he could see was actually built with stone slabs, cut just so and interlocked with no mortar in the seams. It was a feat of masonry that most on Earth would not in these days consider doing. *We build with steel,* he thought. *Steel, and concrete and chalk. A mason wouldn't have the skills to build something this intricate. Not anymore.*

He hadn't gone back to sleep after his short conversation with Greenway. It had become clear to him then, that the man had lost it. He hoped it was temporary.

The trees before him swayed in another gust of wind, then settled. A few leaves drifted slowly down to join those on the ground. The breeze brought with it the smell of cooked meat, faint as it was, and Harvey's stomach growled in response. He'd not eaten anything but a single piece of fruit in over twenty-four hours, and he'd only managed to drink a few handfuls of water during the light downpour the previous night.

His left knee cracked and buckled a little as he rose from his squat. He twisted his neck from side to side, tensed his fingers and folded them into fists, moved his arms back and shoulder blades together until all the joints popped. He sighed as he relaxed his stance. *The price of getting old.* The hip that Weiz had landed on when the ship had shaken the previous day, was bruised but nothing more. Which, he considered, was surprising given all the running they'd done.

He looked back to the entrance at the sound of boots shuffling through dirt. Kristin came out, her uniform covered in dust and dirt, as was half her face. One hand rubbed an eye as she yawned, the other her stomach.

"Morning," he intoned.

She blinked at him. "Morning," she breathed.

"The others?"

"Still asleep," she squinted as she scanned the area. "I'm not inclined to wake them yet."

"So, Greenway finally got some rest?"

"Seems that way."

"You saw him last night?"

She shook her head. "No. Why? What did he do?"

"Doesn't matter." Harvey would keep it to himself for the moment. Give the man some privacy.

"Well, since you're up first; did you catch us any breakfast?" He was ready to reply to the jest in kind, but then he saw she was serious.

"I have nothing to catch an animal with," he gestured to the empty gun in his thigh holster.

She raised an eyebrow at him and breathed an agitated sigh. "Hopeless, you are." It was barely a whisper, but he still heard it. Louder, she said, "Well I guess you've left it to me, then."

Kristin strode into the woods and disappeared behind the trees. He'd not seen anything worth catching in these woods as yet, and despite his hunger, he found himself hoping she didn't bring back one of those giant snake-rats.

His thoughts turned to Weiz. To whether he should call in and let the Commander know that they'd made it through the night and would attempt to make their way back toward the camp.

He was about to press the button when Lance crawled out. "Brian's dead," he said. It was so matter-of-fact it took a moment for the words to sink in.

Harvey wasn't sure what to say. He just stared at the man.

"Where's Kristin?" The Pilot queried after a moment.

Harvey gestured toward the trees with a lazy wave. "She gone to find us something to eat."

A look of disgust crept across the man's face, an expression to match his own thoughts. "Not one of those..."

"I hope not," the Captain agreed. "I might be hungry, but I am not that desperate. Not yet."

The Pilot nodded. "Do you think we'll run into any more of those Shadowmen?"

"I couldn't say. Depends if they'll come out during the day, and what they'd hoped to achieve by herding us the way they did."

"You think there was a purpose behind it?"

"I've been thinking on that," Harvey nodded. "Why they didn't kill us. It's baffled me."

Lance sat down against the outside wall and grabbed up a

handful of twigs. "Can't say I haven't had the same thoughts. What did you come to, then? 'Cause I have nothing."

Harvey leaned back on his haunches beside the man. "Well, for one, we didn't see them until after Kristin killed that rat thing, right?" Lance shook his head. "And that was not long after we left the village, too. And, as far as I can tell, no one else saw them 'til after then as well."

"So, you think they're after us because Kristin killed a rat?"

"No. It's more likely something to do with the Village, it just took them some time to work out where we were, maybe."

"So, what were they doing?"

"I think they were trying to keep us away from any populated areas. A good distance away." Harvey cleared his throat and spat again.

Lance broke a twig and flicked the smaller piece toward the trees. "You think they're protectors?"

"It's just a thought. But, so long as we kept moving in the direction they pushed us, and didn't stop to fight, they'd have no reason to kill us, right? And for what other reason would they do that, unless they're protecting people?"

"Why would those things bother protecting mud hut villagers?" Lance scoffed. "Do you think they have some sort of pact? Do the villagers even know about them?" He stood then, and tossed his handful of twigs to scatter on the mulch. "And the other teams would have run, same as us."

"Well, I been thinking some on that, too," Harvey said.

"Look, sir," the Pilot growled, "save your garbage for someone who, cares, alright?"

Harvey shot up and moved so close to the man their noses almost touched. "Manners, boy," he told him in a low tone, then took a step back. "What's got you wound so tight?"

Lance's teeth ground together, his nostrils flared, his dark eyes stared daggers into Harvey. But he didn't say anything.

They stood like that for a good few minutes before Kristin returned. "What d'ya know," they heard her say before she was visible. "They do have rabbits here. Or, something very like them."

She exited the trees about four feet from where the two men stood. Both sets of eyes moved to her, and the three rabbits she held upside down by their feet. All of them had had their skulls smashed by something heavy and sharp. Blood leaked rivulets down their ears and landed in drops on the ground.

Kristin eyed the scene before her and shot them both a glower that made it plain, she was not impressed. "Viatri," she said in a stern warning tone, "You've had a bug up your butt since the Shadowmen turned up. Out with it now, or I'll make you gut these rabbits." She lifted them high as if to throw them at him and he flinched back.

Harvey let his eyes fall to the ground. He was the Captain. *He* should have been the one to say those words. He should not have got up in the man's face and let anger overtake him. *Again, she does my job, and I allow it.* The more he got to know this girl, the more she reminded him of a young Weiz.

"Well?" Kristin prodded.

"We're not going to make it home," Lance spat. "But you all keep acting like we will. Like everything is normal and tomorrow is just another day. But it's not!"

The vehemence of the words broke through to Harvey. To his own sense of what was happening. *Are we in denial? Has it not settled in yet?*

The Pilot pointed back toward the building. "Brian is dead," he continued in a more controlled voice. "Half the rest of the crews, are dead. And we sit around and pretend that a thing we say matters? Because tomorrow we'll be home?" His voice rose to a shout. "You don't know that! None of us knows!"

Kristin lowered the rabbits slowly until they rested at her side, the blood making a track down her leg. She didn't try to soothe the Pilot, or argue with him. She just lifted her brows. "Feel better?"

"Yes!" he screamed. Suddenly, like a damn released, all the anger left his face, and he began to laugh.

Harvey's eyes bulged. Kristin stepped forward, her lips twitched in a slight smile. She pushed the rabbits against Harvey's chest. "Guess you get to do the gutting," she told him with a wink, then continued past him into the building.

He looked down at the three sorry looking creatures in his arms. *Bet you didn't expect to die today.* He thought sourly.

Harvey spent the better part of the next hour preparing and cooking those rabbits. Lance, while not his usual humorous self, had stopped with the dramatics, and was now busy burying Brian. Greenway, awake now, stared into the fire as if flames held the key to his salvation. And Kristin scouted a path back to the ships.

By the time the food was ready, they were all seated around the fire.

"No sign of the Giants," Kristin said before she hoed into a leg. The grease dribbled down fingers and chin, which she wiped away with a sleeve.

"They'll wait until we all come out," Greenway intoned.

Harvey took a mouthful and eyed the other Captain. His mouth was still half full as he answered Kristin. "But you did find us a path back?"

The woman shrugged. "More or less. It's not exactly straight forward, but I'm sure it's in the right direction."

"How long?" Was all Lance asked.

"Half a day, at least." She took another bite from the leg she was holding, and continued once she swallowed. "After all the running we did last night, I'll be surprised if it's only that far."

They all sat in silence for a while.

Once they'd finished the meal, and his stomach finally settled, Harvey dug a small hole and filled it with the bones. Then, he kicked dirt over the dying embers of the fire and looked around with a nod.

"I'd judge it to be at least eight, in our time," he said to the rest of them. "If it's half a day, then we'd best get moving."

No one argued.

~

Bleary eyed from lack of sleep, and still smarting at the losses of the day before, Weiz looked out on the Giants who still stood where they'd arisen the previous night. The corpses of several airmen lay at the feet of the one she'd personally punched. The others, who'd been unceremoniously thrown by the monstrosity, whole or in pieces, were now joining their comrades in their off-world graveyard.

She glanced at her bandaged hand. It didn't seem enough in penance for the damage it had caused. Perhaps if she'd shattered her arm, and not just broken her hand... But no, she knew they still would have done it.

Along the perimeter of ships, none more than a few steps from the hull, Fields' crew kept watch. Like her, she knew, they mourned for those who'd thrown their lives away.

Fyord stood silently at her shoulder. She knew he had something to say, but he waited patiently.

"Did you see?" she asked him.

"No, Ma'am. I was in the ship."

She nodded and turned to him. "What was it you wanted me for?"

"Pilot Zim called in from Io Station," he told her. "They've taken one of the scientists prisoner, Ma'am. Seems he's the cause of this mess."

"Is that so?" *Why am I not surprised?* She shook her head. *Scientists are a different breed.*

"They've no solid proof, Ma'am, but they plan to keep him

confined to the gun hatch on MM238 until we get back to Earth."

The gun hatch was a small store room near the aft that housed the ammo boxes for the Gunners. She couldn't imagine the scientist would be very comfortable. "Surely they'll transfer him to cell once we're on a Docker?"

Fyord shook his head. "Perhaps, but I can't say for certain."

She raised her brows, but probed no further. "So we have a time frame yet?" She felt better knowing that she was having direct communication with one of her own. Deidra was full of useful information, but she was still a scientist, and as far as Weiz was concerned, she'd learned all she needed from the woman.

"More or less," the comms officer replied. "Zim thinks maybe five to six hours before they're ready. No more than that."

"You told him we'd have to wait until the other teams got back before we can rendezvous at the moon?"

"I did."

She gave the Giants a final glance before she began her walk back to the ship. "We'll need to find a way to get those bodies," she breathed.

"Maybe when they realise we intend to leave, so will they," the man replied as he walked alongside her.

Weiz grunted. *Might as well wish we were all well fed, sitting at our desks on the Docker. Or better yet, home already.* But she felt herself fervently hoping the airmen was right. Though, if it came to that, they may not have time.

She entered the hatch of MM294.

"No word from Harvey?" she asked as she sat down at the console.

"Not yet."

Weiz adjusted the dials, pushed down on a button and spoke. "Harvey, can you hear me?"

~

They'd been on Kristin's trail for at least an hour when the call came through. "Harvey, can you hear me?"

Harvey didn't stop as he pressed the button on his cuff. "Loud and clear, Weiz."

"What's your situation?"

His eyes shifted across the trees that surrounded them. "We're on our way back. Probably take us half a day, Kristin says."

"Kristin says?"

"She's on point."

"No other — *confrontations* — with the Giants?" Weiz's voice took on a sadness that Harvey had heard only once before.

"None as yet. What's happened?" He stepped over a branch that had broken off the tree beside him, his eyes on Kristin's back.

There was a pause from Weiz, one that held so many feelings. Harvey wanted to wrap his arms around the woman. *When I get back to camp, I'm going to say it outright, woman. And you are going to hear me. No more skirting around this business. I will retire, spend some more time with my son. And you. You could come with me. If you wanted.*

"We have three of them at the camps edge nearest the woods," she told him finally.

There was more, he could feel it. "And?"

"We've lost nearly thirty more." He could hear the lump in her throat.

He didn't know what to say. He never did when people told him of their losses. Just as he had only stared at Lance earlier when he'd informed him of Brian's death. Or worse, as he'd stood, blank and emotionless in front of the police officer when he had learned of his wife's death. He was no good at these things.

His mind raced as he tried to think of something — anything — to say. "We'll be back, when we're back." It came out gruffer than he'd intended. He tried to soften his words, but didn't think he succeeded. "I'll call in if we run into any trouble."

When Weiz answered, she sounded sadder than she had before. "Fair enough." And he flipped the comms off.

Ahead of him, Kristin crouched as she closely studied the ground. He didn't know what she was looking at or for, but he joined her none-the-less.

Her eyes flicked to him then away. "I don't think those Giants make tracks, Sir."

"Why is that?"

She pointed to the ground all around them. "Our prints," she said, "are everywhere. But there is no sign of the Giants. Also, I don't think I even once saw their feet touch the ground."

Harvey snorted. "Didn't look like they were flying to me."

"Not flying, just not touching the ground."

"Is there something we can't see?" He'd intended his tone to be encouraging, but it had the opposite effect.

She rose to her feet and looked to the west. "We won't end up in the village, but that place crept me out anyway. We'll probably come out of the woods four hundred or so metres from the ships. Should be a clear run from there."

"You've no more to say about the Giants?"

She turned to him there, her brows drawn in thought. "Nothing solid, Captain. And they don't make much sense in my mind. Less, when I actually say it out loud."

Harvey stood up. "Well, when you're ready to share, you let me know."

"One thing I'll say," she told him, uncertain.

"Hmm?"

"Grab some branches," she suited her own words by taking up a large fallen branch, roughly eight feet long and covered in a desiccated layer of bark. She snapped off an end, examined the wood inside, then discarded it.

"Grab some branches?" he queried as he watched.

"I've a feeling, sir. Nothing solid, like I said before." She pulled up a branch that was slightly smaller than the last from underneath the mulch. Repeated the procedure. This time she nodded and stamped it into the ground like a walking stick.

The others had gathered behind them, and were even now finding some suitable wood. Harvey didn't know what he was looking for, but soon enough he had a four-inch thick, six-foot-long branch, that didn't look like it would break in a single swing.

Delegation was a part of leadership, and that was what he was doing, having Kristin on point. He knew he was probably giving her too much leeway, but he also knew that she was their best shot of getting back to the ships alive. He had to let her have her head, as the saying went.

You know you wanted to step back, he told himself. *So just let her have it for a while. You were never really cut out for Captaincy anyway.* That wasn't entirely true. He was fully capable of the leadership necessary; he just didn't like it.

Once they all had their branches, Kristin moved on. As they walked, she slowly pulled the bark from the outside of hers, revealing a hard, dry inner core. Harvey followed suit, and imagined those behind him did the same.

This was going to be a long walk.

~

Deidra fell back in her seat and closed her eyes with a triumphant, "Yes!" hissing past her lips. They'd done it. They finally had it.

She sat up, a smile so wide on her face that it hurt her cheeks and looked to Ulrich. "So that's it? We're done?"

The young genius put down the tablet. "We're done."

Richard had left them some time ago at an order from his superior. He had not come back, and Deidra now found herself wondering where he was.

The charred section of the generator was expanding slowly to cover almost a third of the lower right corner. It was not going to last long, so they had to do this soon.

"We should contact the Commander," she told Ulrich.

The expression on his face was one of incomprehension. She didn't bother to explain, she just got up and moved to the door.

Outside, to either side, stood an airman, at ease but watchful. She was curious as to what they watched for, given that Heinrich had been taken care of, and as far as she was aware, no other scientists or maintenance crew had been found. But she did not ask.

Just as she was about to walk into the comms room, the elevator for Hangar Two hissed open. Richard strode out, the British man who'd ordered them to check the vents in toe. She waited at the door.

"Doctor Ward," Richard gave a nod. "This is our Captain, William Winslow."

The Captain gave her a brief nod, exchanged glances with the guards at her door. "We've interrogated your companion, and I think we should talk," he encouraged her to step into the comms room.

"What has he done?" she asked. *Why can I not have a moment's celebration? A job well done, let's go home. Bah! Even my thoughts aren't making sense any more. I need sleep.*

Deidra sat down at the nearest desk. Her ankle still bothered her.

"He has informed us that he's set a timer for the power output," Winslow informed. "And, that we don't have much time."

Deidra glanced at her watch. It was barely passed three in the afternoon. She'd only just finished the calculation with the help of Ulrich. What would Heinrich have done if she hadn't finished in time? Just let the whole damned moon explode? It wasn't worth thinking about. She was too tired.

"How long is not long, Captain?" she sighed. "I told the

Commander that she'd need to have her ships up here by ten tonight. That's seven hours away. Do we have that long?"

Richard and Winslow exchanged looks. The Frenchman shrugged and stepped forward. "Less than an hour. I'll call them up."

He moved over to the console.

Deidra ran a hand through her hair. "Well, you'd best call your men to board those ships. We're going to want to be far away from here when this goes off."

"How do you mean?"

"Did Richard not tell you?"

The Captain glanced over the dark man as he began his communique. "Tell me what?" His eyes came back to her.

"This whole station will be little more than rubble after the equipment is triggered." Had she even told the airman? She couldn't remember, but she assumed she must have.

He didn't question, he just raced out the door. Deidra peered out after him, but soon even the echoes of his running footsteps no longer reached her. She turned her attention to Richard.

He'd finished his call to the Commander and now stared at her with intense eyes. "We have to find a way to give them more time, Doctor Ward."

She pulled her brows down. "Can they not make it up?"

"Not all of them, no."

"They'll have to find a way and fast," she told him. "All or none, we're leaving."

His face took on an aspect of desperation, though none of it reached his voice. "Tell me where to find this power substation, and I will make sure we have the time," he insisted.

She shook her head. "You can't. Even if you managed to get around Heinrich's coding, there is still the generator. It's damaged and won't remain working for long. I was coming to call the

Commander, as you just did. She'll need to have them up here and soon. If they're not..." She let it hang in the air.

The tall man scowled as he rose from his chair. "Another hour is another hour, Doctor. We must make this work!" He strode past her to the door. "Guide me or tell me, but I will make this happen."

With reluctance, Deidra got up from her chair. The news she'd felt so good about, now felt like a burden on her soul. The ships on the ground were not going to make it.

~

Weiz glared down at the crack in the screen, broken fist throbbing where it rested on the surface. It hadn't broken the console, but she regretted the burst of temper.

An hour to get the ships up there, when she promised me 'til tonight, she thought, furious. *I have to find a way to get everyone home. I have to.*

It was not normal for her to express such strained emotions where others could see, but the events of the last twenty-four hours had left her frayed. Tears of pure frustration threatened to stream from the corners of her eyes, held in check by sheer stubbornness.

She was the Commander. She was here to lead, as she had so many times before. As she had succeeded, many times before. So why was she having such a hard time with this? Everything seemed a misstep.

Fyord stood behind her, silent, gaping.

"We have to find a way," she grated.

They hadn't heard back from any of the other teams. As far as she knew, Harvey's was the only one left out in the woods. All those who were going to come back, were already there, and she had to come to terms with that. There was still a part of her that wanted to deny it, but as the Commander, she knew she didn't have the luxury.

She pushed down a button. "Harvey," she said softly.

What I would not give to have you here now to comfort me. What I would not say to make you mine. You idiot man.

It took a moment, but he replied. "What's the situation?" Weiz rested her head on her arm where it lay on the console, and spoke into it, voice muffled.

"We're out of time. We need to be on the surface of the moon in less than an hour. I need you to get back here quickly."

There was a pause.

She waited.

Fyord shifted nervously behind her. Perhaps he knew that she would not leave them behind. Perhaps he thought he should inform the rest of the crew that they had little time, and would then let them take things into their own hands.

She didn't care.

When Harvey's voice came through it was hard and resolute. "That's going to be a problem."

"How far away are you?" She sat up, her voice clearing. This was not what she wanted to hear.

"At least a few hours. Kristin says we're just about half an hour from the village."

Weiz didn't know what to say. They couldn't fly into the woods and land a ship to retrieve them. For one they had no true coordinates, and for another they'd have very few places to land.

Then a thought occurred. "Could we not just pick you up from there? From the village I mean. You said they had a field?"

Why did it feel like forever between replies? "Go without us," he told her solemnly.

"No."

"Catherine." The way he said her name was like a ghosts embrace across her skin.

"No, Harvey, I will not!" She slammed her fists down on the console again, a tear she'd been holding back escaped to run down her cheek. *I will not leave you.*

But Harvey gave no reply.

She viewed the console, it was still on, still working.

But Harvey gave no reply.

~

Harvey let go of the comms button, but Weiz's voice still came through. He switched off the lapel speaker. Silence.

Not more than a few paces ahead, Kristin had stopped and was staring at him. He caught her eye and stared right back.

Lance grabbed his jacket and spun him around. A fist hit his left jaw, and he spun once before he landed on his side.

"You don't get to make that decision for us!" he yelled down at him.

Harvey blinked rapidly at the ground. A dribble of blood escaped his lips, and he wiped it away with the back of his hand as he rose to his feet.

Lance and Kristin stood shoulder to shoulder, arms crossed. Harvey spat blood onto the ground, glared at the two people before him.

The Pilot smirked, turned in his stance and made his tattooed eyes dance. Harvey shivered. "Lance!" The man laughed.

"Let's just go," he said, facing him once more.

Greenway grimaced at the man, pressed down on his comms button and radioed in. "Meet us at the Village, Weiz. Greenway, out."

Harvey stepped back. Turned to Kristin. And saw a Giant.

CHAPTER TEN

She nearly wept tears of relief when Greenway called in after Harvey. The village, she could manage that, if the field was big enough. If it wasn't...well, she'd just have to figure something out.

Weiz shot out of her chair, a purpose in mind. Fyord moved out of her way as she raced out the hatch, only a step behind her.

"Gather the teams and get them ready to fly out!" she ordered without looking back. He gave no reply, but she heard him run off in the opposite direction.

She moved directly for Fields.

"I need you to fly us to the village, Pilot," she demanded before she stopped in front of her.

Fields peered up at her with hooded eyes, and a slight frown.

"Now!" Weiz screamed in her face, spittle spraying out.

The airman came to sudden attention. "You lot! We're off."

The crew gathered in and followed Weiz back to the ship at a run.

Fields took the pilots seat and got the ship online.

A thought made the Commander hit the internal comms. "Walt!

Dames! Are you still with us?"

"We are." Dames sounded as if he'd just woken up.

"We're going to get Harvey. If you see a Giant getting in our way, unload. We're going home."

There was a grunt from one of them, but it was Walt who spoke. "Took you long enough."

Weiz grimaced and hit button again. She didn't have time for their smart-arsed comments.

The Giants on the field below could be clearly seen as they rose slowly into the air. The ship had been refuelled, siphoning from the ones they knew they would not need. It would be enough for them to break atmosphere and land if they needed to, but no more than that.

As they moved toward the treeline, climbing higher as they went, the Giants disappeared.

Behind them, ship after ship took off into the sky, their occupants ready to go home.

Home, she thought. *Strange that I never doubted we'd get there. But Harvey, you sweet, stupid man. You're coming with me.*

The trees passed below them slowly. They took the exact direction she had sent Harvey's team out in.

She gripped the back of the pilot's seat with her good hand as she stared out of the view port. She had only a vague idea of what to expect from Harvey's description, but she'd know it when she saw it.

"Faster," she instructed, leaning further forward.

The ship picked up speed, but not so fast they couldn't stop quickly. Eyes scanned the horizon.

In less than ten minutes, they had found the spot. Fields spun them around and landed them smoothly on the sodden dirt of the plantation. It wasn't as seamless as Lance's had been, but it was as near perfect as any Pilot she'd flown with.

"Keep the engine running," she told the woman, and rushed to the hatch.

Her boot squelched down into mud at the first step. It clung with suction as she took the next. After a few more, her boots were so covered in the muck, that she had to shake off before she could move further.

She didn't realise that Fields had come out with her until she reached the trees, and the woman entered her peripheral vision.

Her heart raced. They should reach the ship soon. She looked back toward it; irrationally afraid it would not be there. When she faced the trees once more, a Giant came toward them.

~

The screen in the substation blinked a warning. Richard, at the controls, attempted to reset the timer. The action was denied by the system.

Deidra shoved him aside and tried to get around Heinrich's coding, but the controls would not let her. Every stroke of the keyboard was met with a noise that sounded like a buzzer, but nothing changed.

They were running out of time. They had to get back to the hangar.

She turned to Richard. "There is nothing we can do."

He regarded her coolly, and without a word, tried again to affect the desired time. He continued, relentless despite the futility. She grabbed at his sleeve and tried to turn him away from the console, but he merely swung his hips and flung her away, eyes never leaving the screen.

"We have to go!" she shouted at him.

"I am not leaving without Commander Weiz!" he returned.

She gazed around the room for inspiration. She did not want to be anywhere close to the station when the timer got the zero. It might as well have been a bomb. Propped in a corner, near the seat of the console, was a broken section of pipe she assumed Heinrich had left there.

Can I drag him? she wondered. Then decided it didn't matter. She'd try. If she had to, she'd leave him, but not if she had a choice.

"We have to go, *now!*" she tried to reason. "We need you, Richard. You're a pilot, right? Well, I don't know who else you lost, but I'm guessing there was at least one pilot, so I don't think we can afford to go without you."

But if he heard her, he gave no indication.

She grabbed up the pipe and swung it straight at his head. *God help me, I hope this knocks you out.* But it didn't connect. He must have seen it coming from the corner of his eye, as he twisted to grab the pipe right next to her hand. His face was contorted in a snarl, but it calmed when he saw the horror on hers. He wrenched the pipe from her grip and threw it to the ground.

They locked eyes. The intensity of his gaze made her want to draw back, but like a rabbit in headlights, she could not move. Slowly, his features relaxed, and he stepped away.

"I apologise," he mumbled. It would have to do.

"Then let's go!"

~

Kristin had her attention on the boys behind her. In that moment, that was how she thought of them. Boys, not men. It was idiotic to think that a fist fight would get them to camp any faster. She'd heard what Weiz had said. Had heard Harvey's reply.

And he's right. We're not going to make it in time. If we cut to the village, then maybe...

Greenway put the call in. The decision was made. She turned around.

Before her, less than a metre away, was one of the Shadowmen.

Her blood rose. She shot out a bitter laugh. She had to make it home. It was her first mission. Her brother needed her. Random and fractured thoughts raced through her mind as her eyes rose to meet the ruby red glow of the Giant's own.

"Fuck this," she told it. "I'm going home." She planted her feet in a wide stance. Then, as the Giant swept toward her with its immutable stride and unhurried pace, she stabbed out and up with her stripped branch.

The stick punched through sternum, the impact jarred her wrist and shoulder, but she held on. The Giant continued. A wounded roar that sounded like a flight of condors assailed her where she stood. She shifted her weight to the left and heaved. The Giant moved with the direction of her makeshift lance and fell sideways to the ground.

She kicked down on its jaw. Felt her ankle snap. A gasp. Pain.

Kristin wrenched the stick free of the Giant's sternum, and almost lost balance. She angled its tip to the Giant's face and fell with all her weight. The branch bit deep and kept moving. Muscles strained; veins popped out on her forehead. She heard a *crack*, and toppled over, her body falling to lay beside the now dead Shadowman. Well, she hoped it was dead, anyway.

Her breath came in gasps. "I'm going home," she breathed, determined. *Who dares wins.* A chuckle escaped her. She'd done it!

She rolled her head to view the Giant beside her, only to see it evaporate into the air around her. She tried to hold her breath, but it was as if the dark smoke forced its way into her.

Faintly, Kristin could hear the sounds of battle around her. She found herself hoping that the others had fared better than she had. There was no way she was going to make it back to even the village in time, with her ankle the way it was.

The mist that had come of the creature swarmed into her on an in-drawn breath. She felt things stir inside her. A churning that made her want to vomit. She rolled onto her stomach, got herself to hands and knees, then began to dry heave. She needed to get it out.

Her eyes spied a figure on the ground near her, wrapped in a dark cloud. The significance of it escaped her. Her thoughts raced, an invasion of memories that were not her own. This was *wrong.*

I have to get it out. She coughed. *Get out of me!* But as hard as she tried, the most she could bring up was spittle and a bitter string of bile. Even the rabbit they'd eaten that morning stubbornly refused to be moved.

Exhausted, she fell onto her side, breathing hard.

Around her, she heard the others retching. She sat up to view them, and discovered she felt better with every breath. She stood.

Lance was half covered in a dark cloud, struggling to get out from underneath it. But every move he made, it followed, as if it were aware. Greenway and Harvey, facing away from each other, were both coughing up mucous and bile onto the damp mulch. First Harvey, then Greenway, fell onto their sides, much as she had.

An awareness came to her. Sight, smell, sensation. *Just the aftermath,* she told herself. *What a thousand soldiers on a thousand battlefields have described of their first life or death situation.* But even as she thought it, she knew it to be a lie. This was hardly her first tour of duty, just her first with the ATF.

A sudden mind spasm engulfed her, and while vitality returned clarity faded away, replaced by vague and disjointed memories not her own.

Thunder roared in the distance, lightening arched. Mountains rose from plains and oceans. A city, buried in the dust and detritus of ages. A hand reaching out toward a lever, screams and shrieks sounding all around.

Fire burned behind her eyes, and she fell to her knees, hands at her temples, eyes squeezed shut. The vision passed.

Even as the feeling of pressure released, she looked up to see the others on their feet, no sign of the Giants they had each killed. Eyes darted, each silently asking the others, in their own way, *what just happened?*

She breathed hard. How much time had passed? Only moments. "We can do this," she told them, more for herself than for them.

Harvey looked stricken, as he took a step forward, then vanished.

Kristin stood blinking for a moment. Then turned to see the look of shock on the other's faces. *Jesus fuck, what is going on?*

~

Weiz dived to the side, coming up on guard. She was remotely aware that Fields had done the same in the opposite direction.

The Giant lunged at her, soundless. She let herself fall, then rolled with enough momentum that when she found her feet she slid and fell on her arse.

This was the end of it. If that Giant caught her, if it laid a single finger upon her, she knew she'd cease to exist. In any meaningful way, at least. She had no real beliefs in what came beyond, but she wasn't ready to just let go. Not yet. Not like this.

She got up on all fours, covered in mud and manure. The smell clung to her nostrils and made her want to gag. She blew it out forcefully, even as she gained her feet and spun to see a Giant's hand closing on her head. Reflex made an arm go up in a blocking gesture.

They connected. Her arm held firm. She didn't have time for surprise, as the Giant's other fist flew toward her. She moved forward, inside the blow, and sent her fist up under its chin. Pain coruscated down from her hand, and up the length of her arm to the shoulder, the shattered bones grinding.

She swerved off to the side as the Giant staggered back. She didn't know what had changed. She didn't understand why she could hurt it now, but she wasn't about to let the opportunity pass.

Weiz darted after it. She kicked at its ankle, it stumbled. She rammed her unbroken fist into ribs. A solid snap kick with the sole of her boot in the creature's solar plexus, followed by a series of smacks to its face where a nose should have been.

She didn't let up. Refused to let it get its feet. She felt bones break as she stomped on its forehead with her boot.

It stilled.

The Commander took a few steps back, breathing hard, and vomited onto the ground. From the corner of her eye, the Giant became mist.

~

Deidra wanted to run. She could feel the time ticking by, the seconds fast turning to minutes. The corridors, so familiar an hour before, seemed too long, the hangar too far out of reach. Every step came too slow, her right ankle an inconvenience that she could not discard.

Panic welled within her, and she couldn't fight it, couldn't stomp it down. Richard kept pace beside her, seemingly in no hurry to reach the hangar. She wanted to throttle him, to grab him by the wrists and *drag* him. But a part of her knew that he did it for her. So she knew she wouldn't be left behind.

She glanced at the watch on her wrist. She'd set it to count down with the substation timer. They had just over twenty minutes.

They neared the elevator, and despite her ankle she quickened her pace.

Almost there. She swiped her card.

She waited.

The elevator clicked open, and she almost fell in her rush to enter, hands coming up before her as she aimed for the close button. She didn't even consider the man who came in after her. In her mind, he was no longer there.

She had to get to the ship.

The elevator descended. Fingers beat a fast tattoo on the grab bar.

The doors drew back. Deidra's hip collided with something on her way out, and she felt hands enclose on her waist.

"Careful," the Frenchman intoned, and let go. "My ship is the furthest."

She moved forward.

Previously hidden by the other ships, at the base of the ship hatch, stood four crew members, all looking anxious and ready to be gone. Her eyes widened in silent agreement.

There was no discussion as they all climbed on board. Deidra followed Richard onto the bridge. The available seats were already taken, and she sat cross-legged in the most unobtrusive spot she could find.

Oh, shit, she thought as she sat, and nearly got back up. *Shit, shit, shit.* "Richard!"

He turned his attention to her, though it was hard to see his face from where she sat. "Doctor?"

"Who's going to open the roof?"

~

Harvey spat the last of the mucous from his mouth, bent over, hands on thighs, and looked around. Kristin was on her knees in the duff, hands pressed to her temples, eyes squeezed shut. Greenway lay on his back, eyes to the sky, gaping. Lance was on hands and knees as he lost his breakfast to the damp plant litter.

He'd seen Kristin's branch go into the Giant she faced. But that was all he'd seen, before the other Shadowmen had shown up. *One for each of us. They didn't want us going into that village.* They'd had no time to run.

First Harvey had swung his branch to connect with the things face. From the corner of his eye, he'd seen Greenway do something similar. But from that point, he hardly recalled what he had done to fell the Giant. And yet he must have.

The dark mist was something that concerned him. What had happened there? Why had it happened? What did it mean? Was it the Giants last protection against predators? *Fuck me, but I would hate to think what would hunt those things.*

Kristin was getting to her feet.

Something didn't feel quite right. His head swam. His vision became fractured, overlapping scenes. One where he saw Kristin looking to him in mute surprise, and another where Weiz stood with her back to his ship, head down.

He took a step toward her, and his sight cleared. He strode toward the Commander.

Harvey paused in his stride and looked around. *How the fuck...?*

Weiz saw him. She pushed herself away from the ship's hull. She was covered in mud, he noted, but he didn't care. He ran to meet her halfway.

They collided in an embrace. He lifted her from the ground and kissed her dirt-streaked face, held her close.

"I never want to hear you say those words again," she wept into him.

He pulled back slightly from her grasp, but she held on tight, so only his head moved. "And what words would those be, my love?" *My love. So long I have waited to say those words.*

Weiz breathed a sound of contentment into his chest. "To leave without you."

"Never again," he promised.

She released him and stood back, then. Her ice blue eyes looked deep into his own. "Where are the rest of your team?"

He blinked down at her. A part of him was aware that what just happened should not have been possible, but another part of him instinctively understood why. *And how.* "I don't know." And that was the truth.

~

They were far enough away now, that should the entire station collapse, they'd not be affected by spewing jets of lava. Richard had explained to her that the Captain had taken care of the roof mechanisms, rigged up a control module. Because they hadn't needed to fly out the same way they'd come in, being re-pressurised, they could simply leave it open once they were on their way.

They flew now, just over a kilometre above the surface, in case there was a crust expansion when they re-entered Jupiter's orbit.

Deidra kept her eyes on the Pilots view screen. Along the bottom it had several camera angles in small sections, through which she saw the dwindling station. Her home for four years, that was about to be destroyed. *Will I miss it?* she wondered.

She glanced down at her watch. The seconds flashed. Three. Two. One. She squeezed her eyes shut, waited for the explosion, the roar of collapse. But it didn't come.

Her eyes opened to see the Captain staring at the view screen, mouth agape. She followed his gaze, and saw only empty space there.

Deidra bit back her tears. Io was gone. And they hadn't gone with it. They were stuck.

Oh Dane, please forgive me, she thought. *I will find my way back to you, I swear.*

Part
Two

~ The Becoming ~

CHAPTER ELEVEN

Somehow, in the midst of a nightmare, they'd managed to make a home on the ground of the planet they now called Eridu. It had been difficult to start with, everyone coming to terms with the fact they weren't getting home any time soon.

On the day they'd killed the Giants, everyone who hadn't been with Weiz or Harvey had broken atmosphere, only to suffer the bitter disappointment of a disappearing moon. And while those on the ground found some satisfaction in their triumph over the Giants, they were left with some confusion as to the how. And a little dismay over the consequences, which were yet to fully express themselves.

The scientists, and the remaining ATF crews that had been on Io Station during that time, had landed not long thereafter. Since that day, they'd spent a great deal of time butchering abandoned vessels to find the parts they required to make a new device that could get them all home. So, they had not given up hope, yet. Though, at times, one might be forgiven for believing they had.

Every day, teams were assigned to go out on hunting and

gathering missions, and it had become something of a joke to go into the village and steal their food and supplies. It was no surprise to him that Kristin often lead these parties. And, the huge snake-rats, he had to admit, made quite a good stew.

Harvey sat now at the edge of the ship line, facing toward the forest. Since that day, everything had changed. It wasn't just because they were stuck on a planet far from home with no idea of how long they'd be there, but because of what the Giants had given them.

Weiz, Fields, Lance, Kristin, Greenway and himself had all been blessed with a kind of vitality that an athlete would be jealous of. Speed, strength, vision all increased to super-natural proportions. They all also seemed to have their own aspected — *power* for lack of a better term.

Harvey grabbed a handful of dew-wet grass, looked up to the grey sky and breathed in the smell of fresh morning air. *Sometimes the simple things are all we need.*

Behind him, footsteps that he would not have heard a month ago, sounded loud in his ears as they crunched through the grass toward him.

Without turning, he said, "Had another vision?"

Kristin grunted and sat down beside him. "If you can call it that," she replied.

"What would you call it?"

"A bad dream."

"You knew that the scientists would come down before they did. You knew where the lightening would strike last week," he tried to encourage.

She shrugged uncomfortably and stared out into the distance. "Most of them are just like the first," she told him after a while.

"A city buried? A hand on a control?"

"That would be the one."

"You don't think it means anything?"

"I don't see how it can."

They sat in silence for a while. Harvey's mind drifted. He could move where he willed, it seemed. No matter the distance. He hadn't got the courage yet to attempt to will himself back home, but he felt the day was approaching. He missed his son and often found himself wondering if he'd been informed of his disappearance. Or if the ATF had classified them as presumed dead.

A chill breeze swept across the plain, the grasses swayed toward the north. A light rain began to fall. It was definitely spring.

"How's Weiz?" Kristin asked.

It took him a moment to realise that she had spoken, and when he answered he chose his words carefully. There were some things that were just between them. "She's healed up well, as we all did," he told her. "But she still has nightmares about that first night."

Kristin nodded as if she had expected no different. "Lance has finally gotten his sense of humour back," she informed. "He's still not the same, I guess, but he's getting there."

"So has he shaved his hair off yet?"

"This morning," she grinned. "The eyes are back."

Harvey chuckled. "You know, I really hated those things. But if he gives them a dance in front of me, I promise I won't go off at him."

"Better if you did. If you don't treat him normally, he won't act it."

There was wisdom in her words to which he nodded. Lance had not taken the victory against the Giants the way the rest of them had. He had yet to find his aspect, as it were, and he was concerned that they had just not yet felt the negative side effects of the curse. To his mind, the other shoe had simply yet to drop, and he spent most of his time worrying about what would happen when it did.

While Kristin and Harvey both chose to take it a day at a time, Weiz pretended their new power did not exist, and Fields walked around confused all the time. Greenway had gone off by himself into the woods, day after day, returning after night fall with not much to say. It was a sorry group they made.

"You going out again today?" he asked.

"No. Think I'll spend some time with Viatri, make sure he's not just putting on a show for me." She smirked and stood. "Actually, I should probably get back there now."

Harvey grinned back at her and rose to his feet as well. He swiped at the back of his pants to dislodge any grass that might have clung. "I'll go check on Weiz."

Together they moved into the row of ships.

Kristin left him when they reached MM294. They all shared the bridge, technically, but most nights Weiz and he elected to sleep under the stars, unless it was raining too heavily. It was something they used to do, back during their Earth days when they'd first joined the ATF.

Harvey continued on until he came to the centre of the camp, where had been erected a structure of sorts, made from the outer hulls of abandoned ships, and debarked logs from the forest. It wasn't much to look at, just a thatch work of grey and black metals, arrayed in no discernible pattern, attached to the butt end of several wooden posts using electrical wires and tape. But it kept the rain off the communal fires, and became the place for the crews to congregate when they had nothing better to do. Which wasn't too often, he had to admit. Living off the land kept them busy and tired.

He crossed through the now largely empty space, as most had not bothered to come out of their ships yet, and made his way to the outer perimeter, where Deidra had set up her Lab. Four ships parked with their hatches facing a centre point. A structure, much like the one in the centre of the camp, was in the middle of the clearing between the ships, but on a smaller scale, and with sides.

The crews that had been on Io station on the first day had taken it upon themselves to be protectors of sorts. And Fields, whom Harvey suspected was having a less than professional relationship with Zim, was often seen in the area also. Not that he was in a position to judge, of course, as most people were now aware of his and Weiz's relationship status. But gossip would always abound, wheresoever humans congregated, he was sure.

He entered the structure, expecting to find Weiz with Deidra as she went about her work. The Commander came by for updates of a morning and an afternoon, to gauge how the project was coming along.

But Weiz was not there.

Fields sat cross-legged on the ground against one of the sides, and as he closed the hatch behind him, Deidra looked up from her work on a circuit board.

"She's not here," she said simply, and put her head back down.

"Do you know where she might be?" he queried.

It was Fields who answered. "Went back to your ship to check on Lance."

He sighed. He hadn't expected that. Weiz had been avoiding the man as much as possible for the first month. She found his disposition "too depressing". But if he was getting his sense of humour back...

Harvey grunted his thanks, then walked out the hatch. If there was any kind of reply, he didn't hear it.

The camp was beginning to stir. It was almost like an alarm bell had gone off as crews began to emerge from hatches, barefoot or booted, their footsteps crunching the grass beneath. Whispered conversations and laughing asides warred with the sound of rain drops on metal.

Harvey moved back toward his ship at a hurried pace. Two crew members had lit the cook-fires and were tending them keenly, as he passed back through the camp centre. Another hundred metres, and he was climbing into his ship.

On the bridge, Kristin sat in her comms chair, facing Lance, who was in his pilots seat. Harvey could see the tattooed eyes on the back of his once again bald pate, and he cracked a grin.

"Did I interrupt?" he wanted to know.

The eyes danced. Harvey cringed. "Not at all, sir."

"God damn it, Lance," he said, but without the usual venom that would have accompanied the statement.

The Pilot laughed. "What brings you here?" The brow of his left tattoo lifted a fraction.

"I was looking for Weiz. Deidra told me she'd come back here. Where is she?"

"Left a while ago, Captain. Before Kristin came in, even."

"Any idea where?" He was becoming concerned. Catherine Weiz was a woman of routine, and she was off course.

Lance actually turned toward him, then. "Said something about going for a walk. Think she just wants some time to herself."

There was pity in Kristin's eyes. "Don't take it too personally, sir. I'm sure she's just trying to sort some things in her own mind, like the rest of us."

He sighed. "Has she sent anyone out to scrounge, yet?"

Kristin shook her head. "Not that I know of. But that's not to say she hasn't."

"Think I'll go out myself." He decided. "I haven't been too useful with these things of late." At all, was more accurate, but he wasn't about to admit that.

Kristin glanced between Harvey and Lance, an expression of apology and desire, and he couldn't tell to which of them each look corresponded, until Lance said. "Go on then. You'd get miserable just sitting around with me anyway."

She smiled and patted his arm as she rose. "And you know it, you freak."

His hand caught a hold of hers before she could drag it away, and she looked to the pilot seriously. "Come back, though, Belle."

She pulled her arm away and slapped him upside the head as he laughed at her. "You'll never give up on that, will you?"

"Not until I die," he informed.

Kristin strode past Harvey toward the hatch, and he was forced to follow at a quickened pace.

Outside, he said, "I thought you wanted to spend the day with him?"

She glanced sideways at him but continued her quick pace in the direction of the forest. "Oh, I did. Before I got there. And then I remembered that his sense of humour also included a great deal of flirtation."

Harvey found himself chuckling at that statement. "As it was with our last comms officer," he told her.

She stopped then, hand to her chest with an expression of mock indignation. "So, he doesn't have feelings for me?" she opened and closed her mouth silently a moment, then cracked a grin and resumed her walk.

"Not offended, then?"

"I'd already gathered as much, Captain."

They walked the remaining distance to the tree line in silence, content just have someone else for company. The clouds overhead were clearing, the rain drying up, even as they entered the forest.

"You want to take the lead?" Harvey asked.

"Race you to the village?"

Harvey guffawed. "You know that wouldn't be a fair race."

"Not using your special little trick," she clarified.

"Still wouldn't be fair," he mumbled under his breath, but of course she heard him, and he got a painful punch in the shoulder for it.

"Don't be a pig," she told him, and ran off into the woods.

~

Deidra examined her work closely. *As good as it will get out here,* she thought. She pursed her lips together, brows drawn down, and tested the edge of the soldering. It flaked off, and the wire popped loose.

She had to restrain herself from throwing the circuit board against the dirt floor, and thereby ruining all the work she'd just done.

Fields leant over her, put a hand down over one of her own. "It'd be easier if you didn't have to solder," the woman said.

"Give me a way around it then."

The pilot had been helpful over the last few weeks, giving her bits and pieces of advice that sped things along quite nicely. But sometimes, she felt, the woman could tell her some things *before* she had a problem.

"Drill a hole," the woman shrugged, then sank back on her haunches.

Deidra stood and looked to the roof of her makeshift lab. *Why, dear God, do you challenge me so?* "How would I drill a hole, without a drill?"

"A screw."

"Do you have a screwdriver? Or a screw that small? I'm already at a disadvantage here trying to build a chip at more than a thousand times scale, here. Millimetres over nanometres. I cannot do it with the equipment I'd usually have at hand in an ATF RD Lab, and now I have to use things that would have suited a supercomputer in the mid twentieth century!" she growled. "I've not the knowledge of such archaic means of sophisticated machinery creation."

Fields got to her feet slowly, wiped the dust off her pants. She cocked her head toward the door. "Let's take a walk before Heinrich gets here and your mood darkens."

She has a point. Can't be around that old man in a mood like this.

She acquiesced. More than anything, she could not believe that the crew had let him out of the damnable gun hatch. She had thought for certain that everyone who'd been stuck in this place would tear the man's throat out. Possibly fight for the privilege to cut the scientist personally. She'd expected that she would have to fight the crews off, however she might, to make them understand that she needed him, no matter her feelings on the subject. It would not be unreasonable to say she had expected the ATF crews to be more feral than they actually were.

The day outside was warmer than inside the structure. It was mid-morning by her reckoning, and only a few wispy white clouds remained, just on the horizon to the west.

She could smell fires burning, and knew that it was time for breakfast when her stomach rumbled. She took a step in that direction, but was pulled around by Fields.

"What are you doing?" she asked. "I was going to go eat."

"Worry less," the woman replied with a smirk. "You can eat after. Come on, it's not far."

Deidra relented and the Pilot let go. Together, Fields slightly in the lead, they made their way in the direction of the river.

A few minutes later they stood at the water's edge, gazing down on a school of freshwater fish as they struggled up the current. It was a mountain stream, she knew, made of snow and ice as it melted to descend down a long and winding bed of rocks before it widened out and fed into the plain.

Deidre was fascinated by the existence of such Earth-like creatures on this planet. It raised so many questions about evolution throughout the universe. Were the planets separately developed? Or did they share common ancestors? If they did, who came first? Which planet held the originators of their shared DNA?

She cocked her head and looked up at the mountain range a few kilometres distant.

"Peaceful, isn't it?" Fields inquired.

Deidra found herself nodding. "It is, yes."

"That school of fish," the woman pointed, though she needn't have. "We're like them. We struggle to push our way upstream. If we but turned, things would come easier."

"Turning seems an awful lot like giving up, and I have too much to —" She was cut off by a raised hand.

"I did not say, give up."

"Then what do you mean?" Deidra implored. *I just want to go home and see my parents. I want to fall into my fiancé's arms and just sleep without this constant fear hanging over my head.*

"We simply need to try another approach to the same problem." The woman shrugged and turned back toward the camp.

"How do you figure?"

"Well, we're doing it one way and getting nowhere pretty fast, I'd say. If we but try another, would it hurt?"

"If I knew another, believe me it would be getting done already."

"But you are basing your assumptions on what you already know and not on what you might learn." The woman smiled and glanced sideways at her. "You learned to do things on a molecular level. You excelled in your field, yes? You created the things that go into our computers and make things run and do as they do. Things that people like me do not understand."

"That about sums it up," Deidra murmured to herself.

"So, you see it only how you learned it."

"How else am I meant to see it?" She felt like she was missing the point of the conversation, and worse, the smell of the food being cooked in the camp common was making her nose twitch and her mouth salivate.

"Basic core components," the other woman offered. "You see solder only as solder. And not just that, but also a primitive means of achieving the same goal. The things that you make now are massive and ungainly compared to the finesse required to build a *microchip* named so only for its size. What basic elements go into a microchip, and how would you array them in order to get the same effect? Do you use solder on it? No, you use laser etched crystals."

"How do you know all this?"

The Pilot shrugged and looked slightly abashed. "I don't know. I just do, I guess."

"Anyway, if I understand what you're saying, you want me to make the microchips on a larger scale using the same essential methods as I would in a lab. And that is impossible. I simply don't have the equipment. If I did, it would be done already."

Fields shook her head. "Tell me what you need. I will find a way for you to have it. Remember that we have a whole world at our disposal, not just what lies upon these ships." She gestured to the rows of stripped vessels as she began walking back toward them.

Deidra kept pace beside her. "But how can we possibly know what is on this planet? Again, it becomes a question of the equipment we have available. I see no way around this. And unless I missed something the inhabitants of this planet are a little primitive. I don't think they'd help, even if they could tell us."

"Like anything, Deidra Ward, you need only know where to look."

"And I suppose you do?"

"If you tell me what I am looking for."

She used a finger for everything she listed. "Glass, lasers, silicon crystal and or pure quartz crystal. Silicon dioxide, ultraviolet lights, aluminium and a sterile environment!"

"Done, then." Fields smiled at her.

"What do you mean, 'done'? If I took only one thing off that list the chips would be useless. And some of that is equipment, not components, but I can't break it down more than that." She was reminded of an early twenty-first century article explaining the difficulty of a single person making a toaster from scratch by themselves, largely due to the new hyper-specialisation of industry caused by the growth of computers in their modern society.

"One thing at a time."

"And we're going to need to find a way to produce a lot more power, too," Deidra mumbled. "The more I think of the larger picture, the harder this goal becomes. I'm as motivated as anyone could be, to get this done. But I'd be lying if I said I don't have my doubts."

Fields eyed her sideways but said no more.

They were through the first lines of ships and in the food lines, being handed bowls and spoons carved from wood, before Deidra spoke again.

"I am sorry for taking my frustrations out on you," she said sincerely.

"It is what it is," the woman replied, taking another step forward in the queue as the person in front of her advanced. "Think nothing of it."

But she couldn't do that. As she reflected back on the conversations that she'd had with the person in front of her, she realised that they all pertained only to her work. She'd been helpful in her suggestions, with a surprising amount of knowledge for someone who'd not obtained any kind of secondary schooling. For someone she worked so closely with, she knew very little about her.

"Why do you stay with me, when the rest of your crew is off doing other things?" She didn't mean for it to sound accusatory, but the words were out before she could take them back.

The Pilot turned her head, advancing another space. "I'm not a hunter."

"You're not a scientist, either." Deidra shook her head. All the wrong words were coming out.

The woman stepped forward again, and food was served into her bowl. She shuffled a pace to the side and waited for Deidra to be served, then led them over to a corner of the structure where warm mid-morning sunlight bathed the grass. She sat down, and Deidra did the same.

"It's true, I am not a scientist," Fields said around a mouthful of hot stew. She looked down at the bowl and smacked her lips after she swallowed. She put the bowl next to her and glanced at Deidra before she continued. "But I know things. I am not sure how, but I do. It came, after the Giants."

That was a point of curiosity for Deidra. The Giants. They'd been explained to her somewhat by the crews that had been on the planet while everything was going on at Io station, but had heard nothing of them from those who had defeated them. Six, in all, as far as she could tell. There had been no sign of others for the month that they'd been there, but that wasn't to say there weren't more lurking around somewhere.

Deidra's bowl was half empty before she got the courage up to ask, "How did you defeat the Giants?"

The other woman drew her brows in thought and picked up her bowl again, only to stir through it, eyes on the small trails the spoon made. Then she sighed. "It was the life of the planet. They were not affected by our weapons, by us, because we are not of this world. They could only be harmed by this world. But more importantly, they let us."

"How do you mean?"

She rolled her head from side to side, rolled her eyes, blew out a breath. "They were the gods of this place. If they had truly wanted us gone, we'd all be dead."

Deidra dropped her spoon into the small remains of her stew, a spray of thick gravy splashed onto her cheek which she wiped away with a sleeve. "The gods? How do you know that?"

"A side effect. We don't talk much to one another, since then.

Well, Harvey tries, but it's hard. If they asked me, I would tell them. They want the answers, I can get them. But I will not seek them out, because I feel a part of myself dying with every new piece of knowledge."

The Pilot put her bowl down and gazed in the direction of the forest, though they couldn't see it. "I wonder if they, too, are losing themselves. But, in answer to your question of earlier." Her head swung back toward Deidra, her brown eyes intense. "I stay with you, Doctor, because what you do is important. Because if I am to lose these pieces of myself, this is a goal worthy of that loss. These people all deserve to go home."

Deidra found herself nodding to every word. *Can I imagine the sacrifice she makes? Could I choose to make it?* "I do not envy you." And it was truth. As much as boundless knowledge appealed, the thought of losing herself to it was another thing altogether.

"It is what it is," Fields told her, as if she could read her mind.

~

The earth trembled beneath him.

Eyes shut, face to the sky, he clenched his fists. Power surged through him, raw, untainted, awaiting only a direction. This was his gift, a reward for the destruction of the Giant. He twitched his wrists a fraction, and clumps of dirt sprayed up in front of him.

He couldn't yet let it all out, though he felt it building inside of him, demanding release. If he were to make his presence felt, they would try to take it from him. Try to strip him of his gift. But he had earned it.

The trembling subsided. He unclenched his fists and opened his eyes to view through the forest canopy, a clear mid-morning sky.

He looked around the small clearing he'd found some days after the Day of Giants, and scrutinised his work. Mounds, no taller than a foot, tapered at the top like tiny mountains, surrounded the clearing without break. Each mound base touched another on both sides and were arrayed in such a fashion that they resembled shark teeth. It some strange way, it had been difficult to contain the power enough to make these monuments. But if he was to have this gift, then he needed to control it.

Satisfied, Greenway sat down.

Not one of his own crew members had survived the first night on this planet. Those he'd so wanted to help get home, enough to war with his own defeatist attitude, had proved unworthy. While he, who had so long ago given up on the thought of life, was now a being of power.

He let his hand hover a foot above the soil in front of him, and like a magnet attracting iron shavings, it drifted into his palm and stuck there. He turned his palm up, studied the pile, then blew it. The force the minuscule particles of dirt exuded as they hit the mound directly across from him, caused a fireless explosion.

A smile crept onto his face. For all his prior flaws and weaknesses, he had survived where the others had not, and he was now something more. Weiz, Fields, Harvey, Kristin and that pilot boy Viatri, were now his only equals. He had not shared his particular power with them, and aside from Harvey's disappearing act, he had no idea what theirs were either. It was a fair exchange. *Power lies in secrets.*

It was time now, he knew, to return to them.

He levered himself off the ground, prepared to make his way back to camp — the first time he'd made the trip in day light hours — when he heard a movement in the undergrowth to his left. He stilled, prepared the flow of power within him.

I'll not run again, he thought. *Not ever again.*

Trees rustled, leaves crunched under careless feet, the rhythm of a heartbeat, steady and strong. A booted foot showed through the trees, followed by a body, and then a face that he recognised.

He relaxed with a grunt. "Weiz," he intoned as his only greeting.

To him, she was no longer his Commander. But she was his equal, and that demanded courtesy.

She stopped on the outer edge and looked down on his work. "I had been wondering," she said with a frown, "what had you out here, day after day. This view, I think, is sufficient to answer the question."

"How did you find me?" While he knew that he did not have the level of skill in bush craft as some of the others, he knew he did not leave any obvious tracks. He'd made sure of it as he'd not wanted anyone to find this place.

The Commander met his eyes, then turned away to continue her study of the mounds he'd made. "Marvellous work. I assume it's yours? You need not answer, of course, just a curiosity."

He kept his eyes on her as she moved around the outside of his mounds. *And nor will I, since you do not care to answer mine. I have extended you the courtesy of an equal, woman, but you show me contempt. I will abide this only once.* He waited.

After a full circuit, she stepped over the mounds at the place where she'd started and strode over lazily to stand beside him. *What is your secret? Your power? Is it one to rival my own?*

The silence stretched on, but it was a game he knew well, a feeling he was comfortable with. He'd used it more than once to his advantage, to intimidate those afraid of no words.

A bird flew overhead, and they glanced up, followed its flight to the south as it disappeared over the treetops. A small flock joined the scouts' tail, one loosing its bowels, its guano hitting the ground just beside the Commander's boot. She glanced down at it, but did not move or express disgust.

"I find it difficult, at times, to speak with the others," she breathed, her eyes focused somewhere in the distance. "I had hoped I would feel differently with you, Greenway, as we've never been close, nor did we share our trials of the first two days." She looked to him then.

Not what he'd been expecting. "A stranger is sometimes easier to talk to than a friend," he acknowledged. It was a truth that he understood well. "But I doubt that I am the stranger you seek."

"Then I shall move on," she gave him a nod, and made to move back the way she'd come, finishing as she disappeared into the trees, "Thank you, Greenway."

Baffled by the exchange, Greenway stared after her for some time. It was true, they did not know each other well, and perhaps it hadn't helped that he had held himself aloof for the last ten years. But, despite that, she was the last person he'd have expected something like that out of. He was aware of her relationship with Captain Harvey. Surely she could have spoken to him? But then...

Lovers are the hardest people to speak to, the most comforting to be around. There is a desire not to leave them feeling guilty or pained. It is this that she seeks to address. A stranger does not always sympathise.

Greenway had been in love once. He'd thought he'd never want for anything again. He was sad to leave and happy to arrive home. Until that day, just over ten years ago, when he'd gotten home to Nova Scotia after a three-month mission to find his fiancé dead in their small apartment. She'd been on the floor of the living room, her back against the couch, a meat knife in her right hand, head fallen to the right and rested on the couch cushion, dried blood forming a river from neck to feet. A suicide he had not seen coming, and never explained. He'd lost faith then. In just about everything. He could not make himself join her, though he'd tried a few times. His survival instincts were too great. Instead, he'd become one of the most daring Captains of all time.

He shook his head to clear it of the memory, though it was one he re-lived on a daily basis. He had other things to do now, other things that required his attention. But he had always had trouble letting go.

Greenway took a step in the direction Weiz had taken, thought better of it, spun on his heel, and headed to camp.

~

They hadn't seen him, he knew, or that damned pilot would never have spoken as she had to Deidra.

Gods, is it? The thought appealed. He had noticed her uncanny ability to know exactly what was needed to keep the project moving. To know that it was a *side effect* of her having killed a *god*? It created images and ideas in his mind that pleased his sense of self-importance.

Heinrich had gotten off light, all things considered. He had an escort of crew members from Io Station with him every time he stepped foot outside the ship he'd been assigned as quarters. Since there was only one entrance and exit, it made it difficult to get out from under their scrutiny, but on occasion, he managed. Like now, while he ate his breakfast in the common.

The problem was, they needed him. This was his work. His idea. He knew more about it than even Deidra, so they had to put up with him. A sacrifice that would get them home. Did they have a clue? A suspicion that perhaps he would find his way without them if he could? It was likely. But it was the fact that they saw him as a prisoner, a murderer awaiting trial, that he had the guards stationed on him.

He ran a hand through his almost completely grey beard as he deposited his empty bowl on a pile. He'd never liked the things, had always shaved. But, after the first couple of weeks, when it finally stopped itching, he found that he didn't mind so much. In fact, he was beginning to like it. It was a nice change.

Though he would have liked to have stayed and further eavesdropped on their conversation, Heinrich made his way back to the 'Lab'. It was best if he was seen to be there before them.

Two airmen broke off from a group near the edge of the

structure and followed at a respectable distance.

He was still very impressed with what he'd been able to achieve in getting them all to this place, however things turned out. He'd placed the coordinates based on myth, and rumour, of a world that had, potentially, seeded life as they knew it, on Earth. From cave art and ancient writings, he had deduced the most likely area of space. But he hadn't been sure. But the very existence of this planet gave all those myths and legends great weight, and the potential of the discovery was exciting.

The truth was, as much as he'd have liked to have been of vital importance to the project, at this moment, his presence was worth very little. He could affect none of the changes, various adjustments and fine tuning until Deidra had built the equipment. And despite the Pilot's words of earlier, he saw that as becoming less and less likely.

No. What he needed was to find a way to get it done himself. And he thought he had the answer.

Being a god is a most excellent idea.

CHAPTER TWELVE

The race to the village had ended as a tie. The crops in the field they had first looked upon had now grown to saplings, and while some of them were a mystery, others were familiar. Tomatoes, carrots, lettuce and various other things. On trellises at the back of some of the mud huts were grown squashes, zucchinis, pumpkins and other vine vegetables.

Though the villagers seemed more than capable of communal production, they were yet to farm cattle. Largely, they hunted in the woods, much as their own teams did. Whether or not that was indicative of other such villages was hard to say.

Kristin had noted, as they walked through, that the language the people spoke was becoming oddly familiar. A niggle at the edge of her memory, as if she should know what they were saying. Only she wasn't hearing properly, and she found herself pushing at the back of her ears and moving her jaw waiting for the pop.

Like other crew members, she'd made a practice of stealing from the villagers. As she saw it, they provided well enough for themselves, and if a few things went missing now and then... She wasn't proud of what they were doing, but she had to admit it could be fun.

Down the main street — the only one, really — she saw children play with a ball, much as the children on Earth would. Good wives cleaned clothes in soapy water, eyes shifting back forth between them and the children while they gossiped with those close by. The men sat at the far end, repairing tools and carving out new furniture mostly on the silent side. Some were indoors, cooking what smelled like pies and pastries.

She glanced at Harvey. "As different as it appears at times, it's still a little too much like Earth."

The Captain nodded, his eyes on the children. "I imagine my son here, sometimes," he confessed.

The man rarely spoke about his son, at least not to her. She didn't even know his name. But she imagined that he thought of him as often as she thought of her brother. Every day.

They passed through the village and into the forest without incident. They took the path of the game trail that they'd found the first day.

"Have you ever thought about other villages?" Kristin asked.

"Can't say that I have."

"It's just that, what you said, about the Giants herding us away from populated areas and all. Sometimes I think there is probably another lot of villages out there, and maybe they have cattle."

Harvey turned his head toward her with a frown. His sandy beard was shot through with grey, his hazel eyes glassy as if he'd held back tears. "In the month that we have been here, have you seen any animal that you would farm?"

"Well, no. But that doesn't mean that there isn't any. Only that we haven't seen them. You don't exactly find too many cows in the wild, back home, but they're farmed by the thousands."

Harvey grunted, put his eyes back on the trail.

They weren't really hunting, just walking in each other's company. Both of them afraid to be alone, and afraid to admit it. She didn't know what his reasons were, but it seemed that as long as she was around one of them, the visions did not come. That, to her, was a mercy.

The first few times she'd experienced them, she'd not understood them for what they were. In her mind, they were just fractured images, without context. Some, though she'd had them repeatedly, still made little or no sense. But each of them, in their own way, had to come to terms with what they were becoming.

Speed, strength, vitality, an increased awareness of things through the mundane senses. They all shared in these small changes. But there were other things that they did not share. Things that the Giants had burdened them with. What choice had they, but to live with it? To accept it and use it to their advantage?

Harvey took one step forward and was suddenly a few metres ahead, just before a bend in the trail. He took another step and was beside her once more.

"I'm not sure I'll ever get used to you doing that," she frowned.

The Captain sighed and mumbled, "I'm not sure I'll ever get used to doing it."

Despite the amount of time they'd been on the planet, she suspected that Harvey did not have full control over his strange ability. Though, she had to admit, nor did she. She was not sure she could control it. Or if she even wanted to. If she could make it stop altogether, she'd take it.

"Should we head back to camp, maybe? See if Weiz is about?" The way his expression fell, she was sorry she'd asked.

"I think I'd like to stay out here a little longer."

"Then we should probably do something useful. I'm getting bored."

Harvey chuckled. "Your curse, I think. An inability to sit still or remain in silence. Always having to do something."

"What's wrong with that?"

"Nothing. Nothing at all. Just an observation."

Kristin kicked up some dead leaves and shot Harvey a glare. "An observation? Would you like me to start making some about you?"

The Captain cocked a brow. "By all means, Lieutenant. I am sure you've been storing them up all month. Just do me one favour."

"What's that?"

"Keep them to yourself," he took a step, and vanished.

Fucking hate it when he does that! "Grrr." She stomped a foot and the ground shook. She winced and pursed her lips. "That was your fault, Harvey!" she shouted. But if he was close enough to hear her, he made no reply.

Kristin continued along the trail. They'd not once made it to the end of the thing, and she was curious to know what might be there. Another village, perhaps? Or, if it was truly just a game trail, a hunters cabin or blind. Then again, it might just taper off, fall into heavy scrub, or end in a lookout.

Time passed slowly; her pace quickened but her heart rate remained steady. Everything was easier, now. She barely felt the need for sleep at the end of a day, but she forced herself to do so for at least a couple of hours. If she was being honest with herself, she wasn't sure she actually slept, as every time she closed her eyes and took those shallow breaths, she was plagued by images she did not want to see.

Harvey did not reappear. She suspected he'd gone after Weiz, or had perhaps decided that being alone wasn't so bad after all. But as she continued along the disused and grown over trail, she began to wonder if she'd make it to the end. Her curiosity remained, but the desire to be around people grew stronger with every step.

The sky was still clear, though the ground remained damp, the forest canopy hindering the heat of the sun from drying the duff.

Dead leaves clung to her well-worn boots, old weathered and dead branches had grown turgid, and the air smelled of moss. The sun had arced passed its apex and had begun its downward slide to the west.

She stopped on the trail and took a breath. Forward or back? *I have become so afraid of my own shadow,* she thought. *I should just keep going forward. Always forward. Never have I so baulked at the prospect of solitude.* In fact, most of her childhood years had been dedicated to seeking it out, as a means of getting away from her drunken, abusive parents. Joining the military had been her way out of that destructive behaviour, and was also a way for her to make sure that her brother had a better life than her.

Kristin had not seen Mitchel much when she'd been on Earth, and now she was here, she didn't know that it changed anything. Except that maybe the Army had stopped paying her, and her ATF bonus would go straight to her brother as was agreed to in the 'in case of death' section of her contract. She did wonder occasionally if he thought of her as much as she thought of him, and if he'd miss her. She'd done the best she could, all things considered. But he was nineteen now. He could look after himself. He wasn't her responsibility, she knew, but she didn't think she would ever completely forgive herself for leaving him alone with their parents.

If thoughts weighed nothing, then why did she feel so heavy?

With a sigh, she turned around and started back to camp. She'd take the long way, skirt the village.

"I was thinking," Harvey said as he came in beside her. She jumped high, startled. When her feet hit the ground, she punched him as hard as she could in the shoulder. The Captain rubbed at the spot and frowned. "Ow."

"Serves you damned right, sneaking up like that," she growled. She quickened her pace, more annoyed at her own reaction than the fact the man had come back. *Right after I decided to head back to the camp. Significant?*

Harvey kept stride and continued. "Like I said, I was thinking."

"A new experience for you, I am sure."

"Oh ha ha."

"Does it hurt?" She knew she was pushing it, but she couldn't help herself.

"Will you slow down a minute?" She stopped on the trail and faced the man. "Good. Thank you."

"What were you thinking, Harvey?" she asked in a more moderate tone.

"Well..." He shot a hand out and grabbed her coveralls at the waist. She made to pull back, surprised, but he held tight.

Vertigo gripped her. Her stomach churned, her vision swam, and her feet felt less than steady on the ground. Worse, it was like she could see two places at once. Where she was, and the graveyard. Finally, though, it resolved itself into the graveyard, and she fell to her knees with a wave of nausea as soon as Harvey let go.

"Fuck me," she breathed.

"So, it works, then." Harvey seemed pretty pleased with himself.

If she'd had the reach to hit him again from where she knelt, she would have. "Little warning maybe could have helped. Jesus fuck, Captain, how do you not vomit every time you do that?" She got slowly to her feet.

"Guess it might have a different effect on you than me. But it worked, right? I held on and now you're here."

Kristin looked around her immediate vicinity. There were a few airmen in sight at the river, all going about their own business. If any had seen them, they pretended not to notice. The graveyard, as always, was empty. From where they stood, close to the remains of the butchered ships, a spring breeze carried to them the stench of the latrine pits and sounds of conversation from the common.

"Could have taken us to a better place," she muttered, making a face.

The Captain shrugged and looked around. "It seemed as good a place as any, Belle."

She scowled at him. "You've been talking to Viatri. But I'm going to tell you this now, it might save your arm. Don't call me that. I think you and I have developed a kind of mutual respect, hell, even a friendship, so if you want it to continue along that line, I am Kristin to you, sir. Or Anna, if you must."

Harvey snapped a salute, with mock solemnity, "Yes, Ma'am." She punched him. In the face.

He dropped to his knees, holding his nose, his voice came out muffled through his hands. "Kristin, you got some problems."

"Oh, get up you big wuss, I didn't hit you that hard, and you know it."

He grunted as he got to his feet. "Hard enough," he told her. "If I wasn't such a forgiving guy, you'd have been in a lot of trouble for that."

Kristin shook her head and breathed a sigh. "Sorry, sir. I don't know why I am feeling so violent today."

"Probably cause you haven't had breakfast."

They stood in silence a moment, each feeling awkward and looking at anything but each other.

Thing was, she didn't feel hungry. There were parts of her that were different, and not just that she had some insane visions. *Don't really need sleep. Never get hungry or thirsty. Shit, I've barely had to go to the bathroom all month. And Harvey knows this. It's been the same for all of us. Why would he say something like that?*

I could never have guessed that my life would turn out like this. My first mission! And now I wonder if we'll get home.

Harvey coughed. She glanced at him. "I'm sorry I pulled you through without asking." His tanned face had turned a delightful shade of red. Clearly, apologies did not sit well with him. She smiled.

"I forgive you."

~

The rest of her day had been spent doing not much of anything at all. She was restless and bored.

Viatri had finally set foot outside the ship and was actually speaking to people, which was progress. She could not fathom the man's constant negativity, especially since he was such a joker. But she guessed they all carried their own kinds of damage.

The clear skies remained as the sun fell over the horizon and stars appeared in the sky. The moon was bright and almost full, as it had been on the first night.

She felt bad for Harvey, for having avoided him all day. Then again, she'd avoided everyone, really. The memories too vivid in her mind.

Weiz found herself now, at the foot of the mountain range, next to the river and facing the trees. The only sounds were those of a few birds, the steady flow of the river's current, and her own breathing.

No one else yet knew what power she'd been given by the Giant. Though, she supposed, she was not alone in that. Greenway, she could guess from what she'd seen, controlled the Earth, at least to some degree. But he'd been reclusive, and he'd not spoken to anyone since that day. *Till I showed up. But he's ready to come out now, I saw him back at camp. Right when I am ready to disappear for a while.*

She sighed. Kristin had her visions, Harvey had his re-location, the others had whatever they had, while Weiz... She put a hand in front of her, palm up, and there, colours danced in a light of their own making. They had no form, and they did nothing of great importance — unless she wanted them to.

Harvey and Kristin's powers were benign and non-destructive. But a single thought, for her, could prove the very opposite. *Flames.* The colours swirled, merged, became a ball of fire, heat pouring out of it. She moved her hand away, and the ball remained where it was.

Big light. And the colours came, and a light appeared, twice the size the flame had been, and illuminating the area all around her.

She saw a sturgeon swim passed, unconcerned by her show of power. She stared down at it until it vanished into darkness, envying its ignorance.

Papa, she thought.

The colours took on a buzzing sound as they expanded and quickly took form. They coalesced into the form of her long dead father. Old, lines marred his features, blue eyes stared from a gaunt and angular face. He wore a tan cardigan and brown slacks but was barefoot. His thin, grey hair fell in short wisps, large ears twitching.

Many times in her life, she had imagined seeing him again. Her mother and father had died of old age a long time ago. She'd been their miracle child. Her mother had been over fifty when she was conceived.

"Papa," she said, and extended her arms.

Her father came forward with a smile and they embraced. He was warm, and strong, his arms gentle and comforting. His breath smelled of liquorice and vermouth as he leaned back to say, in German, "My daughter, I have missed you."

A tear fell. She couldn't help it.

For her entire career, first in the Luftwaffe, then in the ATF, she had been known for her steady head, perfectly controlled temper and self-discipline. She'd been called cold by many who shared her station, but not as a bad thing. To be other, was to hold weakness. But now, with her father here, surrounded by the darkness of night, she let go as she had the first night.

"Papa," she breathed raggedly into his cardigan. He rubbed a hand up and down her back and made a soothing noise. "I cannot forget."

As much as she wanted to wipe the memory from her mind, she knew that it would haunt her for the rest of her life. All those airmen, dead, for nothing. And worse, she didn't even know how Fields and herself had managed to defeat the Giants. All pure luck, as far as she was concerned. Not that she wanted to join the airmen in their graves, but a part of her felt that she deserved it.

"Do you truly wish to forget?" he asked her.

She pulled back from him and wiped her eyes. They sat down together, feet extended toward the river.

"I do not know that I have a right to," she confessed. "They were under my command."

"Could you have stopped them?"

"I didn't try. Not hard enough." The sadness in her father's expression echoed her own. He reached out and wiped a stray tear from her cheek with a thumb.

"The daughter of Wolfgang Weiz does not need forgiveness from others," he said softly. "She needs it only from herself."

"But I did not try! How can I forgive myself that?"

"You must find a way."

Had I run to bar them, would it have made a difference? Then it had seemed futile, but now I wonder. What stayed my hand? Shock? Pain? Does it matter?

The likeness of her father became spectral, and once more the colours swirled. They grew larger and multiplied, performing an increasingly more intricate dance as they floated over the river and became the scene of the first night on the other side.

She forced herself to watch, hands clutching at the dirt beneath her. She deserved no less. Every time the scene played out, she started it again from the beginning, like a holo-recording. Only this was real. Every time.

~

People treated him differently. It wasn't even subtle. From the moment he'd stepped foot outside his ship, people had stared and whispered, avoided eye contact and proximity. To them, it seemed, he was no longer one of them. He was a legend, someone who'd defeated a Giant. And everyone knew that they'd changed because of it.

Lance was a vain man. His entire childhood people had labelled him as fat, had made fun of him and most other children would not speak to him. Unless they wanted something, of course. His parents were wealthy, and he had everything a child would desire at his disposal. But that taught him the worth of the people around him. It was all about what you looked like.

During his early teen years, he'd started to bulk up. Instead of fat, the weight he carried was muscle, and for a while, people liked him. They saw his personality, not just his face, which was less than handsome. But his pride in his own body and his extreme discipline, made up for that short coming. Until he hit puberty, and he started growing more than just chin hair.

The girls wouldn't look at him. He was nowhere near attractive enough to be seen with. He was funny, he knew, had been told many a time, but it was not enough for the girls to notice him. More often than not, they'd laugh at him, not with him. So, he'd shaved it all off. Every single hair. It hadn't helped, because they already knew. But he could see, they liked the look of him now.

The way the people in the camp were treating him now, reminded him of those times. Brought back all the feelings of inadequacy and self-doubt.

It was night, and dinner was being served under a structure that looked to be made from the hulls of several ships. He took a place at the end of the line, and everyone went silent. Their eyes all swung to him.

People in the line in front of him started moving to either side, and someone waved him to the fire. His eyes darted this way and that, a frown on his face, but he moved forward, one slow step at a time, and as he did, the line filed in behind him, and conversations resumed.

Xavier was at the fire, a large wooden ladle in his hand, ready to dip into a giant cauldron that also looked like it had been made from a hull. Lance cocked an eyebrow at him.

"What's this all about, then?"

The Navigator smiled. "Well, if you hadn't have been moping in your ship and feeling oh so damned sorry for yourself, mister 'I'm so much better than everyone else', you'd know, wouldn't you?"

Lance grabbed the bowl of stew Xavier offered him and stepped off to the side. The line, made of about twenty airmen, most of whom he'd never met, and all wearing the same uniform they'd come down in, moved forward at a steady pace. It didn't take long until they were all served, and Lance waited until Xavier took up his own bowl before he said anything.

"So, tell me." They walked toward the edge of the structure facing the woods.

"Feel like I lost my whole crew, you know," Xavier said as he sat. He looked up at Lance until he took his own seat.

"We haven't gone anywhere."

"No. But you've changed."

Lance grunted and took a spoonful of stew. It was tangy and held some interesting flavours, but he didn't ask what was in it. He was a notoriously picky eater, and he did not like the idea of the giant snake-rat popping into his head. He almost gagged around his mouthful, swallowed quickly, and put the bowl down in front of him. *I hope it ain't rat.*

He looked to his crew mate. "I think everyone's changed," he said. "No way we could all be here and not have. You seem more serious."

"I think it's just that none of us expect to get home anymore." The man shrugged. "That first day, it was like 'we could be here a while, let's do what needs doing and let the scientists worry about the sciencey stuff'. All well and good. But now," he glanced around him as if something in the gloom might give answer. "Now, it's too real. We've lost more than half of those who came here with us. We're stripping their ships for parts, and that's almost worse than digging a grave to some. We're settling, almost. Nothing really permanent, but if we don't hear that Deidra has finished soon, that's likely to change." He lapsed into silence as he ate.

Lance stretched, cracked his neck. "But me?" he wanted to know.

Xavier licked his lips then wiped them with a hand. "You're a Giant Killer," he told him, as if it were the only explanation required.

The Pilot supposed it was. The Giant Killers. That's what people were calling them. It set them apart, put them on a pedestal, made of them something more than the desperate team they'd been on the day. They'd just wanted to get back to the ships in time to make it home. Kristin's little inkling about the branches had given them all a shot, but they had all suffered wounds, too. They didn't get off clean. *But it would seem that way to everyone else. Miraculously healing after the encounter.* He felt the curse settle heavy on his shoulders. After all, he could have sworn he'd died that day, before the mist revived him. Sure, he'd got his kill shot in, but the thing had gutted him. *Could have sworn.*

Conversations died off behind him, the shuffle of feet and the stamp of boots on trampled grass faded away as those who'd finished their meals sought the familiarity of their ships. Lance hadn't felt the time pass, but as he looked over at Xavier, he saw that the man had long finished and was lost in his own thoughts.

"So, who have you been bunking in with?" Lance queried.

The Navigator looked to him. "Ellen Rich, from Captain Walter's team." While he said no more, his tone encouraged questioning.

"I don't believe I know her." *Then again, I don't really know anyone on this god forsaken rock.*

"About my height, short brown hair in tight curls, creamy white skin, curves in all the right places." His smile said it all. "She's a Navigator too. We've spent the last few weeks mapping the stars to see if we can find a correlation to Earth. She thinks that the scientist, Heinrich — the one we're having followed?"

Lance shook his head. "I don't know who that is." He had spent too much time in the ship. "Get to the good part," he urged.

"Well, she thinks Heinrich must have known where we were going. That he had to have had a trajectory program running when we ended up here. He denies it, of course, but if we can just crack him, we might be able to plot a course home by ship. As it stands, some constellations look very similar to what we're accustomed to, but time and distance can make a huge difference."

The Pilot turned his head and made his left tattoo raise a brow. The Navigator chuckled.

Lance turned again, his face more serious. "Getting home by ship will take a lot longer, and we know that these ships aren't made to last more than twenty-four hours in space. There wouldn't be near enough fuel. Besides, didn't we use it all?"

"There is that," Xavier conceded. "But we have considered building another. Use the scraps, like Deidra's done. We could build a roof, why not a ship?"

He slapped the man companionably on the back. "Two very, very different things, my friend."

They talked for a while longer, Xavier explaining his theories, and Rich's. They wanted to get home, they both had families the wanted to see again, and settling down on some remote planet who knows where did not appeal much to either of them.

Lance realised that his own desires were a little less people orientated. He missed flying. He was a pilot and had been for a long time. He rarely went a day without flying somewhere, even if he wasn't the one at the controls. And now he was here, stuck with a group of people he hardly knew, and the people he did know were becoming strangers.

"And Dames has finally decided to come out of hiding," Xavier told him.

His head shot round to look Xavier in the eye. "Has he?"

"Turns out, Walt didn't want to stay in such a confined space, and Dames wont go far without him. They were different on the Docker, too. But I have never seen Dames around anyone but our own crew. He's managing, though."

The conversation petered off after that revelation. Lance just didn't know what to say.

~

Heinrich kept his breath shallow and lay as still as possible. He'd feigned sleep for the past hour, while Zim and Fields spoke in low voices on the other side of the bridge. It was hard to not actually fall asleep, despite the way his mind raced. He felt quite relaxed.

For the last half hour or so — possibly longer, it was hard to tell — there had been silence. The lights were off, and he could hear breathing. One of them had left, it was hard to tell whom, but he guessed it was Fields who remained. She often did.

Heinrich opened an eye and glanced at the space where he thought the woman slept. The only light was what filtered through the hatch and down the short corridor, so he could barely see more than a lump on the ground. Though it did vaguely resemble a womanly figure.

Careful not to make too much noise, the scientist softly rose and laid his hand under the comms console, then slowly swept his hand just above the surface of it until he found the knife a careless airman had left within his reach some days ago. He'd not known then that he would have cause to use it so soon, but it was fortuitous.

He did not have much time. He needed to get this done and be away before anyone had an inkling of what he intended. He hoped this worked.

Silent across the deck in bare feet, Heinrich lowered himself over the sleeping form of Fields. He breathed a silent sigh of relief. Zim would have been useless.

Caution made him look around, though he knew he should have nothing to fear. Not yet. Then the point of the knife descended, carefully held above the jugular. The woman did not stir. He plunged the blade deep.

Fields' eyes shot open, their whites reflecting the light from the hatch. A hand grabbed him, strong and steady, then before he knew what was happening, he hit the edge of the hatch, fell outside, landed on his back, and was gazing up at the shocked face of Deidra.

Someone's boot connected with the side of his face, and he tasted blood well in his mouth. But he laughed. It was too late. He'd done it. The woman was as good as dead. All he had to do was wait for the mist to take him. That was how he'd heard it described. Many times, from many different people. He hoped it was true, or he'd risked it all for nothing.

Eyes closed, he didn't see Deidra enter the ship at a run, or the boot that clipped his temple and sent him into unconsciousness.

CHAPTER THIRTEEN

Deidra hurried inside, heart a-flutter with the thought of what she might find. She paused only long enough to bring the lights on.

On the bridge, neck scrunched forward, hand clutched to her throat, another holding a bloody knife, sat Fields. Her breath came laboured, and her face betrayed her shock.

The knife fell from her grasp, her eyes lost some of their acuity and she fell sideways onto the floor. The hand that held her neck had loosened, and the blood flowed free.

Deidra knelt beside her and pushed her own hands onto the wound, and attempted to stem the flow. The woman drew a ragged breath, groping fingers found her sleeve. "For," she breathed, "you." Her last breath came out as a hiss, a stream of black smoke came forth.

The scientist was aware of only two things at that moment. The pilot who had been helping her with her work was now dead. And the mist that now escaped the corpse, was headed directly for her. But she didn't move.

She said it was for me. She would have stepped back, let it flow past her off into the night. Except that she knew that would not happen. There was no choice. If she left it would follow her. She didn't know how she knew that, but she did. And though she wasn't sure what to expect, based on the little she'd been told by Fields, she swallowed her fear, and waited.

Had it already begun? Was it already in motion? She could no longer see the smoke, but she felt no different.

Deidra leaned back on her haunches and rubbed her chin. Behind her, she heard some airmen enter. She turned her attention to them and saw the look of horror on Zim's face. He was stock still, blinking down at the corpse. Without a word, he turned and left the ship.

The other man, a tall, lean Navigator named Harlow, squatted down next to the body and closed her eyes with gentle fingers. He glanced at Deidra, a silent question in his eyes. She didn't have it in her to answer, so she turned away.

It's just one thing after another. How are we going to get home now? A flood of images shook her. They moved so fast it was hard to comprehend. But as they continued, she noticed a pattern to them. The more she noticed the clearer it all became.

She felt her mouth start to sag open. Heard Harlow ask if she was alright. She didn't answer.

Is this what you saw, Fields? When you said that you knew things, though you didn't know how? A side effect, you said. But at a cost. The price only willing to be paid if you could help the others get home. I guess that's my job now. But then, it really always has been, hasn't it?

Dane, forgive me. If I get back and I don't remember who you are, you are going to have to remind me. Don't give up on me. I need you. The memory of her fiancé was all that held her together at times. It was what made her keep going. Someone to return to.

She moved into a crouch, swatted Harlow away from Fields' body, and picked the woman up almost effortlessly. The Pilot's head was cradled in one arm, while her knees were draped over the other.

Silently, she walked out the hatch, and strode toward the graveyard. In her wake, the entire camp. One at a time, airmen popped their heads out of their ships, others merely looked up to see, and each one who saw, started to move.

There had not been a death since the Day of the Giants. And this was one of these Giant Killers. If they could be killed, what did that mean for the rest at them?

Solemn faces followed as Deidra took Fields toward the graveyard.

~

Weiz could see the procession from where she walked along the river, back toward camp. She'd tortured herself enough for one day.

It was a mere curiosity at first, but once she realised where they were going, she started running. Something had happened. *Who is it this time? Please, don't let it be Harvey. Please.*

As the Commander, she knew that she should not have valued his life above the others in the camp, but it was no secret to anyone the feelings they shared.

It took her only a couple of minutes at a hard run before she got to the outskirts of the graveyard. Headstones had been mocked up by some of the airmen, names inscribed, flowers wreathing their bases. No one had asked her; they'd just done it. For that she was thankful.

At the other end, Deidra stood with a warm corpse in her arms. Every airman in the camp was arrayed behind her. She spied Harvey in the first row, as well as Lance. Greenway was in the back, his attention hardly on the scene, though he stepped forward, the others making way for them.

Weiz slowed her pace and got to the other end in time to hear what the man said. "Of the deaths here, on this world, this is the most tragic."

The scientist looked up at him. "Build her a monument, Maker of Mountains," she intoned, loud enough for the entire congregation to hear.

The Captain looked startled by her proclamation, and a little annoyed, but he gave a single nod. "Where would you have it?" he asked.

Deidra laid the body at her feet and stepped back. "Just here, Bringer of Quakes." The way she spoke had Weiz wondering if Deidra was trying to get a rise out of the man.

He grimaced at the name, but turned his attention to the crowd. "All of you step back some. No, a little further. That's good." He faced the body of Fields.

That woman had been one of them. A Giant Killer. The significance of that was not lost on anyone, she suspected. They were still mortal. They could still be killed as easily as anyone else. Despite their power, they were not invulnerable. And she thought she saw that understanding reflected in Greenway's face as he gazed down upon the woman.

He closed his eyes and took a stance, feet together, back straight, elbows at waist, fists clenched tight in front of him. Slowly, he bought one hand down, and as he did so, the whole section of earth below the dead woman sank. The ground trembled, dirt fell in on the corpse, a small mound rose where a head stone should have been placed as the Captain raised his other hand toward the sky, as the first continued its slow trip down.

Silence. Birds, breeze and the sound of a few shuffled feet, but nothing more. All eyes stared toward Greenway, not in admiration for the service, but in fear. What this man controlled could devastate a continent.

The Captain looked back on them all, just as silent, until his eyes found Deidra. "You have become as us, now. I welcome you to the pantheon." And then he strode off.

Deidra's were not the only set of eyes to follow the man as he disappeared into the camp.

Weiz came forward then, and laid a hand on the pilot's gravestone. "Had I words of comfort, had I a belief in anything, I would give them to you. But I possess nothing of value for your journey. So, what I do now, is all I have." She did not know what had actually happened, but this was something she could do.

She was one of us. She opened her hand palm upward, and the coloured lights became a laser cutter. With this, she inscribed the woman's full name, date of birth, and date of death, as she had seen others do on the gravestones behind her.

When she glanced up, she saw Harvey looking at her, surprise etched on his handsome features. *And hurt. He's hurting too. The first time you show anyone your power, and you use it in front of the whole damn camp. You should have told him first, woman. He deserved to know.*

Deidra stood in front of her staring at the laser cutter in her hand as it slowly disappeared. She didn't say a word, but she could see knowledge behind those dark eyes.

Others were stepping up to the grave, now, and Weiz moved out of the way, Deidra a step behind. The airmen were paying their respects, one by one, laying a hand on the monument Greenway had built, and saying a few words. Some of them even left something on top of the grave. A gift of small remembrances.

"Ever felt you were witness to something that you had no right to?" Weiz asked the scientist.

"More than once," she replied.

"How do you shake it off?"

"You cannot." The woman turned toward her area of the camp, past the ruined hulks of ships. Weiz only followed with her eyes for a moment, then decided to join her. There was something in the way the woman had addressed Greenway that said she knew far more about him than anyone else. Perhaps the same was true for her.

"A moment, Doctor Ward," she said, catching up.

The scientist paused momentarily in her stride, then continued. "What can I do for you Commander?"

"What *happened*? To Fields? To you?"

The woman took a deep breath. "Heinrich killed her. I assume he meant to take her powers. I mean, that's how it worked for you and your crew, right?" She shook her head and mumbled something under her breath. Then sighed. "But she had a choice. And she chose me."

"She told you things?" Weiz pushed. Perhaps she shouldn't have, as the woman turned on her and stood, fists planted on hips, anger a dark crease across her ebony face.

"She just *died*, commander. Can the interrogation not wait until later?"

Weiz cursed inwardly at her own stupidity. *Way to show some empathy, Commander.* She gave Deidra a nod, an acknowledgement that the woman was right. "Of course."

Deidra stared at her a moment longer, then turned and continued her march back to her Lab.

The Commander glanced up at the sound of movement. On the inside of one of the desiccated ships, Greenway was sitting, legs hanging over the side. His eyes locked with hers.

"She's one of us now," he said as he jumped down.

Weiz stared at the retreating back of the scientist. "She always was, to me."

The Captain came to stand beside her. "So now they all know what we can do."

"Does that bother you?" She turned to him now. If she was being honest with herself, she hadn't wanted them to know. There was already a distance between them because she was their Commander, but this made her feel more isolated than she ever had been in her life.

He rolled his shoulders. "In some ways, yes, in others, no. I wasn't quite ready for it. But... did you see her eyes?"

"I did, yes."

"I don't know what Fields had; we've all kept to ourselves somewhat. But, Deidra, whatever she took, whatever she was given, she understands it instinctively."

That was something none but Harvey had had in the beginning. She found herself envying that. "Maybe Fields prepared her for it?" she said more for herself than for Greenway.

The man used his chin to point behind her. "My queue to leave, Commander. But first to answer; Fields wouldn't have had time to prepare Dr. Ward for anything. I don't know if you saw the body, but her throat was slit deep." He glanced behind Weiz again, gave a nod, and left.

Weiz turned to see Harvey approach.

His uniform had worn thin, the patch of his rank half peeled off, the navy-blue sun faded. His sandy blonde hair was getting long and had begun to curl at the ends.

"Heinrich's been locked back up in the gun hatch," he said as he stopped before her. "Doubtful they'll let him out without a leash, now."

Not what she'd been expecting. "If we could do without him, I think he'd have joined those in the graveyard instead of Fields."

"More likely an unmarked one somewhere out in the bush. A man like that deserves no respect."

They watched the slow procession of airmen as they began to disperse into their own small groups. She could see Lance, standing by himself at the foot of the grave.

"She was one of us," Weiz said.

Harvey looked at her, but she stayed focused on the graveyard. She couldn't face him. Not yet. "You say that like we're separate from the others trapped here."

"Aren't we? We're the Giant Killers!" She invested scorn into the sentence, and a grimace grew on her face.

"That doesn't make us something other," he replied softly. "We're only as alone now as we were as Commander and Captain. Price of leading and all that other jazz."

"I think Deidra might see it differently."

"That scientist?" Harvey looked behind him toward the Lab, then back to Weiz. "Why would she see it any differently? She was never one of us to begin with. Yeah, she had a few crews looking out for her because she's the one who's got to get us home, but the only person who belongs in her group is that Ulrich fellow, and that guy hardly ever comes out of his ship. She was alone from the start."

Weiz nodded. She had nothing more to argue her point. She just didn't feel as if she belonged, as if she *deserved* to belong here with these people. She had let them down.

Ask me Harvey. Why have you not? Do you expect me to say the first words? I do not have a satisfactory answer for you. I cannot tell you why I did not share my power with you before tonight. I do not know it. Why will you not ask me?

"You should shave," she told him.

If the change in subject surprised him, he didn't show it. He shrugged. "I grow a beard every time I'm on leave."

She raised a brow in his direction. "You do, do you?"

"If you want me to shave it off, Catherine, I will. But if you're asking me to do it as the Commander, then I will have to respectfully decline."

"As a woman, John."

He nodded and began to walk off, she watched him for a moment, then took a step, stretched her hand out toward him, "John." He turned his head.

"What?"

She sighed, let her hand drop and shook her head. "Never mind." He stared at her a moment longer before he walked away.

I am such a coward. I love you; you fool man. We know it of each other, and yet neither of us has ever said it. Is it enough? The feeling, not the words. Twenty years I waited for you. Twenty years. Was it too long? Have I been fooling myself this whole time? That the idea has become worth more than the emotion that lay behind it?

I love you.

It was the little things. Silent conversations, brief contact, the passion of the night. Exchanged glances and smiles, a way of knowing what the other was thinking. Things that had only grown over the years that they had worked together. And now that they had it, did she take it for granted? Did it not live up to expectation? Or was it simply that they were not on Earth? That the struggles they had faced here, were too great a challenge for them to address their own needs as a couple?

Is it just me?

~

Deidra had spent the remainder of the night deep in thought. It was hard not to be, with everything that flashed through her head. She needed to use what Fields had given her, and she knew that the consequence was worse than the woman had first told her. Much worse.

Pieces of myself, gone. Holes in my memories, the gaps filled with knowledge that could be useful but yet to be tested.

She found herself wondering how Fields had managed to keep so much of herself after a month with this in her mind. Every thought she had, a curiosity the dark mist tried to answer, leading to yet more questions. A cycle she did not foresee stopping any time soon.

Morning was on its way. A golden line, edged in red across the eastern horizon, the landscape bathed in shades of grey. She sat on the roof of her Lab, knees held to her chest, hands clasped and fingers twiddling, as she watched the day take on colour. It would be another fine one. No clouds visible in the sky.

She understood, now, why Fields had not gone to the others. Just moments in their company had given her knowledge of them and their powers, had created large gaps in her memory. Everything she thought about she had an answer to. She already knew how they would make the device to take them home. It was simply a matter of getting the equipment they needed, and for that, she'd need Weiz. It was doubtful that the woman understood the nature of her powers.

Maker of Mountains, Bringer of Quakes. I know you now. In her mind, the image of Greenway. Then the others, though she'd only glanced at them, her natural curiosity had answered every question. Weiz was the Creator of Life, Breeder of Illusion. Kristin, the Seer, Master of Fates. Lance was the Bringer of Seasons, Maker of Rain. Harvey was the Keeper, the Seneschal, and he held powers he had not yet tapped. And Deidra, she was the Maker of Words. That they all had *titles* meant that it was something greater than they'd first assumed. She now understood what Fields had meant when she'd told her they were gods. Essentially, they were, but only for lack of a better term.

She extended a leg, put her hands behind her to rest on the roof, and looked up to the sky. The stars were fading, the sky a murky dark grey, and slowly, even as she watched, brightened into blue.

The others would start to wake soon, and she knew what she had to do.

Deidra jumped off the roof and landed softly in the grass. As she'd never been any kind of athlete, and disliked heights, it was not something she would have done even the day before. But there was also a confidence that grew inside her along with the gift of knowledge. A change, rapidly occurring.

Gift or curse? It could be either one. But is losing Dane or my parents a worthy price to pay? Can I do this? Is it too much? Somehow, she knew there was no choice. That no matter what she decided for herself, unless she could give this power away to someone who did not mind the sacrifice, then she would become... She did not know. And that, she decided, was the scariest prospect.

In no great hurry, Deidra walked toward the graveyard. To the monument she'd had Greenway raise. She didn't know what had compelled the others to follow her. *So, I'm not omniscient at least.* It was a bittersweet thought. Perhaps it had been that she was a Giant Killer. Or the method of her death. *Or maybe she was just well liked.* The woman had been a Pilot for the ATF long before they'd found themselves in this current predicament.

When she arrived at her destination, she could see Richard, sitting back to the gravestone on the other side. His head swivelled at her approach, and he watched silently.

"You and she were close." A statement, something everyone knew, but she didn't know what else to say to the man. How did one empathise with such great loss?

"Only since this mission," he confessed. "We'd not met before we landed here."

Deidra nodded. "Some of the greatest bonds are formed through adversity."

"We were not lovers."

"A close friendship is no less profound than a life-long love. It is simply different."

He wiped a tear she had not noticed from his face and smiled up at her. "Had I my way, it would have been different, Doctor Ward. But she wished for someone to know her, before she forgot who she was. Someone who would speak to her family when we got back to Earth, who could explain what had happened to her."

Deidra was only mildly surprised that Fields had told him what had happened to her. "And you believe I should do the same?" It was an idea that held merit, but she did not know who she could speak to on that level. She'd been alone in the beginning and saw no reason why that would change. She'd always struggled with close bonds, and it was why the ones she had were so important.

"That is up to you." The man levered himself to his feet and glanced at the grave. "But would you rather your loved ones knew why you were no longer the person you were? Or would you prefer they always wondered, forever without answer?"

He strode away before she could answer.

~

Harvey didn't come back to the ship that night. For that matter, neither did any of the others. So Weiz had sat alone, as she had many times before.

It was early morning; the first hunting parties of the day had gone out. She sat at the comms console, looking down at the cracked screen. It hadn't been used the last few weeks, and strangely, it was this more than the way the others looked at her, that made her understand she was no longer in charge.

No one called in to update her on situations, to give her a rundown of goals achieved and those to go. They didn't need her anymore. Not as their sole leader. They had themselves now. They'd become self-sufficient, worked as a team of equals, and the Giant Killers were on the outside of that.

Except Kristin. She often went hunting with the others. That was probably where she was now.

Weiz considered calling Harvey, thought better of it, and got up from her seat.

MM294 was only one of two ships left with fuel in it. Quite a few had run out of charge, and the equipment no longer worked. While this ship still ran, it would not last forever, and she could not afford to be making personal calls just because the stupid man would not talk to her.

Maybe it's that I am not speaking to him.

With a sigh, she turned to leave the bridge, when the speakers cackled on. "I hope someone's listening!" She didn't recognise the voice. "The natives can see us! My team's been captured."

Weiz turned back to the console and pushed down on the button. "This is Weiz. Report!"

"We're in a cellar, Commander. Not sure which house. The natives caught us stealing some supplies." He paused. "Look, we can't understand what they say, the language isn't even close to one I've heard before, but I get the impression they mean to deal with us harshly."

She heard someone enter the bridge behind her, but did not turn to see who it might be. *Serves you damned right for theft,* she thought. It was not a game that she'd approved of, but she just shook her head. "Your name, airmen?"

"Captain Oswald," he said as if she should have known. "I don't know how long we have. With me is Senka, Ramirez and Porshenko. They've stripped us, and there's nothing in here we could use to bust the lock on the hatch. So, I'd appreciate it if you sent some help."

"Hold tight, Captain. I'll get someone on it. Weiz out."

She turned to see who had walked in to find Deidra, nodding to herself and muttering something incoherent under her breath.

"Doctor, what can I help you with?"

The woman looked up at her. "Seems we've fallen out of tachyon frequency," she said. "I'm actually surprised that didn't happen sooner. But then, the amount of power that Heinrich flooded the machine with..." She shrugged.

"Yes, well, unfortunately my airmen weren't thinking too hard on the subject." Weiz pushed herself away from the console and moved toward the hatch. "But that isn't what you came here to speak to me about, is it?"

"No, it isn't."

Deidra followed her as she left the ship and made her way through the camp in search of the others.

"So, spit it out."

"I know how to get us home. But I am going to need your help to do it."

Weiz stopped dead in her tracks and gave the scientist her full attention. "That is the best news I've heard since... Well, I cannot remember. Tell me what you need me to do."

"I need you to make the tools I need with your powers, so I can create the machines we have to make."

"You need me to make tools?" An airman who'd been looking at her feet almost bumped into her, but skirted around with a muttered apology. Weiz glanced at the woman, but otherwise paid her no mind. "Why don't I just make the damned machines?"

Deidra shook her head. "It won't work like that. I'd explain it, but it would take some time, and I think you're busy."

Oh, right. She continued her walk, eyes roving over figures both grouped and alone, trying to find the people she needed.

"I'm going to want to negotiate with these villagers," she told the scientist. "I don't really want to waste what ammo we have left on people who don't stand a chance against us."

"Not when you're using that ammo for hunting," Deidra murmured. "But who would you send that could understand them?" She paused. "No, you're right. We can understand them."

Weiz grunted. It had only been a theory, and one she hadn't voiced out loud. If the woman started doing that too often, it would become an annoyance.

As she hit the other side of the common, heading toward the graveyard, she saw the people she was looking for in a huddle at one of the scrapped ships. She frowned over at them, though they weren't looking in her direction. Greenway, Lance, Harvey and Kristin. All four of them. When they'd all spent so much time avoiding one another. And they hadn't invited her or the good Doctor to the conversation.

There was a hush when Greenway glanced up and noticed she was headed toward them, the scientist in toe. His eyes did not leave her, and the others shifted their stances to watch. She glared at each of them in turn, but not a one of them held an expression of guilt. *What were they talking about?*

"I need you four to go to the village and get Captain Oswald and his team out of a cellar," she said. The simple act of giving orders again made her feel more like herself than she had in weeks.

They each looked to the others, then back at Weiz, confusion writ clear on their faces. "Get them out of a cellar?" Kristin said.

Weiz nodded. "Yes. Seems they can all see us now, and the good Captain has gotten himself into a spot of trouble."

Harvey snorted a laugh. "Surely they can get themselves out? Those villagers don't exactly strike me as masters of engineering."

Greenway moved to the front and put a hand on Harvey's chest. The Captain looked at the other man with a frown, but said nothing. "We'll go, Commander," he told her. "We'll get them out."

"Good. See that you do." She measured the four with a critical eye before she sighed. "Keep me updated on the negotiations."

"Negotiations?" Lance raised a brow.

"Yes, I want you to speak to them."

"Could be difficult," Kristin intoned.

Deidra coughed into a hand to get their attention. "Actually, you should all understand the natives. A *gift* — for lack of a better word — from the Giants."

Greenway nodded to her and then strode past them all in the direction of the woods. Weiz caught Harvey's eye, *we'll talk later* was the thought she got from him. Then they were all off, headed for the village.

She had a feeling that something was about to go terribly wrong.

Only, she could not put her finger on what it might be. On how she might change it. Just that, after today, things would once again change. And she didn't think she was going to like it.

"Come," she told Deidra. "We can talk of the things you might need while we await a report in the ship."

Weiz didn't bother to see if the woman followed. *Something just doesn't feel right. But then*, she reflected, *nothing really has since we got here.*

CHAPTER FOURTEEN

The walk to the village had not taken them long. At a steady pace, it was usually about two hours from camp, but they'd made it in less than thirty at a good run. Sometimes they all just felt the need to stretch their legs, let the wind flow through their hair. Even Lance was enjoying their outing.

They walked now in lock step, down the northern end of the field where the villagers grew their vegetables. One of the men who'd been hoeing a small patch of ground near the centre of the field, stopped in what he was doing, leaned on his hoe, and glared at them with his brown eyes.

Harvey avoided that gaze. There was something in it that didn't sit right with him.

So, this is our first contact with an alien race. And they look just like us. Behave, just like us. In his twenty plus years of fighting off hostile alien incursions, this was nothing close to how he might have imagined making contact. He wondered if there were people on Earth who knew there were humans on other planets. The previous five hundred years had certainly been full enough of sightings and stories of abductions. He had no doubt there were governments who had known about such things long before they were brought to public consciousness.

The village seemed to fall into a hush as they stepped foot into the broad street. Eyes followed them, mothers clasping children, men holding weapons or farm tools. Most were out front of their houses, though some were gathered at the other end, where a pyre had been erected.

Harvey's eyes widened at that. Did the people of this village intend to burn Captain Oswald and his team? But then he saw, a little off to the side, laid out on a table, the body of a young woman in a ragged, faded pink dress. Her feet were bare and dirty, her hair long and the curls uncombed. Her face looked peaceful, lifeless lips painted red, eyes closed, head lolled to the side as if in sleep. One arm was draped over her stomach, and he could see a dark red stain on the dress near her pelvis.

The woman must have died during childbirth. Not an uncommon occurrence even on Earth five hundred years ago. And he did not know why, but he knew, that when he finally left this place, this was the image that would stick with him the longest.

A leader of the village stepped forward from where he'd been laying hay around the pyre. Harvey's gaze shot up to meet his. He had long grey hair, gathered up in a ponytail. His eyes, red rimmed and brimming with unshed tears were a bright green with yellow flecks. His skin was tanned and unlined, and his thin lips pressed into a tight line. Around his left wrist he wore a bracelet woven of hair.

Weiz and that scientist might think that we should understand these people, and that may be so. But can they understand us?

Harvey made to step forward from where they'd stopped a few paces away, but Greenway took the lead before he had a chance. "We demand that you release the prisoners."

Good negotiating skills, Captain, he frowned.

The villager who had stepped away from his fellows, swept his gaze over the group. "I am named Fell," he told them as if Greenway had not spoken. "I am the Garas of this village."

"Garas?" he mouthed to Kristin. The woman shrugged at him, and they turned their attention back to the man. It must have been a title the equivalent of governor or mayor, he assumed.

Greenway cleared his throat. "Fell, is it? I am named Aiden Greenway, a Captain of the Allied Terran Forces Attack Fleet. And I demand that you release your prisoners."

Fell looked to his fellows. There was a young woman who looked like kin to the one on the table, though her dress was brown, and she wore shoes. Beside her, a man that looked to be Harvey's age, muscular and stout, with brown hair and eyes in an unremarkable face. To the Garas' other side, were four old men, one leaning on a cane, his grey beard so long it almost touched the ground, his eyes like blue diamonds. One was bald, with a beard to match the first, and the other two, were gnarled and ancient. Joints swollen, eyes rheumy, backs hunched.

"We cannot do as you ask," he told them.

"Which would have been the expected answer had Greenway bothered to *ask,*" Lance breathed so quietly to his left that he barely heard him. He hoped that Greenway hadn't.

Greenway made to speak once more, but Harvey restrained him with a hand. "Let me," he told the man as he looked him in the eye.

The Captain did not look pleased, but he waved Harvey on. "Do as you must," he said.

One of the old men spat on the ground at Harvey's feet. He tried to ignore it. "We've come to negotiate. Tell us what you would have in exchange for our men."

The Garas said nothing for a moment, but he kept his eyes on Harvey. "We cannot do as you ask," he repeated, finally.

Do they even understand what I am saying? "Surely there is some kind of arrangement we can come to? Do you need more hunters? Help with the crops?"

Fell shook his head. So, he did understand. "We hunt what we need, we take turns with the crops. Everything else we need, we get from Djorik. Our village is a very small one, and we need very little." He spread his hands wide.

Someone behind him erupted into a fit of coughing. Harvey waited until it died down before he continued. "Just tell me what we *can* give in exchange. Those people are important to us."

"There is nothing," Fell insisted. "They stole. They will be taken to Djorik on the next round and will face the Miwari for judgement. This is the law."

Djorik was beginning to sound like a city, to him. Or at least a good-sized town. They had laws, and he didn't know why that surprised him, but it did.

"They had need," he lied. "We have been stranded here for a little over a month." The man eyed him quizzically. "A month is when a moon moves from full to dark, to full again," he tried to explain.

Fell nodded his understanding. "A cycle. You have been here a cycle. But how stranded? You could have easily gone to Djorik, purchased food there. It is not a difficult walk. Just a day down this trail." He offhandedly motioned toward the trail they'd found the first day.

Harvey shook his head. He didn't know how to explain to a man who knew nothing of technology how it was they had happened upon their plight. Nor the games that airmen played to alleviate boredom. Their theft had been such a game. They didn't need what these poor villagers had; it was simply convenient.

He tried again, somehow certain that it would make no difference. "Look —"

"Give them to us now," Greenway demanded, taking the front

of the stage.

Fell glanced at him. "I cannot."

"You can," he said in a low voice. "And you will." He had his fists clenched at his side.

"I cannot," the Garas repeated. It seemed a mantra at this point.

The ground began to shake beneath his boots, and it took less than a second to realise it was Greenway. There was a rumble so deep that Harvey thought the ground might collapse into a sink hole. He didn't have a chance to respond to what was happening.

"I will not be denied!" Greenway shouted, spittle flying. He raised his fists. Clumps of dirt sprayed up, then rained down on all in attendance. Some remained balanced, others fell in a sprawl, the elderly men among the latter.

First a look of shock, and then horror passed across the faces of those arrayed before them. Fell glanced at the corpse on the table. Whether to see if it was still as it ought to be, or a thought they might end up like her, Harvey couldn't say.

Harvey put a hand on Greenway's shoulder, "That's enough," he told the man quietly.

Greenway shrugged him off and raised his left fist high into the air. A pillar of Earth shot like a bullet from the ground, through the roof of the nearest hut, and stood like a piston that had reached its apex and suddenly seized. It sank perhaps a foot back into the ground before all was still.

Harvey glanced around him at all the people of the village. Some looked on in wide-eyed awe, while others had already sunk to their knees and had begun chanting. "Dassun!" they said in reverence. He could only assume that it had been the name of some God they worshipped.

Eyes that bled a kind of insanity turned toward Harvey then, and in that moment, he feared. "I will not be denied," the Captain repeated.

"You're killing them," Harvey said.

"They're dogs who must be trained." More spouts of earth, more ground shaking.

Harvey blinked at the callous statement. This was not the man that he knew. Greenway had always been gentle, kind and thoughtful. "They're people, just like us," he asserted.

"Not like us," the man insisted. His voice rose with every syllable, the earth creaked with every word. "Not like us, Harvey. Don't you get it? They can't be. We are *gods*, Harvey. We — are — Gods!" With the final roar, he took off into the sky.

Harvey watched until the man disappeared into the south, unable to shake the feeling something terrible was coming. He'd known since their first day on this planet that something was wrong with Greenway, but this... It was more than he had words for.

Lance scoffed. "We can fly?" Kristin whacked him hard in the shoulder. The Captain winced in empathy. That woman hit hard.

The villagers were still prostrated, though the tremors had ceased. Those who had not bowed while Greenway was there, remained fixed in their positions, eyes on the sky. Except Fell.

Harvey turned to the man. "Where are our men?"

"Cellar of the first house." He pointed to a well-made hut on the left.

The Captain nodded his thanks and moved toward it, Lance and Kristin close behind. He couldn't fathom the amount of damage Greenway had just caused. Not only in the village, but in their potential relationship with them.

To the Pilot, he said, "We'll need to find out if we can fly later..Right now, I am of no mind to carry these guys back."

"We could make them walk," Lance nodded to himself, obviously excited by the prospect.

"We're their escort, Sinatra," said Kristin. "If we leave them, like as not these villagers would just catch them and put them back.

They were pretty insistent that they go to this Djorik place and face the whose-a-ma-whats-it."

"Come on, let's just do it."

~

They arrived back at camp with four perfectly able, but shamed, airmen. They said very little on their return trip, and less once they'd gotten there, excepting Captain Oswald's mumbled apology to the Commander. Which she accepted more graciously than Harvey would have in her position.

He waited until they'd all left before he gave Weiz his complete attention. "He'll be back, you know."

"Who? Greenway? I am sure he will. And he'll regret his burst of temper." She sat down on the floor of the bridge and patted the ground next to her.

Harvey obliged, sitting so close that their hips touched. He put his hand over hers, and their fingers entwined. It was so natural. He didn't even have to think about it.

"You didn't see him out there. I am sure it's more than that."

"What do you think, then?"

He leaned his head back and closed his eyes, then let it lull to the side so he could look into her eyes. "He believes that we are gods. I think he believes that we deserve *obeisance*. The way they bowed to him in the village... Whoever these Giants were before we took them out, those people down there, they worshipped them, I think. Or a version of them."

"Deidra says they were *as* gods. Whatever that means. That we have become what they were. So, I suppose in a way he might be night." Weiz sighed. "I don't know what to believe. But Deidra seems to know what she is talking about, so I'll try to believe that."

"So, you think we're gods too?"

"That's not what I mean."

"What do you mean?"

She let go of his hand and got up from the floor. Somehow, talking to each other had become more difficult over the past month. Something they'd never before struggled with. Words. Such simple things.

After a moment of having her back turned, she swung swiftly around. "What do you want from me, Harvey?" she asked, blue eyes glaring down.

"How do you mean?"

"I mean, *what do you want from me*? Exactly as I've said it."

Harvey squirmed in his seat. *What is she expecting from me? What does she want for an answer?* he wondered.

Apparently, he was taking too long to answer because she threw her hands into the air with a frustrated growl, did a three-sixty, then leaned over him, pointing with an accusatory finger. "I waited for you, John," she hissed. "Probably a stupid thing to do, I admit. But I waited for you, knowing you were married, that you had a family. I never took a lover that I couldn't easily discard if you decided to come my way. I *waited*. And this is what I get? *This* is what I was waiting for?"

She stomped her foot hard into the ground and the ship shook. She turned to face the other side of the bridge as Harvey got to his feet.

"Now hold up, woman," he demanded. "I never asked you to wait for me, and I never expected it either, so don't you try and lay that at my feet. You ask me what I want from you, but what the hell do you want from me?"

Her head lifted, and she breathed deep. "I don't know."

"Then why do you expect me to know?" He put a hand on her shoulder, and another on her waist. She didn't move and he slid forward until their bodies touched. Her head leaned back into him. "The beauty of such things lies in the unexpected," he said softly into her ear. "And expectation breeds disappointment."

"We don't talk," said Weiz, just as softly.

He wanted to chuckle at the comment, though he knew it wasn't funny. "We've all been a little preoccupied, that is all, my love."

"Hmm. Say that again."

"Which part?"

She raised a hand to stroke his cheek, let her body fall completely into his, and turned her head a fraction so he could see her eyes. "My love."

He smiled down at her. "My love. My love, my love."

She raised her head for a kiss — and someone bounded in the hatch.

Weiz pulled away quickly, and Harvey grimaced at Lance. "And the worst timing ever award goes to..." he growled.

Lance turned swiftly to show the wide eyes of his tattoos. "I'd never have guessed," he said.

If Harvey had something to throw, he would have.

"What do you want, Viatri?" Weiz asked testily.

The Pilot swivelled back to them with a shrug. "Deidra wants you."

Weiz stormed out, pushing Lance out of the way.

Harvey ground his teeth glared. "I was about to win an argument," he told him.

"Looked more like something else to me." Lance strode over to his chair and sprawled in it.

"What were you doing with the Scientist, anyway? Didn't think you'd even met her before."

"She seemed to know what she was talking about when she asked Greenway to build that grave for Fields. So, I thought I'd ask her if she knew anything about our powers. You all seem to know what you've got in your pockets, but I've yet to use mine."

Harvey took a seat against the view screen, arms wrapped around legs. "She's got Fields' power now. What did she tell you?"

The Pilot nodded. "I'd figured, though I didn't know what it was. Apparently, we can't fly, and neither can Greenway."

"Damn well looked like he was flying to me."

"She doesn't know how he did it, but only because she wasn't there to see him. But me, in my incredible uniqueness, and awesomeness, am the Weatherman." He wiggled his brows with a big smile as if the name held significance.

"Say what, now?"

"I can control the weather. She gave me another name, but it was dull."

"And the weatherman isn't?" The Captain shook his head. Dealing with Lance was sometimes a trial. He was glad that the man was back on his feet and had stopped feeling sorry for himself, but his sense of humour sometimes grated.

It's just your mood. You don't feel like being happy, so those who are, frustrate you. It's a jealousy thing. You know this. He tried to smile. "I suppose it suits you."

"She told me a bunch of stuff about all of us." The man shrugged.

"What did she want with Weiz?"

"Don't know, but figured it was important. She was working on some plans or something."

"And where's Kristin?"

"No offence, sir, but you're beginning to bug."

Harvey scoffed. "You're the one who busted in on me, if you remember. I get to do that for a while."

"Good point." But he still didn't answer about Kristin.

She's probably out with a hunting party or something. That woman does not know how to sit still for long.

The Captain levered himself to his feet. "I think I'll go see what Kristin is up to."

"Good luck," was all Viatri said as he made his way out the

hatch.

The world moved around him, and when his boot hit the ground, he was standing next to Kristin.

She was sitting at the edge of the water, looking across at the empty plains. "Harvey, you have to be the single most difficult man to get rid of."

He faltered in his step, glanced down at her. "If you want me to leave…"

"No," she sighed. "Just… I am thinking. What happened with Greenway?"

That is exactly what all of us have been thinking in our down time, when we haven't been distracted by other things. Thing is, none of us knows, we can't know, 'cause we don't share a brain. Maybe Deidra. Hmm. Would it be too much of an imposition? I wonder if she has time.

Kristin clicked her fingers in front of his face. "Oi! You! If you're going to loom like that, you could at least be useful. Thoughts on Greenway?" She blinked up at him with an innocent half smile.

"He'll be back."

"But you kind of get the feeling we're not going to appreciate his coming back, right?"

He sat beside her in the grass. "What did you see?" he asked.

She shrugged uncomfortably, many expressions warring for precedence on her face. "I think we'll have a fight on our hands before it's all said and done," she said at last.

"That's what you saw?"

"Not exactly, but it was the feeling behind it."

Harvey pushed out a sigh. "You tell Weiz?"

Kristin glanced sideways at him. "She's not been the Commander for some time now."

"Of course —" He started, but she cut him off.

"No," the woman insisted. "She's been in her own head too

much. She's a legend, she's excellent at her job, but not lately. Lately, she's been absent and useless. You distract her. And you're not the only thing on her mind."

"But —"

"But nothing."

"Will you let me finish a damned sentence!" Kristin waved him on, her eyes still on the vista before them.

"She's not commanding 'cause no one is looking at her for it, not because she doesn't know how. She understands that this is not a normal situation, and that in a lot of respects she has to give us our freedom. It's not about control, or power, or even leading. It's about respect. If you speak to her, and let her know the danger, then she will do what needs to be done."

"Are you sure about that?"

Am I? "Yes." *She just needs people to start looking to her again. She's lost her confidence. She got us to go get those team members from the village, right? She ordered us then.*

"I wish I shared your confidence," Kristin murmured.

So do I. "She's with Deidra, at the moment. They're plotting something between them."

"If it amounts to anything, then I am sure we'll be informed." Though her tone suggested she did not believe that.

"Maybe —"

"He's coming." Kristin got up and looked down at him expectantly. He stood.

Harvey bit back some frustration. He didn't think he'd ever been interrupted so much in such a short span of time.

She led him through the camp, past the ships, skirting the common, and facing toward the woods. He couldn't see anyone down there. But he trusted in the woman next to him, and instead of asking stupid questions, he just waited.

Close to ten minutes later, a man emerged from the forest.

Kristin turned back toward the ships and hollered at the closest airman, "Get Weiz!" then returned her attention to the man walking toward them.

From this distance, Harvey couldn't clearly tell if it was Greenway, but there was no one else it would have been, either. He strode slowly, in no rush to reach them. He appeared aware of their presence, their eyes on him, but unaffected by it.

Footsteps behind him alerted him to Weiz's arrival. A few others, too, had come to watch, but he didn't take his eyes off Greenway.

We — are — Gods! The man had screamed. Harvey knew he believed it too. *But so what if we are? That doesn't give us the right to do whatever we want. It doesn't automatically erase the moral compass. We're still people. We still came from somewhere, still owe an allegiance to our race.* He just could not fathom Greenway's insistence that they were somehow *better*.

Greenway stopped a few feet away and shared a glance over all who were there. Harvey looked back then, to find that a good half of the airmen were there as well.

"Good start," the gaunt Captain said. "I'd only planned on addressing Weiz in this, but the more the merrier."

"Get on with it then, Greenway," Weiz told him.

He inclined his head. "We are Gods, now. You, Harvey, Kristin, Lance, Deidra and myself. We make the Pantheon. We already have worshippers. That was obvious in the village, was it not?" He directed the question to Harvey.

"They weren't exactly chanting Greenway," he growled in defiance of the man's claims.

"Ah! But they were chanting, no?" He waved the question off with a hand. "I have come to invite you all, to join me. I have already gathered for myself some acolytes. You could do the same."

"You're mad," Kristin spluttered.

"A matter of perspective." He addressed them all now. "Come

beneath my banner, and I will afford you anything at all you might wish. It is within my power to grant such things, while you all wallow here hoping you'll get home. But I have news for you. You're not going home." He gave them a moment to let that thought sink in. "So, you have a choice to make. Follow, or die here." Silence greeted him. "I'll come back in twenty-four hours; you can make your decisions then." Then he turned on his heel and strode back toward the woods.

Harvey turned to Kristin, then Weiz. "He means it, doesn't he?" she asked him.

"I'm sure he does."

"He'll try and sabotage what work we've managed to do, in order to ensure his words are true," Deidra said from beside Weiz.

"Then we'll need to do something about that." The Commander faced her airmen. "What he has said," she told them, "is not true. The Scientist and I are already working on a way to get us home. Have faith. It will happen."

But it was clear by the look on some of their faces that they did not believe her. Harvey was of half a mind to back her up, to say a few words to add to her assertion. But he didn't have any.

Kristin fell to her knees beside him, and he dropped to make sure she didn't land face first. Though he needn't have. She held her head in her hands, eyes stared sightlessly into the crowd. She was having a vision.

The airmen had begun to drift off, talking amongst themselves, already halfway to making that decision. Harvey was sure that some, at least, would follow Greenway in his madness. He saw no way to avoid it short of locking down the camp, and that would not go down well.

We have things to go home to, Greenway. And you've no right to take that choice from us. Though he had addressed the other Giant Killers as equals, his tone had indicated he saw the others as no more than servants at best. Favoured servants, perhaps, as they were from his home world, but servants none-the-less.

Kristin gasped and breathed hard. She dropped her hands from her head and stared into the ground. Only Weiz, Deidra and he were left. He briefly wondered where Lance was but said nothing.

"What did you see?" Deidra asked.

Kristin punched the ground hard. Breathed hard, punched it again, then let loose with a string of punches that caused a small tremor. She was cursing under her breath, and she looked as if she might throw up. They waited it out.

"It was the same fucking one!" she yelled in frustration as she got to her feet.

"Which one would that be?" Weiz queried.

"The same one I had the first time and just about every night since," she spat.

Harvey patted her arm. "Calm you're shit, woman," he said softly. She shot him a glare. But she didn't punch him, for which he was immediately grateful. Seemed she gotten all her anger out on the ground.

"The Mountain," Deidra said. Kristin glared at her.

Weiz faced her. "The Mountain?"

"It was a thought only. This world wasn't always villages and empty spaces."

Kristin breathed deep, then said normally. "I cannot say it's a mountain. Just a very broken and very old place."

"And you've been seeing it since the first day?"

"I said that, didn't I?"

"Just making sure." Deidra turned to Weiz. "I think we should go there. It's hundreds of kilometres from here. But we can get most of what we need, and Greenway would have no idea where we are."

"It's a long fucking walk!" Harvey interjected. "All well and fine for me, or those who could fit in my ship, but what about the rest of them?"

There was some kind of silent communication going on between these women, he was sure. The way they glanced at one another spoke of an agreement already made.

"We might not have a choice," Weiz told him, but would not meet his eye.

He stared down at her. "You think they're going to Greenway?" *You think the same thing. You know you need to make the move before he can damage the equipment.* And it would be easy for the man to do, he knew. A few well-placed mountains shooting out of the damned ground and that would be it for all of them.

Kristin brushed his arm, then. "Most of them," she said. "But it doesn't mean we can't come back for them once we've got it all done. We just can't let him destroy the hope."

Harvey kept his eyes on Catherine. "We do this, and you realise they'll see it as abandonment? They'll not forgive you, even should you get them home."

"When has being a leader ever been easy, Harvey? That's why you never took up a Commandership. I know it was offered to you more than once." He could only grunt in reply.

"If we're going to do this, then let's do it. I hope you know where we're going, Doctor, 'cause when we come back, we'll be facing the wrath of a god, apparently."

Kristin started for the common. "I'll get those who will come, and I'll meet you at the ship."

"What more can we do?" From Weiz it was not just a question, but a plea. If he could give answer, then she would listen.

But I have none. All that will come, will come.

They went to the ship.

CHAPTER FIFTEEN

It was an exercise in torture. To wake up here, blind from lack of light, sweat dripping, joints aching, head thumping. He had come so close, only to end up back where he had started. The gun hatch.

Heinrich growled out a string of curses that echoed off the thick metal hatch and whacked at his head like a kick from steel capped shoes. Saliva sprayed from his mouth only to land on his face. The indignity alone was enough to stoke his temper. Even on Io station he had not *wanted* to hurt anyone. But now, he did. He most definitely did.

Knowledge! It was mine! Deidra, I will have you for this. I will have you! He didn't know which ones had kicked him in the head, but he would solve it by killing them all. Only he could go home. That was how it was meant to be in the first place, now that they all knew what he had done. *I was going to let you live. I was. But not now.*

He felt a chuckle escape him and somewhere on the edge of thought he wondered if perhaps he'd gone mad. It was laced with hysteria, he was sure. But did it matter?

He couldn't stand up, he couldn't lie comfortably, he couldn't even sit up without hunching his back. His fists slammed ineffectually into the hatch door. It didn't even rattle.

There was no point in yelling out to whoever was guarding him, they wouldn't hear it. At least not as anything more than a soft murmur, and they'd have to be close for that.

Heinrich lay on his back, hip pressed to the floor, knees bent, toes touching the far wall, head scraping against the other. His hands hovered a few centimetres from the hatch. If he'd succeeded in stealing that woman's powers, then he would have had no difficulty in getting out, he was sure. He'd have *known*. Known everything.

As it was, he'd just have to be patient. They would let him out when they so judged he should eat before he starved. It had taken them two days, the first time. With the blow to his head, he was not sure how long he'd been in the hatch already, but from the way his knees ached, he had to assume at least half a day, perhaps more.

You could be in here forever. They might forget about you. You'll die alone here. "Shut up!" *You do not deserve to live, do not kid yourself.* "I said shut up!" He whacked the hatch.

The absurdity of having an argument with himself was not lost on him. But he had no one else to talk to. Truly, no one had spoken to him since Io station. They'd stared, they'd handed him things, they'd done things for him if he explained to satisfaction that they were necessary. But it had all been silent. No words for him.

Because it all would have been wasted breath, old man. You let yourself down. It wasn't supposed to happen like this. "No, it wasn't supposed to happen like this." *Just a test. If the dome hadn't exploded, we'd be home already, none the wiser. None of this would be happening. And we could have come back here. A grand accidental discovery made by Heinrich Faets!*

He felt a tear spill down his temple and fall into the side of his ear. There was nothing left to him now but —

The hatch opened. He was struck by a light so bright it burned behind his eye lids. Heinrich thrust up his hands to ward it off.

Rough hands grabbed him by the upper arms and hauled him out. He was thrust forward on his unsteady feet. The hands let go and he fell, his weak knees betraying him.

Heinrich blinked rapidly to adjust his eyes to the light. Boots thudded on the deck in front of him, stopped right in front of his face. He looked up.

He couldn't have said he knew the man who stared down upon him with a scowl. He was average in height, hazel-eyed with sandy blonde hair and a beard that ill-suited him.

"We no longer need you," the man said. "But of necessity we must leave, and we have no room for those who would not be useful. In this, I must give you a choice."

He didn't understand. *Are they letting me go? Have I served my sentence? Am I to wonder these wilds alone, forever? Are we going home?* "This is my work!" he found himself shouting before he knew what was coming out. "You have to let me go home!" *But is there anything left for you there?* "You have to let me go home." This came out softer, and tears flowed free.

Heinrich was embarrassed at this show of weakness, but he just could not help himself. If he faced madness, then he was no longer sure he cared. It was his project, and he deserved the credit for making it work. If they left without him, they would keep it for themselves.

The man in front of him shuffled back. He didn't say anything further, but he must have given silent instruction, as the men who'd hauled him out of the gun hatch dragged him out into fading daylight.

~

From his position in the tree at the edge of the forest, Greenway watched as the airmen separated. Some had gone into Harvey's ship, but for the most part, they stayed in the common.

Beside him, on a neighbouring branch, was Odden, a man from the village who had bowed to him that morning. His dark hair hung loose about his shoulders, his face blackened with soot, dark blue eyes searching. This, then, was his first acolyte. The one who would be his High Priest. He'd fought for the honour with others in the village and had come out the clear victor, with blood spilled.

Greenway found that he did not mind that. Life was almost meaningless to him. It had been for a long time, though it had taken this month to realise just how little regard he gave it. He'd always assumed it was just his life he'd been careless with. But when he'd really given it some thought, as he'd practised so diligently in that clearing, he realised that every time he'd gone on a suicide run, hoping to join his lost love, he'd taken his entire crew with him, and had never once thought about how they might feel. And it was because it didn't matter.

The sky had begun to darken, the sun setting in red tones over the western horizon. The near full moon was a misty orb in the sky, and the brightest stars had already begun to glow.

"They've made their choice," he said to Odden as Harvey's ship began to climb. "Either they've abandoned those who're left behind, or they chose to stay."

"As you say, M'lord."

"Go back to the village. Take word that there will be guests this night." He didn't wait for the man's acknowledgement of his words — he knew he'd heard and would heed — he just jumped from his branch and landed with an earth shuddering thud upon the ground.

It was time to collect his new recruits.

It did not take him long to reach the common, and when he got there, they all just stared. The fire was not lit, they'd prepared no evening meal. The stripped carcasses of a few rabbits and a giant snake-rat lay on a slab near the fire pit, but the cauldron was empty.

He looked them over. They didn't stand to attention, or gaze at him in admiration or adoration. They assessed him as he assessed them. They were airmen. They were equals. He would have to disabuse them of that.

"Who," he said after a few moments, "has chosen to follow me?"

There was no movement in the crowd. Not even a shuffle of feet. None of them looked to each other for the answers, they just stared at him.

He let the silence stretch on for a time. Then softly, "Do any of you deny my power?" He made the earth quake beneath them.

Still, they did not move, except to keep their footing. And none spoke. But none walked away, either. What did they wait for?

He gestured toward the outer edge of the camp, to where Harvey's ship had been less than fifteen minutes ago. There, a mountain slowly began to rise. It would change the landscape for kilometres in all directions, the village would live at its foot. The plains would roll around it, and the river would come to meet it. This then, would be his epithet. It would take weeks to form, for he did not want to ruin its surrounds. But form it would.

"Step forward," he demanded. "Step forward and I will reward you." He knew he didn't have the power to give them all that they wanted. But he could give them a close second. "You have been abandoned by your leaders. You have been set loose upon this world. Choose now if your new beginning would start with power. Or with need."

Finally, one of them cleared his throat to speak. He looked to the airmen, and thought he recognised him. White-blonde hair, dark grey eyes, honey skin. He was clean shaven, and his uniform looked little worn. "Speak, if you would, Pilot Reeve."

The man's eyes shot up in surprise. Likely he didn't expect Greenway knew his name. "You gave us twenty-four hours. It's barely been three."

"You did not go with the others."

"There was no room."

"So, you would have if there were?"

Silence. The others continued to just stare at him. He had given them twenty-four hours. Had said it out loud and meant it at the time. But his curiosity had gotten the better of him, and so he'd watched. This had lead him to believe that they'd chosen. To stay with him...

"So be it, then," he told them. He gestured to his epithet. "Witness." And he strode back toward the woods.

He would give them the time. The time to choose right. To choose him. He had said it, and it would not have sat well with any of them had he taken those words back. He knew airmen, had been one long enough. It could not be forced.

At the edge of the woods, Greenway sat with his back to a spruce, so he could view the proceedings, though giving them their privacy at the same time. While he could see those who were closest to him, unlike the vantage he'd had in the tree, he could not discern their features or movements. And he definitely could not hear any of them.

Patience, Greenway. You are immortal now. This is a trait you must learn. Patience.

~

His hands were tied, his mouth gagged, and blindfold placed. Then he was shoved into the gun hatch of a new ship. He'd have struggled out of the bonds if he'd had the space, but as things stood, he saw no point.

The ships engines had whined on at some point, and wherever their destination, it had taken a good couple of hours before they landed.

The ship had been cleared before he was dragged from the hatch and deposited on the ground outside. It felt like gravel and smelled of dust and dew. The air was cool. From this, he assumed that they'd risen in altitude.

No one spoke to him or removed the blindfold. But he was not deaf to the work that took place around him. Murmured conversations muted by rock fall, and the hurried scuffle of boots. It was dark out, now, that much he could tell, though the knowledge did him little good.

I wonder if they bought food. His stomach rumbled, reminding him he'd not eaten since breakfast the day before. He'd been too excited about his plans. Too focused in his hunger. The power that should have been his.

Boots crunched on the gravel near him, and the blindfold was removed. It was the man who'd spoken to him before. He crouched down, resting one arm on a thigh.

"Doctor Ward and Commander Weiz both agree that it would prove expedient to just kill you and get it over with. Especially after what you did to Fields." He grimaced and spat. "The other you might have been forgiven for, eventually, a scientist too enthusiastic about his work, but the murder..." He shrugged. "But you want to go home, so I'll not deny you that right, because *I* am no murderer. But understand this; one foot wrong, just one, and nobody will hesitate to slit your throat. And not one among us would stay that hand. You understand me?"

You talk too much. But he could say nothing around the gag. He nodded.

"Good. You'll be bound and gagged every night, no complaints or I'll deposit you somewhere out there in the wilderness to fend for yourself. We might give you a short leash, but don't imagine you've earned any trust." The hazel eyes searched him. "You got me?"

Again, Heinrich nodded.

"Right then. I'll untie you in the morning."

If he could have sighed, he would have. Instead, it came out as a snort. The man looked back at him with an arched brow, but Heinrich just twitched his nose. The airman moved on.

He didn't know how he was going to get himself out of this one.

Hours passed. Eventually he fell asleep, still where he'd been dumped, head against the ship. Saliva had soaked the gag and had started to dribble down his chin. Because his hands had been tied behind his back, he was forced to wipe it on his shoulder.

His eyes flickered open to an early dawn, the sky still dark though the horizon showed a streak of yellow and pink.

He couldn't see much other than silhouettes, and those mostly of trees and rock. Though he spied some movement out of the corner of his eye, when he tried to focus on it, he saw nothing.

Heinrich waited.

If he couldn't have Deidra's power, then he needed to find a way to take one of the others. They were not impervious, that much was obvious. *But the knowledge. We could have had that. We could have been celebrated back on Earth for our triumphs.* The fact that he thought of himself in plural form had not yet truly penetrated his inner understanding. It was simply how things were.

As the sun began to brighten the sky, someone came over. A guard, no doubt. The man lifted him effortlessly from the ground with a single un-sleeved arm and looked him directly in the eye. He was shorter than Heinrich, so his feet still dangled close to the ground, but it was an impressive feat.

"Right," he said, an odd mix of Italian and British accents in his words. "I've been told you're the one we have to thank for this sorry situation we've got ourselves in. I've also been told that I am not supposed to talk to you, that Harvey has already taken care of the understandings, as they are." He looked back toward the sleeping figures huddled against the cliff face, revealing an eye tattooed on the back of his bald head. "But you and me, we're going to have a little understanding of our own, you hear me?"

Heinrich widened his eyes and nodded. *Untie me already, you twit.*

The man lowered him so he was standing, though he was still tied at the ankles and would fall if he let go. "I am the Weatherman. And I've eyes in the back of my head." He turned to show them off, then resumed. "Foot wrong, Doctor, and I won't bother with a knife. Capisce?"

I got it. Du bist doch zu dumm zum Scheißen! Now untie me! He nodded so profusely that he shook in the man's grip.

The Weatherman gave a single nod, then let him drop. He unceremoniously rolled him over, then first untied his legs, then his hands. Must have figured that Heinrich would be able to take care of the gag himself, as he walked away before he could even roll onto his side.

He removed the gag, inhaled deeply, and immediately began coughing. "*Scheiße.*" He wheezed and spat out dust.

Now he was untied, he would be closely monitored. Or so he'd thought. As he turned to face those who'd made the trip, he saw only a handful, and none were looking his way.

Heinrich almost laughed. Again and again, they underestimated him. There were no eyes on him. Even that tattooed man had moved out of his eyesight.

A grim smile edged onto his thin lips. He took a good look at where he was. On the side of a mountain, so far as he could tell, though not too high up. They were on a ledge — a rather large one — and as he kicked away some of the gravel beneath his shoes, he saw tiles. *Nun, werde ich gefickt zu warden.* Seems there'd been some smart people here.

He continued his observation of the surrounds. Lots of trees, not something he was particularly fond of. Gravel and dust, dried leaves and bracken. The ledge they were on had a scree slope on one side that ended in thick forest, part of it formed an overhang, while another section dropped directly down at least twenty feet. He saw no trail to follow, nothing that wound around the mountain from whence he could slowly make his decent. It would have to be a jump or a climb, neither of which appealed.

His smile turned to a snarl at his limited options. No wonder they weren't guarding him as they had at the camp. They didn't think he'd have a chance of escaping them, nor likely thought it mattered if he tried. It was he, after all, who'd insisted that he needed to go home, not them. But he was a murderer, and he couldn't understand why they were unafraid. They were as vulnerable as anyone else...

He couldn't underestimate them as they had him. They must have thought of something he hadn't.

Heinrich sat down on the ledge, feet dangling over the sheer drop. The trees below might cushion his fall somewhat, but he doubted he'd be in any state to move beyond that point if he tried. If he managed to get the powers of just one of them...

"Thinking about jumping, old man?" Heinrich turned his head sharply at the sound of Deidra's voice. "Save us all our moral dilemma if you do."

He snorted then looked back down on the treetops below him. "Moral dilemma indeed. You all seem to want to talk to me today. Or threaten."

"Call it nostalgia," the woman replied as she sat down next to him. If he'd had a knife...

"So, you miss working with me?"

She glanced at him. "I've always been a little suspicious of you, Heinrich. Even at the Paris Institute. You have to admit that you're a strange man. You get very focused on your work, you don't form bonds with people, and you had some very odd rules on the Station. But I find myself... forgetting."

He frowned over at her, though she wasn't looking at him. "Forgetting?" Not what he'd expected. Did she want comfort? He'd always liked her, but she'd never expressed such vulnerability before.

"It's the price, for this." She gestured to her head; eyes focused on the western horizon. "Soon, I'll no longer be the person you knew. Or anyone knew, to be fair. I hold to some things, but others are already gone. It's barely been a day, and judging by the rate of decay, I'll be incredibly lucky to make a month, as Fields did. There is a price, Heinrich." She looked at him then, and what he saw in her dark eyes terrified him. "Understand that you were spared, and be thankful. Everything you hold dear to your heart would mean nothing. Perhaps it would have been best had you taken this. Had she let you. Could you have lived with that sacrifice?"

He found his jaw was slack and his lips moved without sound. *Everything we hold dear to our heart would mean nothing. But we would have survived. We would have found a way home. But at what cost? Would it have meant anything? Are we thankful? We are thankful.*

Deidra gave him a tight smile, and the unexpected comfort of a pat on the arm. "I see the answer there in your expression, Heinrich. Remember, there is always a price."

She left him then, alone on the ledge, staring down at the treetops but seeing nothing. She'd given him something to ponder. Something that could change his world.

~

Greenway glanced up at the sound of boots. *Not all of them, but enough.* He arose from his position on the ground and swept the clinging leaves and grass from his damp pants.

From the camp, just over thirty odd airmen walked toward the woods. He wasn't quite close enough to know, but he thought their eyes were on him. Their stride held purpose, their expressions defiant. Not defiance against him, he knew, but against the others.

This pleased him.

He waited, arms crossed, until they reached him. He noticed that Pilot Reeve was not with them and felt his cheek twitch. The Captain disliked the idea of the pilot going home. He disliked the idea of any of them going home. He was a god, and he hadn't said they could leave.

"You will bow to me," he told them as they lined up in front of him.

They didn't even consider it, they just bowed. Greenway smiled. *They are mine. Let's see how much.*

"Rise. Your first task, as my favoured acolytes, will be to destroy the camp you leave behind."

The expressions that spread across their faces were priceless. Though some managed a modicum of restraint in facial movement, others were clearly distraught at the idea. It did not matter to him, as long as they followed his orders. There would be no discussion.

And there was none, they merely all turned and headed back toward the camp. Greenway followed a step behind.

The others from the camp, no more than had come down to him, were preparing a meal over the fire. The mountain that he'd set in motion was now perilously close to knocking the wooden posts loose on the south side. The whole common would be obliterated by days end. He could have let that take care of things. But he needed to see. Were they loyal to him?

Reeve stepped forward upon their arrival. "We have made our choices." He addressed the airmen who had chosen to come to him. "We have respected your decision. What would you have of us now?" The others near the fire watched with resignation on their tired features. They knew what was coming. Understood that defiance would avail them nothing.

"We are going to destroy the camp," said the acolyte directly facing him. His was tone strangely inflectionless, as though he took no joy from it, but nor did he feel the horror of it. He had been asked to do this by his God, and he would do so. "If you choose to get in the way, you too, will be destroyed."

And so, he took a step back and observed as Reeve punched the man square in the face. He dropped to the ground and lay unmoving. The Pilot looked over the others, a challenge in his gaze. "Who's next?" he asked.

Greenway had to admit he had not expected them to defend the camp when it was so clearly futile. He toyed for a moment, with the idea of giving them a second chance to leave. There would be no benefit in fighting.

There was a moment of tense silence, and then the brawl was joined. Greenway just let them have at it. Whoever were the victors at the end of it, would have earned their place at his side, or their freedom. Short of killing them all, he didn't think he'd stop them. And that surprised him.

He would need to begin grooming some of his acolytes to take on the mantels of the other Gods. If Weiz, Harvey, Kristin, Lance and Deidra would not do what was right, then he would find those who would. And he would deliver them. Every Pantheon required a leader. The Greeks had Zeus, the Romans had Jupiter and the Egyptians had Ra. This world would have Aiden.

The first thing he needed to do, was find out where they'd gone. Once that was done, it would only be a matter of time.

I offered you all a place in the pantheon. I gave you all a choice. Do the right thing. Become as one with this world. But you defy me. You strip this world of its gods and then you flee from it. What cowards you are that your home *is more important than the people who live here. This* is your home now. *This* is where your body will lay. For this world needs its gods, and if you will not oblige, then I will see to it someone else will.*

CHAPTER SIXTEEN

He'd wanted to be helpful. *Turns out that was a bad idea. Let's not do that again.* He felt a little abashed at his efforts, smiled nervously over at Kristin, now completely covered in dust and fine powdered stone. On the upside, they had uncovered a wall, though they'd been hoping for a door. Deidra had told them there was one here, and they trusted her.

Kristin spat a string or dark sputum on the ground at her feet, eyes still closed because of the debris caking her eyelids.

A hand clapped down on his back, and he jumped. Harvey kept his hand placed there as he moved to Lance's side. "Got her good," he nodded.

"Not what I'd meant to do."

"But it serves a purpose."

"It does?" He couldn't imagine what. The Captain looked to him with a smile and a wink. "It's funny."

Lance stared blankly at the man. Harvey gave him another clap on the back and moved on, laughing. "Maybe to you!" He yelled after the man. "But you're not the one she's going to punch in the face!" To this the Captain replied with a louder laugh than the first.

"Glad you think my pain is so funny, sir," he murmured to himself, arms crossed, lips pressed together.

"Lance." Kristin, finished with her spitting, rubbed a hand over her eyelids in an attempt to dislodge the dirt. It did her no good. "I am going to kill you."

He took a step back. "But you love me," he said, hopeful.

"Lance!" Her roar said it all.

He thought about going to her and helping her to get the grit out of her eyes, but decided against it. "Nope. Don't have a death wish." Instead, he turned and made his way to Deidra. He thought if Kristin came toward him, he'd use the Scientist as a shield.

She was on the edge of the cliff, sitting with that Heinrich fellow who'd caused this whole mess. He didn't understand why she did that. Everyone else wanted to kill him, and she just sat there and spoke to him as if they were old friends. *Maybe they were. They did work together for a long time.* But if he was being reasonable, he'd have thought the betrayal would have hurt more coming from someone you trusted.

"Found a wall," he told her as he approached. Kristin was still yelling behind him, and Deidra spared her a glance. Whatever she thought of it, it didn't show on her face.

"Excuse me, Heinrich." She got up, dusted herself off and moved toward the excavated piece of wall. Lance followed, scratching the side of his bald pate as he neared Kristin, muttering obscenities between spitting and unsuccessfully attempting to clean her face.

Deidra stopped before the woman and shook her head. "Hold still," she said, and Kristin obliged. With the sleeve of her fairly dirty lab coat, she wiped at Kristin's face until she could see at least some of the skin. There was no stream up here for the woman to go dunk herself in, though Deidra insisted there would be water in the buried city.

Annabelle opened her eyes. They were red and limned with grit and mucous, but when her eyes fell on Lance, they glared bloody death. He'd have run, if he'd had somewhere to go. He didn't even see the fist that flew at his face. He landed on the ground with a reverberating thump.

His nose felt broken, and it was definitely bleeding. He clutched at it, groaning. His eyes watered and his elbow hurt from the impact with the ground. He blinked to glare up at the woman, but all he could see was her back, surprisingly clear of dust. Deidra looked down on him with some sympathy, he thought, but she didn't offer to help him up.

Save the princess some damned work, and she punches me in the face. I knew that was coming. I knew it. Violent bitch. But he kept the thoughts to himself as he got up, and with thumbs squeezed together on either side of his nose, he set it straight. He'd had it broken before, and as much as it hurt every time, it was never as bad as the first.

He wiped the blood away with his forearm, careful not to touch the tip, and tried to focus on Deidra, who was now inspecting the wall. Her fingertips trailed lightly over the brickwork, where a few cracks could be seen in the smooth grey surface, but the mortarless seams were almost invisible.

She stepped away and turned to him. "This will do," she said. "For this, Greenway would have been more suited. But, I am sure that you can manage."

He knew there was a question in his eyes. "You sure you want him to do it, Doctor?" Kristin scoffed. "'A light breeze to scour the wall,' he says. He gives us a gale strong enough to lift a house." Deidra was between them now, for which he was thankful. He wasn't entirely sure that she wouldn't hit him again.

Deidra was either unaware of the tension — which was unlikely — or she just didn't care. "A gale would be fine. Enough directed force and it should topple inward. This particular space should lead into someone's house. The mountain is mostly hollow, and the city was built inside of it. On purpose. The streets will be clear, though the air will be stale."

Blow a hole in the side of the Mountain, Weatherman. You can do it. From the corner of his eye, he saw Xavier come to stand with his new girl and Weiz. "How is it," he asked the man. "We've been calling you superman for years, and you're the only one who didn't manage to get any powers?"

The Navigator shrugged at him. "Just lucky, I guess."

Lance grimaced and turned his attention back to the wall. *Just lucky, indeed.* As he'd done before, he sucked in a slow deep breath and focused on the area he wanted cleared. *But they don't want an actual gale, just enough pressure to cave the wall.* He thought a moment, then moved closer, till he was standing almost lips to stone. Then he heaved.

All of the pressure in his chest came out on the single, short exhale. But all it did was put a ball sized hole in the wall. He stepped back, did not let the others distract him from this task, kept his eyes from their looks of disappointment or encouragement. He hadn't spent time practising as they had. Up until yesterday, he hadn't even known what he could do. Wasn't even sure he'd wanted to know.

This time, when he blew, he cupped his hands around his mouth. A finger jabbed his nose and caused a squint, but he didn't let it halt him. He blew. The wall came down in a clatter. Dust and debris burst out in a cloud that engulfed him and anyone else standing too close. He coughed, spat blood, and stumbled away from it blinking rapidly.

Kristin bore an expression of immense satisfaction, while Deidra looked on in wry amusement. Lance turned but could not make out the others through the haze. *They probably all think it's mighty funny.*

"You know," Deidra ventured. "You don't have to blow to create wind."

He stared at her, eyes partially hooded, face blank, his voice monotone as he spoke. "You couldn't have told me that before I did it?" His mouth twisted. "Did you want me to clear this?" He gestured to the dust.

The Scientist shook her head. "Best leave it to settle."

His eyes fixed on Annabelle. She was chuckling under her breath. "Are you appeased, Belle?"

"Quite," she answered, her chuckle growing louder.

He glanced down at himself then, and saw that he was covered in about as much dust as she'd been. Though he'd shielded his face.

He clapped his hands together, and they created their own small cloud of dust. "Right," he addressed Deidra. "Is there anything else I can do you for?"

She shook her head slightly. "You've done just fine, Pilot Viatri. When it all settles, we'll have a look inside. We've an entire city awaiting us."

Whether there was something in the way she said it, or just the suggestion itself, Kristin's face paled. They may just have found that thing that she dreamed of every night.

He tried to pet her arm, a soothing gesture, but she pulled away. After a few moments, he decided to leave her be. That woman was more confusing than any other he'd known.

Lance walked over to Xavier and the others. It seemed strange to him that he should feel such a loss over the friendship he'd had with the Navigator, when in truth it had not been one. A camaraderie as between co-workers. A mutual respect and competitiveness that made them very good at their jobs. But even after four tours together, they hadn't been friends. And he hadn't noticed that loss until Xavier, his long-time equal, was no longer so. Now, he found himself trying to make up for it.

"So, what do you think, Superman?" he asked as he strode up. His girl, Navigator Rich, studiously ignored him, while Xavier gave him a tight smile.

"She doesn't like that name," was all he said.

Lance nodded. "Fine. Xavier — or Rouse? — what do you think?"

"Good job?" It was clear that the man didn't know what to say about it. Like he wasn't aware of the difficulty of what he'd just achieved.

The Pilot slumped in his stance. He was disappointed. He'd tried to include the man. He said he felt like he lost his crew, his team, because of the Giants. But when Lance reached out a hand, the man slapped it away. Not intentionally, he was sure, but the effect was the same.

"I'll see you inside, I guess," Lance told him, and moved over to Weiz and Harvey.

Harvey shot him a pursed lipped half-frown in commiseration. He'd obviously heard the exchange. Lance wondered if he or Kristin had even bothered trying to include the man.

"So, we're in," said Weiz.

"We're in."

"And it looks like Kristin got you good, too." Harvey put in.

Lance touched the tip of his nose tentatively. It was swollen and bruising, but he knew it would set right. And quickly. "That she did. I knew she was mean, but I really wasn't expecting that," he confessed.

"Neither was I, when she got me." Weiz looked back at Harvey, mouth turned down in a frown, eyes glaring. The Captain ignored her.

"She hit *you*?" he was a little shocked. Only a little. He touched his nose again.

The man nodded. "Damned hard too. Though she swears it was

just a tap."

Lance shook his head. "She's got some issues, I'd think."

"I'll not disagree with that."

The cloud of dust had mostly settled, just a few light strands still floated in the air, reflecting sunlight and causing a shimmering effect. *Like the dust motes you see through the light of a window in a dark, unused room,* he thought. *I can be so poetic.*

Deidra was already climbing over the broken bricks and into the side of the mountain. Others had gathered in her wake and merely awaited word before they followed. They had no torches or brands for fire, so he wondered how they were going to see in the darkness. Weiz answered that question before it was asked as she marched to the wall, coloured lights shimmering above her palm.

"She got a pretty good one," Lance told Harvey as they moved to the front.

"A pretty good what?"

"Power."

The Captain snorted. "Fairy lights and illusions."

Lance glanced at the man. "Seemed real enough to me when she was etching with a laser cutter she'd made into Fields' gravestone."

Harvey didn't answer.

The inside of the place where he'd toppled the wall was large, but not big enough to fit all of the airmen at the same time. Tiles were visible beneath the fallen stonework, a faded red. Broken furniture littered the floor, chairs mostly, the wood brittle and split, whatever fabric that had covered them tattered and clothed in detritus. A piece of paper, ancient and yellow, lay on the floor close to the only door. When Deidra attempted to pick it up, it fell to dust in her hand.

Weiz walked next to the scientist, arm extended. The colours in her palm separated from her and coalesced into a large round ball of light that was too bright to look directly at. She put her hand on the door, and it fell from its hinges, making an echoing clatter.

If anything was asleep in here, then it won't be any more. But a part of him knew there was nothing alive in this place. *Could be bats. Bats love caves and mountains and stuff. I hate bats.*

He followed behind Harvey, Kristin to his right. Those two had become a tight pair, he noticed. How was a guy to have a chance against the Captain? He took all the women.

The next chamber turned out to be a street. Lined with cobbles, woven together in a tight and colourful mosaic, and like the walls, there was no mortar.

On the other side of the wide street, he could see houses, lined up in rows, small gardens — or what he thought were meant to be gardens, though they were long dead — reached from the face of the houses to the gutter of the street, and the houses themselves were fenced off. It reminded him of the photos of old places, when there'd been enough land that not everyone had to live in tenements. Now it was only for the extremely wealthy.

Weiz's globe of light expanded and rose above them, illuminating the city from end to end in a kind of false daylight. His senses rebelled somewhat at first, but after a few minutes, they adjusted.

In the distance he noticed buildings much larger, much higher, and much more familiar in structure. Skyscrapers, though he supposed in here, they'd have called them something else.

Deidra started in the direction of those tall buildings, her steps unhurried. She began speaking of the place to all and none, as if she were taking a group of unruly school children on a tour of an historical village.

"They called themselves Enatwa," she told them, her gaze sweeping the street, the houses, and buildings they passed. "They were a singular nation, apart from the others of this world, for they had developed technology."

She paused at an intersection, looked down a large boulevard lined with shop fronts and three and four storey buildings. The other way led to more houses, and directly ahead the street began to narrow and wind. Deidra chose the boulevard, and upon resumption of her walk, the words began once again, too.

"So, the Enatwa found this mountain, that had a great deal of its side missing, the cap a giant overhang. And they built into it. Made the mountain whole. They hid from their would-be destroyers and created for themselves a paradise. They enjoyed the wonders of plumbing, the magic of electricity, and the progress of science. What became their downfall, however, was their need to grow crops outside the city."

Deidra's lecture continued as they walked at an undemanding pace through the streets of the dead city. The buildings were in remarkable shape, built to withstand the weather of time, though all the wood had rotted or dried out. They were old, but not old enough to have yet turned to stone, as Deidra explained.

The Enatwa had suffered a regime collapse that led to rioting, starvation and eventually, civil war. Because all of their resources were so dedicated to eradicating civil unrest, and their food supplies were rotting in the fields outside the mountain, those who survived had been forced to flee to villages and smaller enclaves of the Enatwa who'd not joined them in their city. It was possible that some had escaped to the stars, but Deidra doubted those who had would have survived long.

The science they used in their engineering shows a skill that we have yet to master. And while the structures themselves are incredibly Earth-like in their purpose and design, we cannot say what they were intended for.

Airmen were beginning to mumble behind him, conversations so low that he could not understand a word. He was not sure he cared.

The Scientist halted in front a building that looked more desiccated than the others. Large chunks had come away from the sides and rested on the street. She glanced up, then side to side, and appeared satisfied. She turned to Weiz. "Bring down your light, Creator of Illusions. We enter here."

Lance had not heard her called that before, and resolved to find the woman a better nickname. From the look on the Commanders face, he figured she'd appreciate it too.

Weiz complied, reducing the light in size until it illumined only those who stood before the building. It wasn't much larger than her head.

Satisfied, Deidra turned her attention back to the building and pushed open the door.

~

The air inside was so stale Kristin thought she might choke.

Silently, they'd listened to Deidra's recount of the Enatwa, but Kristin couldn't bring herself to care. Her mind was on the collapse of the wall. On the similarity it had to the visions she'd had. It wasn't the same. Not exactly. And she kept waiting for *that* scene to arrive. She felt inexorably drawn towards some kind of inevitable conclusion, though she didn't understand the journey or its reason.

Throughout, Harvey had walked at her side. Weiz and Deidra were ahead and to their left, and Lance behind. But the Captain instinctively understood that she didn't need to talk. He had not asked her fruitless questions or engaged in useless chatter. But he was there. As he was always there. Almost like an older brother. Or the way an older brother *should* behave, as she saw it, since she did have one, but she hadn't heard from him since she was nine. At fourteen he'd run off, never seen again by any of her family, as far as she was aware.

As they walked through the close tunnel, concrete on all sides, Kristin kept her eyes on Deidra's back. The whole situation made her feel a little claustrophobic, though she'd never felt that way before. *Spend days at a time on a ship in the middle of space, in small, confined quarters with no windows, and where going outside would mean death in seconds, and I baulk at a little concrete.* But on some level, she knew it was deeper than that.

It took her some time to realise that they were descending along a ramp. That at each bend and turn, the degree at which they descended increased, until they hit stairs.

"This is the place," Deidra muttered to herself, though loud enough for those close to hear.

Kristin counted fourteen flights before they hit the bottom. A wide area had been cleared, large enough for a room, and the door that they approached took up the entire wall.

The Scientist stopped in front of it. She turned to face all those gathered. "What we do in this place," she told them. "Will get us home. It will not be quick. It will not be easy. But it *will* get us there. And I need everyone here to help me with that." She glanced over them all, face expressionless.

She thought she heard Lance say something, but at the same time a roar so loud it was like an explosion, filled her ears. Cold crept in behind her eyes, and pressure filled her head. She grabbed it and fell to her knees, the only thought before the vision began, *fucking hell.*

Deidra's hand reached forward; the door opened before her. Sounds, like an automatic rifle fired at close range, pinged against the thick metal door. A bright flare of fire flashed through the small gap in the door to engulf the Scientist. Weiz pushed her out of the way, yelled something at Harvey. A door behind them slammed into the ground sealing them in.

"Stop!" she said, still clutching her head. Harvey was on the ground beside her, watching her face, a hand on her back. "Stop!"

Deidra looked back; a hand half raised.

"What is it?" Harvey asked.

"They've some kind of guard system. We have to disable it before she opens that door." Deidra dropped her arm back to her side.

"I had thought it disabled," was all she said before she moved to the right-hand wall.

Kristin kept her eyes on the woman. *She doesn't see the future,* she reminded herself. *She wouldn't know. But she knew it was possible, and never said a word, didn't even bother to check.* Kristin shook her head. She'd have thought making sure the damned system wasn't working would have been common sense. '*Common sense isn't that common', as Commander Fforde used to say.*

Slowly she got to her feet, while Deidra removed a section of wall that before had seemed of a piece with the rest. She was fiddling with some wires, then she scraped a pair together, creating sparks.

The door made a whirring sound. A machine coming to life. The Scientist picked up a second set of wires and repeated her procedure, causing the doors to move inward into darkness.

Nothing of her vision occurred. *Warning given; disaster averted. This is my purpose now.* While she didn't appreciate the pain or the vulnerability she suffered for the visions, she understood her place among them. If they were Gods, the board was evenly set. They all needed each other. *But we are missing Greenway, and he us. What will he do in our absence?* An idle thought, one she'd rather not spend too much time with.

Weiz was the first through the doors, globe held up before her. They waited until Deidra had joined the Commander to give them direction, then the party followed behind.

If the mountain city could have been thought of as a giant cavernous space, what they entered now was of similar quality, though on a smaller scale.

The roof, she could see, angled all the way up to what must have been the top of the building above. The sides were a mass of offices and labs, as far as she could tell. They had no doors, but she could make out workstations, scattered papers, and some unfathomable equipment. But what caught her attention, was what was in the centre of the giant space. What looked very much like a medium-sized spaceship.

"They lived inside a mountain, but they made a spaceship? Makes sense." She eyed the Scientist with a raised brow.

The woman turned. "Just because the way they pursued their sciences is different to how we did, does not mean they didn't find what was necessary for the same things. In this case, they never finished the project. But it is not a spaceship, just an object designed for flight."

Kristin knew that flight had been a human fascination for centuries before the first plane was made. A simple desire to view the world as a bird might, or to overcome a fear of heights or falling. But there was progression in it. These people, the Enatwa, they had gone from A straight to Z without bothering to check out all the letters in between. Or at least it seemed.

"So, what are we supposed to do with it?" Harvey asked.

"We use it. The shell, some of its inner workings. We strip this city for all the parts and things we'll need to get it working. They've done most of the work for us. I'll just have to start again on the frequency generator and the propulsion device."

"And a coordinate system." Kristin turned to see the owner of this voice she did not recognise, and saw Heinrich, stepping forward from the back of the crowd. She had not expected him to join them down here.

"That," Deidra said, "They already have. You are welcome to check the data yourself once we get some power going. I am sure I can find a way to sync our tablets to these machines. Their language is different, but I'll try and write an algorithm that will decode everything, so everyone can understand."

It was hard to tell what the old man thought, since his eyes never strayed from Deidra, and his face remained impassive. *Doesn't look like a killer. But he damned well is. They're the hardest ones to catch, and we let him walk around unsupervised like he's done nothing.*

"Thank you, Deidra," he said, and moved himself back through the crowd.

Kristin eyed Harvey who in turn eyed her. There was a silent question between them that neither had an answer for. *Did he actually say thank you and mean it? He really sounded like he meant that.*

Deidra spoke a few soft words to Weiz, who nodded, and then took the floor. "Groups of two!" she bellowed. "I don't care who's with who, but you're all in pairs, I don't want you getting lost down here."

There was shuffling in the crowd, Kristin figured she'd just be with Harvey, though Lance sauntered over. Perhaps a group of three? She didn't mind. Weiz spared them a frown, but said nothing. The numbers were otherwise even, and Heinrich also had a supervisor in that weedy young scientist she could not remember the name of. That kid did not speak, she was sure of it.

When it was clear they'd all sorted themselves out, Weiz pointed to the first pair, then out to her right. "Search for lights, or something we can burn. This is what comes first." From then, she just pointed to a pair and indicated a direction. There was only a dozen of them, not including the scientists or Harvey's group, and they were quickly dispersed.

That done, Weiz and Deidra approached them. "I find myself tiring the longer I maintain this light," she said with a sigh. "I could let it go, and it would become a lingering presence that does not diminish or require any form of sustenance, but then it would take on a life of its own, and the consequences..." She shrugged to finish her sentence.

Harvey grabbed a hold of her hand and held it gently. "Don't worry yourself over it. We've lived without powers much longer than with, and I personally wouldn't mind ridding myself of them if I could." *Liar, you just want to make her feel better, and she knows it too from the way she's looking at you right now.*

But she doesn't mind the lie. And here I am, a younger sister jealous of her brother's attention. The thought chaffed and she shook it off.

"We're going home," Lance whispered beside her. "I never really believed that she'd be able to make it work, you know. But now, all this?" He gestured to what lay all around them. "There is no way we're not going to make it. She has it in here." He tapped his head.

She slapped his bare shoulder. "Sinatra, have I told you lately how much I want to kill you?"

"Why, Belle, of course you have." He shot her a look of such solemn sincerity that she had to laugh. He smiled.

"You realise, when we get back, that people like Deidra are going to want to perform all kinds of experiments on us?"

Lance's face dropped and showed a sickly pallid expression. Weiz, Harvey and Deidra all turned their attention to her.

She raised her brows at them. "You've not all considered this before now?"

"Not really, no," Harvey breathed.

Deidra looked thoughtful, biting at her lower lip, eyes staring at something behind Kristin. Like she knew she should have realised it. But, she had to admit, of all of them, Deidra was the only one doing any real work.

"And I have to ask. How did we plan on getting fed down here? I didn't see a single living creature in this place, and if we have to get down that scree slope and back up again it's going to be a pain in the arse."

The way they all stared at her right then, she wondered if she was the only one with a brain.

"We have water, at least," Deidra offered. "That would have been a lot harder to haul in your hands."

Harvey grunted. "I'll take us, Kristin. You just tell me where to go and I'll get us there."

"Take me too," Weiz half asked, half demanded.

"No." From Deidra. "I need you here still. Even with everything that is down here, they won't have everything I need."

The Commander sighed. "Fine."

Harvey looked to Lance. "How about you, Weatherman? Up for a hunt?"

All eyes on him, Lance squirmed. "Can't say I know how, but I'll give it a shot. Just tell me one thing."

"What's that?" Kristin asked.

"We don't have to eat those snake-rats, do we?"

CHAPTER SEVENTEEN

Reeve and the others had gotten away, beaten but alive. They'd survive, if they were mindful of their surroundings. Greenway knew they were going to the Scientist and the Commander, wherever they'd holed up. But whatever those few knew, so too did his new acolytes.

His followers had fared well. They were bruised and bloody, but unmindful of their wounds as they strode through the woods toward the village.

The sun was still low in the morning sky, the forest itself still dark, and though he had no trouble seeing the path before him, his new followers did, and so progress was slow.

They are mine now. He nodded to himself. *Five of them, at least, will join the pantheon. If they prove worthy.* They'd already shown their dedication to him with the spilling of blood.

They had no weapons. They'd used fists, feet, teeth and whatever happened to be lying around. It got the job done, and the camp had been destroyed.

They all had their own reasons, of course, and he was not blind to their ambitions. But so long as they did what they were told, then he would reward them as they wished. Home was no longer an option, and each one here felt it.

The village was already a bustle of activity as they arrived. Cooking, gardening, tool making and mending, children playing in the street. All normal things. But on the far end of the village, near the trail to Djorik, work had begun on a temple. A temple dedicated to him.

He still marvelled at the fact there were humans here. That they were so similar. That so much of the world was almost exactly the same as what he was accustomed to back home. If a few centuries out of date.

Some of the villagers still looked at him in defiance, refused to bow. At first, he'd wanted to show them the error of that, but in a moment of curiosity he'd asked one such why they had not joined their fellows. The answer he had given was simple, and Greenway had let him go. "I worship Hu'ral, God of the Seasons." It was often that he forgot he was not the only god, if only because the others were not behaving as they should. And they would need their worshippers, he could not take them all for himself.

Odden was at the temple, overseeing the few who had already started work on its foundations.

How long had it been, he wondered, since their gods had walked among them? Had they ever? Did that also mean that perhaps there were gods on Earth? That the myths and legends were true? A curiosity, one that may never be answered. It didn't matter, for this was his home now.

He stopped next to Odden and crossed his arms, surveying the work. His trail of acolytes remained a respectful distance behind him. The villagers stared at the newcomers, dragging curious children away from them.

"Today we go to Djorik," he told the man.

"As you wish, M'lord."

"Prepare all those who would wish to come. We need to raise an army."

"An army, M'lord?" The man looked genuinely confused.

"A group of people with weapons, who work in formation to defeat other people." Odden stared blankly. "Fighters, Odden. Fighters who will learn to fight together."

Sudden understanding lit in his eyes. "Of course, M'lord. I'll ready those who'll join us." He walked off.

Greenway turned to address the airmen. "You all require rest, but we are not done. You all require food. But we are not yet done. Today, we walk, we gather. Tonight, you may eat and rest, for tomorrow we will train." They were less than enthusiastic. "Your rewards will come when you prove your usefulness."

A woman stepped to the front, her face a swollen mass of bruises, knuckles mauled and caked with dry blood. He didn't know their names or care to learn them. That could wait for their ascendancy. Only then would they earn the right in his eyes.

"Due respect and all that, Captain, but what exactly do you want us to do?" She glanced at the others around her. "Shit, sir, those people you had us deal with back at camp, they were our friends. I'd not like a repeat of that."

"Do you regret the path you chose?"

The woman shuffled uncomfortably, but plunged on. "Do or die, Captain, as we all see it. We're not blind, you've got power. Some of us were offered a place on the ship with the others, but most never got that much. They just took off without us. Abandoned us. So, what were we to do?"

Blah, blah, blah. But you have to listen to them. Like a Navigator, like a Comms Officer, you might not always care what they say, but it doesn't mean it isn't important. "What would the others have done? Those who did not join you."

"They'd planned on joining the others at the mountain. They promised to wait for at least a month, to give them time to get there."

And the wait was not long before the important words were said. I must remember to listen and not let my temper take over. Listen. "You don't believe they'd wait?"

"Why should they? Besides which, I doubt any of us would make it inside the month. It's a long way off, and we don't know this world. We're limited to daylight movement because we haven't mapped the stars. We could easily get lost, thrown off course. Simply misunderstand the where, and we could wander lost for years." The rest of the airmen did not even look at her. Had she betrayed them, in their eyes? Had they secretly held onto some hope? Did they really come to him out of belief, or simply necessity? How much did it matter?

"You," he said, decision made. "Are now in charge of this lot. You would speak for them, then you can be responsible for them. When I build my army, you will be my first officer. For now, prepare my rear guard."

The villagers who would come held hoes, scythes, sickles and machetes, and walked the broad street toward them. The airmen parted to allow them through, Odden in the lead.

"To Djorik!" he told them. And they began the long march.

~

The town was much as Greenway would have imagined a fifteenth century town to look back on Earth. They reached the end of the trail near dark and found themselves on the side of a large compact dirt road. Across from where they'd exited the forest, were farms, spread out in a patchwork of colours from bright green to dull yellow or cream. Each, he knew, yielded commercial quantities, though he had never been a farmer to know what the fields were planted with.

While the villagers had marched on ahead of him, solemn and single minded, the airmen behind had begun to drag their feet, postures slumping. They seemed as if they might just fall over and die where they stood.

He looked back on them with a measure of pity, for they were not in the fullest possession of their health, and he had pushed them on. *I am not without reason*, he thought to himself. He wasn't sure if he was trying to convince himself, or truly believed it. *I just have to make sure they understand who is in charge.*

The point that the others had not understood, that they would have to be made to understand at all costs, was that they could not leave this world. They *had* to stay. He'd need an army to convince them. Not because he wanted to hurt them, but because he would need all the help he could get to hold them prisoner long enough to ensure they understood their responsibilities. If he couldn't convince them...

The gates of the town were under cover of a barbican, the walls high and made of grey stone. There were watch towers with arrow slits, and the watchful eyes of guards. Those guards were uniformed in simple brown leathers, with blue undershirts and iron helms. They held spears, carried swords and daggers at their belts, and had small round shields strapped to their backs. It was an organised fighting force, though a small one. He had not imagined that these people would be at this degree of civilisation. Not based on what he'd seen of the villagers.

There were torches lit at the gate, a guard to either side, standing at attention. Greenway let Odden take the lead. It was always best to let underlings do these things. He approached the guards.

"We require entry," he told them.

The one on the left gazed at the one on the right, then answered. "From where do you hale?"

"The village of Gar, near the plains of Ouir."

"Don't look like no villagers I ever seen." The guard pointed to Greenway and the airmen.

"They were visitors to our village. We have escorted them here, for they bring word of the gods."

Greenway allowed himself a smile. He appreciated that Odden had given him a kind of anonymity with his statement.

The other guard snorted. "Word of the Gods, is it? Which ones? Ain't seen none around here, of that I am certain."

Because they chose a benevolent path. That answered that question. *I on the other hand...* He raised a fist and the ground erupted around the doubting guard. But he stayed where he was, while the first guard gaped. Odden simply stood there as if he'd been expecting it.

"Dassun." The villager nodded.

The guard, who looked like he might soil himself, quickly opened the gates. "In you go, then. Please, feel free to avail yourself of any of the fine establishments within. Name's Nick, you just tell any of them that name and they'll set you right. Nick, remember that." The man continued on his ramble as they walked through the gate, but Greenway had stopped listening. A guard too easily cowed was beneath his consideration.

The air smelled of rotten hay, horse dung and piss. The streets were uneven, with patches of cobble, long slabs of granite, and wide stretches of dirt. The buildings against the outer wall were squalid things, made from untreated wood, their thatched roofs in need of repair.

The area might have been a bailey, once. But it was no longer, filled now with shacks and poorly made mud huts. They were a few streets in before the scenery drastically changed. The streets were uniform, square slabs of stone, the edges coming up at a slight angle, with runnels in the centre to contain and direct water into drainage holes every four metres or so. Not how he'd ever seen it done before, but it worked.

Odden seemed to know where he was going, as he led them through the city without a backward glance. They eventually ended up in a large square, stalls on all sides, though they were closed for the night. There were a few people who still wandered the streets, sparing them a curious glance but moving on without slowing. A few of these entered establishments where the sounds of music, merriment and drunkenness could be heard. One man was even busy puking in the street.

The man stopped, and everyone halted behind him. He looked around, nodded to himself, then moved back to address Greenway. "We should take up residence for the night, M'lord. What needs to be said would be best delivered in the morning to clear minds and open ears."

The airmen were about to collapse where they stood, and therefore would be of no use to him as they were. The villagers, while they did not share the exhaustion, did not seem much better. Greenway gave a nod. "Lead us on, Cardinal." The man beamed at the title, though he had no idea what it meant.

He took them to a road just opposite the one they'd entered the square from, and turned into the doorway of a three-storey building. Inside two hearth fires burned, one on each side of the large room. Several clean and empty tables were available, each with six seats. Directly in front of the bar sat a few men having a quiet conversation over mugs of ale.

As they filed in, the men turned to watch, but after a few moments, they returned to their low conversation.

The barkeep stood with his arms crossed over his ample waist, his dark, beady eyes on Odden. "Gotcha a big'un dis tum, Odd," he drawled. "Dunno dat I been hasin' room far sa many, d'ya hear?"

"We'll share what you have amongst us," his Cardinal asserted.

The big man shrugged as if it didn't matter. "If ya do say it, Odd.

Ya know da price. Ya pay or ya leave."

Odden pulled something from beneath his shirt and threw it at the man. He caught it with ease, opened the strings, glanced inside and retied it. He gave a slight nod. "Dinner, eight rooms, and breakfast. But no meat."

Greenway frowned at that last edition, but Odden took it in stride. He'd have to ask the man about that statement.

They were led up to the highest level of the establishment, where all eight rooms were. They were given a key for each room and told to choose among themselves who would stay where. They'd need to be out by two hours past dawn, so he could launder the sheets.

Every room had two beds, a small wash basin, a pitcher of water, and a desk. Between thirty-some airmen, himself and just over a dozen villagers, there wasn't nearly enough beds.

"Cardinal, pick eight among your number. They will each have a bed tonight." He glanced back on his airmen. He knew they'd sleep just about anywhere. Had actually been sleeping on dirt, grass or steel for over a month. They all deserved a real bed for a change. "Four rooms for you and your villagers, and four rooms for my men."

Evens even. Let it not be said that I am not fair.

"What about yourself, M'lord?" Odden asked.

"I do not require sleep, Cardinal. I am a God." *And how many more times will I have to say that, I wonder?*

The airmen who had spoken at the village tumbled sideways into a door, knocked it open and sprawled on the floor. He squinted down on her. She'd made her choice then. The others, too tired to care, took the first four rooms. The villagers followed suit, though Odden lingered in the hall a moment longer.

"M'lord."

Greenway raised a brow. "Cardinal?"

"There are no temples here. The Gods are forgotten, or close to.

There are no worshippers to draw upon, at least not in a pious fashion. No hierarchy, no teachings. Only what one family has passed from one to the next. You may need to..." He made gestures with his hands as he searched for the words.

"Demonstrate?"

The man clapped once. "That's the one, M'lord. Demonstrate. You may have to do just that."

The more time he spent in this man's company, the more relaxed Odden became, and the more he found himself liking him. Gods could have friends, couldn't they? Friends, not among their number?

He shook himself, made his face serious. Odden backed up a step. "I am aware of what might need to be done, Cardinal, and I will take care of things. You just make sure that you keep them in line once they fall to our side. I have great things in mind for you."

The man's face twitched in a half smile, uncertainty flickered across his face. "Of course, M'lord, I did not mean to presume." He backed slowly into a room.

When Greenway turned, he heard that door close. *A god cannot have friends. Only enemies and followers. Friends implies equality. There is no longer any such thing.*

He strode out into the night to explore the city. In the morning, he would start creating his army.

One month. That was all the time he had to get to the place where the cowards had crawled to in the wake of his offer. They hadn't opposed him. Hadn't stripped him of his power. They'd just walked away.

Who here is the bad guy? He wondered. For all that they treated him like one, was he not also the only one who had taken a semblance of responsibility for what he'd become? Who considered the damage it might cause to deprive this world of its Gods?

He wandered the streets without seeing, mind racing.

~

It was done. A new monument to his power, rising up through the stone slabs of the town square, while the people looked on in fear and awe. His eyes scanned that crowd, searching for something in the faces, something he could use.

Odden was in the square, on a dais made for criers to address their decrees. He held no parchment, no weapon, and affected no nobility. He spoke simply. "Your God requires an army, and you shall make its core. All able bodies are welcome, even women." It was clear the man was uncomfortable with that last statement, but Greenway was more amused than angered.

The gathered crowd looked to each other. To perfect strangers, to friends and family. They all asked the questions in their minds, he was sure, though none dared to voice it out loud. *Why should I fight for this god?*

And he would give answer. Though now was not the time. *You will fight to save your world. You will fight to make sure your gods stay where they are meant to be. And if they refuse, then some among your number will become as I have become.* But he could not tell them that. He doubted they'd truly understand if he did.

Odden's voice droned on below him, but he was no longer listening. What had to be done, had been done. Those who chose to fight with him would be treated kindly. Those who did not, would be left to their lives. He cared not what they did. If they were unwilling to give their lives for their world, then he didn't want them. He could show them mercy.

He moved to the barbican where they'd first entered. The Guards there hardly took note of him, except for perhaps his odd clothing. He walked out into the centre of the road, and there, he made the dirt rise. Just a few inches, enough for a small platform.

Some of the airmen had followed him out. They'd lined up in front of him. They understood what he required without his asking for it.

These are my Captains. My Generals. They will train my army, and they will lead it. We have little time.

The woman who had become their spokesperson stood directly next to him. "We are at your command, sir," she told him.

He nodded. "When they come out, line them up. Raid the supplies of this town, and outfit our new warriors. It will not be a large army, but let us hope it will be enough."

"Enough for what, sir?"

"It's going to be a long walk to that mountain."

People began filing out of the gate. One, then two, a few more, then a flood. Whether it was fear, a sense of duty or obligation, honour or dreams of grandeur, Greenway did not care. He counted them as they came out, and only stopped when it was obvious there would be no more.

"Just under a hundred warriors," he grunted. "Not too bad for a middling town. More than I expected," he told the woman.

"And not too many to train. What should we do with those who refuse to follow orders?"

"That depends." But he didn't elaborate, and she asked nothing further. Their attention was on the silent and filthy mass.

One of the villagers was organising them into groups and sending them to stand in front of one airman or another. Odden strode straight toward the small platform and took a knee. "I have done what I can for you, M'lord."

"You have done well, Cardinal."

"What would you have of me, M'lord?"

Greenway reached down and touched the man's shoulder. A rare gesture, and he could tell that the man was elated to have received it. *Always the little things,* he reminded himself. "I would that you spread the word. The Gods have returned."

Odden bowed his head. "It will be done."

The Captain gave him leave, and the villager rose to his feet, gave a small bow and moved to the back of the crowd. He had no doubt that Odden would perform well in his duties. That man was a fanatic. He'd need more of his kind before the end of this.

He turned his attention back to the gathered crowd. The language barrier between his airmen and these people was going to cause some problems. A general could not command an army who did not understand them, and everything they said sounded like English to him, so he couldn't teach them. A problem to think on.

"These airmen, who you have lined up before," he started, gesturing to them. "Will be your teachers in the way of martial prowess. Watch their movements, follow their lead, and in one week, we will march."

As he looked over them, he realised that though they may have heard his words, they did not truly understand.

He pointed to a scrawny, older woman in the crowd. "Have you a talent with language?"

She looked around, battered green cloak swaying, then put a hand to her chest, the question in her eyes. He nodded. "No M'lord. But I can try."

He gave her a slight smile. "Then I would you join my airmen." He waved her up front.

The woman took a hesitant step away from her people, a backward glance, a furtive shuffle of feet. But the more steps she took, the more confident she became, until her back was straight, her stride prideful. *And why not? She was chosen by her god.* Now he just had to hope they could work out between them how they were going to speak the same language.

Chapter Eighteen

Between Lance and Weiz, the view screen was lifted and placed. Butchered from their MM ship, Lance was not happy about it, but Deidra could think of no other way to expedite things. After all, making glass was not a quick process, and she doubted that anyone on the ATF crew would have the skills to make screens. If she did it all herself, they'd be there for months.

Weiz and Lance lifted, their expressions tight, while two other airmen locked and welded the panel into position.

It was the second week they'd been in this place, and things seemed to be going well. Harvey and Kristin had volunteered to do all the hunting, and they'd not gone without. They'd even bought in a goat, which between everyone had lasted a few days. The airmen they'd bought with them were helpful, even Heinrich was showing some initiative. Though, if she was being honest with herself, she wasn't sure that was a good thing.

As the days passed, she lost more and more of herself, and found that she cared less. The logical part of her mind asserted that her own will had to be stripped for the process to go smoothly. She knew her name, where she'd come from, but her parents were vague in her mind, as were other details of her past. Some of it was completely gone, in the gaps where memory should have been, instead were tomes worth of knowledge.

Lance came up beside her. "Just the consoles, now," he told her.

She nodded. "I have been working on the frequency generator. So far, we're on schedule to get it all done by the end of a month."

"That'll be enough time for the others to get here?" Weiz asked.

Deidra shrugged. "More or less. It's not as far out of the way as it might at first appear. Though, granted, it would take Harvey a while to get them up here from the foot of the mountain."

"If Harvey could get them from the foot of this mountain, why not just shift them from the camp?" Lance mumbled. "Are you sure they'll come?"

"Of course not. Greenway probably did something, and those we left behind would have had to make their own choices. Those that came with us were chosen because of necessity. If we could have taken more, we would have. But it is what it is. And for Harvey, perhaps he could have if he'd thought of it. But we didn't." She waved it off. The subtle complexities of emotion, while she understood it on a purely clinical level, she no longer felt them. It was not a fact that she would flaunt, could she help it. She knew it would make the others uncomfortable and therefore less productive.

He clearly was not pleased with her answer, but said no more on it. "We'll get the other parts." He turned and left, Weiz beside him.

Deidra kept her eyes on the ship. Her mind flickered through possibilities and equations until it settled on one that would suit her, and she set to work.

By the end of the month, it would be done.

~

"Has she lost it or what?" Lance asked.

Weiz knew he wanted a comforting answer, but all she had to

give was the truth. "She's doing what needs to be done, and for that alone we should be thankful. The way things had been progressing in the camp, we'd have been lucky to have been done inside two years, much less two months."

The Pilot grunted. "She doesn't sound like someone who would care."

"Maybe not so much now," Weiz sighed. "But she did, before the change."

They walked on in silence for a while, a light that she'd conjured leading the way ahead of them through the mountain maze.

There wasn't much that anyone could do to help the Scientist. She had Ulrich and Heinrich working on small pieces, but the woman had taken charge of most of the project. Of the airmen too, though Weiz didn't mind.

She kicked at a loose pebble, listened as it bumped and rolled its way to a halt on the side of a building, the sounds echoing off the surrounding structures.

"I get that she needs the parts off our ship," Lance said after a while. "But why doesn't she just use two ships? Wouldn't that make carrying everyone easier?"

"No." She kicked another pebble. "That one down there was designed to have passengers. More of a shuttle, if you really think about it, despite its strange design. The MM ships are designed for battle. Though you got some space during the flight here because you're the pilot, the rest of us were quite a lot closer to each other than would be considered proper in most circumstances, and we'll have more company soon enough."

"You hope." The Pilot was sceptical.

"Is there anything wrong with hope?" she queried. "Has it become a taboo while I wasn't paying attention?"

Lance ran a hand over his bald pate. "Not that. Just this..." He spread his arms wide, as if he searched for something in the vista that would give him the words. He let his arms fall back to his sides. "How do you all manage to stay so *positive*?" It was a plea, she now realised.

She shrugged. "A truth then, for a truth. The only person who is certain of anything is Deidra. But she bases things on mathematical certainties, without variation. Give her that variant and she may give you another outcome, one that we won't like so much. The rest of us aren't positive, Viatri. We're *hopeful*. Understand the difference in that. We speak of things as we wish them to be, not as how we believe they'll turn out."

They entered the section of the buried city near the opening Lance had created. There was some natural light coming through. Outside, it should be somewhere close to evening.

"So, what truth did you want to know?" Lance asked as they climbed over the debris and out into fading sunlight.

"What happened that made you hide in your ship for so long without talking to any of us?"

He stared at her a moment, and she wasn't sure that he was going to answer. There was a spasm in his cheek, and his brown eyes watered a little. But, when his words came out, they were clear. And he avoided looking at her.

"I thought I'd died. On the Day of the Giants, when we were all fighting for our lives. The thing gutted me, Commander. Ripped out my guts. But I got it before my life drained away. It was dead maybe seconds before me, and I thought to myself, 'this is it, this is the end'. You know?" He reached into the ship and climbed through the hatch. "And then that mist. I thought maybe we'd all died. Greenway had been saying the whole time we were out there that we were in some kind of purgatory. That there was no way we weren't dead. That those Giants were demons. And in that moment, Commander, I believed him."

There was a long pause while Lance adjusted himself under the navigation console, a set of small tools beside him. He started working on taking it apart before he continued.

"So, I was confused, you see. I'm only a semi-religious man, but I was raised as a Catholic. And, here we were, on this planet god knows where, fighting 'demons'. Then I was dead, but I wasn't dead, and for a while afterwards there was a kind of haze in my head. Kristin said I was just being sulky and moody. But, what can you do?"

Weiz crouched down next to the man, for the first time really understanding why he had such an abrasive sense of humour. *Everything is dark inside, so you have to bring the light in somehow. Have to find something to laugh at.*

"You want some help with that?" She knew she couldn't comment on what he'd been talking about. He might have been ready to express it, but his questions were rhetorical.

"Not really room under here for two." She could hear the smile in his voice. "But if you want to jump on top…"

A laugh escaped her. "You are a horrible flirt, you know that, don't you?"

"Only 'cause I don't need to be persuasive. All you women love me, I can see it in your eyes."

"And they all come falling at your feet?"

"That's the way I see it."

"But I already have my man."

There was a snapping sound and the Pilot grunted and swore. A sucking sound, and then, "What is up with that, anyway? You and Harvey I mean? You know none of us thought it would last this long."

"Us being…?" She let a note of anger slip into her voice. Whose business was it anyway?

"Why, me of course. And the many voices in my head."

She had a sudden urge to slap the man. Hard. And found that

she was relating to Kristin, whom she held no great love for. That woman had taken Harvey further away from her than his wife had ever managed to. *Is this how his wife felt? All those times not knowing where he had gone, or who he was with? Did she even suspect that he had feelings for another woman? Even though nothing had ever happened. He's not cheating on me, he's not that man. Then, why do I feel like he is?* She knew that a part of it was because she finally had him after twenty years, only the having was not as she'd imagined. She was...*disappointed.* But that was not Harvey's fault.

"It is a very long story, and none of your damned business either."

Lance slid out from beneath the console and stood up. He took up the small tool tray and laid it next to the screen. "Hold onto that end, will you?"

Weiz braced the side of the console closest to the pilot's chair. Lance pried back a section of console, then undid the bolts connecting it to the hull. He motioned, and she pulled it slightly away from the wall so he could properly disconnect the cords.

Harvey, come back to me. To think, just over a month ago, she had thought those same words in such different context.

~

Kristin and Harvey were delivering their catch. Weiz found herself watching with eyes squinted, not caring if Harvey noticed. Kristin laughed at something he said, gave a playful punch to his arm, and walked off. Harvey stared after her.

Lance was in the ship, helping Deidra wire things up. She should have been there too, but her mind just wasn't in it. She was finding herself much too distracted these days, and no matter how hard she tried to shrug it off, or convince her brain that her thoughts were irrational and filled with the natural fear of losing someone, she just couldn't.

Harvey noticed her now, where she sat at the corner of one of the office blocks. He didn't wave or smile, he just strode over. It was no different than how he would treat anyone else. "You're spending a lot of time with her." *Shouldn't have said that.*

He stopped in his tracks. "This again? Are you serious? You need me to list all the reasons for it *again*?" The tone of his voice was more than annoyed, and his expression was cloudy.

"I'm sorry. Come here." She held out her arms and he stepped forward into her embrace. He was tense and angry, but he still held her gently.

"It's been over twenty years," he whispered into her hair. "And still my passion for you flares. Still my heart goes to you, who knows me so well. Do you think I don't want to spend time with you? We'll have all the time we need when we get back to Earth, but until then, necessity drives us."

The same argument as they'd had almost every second day. There was a part of her that wanted to let it go, but her mouth just kept going. "But it's the way you look at her when she leaves your side. Like you want her to come back. Like... you love her." She'd never admitted that before.

He pulled away from her to search her eyes, but he didn't let go. "I do love her. But not the same way I love you."

"You love her?" Weiz spluttered and disengaged from the embrace.

"Like a sibling. Yes." He held his ground, did not move, didn't take his eyes from her face.

"I see."

"Clearly you do not." He shook his head and half turned to walk away. "I am tired of this insecurity, Catherine. I love you, but I am not your lapdog. You are not the only woman in my heart, and I should not be the only man in yours. Figure it out." And then he was striding away.

~

Deidra held the chip before a critical eye. *Better*, she thought, then placed it on the board. She looked around for Weiz, the woman was supposed to be there, but too often of late she was not. Instead, she'd been relying on inferior tools. For this, though, finesse was required, and for that she needed the Commander.

She addressed Lance, who was installing the navigation console. "Could you get Weiz for me, please?"

"I could try," the man muttered.

"Please do." She heard him mumble a few choice words, but he left, boot steps fading as he left the ship.

"He doesn't seem to think much of his Commander, these days." Heinrich was working on adjusting the view port controls so they'd blend seamlessly into the ships design.

Deidra turned her focus to him. "Oh?"

"None of them do." He fitted some wires together beneath a panel on the floor. "Not even back at the camp, and things are just getting more strained. Since the first night they landed, she's changed. I've heard it mumbled from more than one set of lips."

"So long as she does what we need her to do, does it matter?"

"I suppose not."

Deidra returned her attention to the board. It was almost complete. She only needed to create two more and the shell, then the frequency generator would be complete. It was time to start thinking of the power source. This place held many treasures, but getting to them would be difficult.

Equations flashed through her mind at speeds beyond comprehension to anyone else.

Several sources of energy were dismissed immediately as being either too bulky, or insufficient. To use geothermal energy, they'd need to create a station, as they had used on Io, and that was not ideal. Thermonuclear was beyond dangerous for their purposes, thorium or standard nuclear would present the same problems as geothermal. Fission, fusion, perpetual motion, theoretical versus tested science versus what she now understood to be true. Which was not everything. What she had access to in her mind was only what the people of this world had learned, though strangely only of the math and science variety, no historical data. No names or places beyond those the original Giant had known.

She wasn't an all-knowing being. Not yet. Not until she been completely stripped of who she'd been, and even then, she doubted she'd know *everything*. But it was the arrogance of powerful beings to believe that they did. Though she was limited by her brain capacity, and that was the reason memories were being pushed out. Something Fields had known but failed to understand.

Knowing is not the same as understanding. She had not understood many things she'd known. As even I do not. I am no longer human, and yet I feel that I am doing something humane, possibly for the first time in my career. Certainly, the only time I remember it. And this will be the issue until the issue is no more. Until the only thing left from my past is my name, perhaps not even that. And the curiosity about what came before will lack in every moment. Each movement or sound swept away and replaced by knowledge, yet not knowing the question that proceeded. I shall be as content as a goldfish, guided no longer by friends but by those who would use me. Not a god, not human, just a tool.

She found no solace in these thoughts. Yet nor did they frighten her as they would have only a week before. How Fields had held onto herself for so long, Deidra could not fathom.

Boots alerted her to new arrivals, and she spun, expecting to see Weiz.

"Just got in," Harvey sighed. "Don't suppose you want to give me something to do? I've a need to keep busy today."

Deidra cocked a brow at him. Harvey rarely helped with the ship. He was hardly ever around. And he wasn't the person she needed.

"No."

He stood for a moment, tongue in cheek, then walked out without a word. Deidra stayed facing the hatch, waiting.

~

She walked into the office behind her. She was sure that Kristin knew she followed, but the woman did not turn around. It was dim, but clear of clutter and it held only one desk with a basin and tap.

Kristin washed her hands before she turned to face Weiz. She shook them to dry. Brown eyes looked directly into her.

Awkward silence. But what am I supposed to say? Stay away from my man? Ask nicely if she has any designs on him? How very... pedestrian. But here she stands waiting. She cannot say the first words for she may stand accused.

"Am I being unreasonable?" She startled herself with that question.

"Depends on who you're asking." It seemed there was no need to specify what they were talking about, thankfully.

"I'm asking *you*."

Kristin pushed herself up into a seated position on the desk. "Yes, I think you are. But, in saying that, I understand why you're doing it too."

"So, he's told you?" *What else does he tell while they're out in the woods? Alone. Together.*

The woman shook her head. "He doesn't need to. You make it quite clear. Since that first week, you've not seen me as an airman, the way you should. You've just come to know me as *competition*. It's not true, but that's how you see it, whether you realise it or not." All this said in such a calm measured voice. Weiz seethed beneath the surface as she continued, hands twitching at her sides.

"You stopped leading the rest of them, and so between Harvey and I, we managed what we could. Neither of us are interested in a Commandership, and we did not seek to undermine you, but you

— were — not — there. For whatever reason, you disappeared into your own head, or sometimes just disappeared in general, and we had to bounce our decisions off each other."

"Well, I am doing what needs to be done, now. So, there is no need for you to —"

"No, you're not, and yes there is."

"Excuse me?" She'd never felt so filled with fury.

"You heard me." Kristin jumped down off the desk and walked slowly to Weiz until she towered over her. Strange that she had never noticed quite how tall Kristin was before.

"The only things you are doing is what Deidra tells you to do. You've got no idea about anything that is going on with the other airmen, the ones who did not kill a Giant. It's like they no longer exist to you. You've got it in your head that you are giving people orders, but you're not. And you've pushed Harvey just about as far as any man should be pushed before he breaks. Or was that your plan? To break him?"

"That is none of your business," she replied in a warning tone.

"Get your shit together, Weiz. Cause right now you are looking less and less like a Commander and more and more like a lovesick schoolgirl."

Weiz swung at Kristin's face, but the woman blocked it easily. She tried another swing, and again, Kristin blocked it, but this time retaliated with an elbow to Weiz's face.

The Commander staggered back a step.

She was about to launch herself at the woman, unaware of just how insanely childish she was being, when Lance walked in.

"Oooo! Cat fight," he jibed. "Don't mind me, please continue." He rested against the door, arms folded, and watched with avid interest.

Kristin shot him a look that promised a skinning later. Weiz took a deep breath and thought about what she had been about to do. It had been long since she'd let her temper get the better of her like that.

"What do you want, Viatri?" Weiz queried.

"No show?" Something flew past Weiz and Lance ducked out of the way. Weiz glanced back at Kristin, but she didn't appear to have shifted position. *Whatever that was I'm sure glad she hadn't aimed it at me.* It had gone so fast she was surprised Lance had avoided it; despite the fact he'd seen it coming.

"Viatri," Weiz said in a warning tone.

"You guys are no fun. Deidra wants you. Now, preferably. But I can wait- OW!"

This time it was Kristin who shot past Weiz and smacked Lance in the arm. She kept going without a backward glance, while the Commander followed her with her eyes.

"God damn that woman," Viatri complained. Though once again in the company of this man, Weiz found herself empathising despite her animosity toward her.

"Lead on Weatherman." She was irritated. Nothing had been resolved. And worse, that woman had stood her ground as if she had every right to be there. The truth was, Weiz was not sure she didn't.

The man shook his head and mumbled something under his breath, rubbing vigorously at his arm, but led the way back to the ship.

Inside, Deidra was seated near where Heinrich was doing his work, a circuit board in her lap. She turned to watch Weiz. Disapproval stained her features.

"I need a nano-bonding laser," she said simply, and held out her hand.

I have become a tool. She made the colours dance.

CHAPTER NINETEEN

They weren't much to look at, but they held the line. Every one of his hundred townsmen was perfectly ordered in marching rows behind their airmen.

Greenway strode to the left of these columns, eyes darting from one to the next. He wanted to keep them on their toes, as would any good general. Each one he walked past puffed their chest up, gripped tighter on their weapon of choice.

When he reached the head of the column, he moved until he was centred and then addressed them all. "We are not ready," he said quietly. "But we will be."

They didn't move. There wasn't a single shuffle. Not a cough or a sneeze, nor a nervous tick. And he watched for all such gestures. For any sign that they were not prepared to do what was asked of them.

He looked to the airmen who had stood up to him that day on the road. She held her eyes firmly on the horizon before them. She knew that this was going to be a long march. She understood what it meant to be a part of a military organisation. She asked no questions. It was time he learnt her name.

"Today we march," he continued. "It may take us the better part of two weeks to get to our destination, and when we get there, you will be tired. You will feel like there is nothing left in you. But I promise you, that will not be the case. I ask each of you to look deep inside of yourselves and find what reserves you can. I encourage each of you to look to the man or the woman beside you, in those times of need, and know that they will be there. Know that your neighbour will have your back when in the thick of it."

Still, no reply. This was a good start. He had never been one for grand speeches. Not the kind that made people stand up and cheer. Not even the kind that made people take notice. But when he spoke, it was always with meaning.

He turned and led them forward.

They were his now.

~

Liza Gordon, South American by birth, was a pilot. A pretty good one as far as she was concerned. She'd been on several missions with the ATF all under Captain Lebedev.

She'd chosen to stay with Greenway, not because of any belief in what he was doing, but because she thought she might get a chance to stop him. No luck so far.

Captain Greenway did not sleep. Did not even hold up a pretence of doing so. He was no longer human, he insisted. At least, not in the way they were.

She'd understood instinctively that he was not the kind of man who would enjoy suck-ups. He did not believe that they were equals, but nor did he expect unquestioning subservience. There was a thin line for him, when it came to what could and could not be said. And she intended to walk it as closely as she could, until she found her moment. It was a precarious perch, but she held her balance. For now.

Gordon did not want his power. Had no desire for it. All she wanted to do was get home, and allow the others a good chance of getting there. If they worked this tech out, then there was a good chance they would find a way back here to pick the rest of them up. If not, then at least she'd know she'd done a good thing before she died.

They marched down an uneven road. Herself and all the other airmen taking positions at the front of the columns. They were the examples, she knew, of what Greenway wanted his little army to aspire to.

To either side of them, thick woods, barely a gap between trees. The road itself filled with potholes, layered with dirt and gravel.

Greenway was in the lead, alone. He walked on, eyes toward the sky, as if he didn't care what those behind did, so long as they kept pace. And it was a gruelling pace. A kilometre at a jog, then one at a run, then one at a walk. Alternating. It was gruelling for the airmen, and she heard more than one of the townsmen drop off to the side of the road. Greenway had told them that if that happened to just leave them. They could either catch up later or make their way back to Djorik. Though if it happened too often, they were to make some examples. It would be no use if they all thought they could just go home.

Hours passed. No one spoke. They did not rest. Her heart raced, her legs hurt, and her lungs burned. She chanced a glance behind her. Some of the townspeople looked dead on their feet. They should have stopped more than an hour ago for a rest.

Gordon made a decision.

She caught up to Greenway with what felt like the last reserves she had in her legs. "Sir!"

He didn't slow his pace, just turned his eyes to her. "What is it?"

"We're losing too many, Sir." She indicated behind them. "You may not require rest and food, Sir, but the rest of us do, or by the end of the day you are not going to have an army." She stopped dead in her tracks, determined to make a point. Greenway only ran a single pace, before he came back to stand beside her.

"Rest!" he yelled to those behind, then gave Gordon his full attention. "It's time I knew your name, Airmen."

There was the sound of rustles, bumps, thumps and groans as those who had remained with them settled onto the road without ceremony. What food there was, carried in packs they'd been given in the town, was not even touched. They were too tired, and it was only a couple of hours past midday. They did, however, drink deeply from the canteens at their hips.

"Pilot Liza Gordon, Sir."

"Gordon. I have things in mind for you." He smiled, and she suppressed a shudder.

"Yes, sir." *Though I'd really rather you didn't.*

"Keep an eye on them. I'll scout out the way ahead." He spared the townspeople another glance, then began running down the road at a pace none of them would have had a chance to keep up with.

At the front of the columns, the airmen had their eyes on her. They thought she was a suck-up. They thought that she was doing this for her own personal gain. All except for one. And it would have been better if he did too.

"We've got an hour," she told them as she came to a stop beside them. She surveyed the townspeople and nodded to herself. They'd held up much better than she would have expected.

"An hour?" Gaulin queried. He was a navigator that she'd never worked with, and had never spoken to until the Day of the Giants. "After that, that's all we get, one hour?"

Winch pushed him into the front row of townspeople, who scrambled out of the way before he could trample them. The airmen had a good laugh.

"We get what we're given and be thankful for that much."

Ainsley, the only Captain of the group said. "And you'll thank Gordon personally, 'cause it's clear to me if she'd said nothing we'd still be moving, so sit your scrawny arse down and rest." His dark hazel eyes challenged the others. None said a word.

She'd wondered a few times over the past week if she'd made the right decision. If she hadn't have been better off making her own way to the mountain.

Ainsley pulled her to the side somewhat, but addressed those behind them. "Gordon and I are going to range out some, see what's what. Winch, you take care of the rest."

And they began walking into the trees, twigs crunching, branches scraping. What light there was in the sky quickly lost beneath the thick canopy. What the Captain expected to see out here was anyone's guess, but Gordon followed until he stopped in a small clearing, large enough for them to face each other.

"What is it, Captain?"

He looked around, eyes constantly roving over the brush. "I'm going to kill him tonight."

Gordon felt herself go cold. Why would he tell her this? Yes, he was the one who knew what she was doing, but she would have thought he'd leave it to her. And not say anything out loud! "Captain, I'd advise against it."

The man snorted. "He's not all knowing. He might not sleep, but his mind isn't always here, either."

Gordon held up her hand to cut him off. "I don't want to know what you plan. Shove it back in your pocket, right now! You're not going to get to him. Not while we're on the march. And probably not after, either. You want to have a go at him, fine. But I'll not be implicated in any way. You feel me?"

"Then tell me what *you* plan," he growled in frustration.

"Why should I do that? The less anyone knows, the better for everyone. I wish you'd not worked it out."

He sneered. "So you can have his power to yourself."

She thought about denying it. It wasn't true, after all. But it would be better if he continued to believe it was a power play. The truth of it, something she carried only for herself.

"Do as you wish, think what you like," she told him with a dismissive wave as she turned back to the march. "I am going back to the road to take my rest. I suggest you do the same."

~

It was the end of the fifth day on the march, and they'd lost the road. It opened into a gorge, which they could not pass, and Greenway wondered why they'd have built a road here, when they'd not bothered to build a bridge.

He stood on the precipice, at least a hundred feet above, watching the swift currents of the white-water river below. Large red rocks and pebbles littered the bottom, and the shores were no more than a few metres wide. The water pushed up against those rocks and sprayed plumes a metre or so into the air. It would be the death of anyone who attempted to jump. Perhaps even himself.

He glanced back at the townspeople. They were arrayed on the road in their columns. No conversation between them in the dimming light. They'd not had a cooked meal since they started, and their packs were getting light. He'd need to start sending out hunting parties.

Gordon and the other airmen were off to one side, eyes darting between the townspeople and the gorge. They would be thinking the same thing as he was. *Why build a fucking road to nowhere? Or did it once lead somewhere? Was it an old road they'd not let grow over?* His frustration was not evident in his face.

He beckoned Gordon with a finger. She gave her fellows are single furtive glance and then came over.

"There is no bridge," he said softly, as if she were blind and couldn't see for herself. "And no evidence of there ever having been one. Am I correct in this?" He was not an engineer, or as full of himself as people might have thought. He did not know exactly what to look for. Perhaps Gordon didn't either. But a second opinion was always the right way to go.

The Pilot looked across the gorge, then lay down on her belly and poked her head over the side, glanced either way. When she got back up, she shook her head. "No sign of one that I can see, Sir."

He nodded. "And that Mountain that the Scientist described to you. You're sure about the direction?"

"As sure as we can be, given that we don't have any maps," she assured. "She said North, Northwest. And we'd know it when we saw it."

How would they know it when they saw it? Scientist, you make no sense. I can already see mountains in the distance. Which one? He gestured for Gordon to re-join the others, and she moved off without a word.

With a breath of concentration, he gathered the earth beneath him. He kept his eyes on the other side of the gorge. He could make that in a single jump. The first time he'd tried this, some trees had suffered. He knew that it would seem as if he flew, but it was just the pressure the earth exerted. Shot like a bullet out of a cannon.

He made the earth push. He angled himself so that the pressure pushed him forward, rather than up. He did not want to be falling that far again. Especially not in front of his troops.

The wind roared past his ears. His vision blurred as it dried out his eyes. Within seconds he was skidding across the dirt and scree on the other side of the gorge.

He looked back.

It was a hundred metres or more to the other side, a distance he had not thought of before attempting the jump, or he may not have done it. As it was, he'd only just made it. *Need to angle it up a bit on the return trip.*

Greenway moved into the sparse forest. There was enough room between each of the trees for two or three people to march astride. If he could get them over the gorge, then they could continue on this bearing.

It was mostly pine. It was the wrong kind of forest for him to find vines to be used as ropes, and he swore loudly at this.

He couldn't get them all over the gorge the way he had. All that pressure would cause a massive earthquake, and the consequences would be beyond his control. If he tried to raise a mountain, it would damn up the river, and again, the consequences would be beyond his control. If he built a bridge of rocks and debris, it was unlikely that it would hold well enough to get them all across, without clay for mortar, and then he could not heat it up to set the seams.

He hit the side of a tree with an open palm, and the pine toppled over. He stared at it for a moment. It was not what he'd intended, but he could possibly use the result. *But even here I'd need tools I do not possess. And rope or something like it. They cannot span the divide on their own.* They were nowhere near long enough, end to end.

Greenway closed his eyes and breathed deep. His people were on the other side, and they needed a solution. They counted on him to lead.

Then it came. Like a bell ring at midnight from a carillon. *I can make a mountain. But it doesn't mean it has to stay there. I can squash the mountain once we're done.*

He grunted and shook his head at himself as he made his way back to the gorge to face his small army. He would not tell them what he was about to do, he'd just do it.

A look down to the bottom showed the river. He turned his head from side to side to scan twenty or so metres to either side of his position. He'd want to raise it like a platform. Not a mountain, but a plateau.

Greenway squinted at the bottom and clenched his fists. Slowly, he began to raise them toward the sky.

A great rumbling sounded from deep beneath the earth. The townspeople backed up. He could see looks of surprise and horror etched on their faces in his peripheral vision. But he was much too busy to care what they thought.

The earth split below, and water rushed to fill the cracks. The section rose, just a few inches to start, but as it loosened away from the edges, — roots snapping, rocks dislodging, dirt cascading away — its ascent quickened, until it reached level with Greenway. Wet pebbles and mud covered the surface, and it would make the footing treacherous, but so long as they all stuck to the centre of this wide aisle, then they would be fine.

Greenway surveyed his work with a nod. He'd not changed a detail about it, only made it rise to meet him.

He looked over to the airmen, and he saw Gordon begin to wave the people past. *Good lass.* With hesitant steps they approached the wide bridge. Tips of toes tested the tenacity, while breath was held deep in the chest. It was clear they didn't think they'd make it across. Greenway chuckled to himself. *They're afraid I'll take it away as soon as they step foot on it.* Though why they'd think that when he'd gone to such lengths to get them here, was beyond him.

It took the better part of an hour before they were all across, the airmen last in line.

Gordon stuck by his side as they walked by. "We should strike camp for the night, sir."

He looked down on her, lips pursed together. "We just had a long rest," he replied. "Can they not stand a few more hours of walking? We've lost almost half the day at this gorge. If Deidra gave you a month, then I would hazard a guess that she means to be gone at the end of that month."

The Pilot shrugged. "You're probably right, sir. No argument on that count. But, the townspeople..."

"What?"

"Their nerves are frayed."

Greenway snorted. Then after a moment said, "I suppose I should not laugh at that."

"Probably not the best idea for morale, sir."

"Very well. Do what you need to do to get them settled. But we'll be moving at the same pace tomorrow. We don't have time to sit and twiddle our thumbs."

She gave him a nod and moved off. He noted that most of the time they'd been speaking, one of the other airmen had been watching, though evincing the air of someone busy with other things. He'd have to keep an eye on that one.

~

Finished with the re-wiring of the ship, Heinrich sat up straight and took a deep breath. It had been a long time since he'd performed any kind of physical labour. But he felt better for it.

From the corner of his eye, he could see Deidra and Weiz working on a piece of the propulsion device. His project, once again being made into a reality, though this time it was taking them less than a month, rather than the better part of three years.

The crews had let him wander as he might over the last couple of weeks. A freedom that he had not expected, all things considered. Not that he would have tried to kill Deidra. No, that was a sacrifice that he just wasn't willing to make. Lose himself, the essence of who he was, for the sake of knowledge? She had opened his eyes to that. And he would respect her choice.

But Weiz... He had seen that woman by Deidra's side, day after day, creating for her the tools that she required to make the smallest components of the devices. She showed no outward sign that she might suffer the same side effects. Indeed, none of the others that he had witnessed did. And while it was not knowledge, the creation of things at his whim was an ability he would not mind having.

He had to be careful, of course. In Deidra's eyes he had reformed. *Or she has simply forgotten what we have done.* He thought about that and shrugged it off as he dumped the wire cutters he'd been using into a toolbox.

Heinrich shifted the floor plate so that it sat flush with the others, then got to his feet. Only that pilot, Lance, ever paid him any heed, and he wasn't here. He could jam a screwdriver in the back of Weiz's skull, and the only one who'd try to stop him would be Deidra.

He walked past and out the hatch.

It was hard to stop thinking of killing people. Hard to continue fooling himself into believing he didn't *want* to, that it just needed to be done. He understood that he just coveted their power, now. That he wanted what they had. True, he'd rather experiment on them, find out what made them different, and create an army full. But he wasn't a biological scientist. He'd not have known what he was looking at, or for. He was a physicist, theoretical and practical.

Outside the ship, Heinrich moved over to his designated office. The airmen had cleaned them out and stripped them bare of any wooden furnishings for the fire on the first day. As far as he could tell, all the offices were the same. One or two work desks with a gas valve and sink. A science lab, configured much the same way as they would appear in schools on Earth.

Heinrich settled himself down on the bolt of cloth he'd found in a storeroom in one of the other buildings. It had held up surprisingly well, considering how long it had been there. Though, given its location, and the fact that they'd not found any other cloth that even remotely resembled the tan weave, it was possible it had been experimental. If the experiment had been in longevity, then those dead scientists had succeeded.

Weiz. The Commander. The woman that none of the airmen

any longer respected. Or if they did respect her still, it was for past deeds only. Would they miss her? Certainly, that Harvey man would. Then again, perhaps not. Things in that arena were not going well.

Heinrich dug under his cloth and found the knife that he'd secreted away. He held it up in front of him. He wasn't supposed to have any kind of weapon, but they'd let him near screw drivers. They'd not been thinking too hard about that.

"Time comes," he whispered to himself. "You have to make a choice. Weiz seems logical, but only because she's a convenient target." He sighed and looked through his open door at the airmen around the fire. Not a one of them glanced his way. "The power to make whatever I want. But what use? I am sure I can find one. Or Harvey, the ability to go wherever I want. That is more to my style, though I doubt I could catch him unawares." He wasn't sure he'd be able to catch the Commander unawares, either, but he thought he had a better chance.

The conversation with himself continued for some time before he replaced the knife beneath the cloth. Still, his decision had come no closer to being made. Each power had its merits. But no one of them seemed enough, and he wondered if he could take all of them. If it was even possible.

But there was also the possibility he wouldn't acquire any, if they had a choice in who it went to, as had been implied by Deidra.

He settled down for sleep. He had a few days left yet. But he needed to make that decision before they left. The only person he could afford to have go back to Earth with him was Deidra, for obvious reasons. And he intended to make good on that promise to himself. He would not go back only to be imprisoned. He would be exalted. He would win the awards that all scientists dreamed of winning. And no one would stand in his way.

~

Gordon looked up at the sound of twigs snapping. Winch strode toward her, his dark hair covered in leaves, a scowl on his face.

The night was dark, moonless, and between a hundred odd people they shared only two fires. Some of the townspeople had been sent on a hunt and had come back with three large boars. Or, they looked like boars, so that was good enough for Gordon. *Enough that we shouldn't need to hunt again before we reach the mountain.*

She was less than impressed that Winch had told Greenway where the others had gone in the ship. But she figured that was more due to a lack of courage on her part. If she could have led him in circles, or in the opposite direction, then she would not have to make an attempt on his life.

"What is it, Winch?" she asked.

"What else? Greenway wants you." The gruff manner in which he delivered this message told Gordon all she needed to know about how the man felt.

She gave him a nod and started on her way.

The clearing they'd found was small, large enough to accommodate them, but only barely. Greenway was due west from the tree line, his back to the fires, his eyes facing a mostly clear sky. He did not turn as she approached.

"Fields was a Giant Killer," he said. "Though I didn't know her well, she had made a sacrifice. Knowledge for self."

Gordon stood still, but her eyes roamed. *Why is he telling me this?* He had a penchant for making obvious statements. But she didn't ask. She let the silence lengthen, but the man didn't turn to her.

"I can respect that choice." He turned to her. "Would you make that sacrifice?"

"I am not sure it's a choice so much as a natural consequence. Whether you bare it with dignity or complaint is another matter."

"So, you understand." His mouth twitched in a grin as he turned back toward the sparse forest.

If you say so, she thought, but she didn't believe she did.

"Would you bear it with complaint, or dignity?" he asked, but clearly didn't expect her to answer, as he continued on. "The villagers, I sent them off to tell their precious world of the return of their gods. I mean for it to be so, Airmen."

Is this to be some philosophical outpouring, then? "I don't know what to say, sir."

He faced her fully. His eyes searched hers, his face expressionless. "Would you take upon yourself a mantel? Would you become one of these gods?"

"If you ask it of me." And she had a suspicion he was asking just that. *Though, I'd really rather not.*

"I note your hesitance in that statement. But I applaud it also." He took a step toward the camp and halted until she turned beside him.

"Who would willingly become something they know they cannot live up to the expectation of?" Simple truth.

Their pace was slow, and they stopped at the tree line to watch the townspeople as they conversed in quiet tones around the dying fires. They were sated by their meal, and while happy to rest, still aware of the gruelling pace that tomorrow would bring.

"We had no choice. Not in what we became. But in how we handled it. They all slunk off and decided that they would go home." A derisive snort. "Home. As if we could ever exist there now. But it has a hold on them. Not us, though. We've made our choice. Integrity. Here we shall stay. Here we shall make our home." He faced her once more. "Think on it, Airmen. Complaint or dignity. I like the way you put that." And he strode back into the woods.

"I'd really rather not," she mumbled under her breath as she watched him leave.

The problem was the man was starting to make sense to her. Despite his methods, which she disagreed with, she saw his reasons. *Understandable* reasons. This, she decided, was not something she cared to think too deeply about.

Better had it stayed black and white. Good guy, bad guy. Person to cheer for, person to stop. The product of choice. And now he is asking me to take something from one of them. To become a God. Stay on this world. I have no desire to do any of these things. And if asked, I will not try my best. It will be with hesitation in every step, for I too, wish to go home.

She found that she could not wipe the grimace from her face. There was no pleasure in understanding this man. She would need to find a way to off him soon, or she may find that doubt clouded her judgement.

And should it not?

~

Greenway stood in the woods, seemingly alone, though he knew he was not. An airman had taken up residence in one of the trees and was watching him. Probably waiting for an opportune moment to drop on him. To finish him off and take the power for himself.

He felt a smile form on his face. They could take it, but they had to earn it. He suspected it was the same one who had been watching him speak with Gordon. He had planned on having a talk with a few more of them this night, but now he decided he'd just wait. Gordon was the only one he was sure of, anyway.

A cool breeze brushed his face, and he closed his eyes as he breathed deep. He was enjoying being outdoors so much. Almost two months now, and he did not miss being confined on the ship. Did not regret the loss of his job. Did not mourn the death of his crew as he had the first days.

Time passed, both swiftly and slowly in turns. He did not move.

The breeze picked up in intensity, and he could hear it stir the leaves on the forest floor to life, a light rustling that would disguise foot falls. He did not tense, as he listened intently for an approach.

It came quickly. The man dropped onto him like a monkey. Arm wrapped around Greenway's throat, muscles expanding as the elbow bent, the result threatening to crush his windpipe. The man put his legs around Greenway's waist and pulled him backward to the ground.

Greenway put his fingers between the airman's arms and his throat, as he was rolled onto his stomach. He bucked his head back and felt it connect with a chin. Though the blow had not had much weight, he heard the airman grunt.

Knees were pressed into his spine, and he felt the sharp end of knife slice against his arm, followed by a curse.

It was time to get this over with.

He let the pressure of the earth beneath him build, then let it loose. As at the gorge, he surged into the air, this time carrying a man on his back. The man's surprise was sufficient for him to relinquish his grip on Greenway's throat, and as they landed, face to face, Greenway grabbed at his knife hand.

With the strength of a god, Greenway squeezed the airman's wrist and heard bones snap. He fell to his knees, the knife dropping from a numb and useless hand.

Greenway turned at the sound of movement behind him. The flicker of a knife, and he leant back, the point slicing only the top layer of skin on his throat.

With a roar, he pulled the first airman into the air and *threw* him into the newcomer.

Greenway looked down on them and spat. "Try that again, and I'll kill you both." He took up the discarded knives and drove them into the bole of the nearest tree.

There was fear in the eyes that watched him. They did not move from their position on the ground.

He stamped a boot next to the first one's head. "Get!" He yelled as he would have to a dog or other domesticated creature. They scrambled upright and made for the camp. He doubted they would try again.

"Their loss, then." And turned back to the trees. Only a few more hours until daylight. And only a few more days to the mountain.

He would have his day.

CHAPTER TWENTY

Harvey stepped away from the alien ship feeling tense and restless. Deidra had asked him in a cool tone to retrieve some things for her from the city that she would need to build a power source. While Weiz had watched in sullen silence, not a word of greeting, not a gesture or smile, nor even a frown that suggested she'd even noted his presence.

He saw Kristin, knife out, whittling away at a piece of wood and throwing the chips into the fire.

"Want to come along and help me find some things for Deidra?" he asked.

Kristin glanced back at him but did not cease her whittling. "Got your woman on a leash yet?"

He jolted in surprise. "Excuse me?"

"The Commander has decided that I am enemy number one." Kristin held out the stick and examined the tip closely. "I tried to put her straight on how things are, but she had no interest in listening. So, I assumed you'd need to explain things to her."

Harvey frowned at the woman as she continued with her work. "I thought I had," he said through gritted teeth. "But now she won't even acknowledge my existence."

"No leash, then."

"I wouldn't attempt one."

"Figure of speech."

"Regardless. Childish." He ran hands through his greasy hair.

"Well, whatever the bee in her bonnet is all about — aside from the obvious jealousy problems — you had best do something about it. Because I tell you now, if she goes for me, I will take her down. I won't hold back on it."

"You just watch what you say about Weiz," he warned.

"Don't be stupid." She held the knife up between them, and rattled its point, her eyes on Harvey's. "She's behaving like a lovesick teen who's never had a boyfriend before. You set it right, or it will settle itself in a way that you won't like."

Harvey ground his teeth and groaned out a note of frustration before he stomped off. *Fucking women.* He knew that Kristin was right though. Catherine had just about admitted it back at the landing sight, hadn't she?

He ran a hand over his beard, one boot moving in front of the other, without thought to where he was going, though he shifted a few times.

'I waited for you, John'. The sentence repeated over and over in his head. *'I waited for you, John.'*

He stopped dead somewhere in the middle of the city, head coming up to stare sightlessly into the depths of the cavern. "Jesus fuck," he breathed.

At forty-six, he'd assumed she'd had some life experience, but if she'd been focused on her work, had never been in a serious relationship, as she'd said... She would have no way to understand the expectations of an adult relationship. The things that required compromise.

He thought back to the first time they'd lain together, after the Day of the Giants, when they realised it was going to take them a long time to get home. But he couldn't remember much more than an overwhelming passion driving him. The sky had been overcast, the night dark, they'd been beneath the hull of a ship, though which one he couldn't have said. It had not been hurried, but he had felt like a hungry man at a feast.

'*I waited for you, John.*' That line continued to reverberate around his skull, and he could not make it leave. It whispered to him like an accusation.

This is not my fault, he told himself firmly. *I can only take responsibility for things that are in my control. Catherine cannot be controlled, for she makes her own choices.*

But he did have to find a way to communicate with her effectively, or whatever they had going was not going to last. Why had it been so much easier when they were just friends?

Harvey growled deep in his throat and took a step forward. Best to keep busy. Best to do as he was asked.

He went looking for the list of things that Deidra requested, all the while wishing that Kristin were with him.

~

She'd wanted to go with him, but he needed to face up to some things. As did Weiz, but she obviously had no interest in listening. Kristin didn't want to be stuck between the feuding parents, as it were.

It was surprising, she supposed, that the situation had not completely disintegrated into a writhing mass of people only out to help themselves. They'd maintained some of the discipline instilled in them by their various military organisations, and respected the chain of command in the ATF. By some miracle, very few of them had gone off the rails. It was just unfortunate that Weiz had been one of them.

Kristin held the stake she'd been whittling out for inspection. She nodded to herself and placed it on the pile. They were not spears, but they'd do the job.

Just as she was about to pick up another, pressure built behind her eyes, and she sat down before she fell.

I could do without this, she thought just before the vision took her.

Parts of the mountain were being stripped away as she stood witness. Daylight bathed down on a city that had never known it, moats of dust swirling in the blinding shafts. Boulder sized chunks of debris fell from the ceiling and crushed houses and building with equal efficacy.

She turned and saw Lance, hand outstretched...

The return to reality sent a shock through her. She inhaled deeply, as if she'd been holding her breath. Her hand was bathed in sweat where it had fallen close to the fire. The airmen surrounding her watched on, concern on their faces, but none of them moved.

She looked up at them with a degree of confusion. They all knew that she saw the future now, that was certain. She didn't know how she felt about that.

Kristin shook off the lingering effects of the vision and rose to her feet. More than a dozen eyes followed her as she made her way to the ship, but not one throat uttered a whisper to ask what she had seen.

If they knew, they'd probably panic. I need to take this to the Commander. But she will not listen to me. So, to Deidra. To the one who has sacrificed the most of any of us, and I'll ask of her one more thing.

She felt a sticky wetness enter her right boot, and she stopped on the ramp to the ships hatch and looked down to find the knife she'd been using to whittle, stuck hilt deep in her calf.

Kristin bent down and wrenched it out, then looked upon the bloody blade. *Why didn't I feel that?* She wiped it off on a sleeve and sheathed it at her hip. A concern for another time.

She stumbled the next few steps up the ramp, and turned her attention to the forward section of the ship where Deidra was working with Heinrich and Weiz.

Weiz noticed her first, her blue eyes boring holes in Kristin. *What are you looking at, bitch?* she wanted to say, but her lips would not move.

Her eyes fluttered a few times, her gaze became unfocused. Deidra turned in her direction, her mouth moved, but all Kristin heard was a roar in her ears like the rushing of an ocean.

She fell forward on her knees, hands hit the metal of the aft deck. The pressure built again. She felt nauseous and dry heaved a few times.

Weiz was prone on the deck of the forward section, life draining away with the blood that spurted from a knife wound to the thigh. It wasn't healing quickly enough, and Harvey couldn't hold it in with his hands.

"You —" she forced out, even as the vision assailed her. "Are — going — to — die!" The last came out as a choked scream.

She was distantly aware that someone had run toward her, and she was being lifted into strong arms. A man's arms.

Kristin let her head lull to the side and rest against the man's chest. *Harvey. You have to save her.* Whatever was going on between the two of them, and despite the fact that they'd involved her in their little mess, she did not want her Commander to die. She was a legend, and she deserved to see this through.

Don't let her die, Harvey. And then darkness stole her away.

~

"—how she meant it," she heard Harvey say.

"Then how did she mean it?" Weiz's voice, a shouted whisper to match Harvey's, was full of hostility.

"How am I supposed to know? You can ask her when she wakes up." Kristin felt Harvey's hand on her shoulder, the gentlest of touches.

She was aware, now. Awake, in a manner of speaking. But her eyes refused to open, her body to move. And so, she was forced to endure the argument between the two lovers. An argument involving her. She'd have given anything to be on the other side of the world right then.

One of them hit something. A dull thud. "You insist there is nothing going on, and yet look at the way you care for her."

Harvey growled beneath his breath. "God fuck it, woman! How many times do we have to go over this? I'd had enough before, and now I'm just about ready to walk away. I never once cheated on my wife with you. Not once. So why would I cheat on you? What, in my history, have I done to suggest that that is something I would do?"

There was quiet for a long time. Kristin struggled to move. To say something. Her discomfit at being a silent auditory witness completely overriding any medical concerns she might have otherwise had.

"You would leave me?" She could tell Weiz choked back tears.

Her hand moved! Kristin forced her mouth open, she wanted to say something but all that came out was a croak. In a rush of pins and needles, sensation returned, and the croak turned into a yelp of pain.

She could feel the attention shift to her. Harvey's hand moved off her shoulder, and he bent close to her ear, she could feel his breath on her neck.

"I'm here," he said softly.

Her eyes fluttered open, but her vision was blurry. The room was lit with a torch that flickered shadows across the wall. A few blinks and her vision corrected. She tried sitting up, but her muscles refused.

"Wh-where?" was all she managed.

"In your office," he told her, some humour in his tone.

Weiz must have left, as Kristin turned her head toward Harvey and no one else was in evidence. "What." Forcing the sentence out was difficult. "Happened?"

The man shrugged and shook his head slightly. "Can't say for sure. Wasn't blood loss. That wound healed quickly after you removed the blade. But we assume you had a vision."

"A few." It was getting easier to speak, though movement still proved a problem.

"You told Weiz — or maybe Deidra, that's unclear — that she was going to die."

"Weiz." There was sadness in his eyes as she voiced this. "You have to save her."

"Can you move?"

"I'm trying."

"Let me help." He moved behind her and lifted her into a seated position. He stayed there so she could rest her back against him. She flexed her arms. They still felt heavy with numbness, but the pins and needles were subsiding, and movement was coming easier.

"Greenway is going to tear the mountain apart." Kristin flailed her right arm out to the side and Harvey caught it. He began moving the shoulder joint up and down gently, then the elbow. She let him.

"Tell me all about what happened," the Captain encouraged.

She explained as he got her arms working for her. He didn't interrupt or ask any questions. He understood. He had from the very beginning.

By the time she was done, Harvey had her standing. She looked up at him with a smile.

"Of course, I can't tell you *when* this will all happen. But I get the feeling that it's soon."

Harvey nodded, then gestured toward the door. "We should take a walk."

Kristin gave her ascent, and Harvey took her under the arm, and they strode into the woods. She wasn't sure she would ever get used to that sensation.

It took her a moment to realise that they were not on the mountain. That the woods around them were on flat land. A few steps forward and she saw that they were near the trail that led down to the village.

"Sometimes it is good to get away," Harvey told her. "But in this case, we're just checking on the progress of Greenway's temple."

"Temple?" As she followed him down the trail. They stopped short of the trail end and edged into the woods. Harvey didn't have to explain, as when she looked, she saw the foundations had already been laid, the frame erected.

"I haven't actually gone into the village, but I *have* heard the workers talking. Greenway ordered that the temple be built. He's taken half the men into town and hasn't been seen since the day after we tried to negotiate for those crew members."

Kristin shook her head. "Wasn't much of a negotiation as I recall."

"True enough."

"So why are we checking on this?"

"To see if he's been back." He shrugged. "Doesn't appear to have returned." He took her by the arm again and suddenly they were in the graveyard.

A few metres to her right was Fields' monument. When she turned, her mouth dropped open. A mountain was *rising* from the ground. Slowly. Several ships had already been upended, pieces torn off, hulls dented and scraped.

"Most were gone when I first returned here," Harvey told her. "I had planned to bring them, one at a time if I had to. But when I got here, it had already been abandoned. Some might have gotten away, but I dare say Greenway has inducted them."

"Why are you showing me this?" she wanted to know.

He looked her up and down, hazel eyes a bright green in the sunlight. "Weiz told me what you said about us leading," he said after a moment, then looked away. "I didn't want to believe that, of course. But, you are right. So, we're leading. Taking initiative. All the fun stuff." Though he certainly did not sound as if he were enjoying it.

"Together?"

"Together."

Kristin chuckled. "Oh, Weiz is going to hate me forever."

Harvey shrugged. "That was bound to happen regardless. But she's either going to put her Commanders cap back on, or we're going to take over. If Greenway is going to make a play for the mountain, then we need to be prepared. We gave those airmen we left behind a month to get there. And we gave them directions. It would be folly to think that Greenway would not put that to use."

"So, what do we do?"

"What we do most times we venture out." He grinned at her. "Get some hunting done."

She slapped his arm. "Not what I meant. Greenway. What are we going to do about him?"

"Not much we can do 'til he shows up. So, I was thinking a discussion with our airmen over dinner."

He grabbed her arm again, and she prepared herself to be drawn to yet another location. *Just along for the ride.*

~

Having the Seer collapse into the ship and utter the words "You are going to die" was not at all conducive to work, apparently. Heinrich had grabbed the girl up, Weiz had followed in toe and Ulrich was, as always, absent. And so, Deidra was left to herself. Again.

Heinrich had returned an hour later, arms laden with the supplies she'd sent Harvey out for, mumbling something about the absurdity of domestic arguments in their current situation. He'd dumped the stuff on the ground next to her and walked out still talking to himself.

She was about to get started on Tesla's Wardenclyffe solution when Weiz came stomping up the ramp. She glanced up.

Deidra thought the woman was going to say something, but she just raised a hand, lips pursed, and cocked her head to the side with a glare. Whatever she was trying to communicate was lost on the Scientist.

I am sure I am supposed to care. But I can't remember why. Should it matter? Do I say something suitably comforting? But nothing came to mind, so she just pointed to a place on the other side of her material pile.

Weiz frowned and looked like she might like to murder Deidra, but she complied. "More tools?" she asked.

Deidra nodded. "Not yet, but it won't hurt you to stay with me while I construct this."

The woman glared, then sat down cross-legged on the deck, hands resting on knees. "What are we making now?"

"Wardenclyffe towers. Smaller than the original, true. But it should suffice."

The Commander cocked a brow. "I am supposed to know what that is?"

"You asked. I answered."

"What does it do?"

"Draws power form the ionosphere." She picked up some of the materials and began her work.

Weiz watched from her position on the floor, saying nothing.

Occasionally Deidra glanced over at her or had the woman pass her something, but for the moment her help was unnecessary.

The ship rattled. Deidra looked up. The ship — *shifted*. Weiz had the question in her eyes, and Deidra answered before it was asked, as she stood. "I don't know what that is." And she moved toward the hatch.

A *breeze* touched her face. It became a gale, and then calmed.

"Lance," Weiz breathed beside her.

"I should talk to him." She wasn't sure what compelled her, she just went with it.

For the first time in days, she left the ship. She looked around in the dim glow from the fires and torches left scattered around the building. It was neither hot nor cold in this place, but she noted that the airmen were huddled together at the central fire, where their food was generally cooked. Probably for the light, she realised.

Near the far end, his back to an office wall, Lance sat. A look of extreme concentration marred his face. He held his hands in front of him and when he extended his fingers, making a popping noise with his mouth, a gale erupted.

Deidra stopped before him. "Stop it."

He glanced up. "I need to —"

"Not in here you don't." She reached down and hauled him up by the elbow. The indignant look she received might have amused another person. "If you want to practice being the Weatherman, then take it outside."

Lance pulled his elbow away from her. "You're all paired off in your own little worlds," he stated. "You and Weiz, Harvey and Kristin. But I don't have that. Maybe for a moment here or there one of you might give me the time of day, but for the most part I am left to my own devices. The other airmen will barely speak to me. Not even Xavier."

She was not completely without sympathy, though the complete loss of emotion was coming close. "We're all just using each other," she told him. That probably wouldn't make him feel any better. "I need Weiz for the tools she can provide. You *all* need me to build this equipment that will take us home. Kristin is a hunter, but she needs someone by her side when she has a vision, and for this she uses Harvey. Harvey is used by all of us because he can go places with ease that we could not reach. Use, Lance. Would you care to be used?"

To her surprise, the man nodded. "Better to be used than be useless." It sounded like he was quoting someone.

"Are you sure?"

Lance didn't even hesitate. "Tell me what to do."

For Lance's particular talent she'd had a few things in mind, but there was one that she thought he might enjoy above the rest. As she explained what she wished, a smile slowly bloomed on his face.

"That," he said when she was finished, "sounds like fun."

"Good." She stayed where she was and watched him until he disappeared up the stairs leading to the street. He would do as asked.

That solves a singular problem. And I had not even considered it until he made the ship move. It made her wonder what else she was missing. The knowledge may be there when she looked for it, but she did have to look for it. And that meant asking herself the right questions.

~

Lance took the now familiar route through the city to the opening they'd made.

Sunlight was fading, another day disappearing without being seen by those who lived below. He was glad it was on the edge of twilight, for even this much natural light hurt his eyes.

How far we have come in under two months. How far we have fallen. It goes both ways. They'd become gods, he was told. Not that any of them acted like it. It was all use and selfish desires that drove them. Just as Deidra had said. That need to go home. That singular purpose that bound them together and separated them at the same time. For their motives toward that purpose varied.

He proceeded to the edge of the ledge and faced the sky. Although it was strictly unnecessary, he threw his arms out and back, puffed his chest out, put his feet together and kept his legs straight. He enjoyed the thought of what the pose may look like, him silhouetted against the skyline, and wished that one of his friends was there with a camera.

Lance kept his eyes on the horizon. What Deidra had asked for was simple in theory, but he didn't know if he could do it. Knowing that rain and clouds were made from dust and water was something most people were taught in their first years of schooling, but he wasn't sure he'd ever been taught how an electrical storm was formed. If he had been, he'd forgotten. So, he hoped that will alone was enough.

Weiz can make things without knowing how they're made, so I should be able to do the same. Just concentrate on the clouds and the winds the not-quite-raining yet muggy and static feel. Electrical storms were a common enough occurrence on Earth, so he knew the feeling he was going for.

On the horizon, just above where the sun now sat, clouds began to form.

~

In his arms was the last on the list of things that Deidra had asked him to scrounge for.

He took a step and was before the ship. He jogged up the ramp, entered without greeting, and left the stuff in a pile just inside the hatch. Heinrich was doing something in the passenger section, and he glanced up at the sound of metal clanking.

Harvey looked to Deidra who was in her usual position, Weiz looking bored beside her.

They'd not spoken since the fight they'd had over Kristin's unconscious form. He had nothing to apologise for, and if that was the cause of her silence, then no more words could be said. *I've done nothing wrong, woman, and the sooner you realise* that, *the sooner you'll find the happiness that has so long alluded you.*

"That's all of it, then?" Deidra asked without turning.

"There is more where I found this, but if it's enough, then it is the last." He waited while she made a few adjustments to whatever it was she was doing.

Weiz made something for the scientist at a gesture, and she continued her work. "Good. I have one last thing that I need you to do, Captain."

He nodded before he remembered she wasn't looking, then said, "What is it?"

"Outside, in the first office on your right, next to where Heinrich's been sleeping?" She turned her attention to him then. He indicated that he understood which place she spoke of. "There are fourteen small antennas. I want you to place them evenly around the mountain. Well, as evenly as you can manage. And high, but not right at the top."

Antennas? But he didn't ask. He just grunted his acquiescence, turned and made his way to the office.

Kristin was by the fire talking to the airmen as he'd asked her to do. Explaining to them what was going on, what they expected to happen, and the state of readiness they hoped they'd be in. Kristin was sure that Greenway would make an appearance before Deidra was finished with her work, and he trusted her on that. But he hoped she was wrong.

The antennas actually looked more like miniature versions of power towers, though with domed tops. Each one was the length of his arm, and as wide as his thigh. Though when he picked the first one up, he realised it had been folded inward like a stand, and that the tops rose out to over double their length like a camera tripod.

Satisfied that this was what Deidra would have him do, he picked four up off the pile and made his way to Kristin.

They all must have seen him, for conversation ceased on his approach. "Help an old man out?" he asked Kristin, his face poking round the pile in his arms.

She cocked a brow. "How exactly?"

He explained to her what Deidra wanted him to do.

Xavier got up and dusted himself off. "I'll do it," he said. "I need to get outside for a while." He looked at the others. "Many hands, light work? Enough of us here that we take one each, it'll be done before daybreak."

The others got up, and Xavier nodded.

"Remember that Lance has a little storm brewing out there, Superman," Kristin said. "So, stick to groups of two. Don't want any of you getting caught in a mud slide or falling down a scree slope without someone there to help you out or call for help. You get me?"

Xavier gave her a tight smile, and smart-arsed but well-meaning salute. "Got it." Then he turned and led the rest to the office.

"They chose the hard way," he murmured.

"They need to get out." Kristin shrugged. "Been a few weeks of no daylight for any of them, it's enough to drive just about anyone mad."

"True enough."

"So where are we going?"

"Other side of the mountain. I'll start there and work back toward the entrance."

Kristin walked over to him and held on to his elbow. "Just don't run me into a tree again. That was not fun."

He wanted to laugh but settled for a grin as he stepped forward and out into evening twilight.

Kristin took one of the antennas from his arms and adjusted it, so it was at its full height and width. Then she looked to him. "If we just stick it on the ground it will fall," she said. "We bury the feet it may be too short. To be honest, I think they may be too short already."

Harvey shrugged and rested the other antennas against a tree. "She wouldn't have asked us to do this if it didn't serve a purpose. And she would not have made them so uniformly short if they wouldn't work when finished."

"Unless she wanted to give you something to do?"

"Then she wouldn't have bothered making the damned things. She could have just kept asking me to bring her piles of junk."

"Maybe she wants us to put them up a tree?"

"Then she would have said so!" He grabbed the antenna off her and drove it into the ground. It was sturdy and absorbed his weight with a flex, though he estimated the feet sank roughly ten centimetres deep.

He stepped back to assess it. It didn't appear to be damaged in any way. He glanced to Kristin.

"Or you could do that," she said with a sour look.

"Indeed." He picked up the rest of the antennas, indicated for her to hold his arm, and moved them to another spot on the mountain.

"It's really not fair you know." She took an antenna from his arms, then opened it and jammed it into the ground in the same fashion he had done before.

"What's that?"

"How you can just move about as much as you like."

He shrugged, tossed her one of the antennas, then lunged at her with his free arm, lifted her off the ground, and moved them to another place on the mountain. He laughed, even as she whacked him hard on the back.

"Put me down!" she demanded.

Harvey let her feet touch the forest floor and released his hold. He took one step back. "No fun," he said with mock solemnity, then ducked as she threw the antenna. "You'll have to go get that now."

CHAPTER TWENTY-ONE

The attempt on his life had not been repeated. Nor, he suspected, had anyone else found out about it. Those two airmen would be licking their wounds and stroking their rage. They'd resumed their places at the head of their columns, and had not said a word in his hearing.

That doesn't mean they're not planning something. He reminded himself that he was not infallible. That knife had come perilously close to ending his life. And though the cut had healed quickly, its initial sting was a memory that would haunt. Even now, his hand reached up to feel at the smooth skin where it had bitten him.

Gordon was up front with him now as he surveyed the mountain in front of them. According to her, this was where the others were holed up. It would take them another day to reach it, but as yet, he saw no indication that there was anyone alive up there.

"Are you sure this is the right one?" There were no other large mountains in view. Next to it, the others were merely jagged spikes thrust up out of the ground.

The better part of the day was spent arguing with trees, as Greenway saw it. Weaving between them, breaking branches, dodging twigs and attempting to pierce the gloom that their canopy created. As if the trees themselves were against them getting to that mountain. An absurd notion, but he didn't brush the thought aside, as he once would have.

I come to face you all with an army at my back, hoping they'll distract the regular airmen long enough to convince you to stay. And in the chance that you cannot be so convinced, I have others willing to take your place. How easily did they come to the decision to take my power? How eagerly did they try? Power for powers sake, and no more. Not one thought for the responsibility it entails. And yet I would use them. For they know that we should stay. Even without a power to hold them to this place.

Dirt and scree dislodged from slopes, showered down on those who came behind. Townspeople fell in mudslides and tripped on branches, aided back to their feet by comrades and allies.

Greenway paid them no mind. His focus was entirely on the mountain. On the glimmering object atop it. He himself need not reach that place. He only needed to see it clearly, to know where to start pulling the mountain apart.

Above, a storm was raging, swirling and stuck in the clouds. Forks of lightning swept the sky, but did not arch toward the ground. The rain would come, and when it did, it was all too possible that those behind him would be caught helpless in these woods.

He felt Gordon catch up beside him. He viewed her from the corner of his eye and saw determination on her face. She would do as he had asked; he was sure of it.

If I can be sure of only one, it should be her.

He ran on.

~

The townspeople were a long way behind them now, but she could still hear them. She'd caught up to Greenway with a single purpose in mind, but she had doubts. Lots of doubts.

The pace that Greenway had set from the start had exhausted them all. They'd lost more than a few of the villagers in the last few days of travel. And yet he continued to appear in good health, despite the fact that he did not sleep, and she had never seen him eat.

A part of her wanted to scream. *He is a god!* But a larger part of her denied it. Wanted to explain it away. Needed to have him removed from the equation, so the rest of them could just go home.

Take up the mantel. If she killed him, she would have to. If that was the way that it worked. After all, Heinrich had tried to kill Fields, but it was Deidra who had ended up with the power. Was there some kind of balance being maintained? A way for the victim to choose who they gave their power to? An *heir*?

Hard to imagine. Not what she had in mind.

She looked at Greenway, his gaunt features hard, a wry twist to his mouth. He had his own plans, his own thoughts.

Her hand reached down to the holster on her thigh. Most of the bullets had been used for hunting, but she'd kept one for herself. *Always one bullet, just in case. Just one, is all a person needs.* She'd have to do it quickly, and if she missed, she knew her life was forfeit.

Gordon saw him glance in her direction and hastily pulled her hand away from the gun. She tried to make it seem like a natural occurrence in her stride, but she could not tell if he'd been fooled.

Fuck. She was going to have to wait now. Only, they were running out of time.

~

They were placing the last of the antennas on the southeast face of the mountain, higher up where the other airmen were not likely to make it.

Harvey looked up to the grey sky above, the blue strikes of

lightning flashed, their sound swallowed by the clouds.

"Think it's going to rain soon?" Kristin asked.

"From a sky like that I would expect a deluge." But it had yet to rain a single drop. At least not that he could see.

"Should we head back?"

"I want to get a better view. Come to the summit?" He looked up, though he knew he wouldn't see it through the trees.

"Don't see why not." She grabbed hold of his elbow.

Snow crunched under his boot. The wind was cold and hard against his face. He felt himself shiver and become lightheaded from the thin air.

With his next step, he took them a little lower. It was cold, but the air was breathable and there was no snow. He looked to Kristin.

"Glad you decided that was a bad idea." She flashed him a nervous grin.

"Well, I never did claim to be perfect."

They looked down on the vista below. It was stunning. The tree tops all shades of blue, grey and green. The distant grasses could just be seen on the far horizon. Birds flew in flocks toward the south, probably trying to avoid the coming storm.

Harvey was all too aware of Kristin's grip on his arm. Normally she'd have let go by now, but while he didn't want to make a big deal of it as Weiz would have, he found the need to pull away. She let her hands drop without shifting or making comment. For that he was glad.

If only Weiz could take things so easily. But thoughts like that only served to remind him of what their relationship had devolved to. *Too many years spent waiting. Layering expectations upon ideals and ideas that have no basis in reality. Jealousies that override passion.*

"Holy shit," he heard Kristin breathe.

"What is it?" He followed the direction of her gaze.

If the mountain was a sheer drop, then the ship they'd landed on it would be a few hundred feet below where they stood now. A little way to the left of that, on a smaller adjacent mountain, he could see movement in the trees.

"That's a lot of people rushing towards us," Kristin asserted. He glanced at her, but her eyes remained on the scene below.

Harvey looked back down. "How can you be sure?"

"There's a small clearing coming up in their path. Just watch."

And he did. Within moments, Harvey saw them coming. He had not expected to face an army, and as he looked to Kristin, he knew she had not expected it either.

"He's found his worshippers, then," the woman said.

"I think he's found more than that." He grabbed hold of her arm. "We need to get word to Weiz."

She nodded, and Harvey took them directly to the forward deck of the ship.

~

Deidra jumped, startled as Harvey and Kristin appeared a foot in front of her. They almost landed on her work, which earned them a frown.

"They're coming," Harvey said.

Weiz, who'd been sitting next to her silently sulking, turned her attention to the new arrivals. "Greenway? And who else?"

It was Kristin who answered. "Villagers for the most part. Though I did see a few ATF uniforms."

"How long do we have?" Deidra queried.

"'Til the end of the day." Harvey met her eyes. "Whatever you've not yet got done, I suggest you rush it now. If they storm this position, I don't know how any of us are going to start again."

"Go." She waved them out the hatch. "Do what you can. Just send in Heinrich, and see if you can find Ulrich. I've a suspicion that he may have offed himself."

The way they all just stared at her then made her wonder if she should not have added that last. She gestured toward the hatch again, and that got them moving.

This was going to be a challenge. A month had been a challenge even with the help of others. This was going to be something else again.

"Half a day at best," she mumbled to herself.

She glanced down at the almost finished circuit board in her lap. It was the last one for the propulsion device, but she had yet to make the housing or connect it to the ship. None of the calculations had been put in, though that was what she hoped to use Heinrich and Ulrich for. But she hadn't seen the younger scientist in some time.

With a sigh, she held her hand out, palm up, and Weiz deposited the tool she'd been thinking of without asking. They'd come to this stage of their working relationship, where efficiency outweighed everything else.

It didn't take long before Heinrich was with them, a harried expression on his face. "Where do you want me?"

"I need you to put the math in," she told him.

"What are you up to?"

"From the beginning! I haven't had the chance. In case you can't tell I am a little busy building it." She wasn't annoyed. At least she didn't think she was. But there was something creating a sense of urgency. "Have you seen Ulrich?"

Heinrich blinked at her. "Did he even come to this mountain with us?"

"No, then. Fine. Go, do the calculations." He mumbled something incomprehensible, pulled at the hem of his shirt, and turned to make his way into the passenger section where they'd installed the frequency generator.

"I still cannot believe you trust that man," Weiz whispered.

Deidra kept at her work. "I don't need to. He wants to get home just as badly as the rest of you, and this was his project. He knows the calculations better than anyone."

"So, you're confident he won't try to sabotage us?"

"Not this ship. Not the project."

"That does not put me at ease, Doctor."

"Nor should it. He'll probably try and kill one of you before it's all said and done." She finished up the board, held it out for inspection.

"Done?"

Deidra nodded. "Last piece done. I just need to put this together, then deal with the power problem."

She got up and took it over to the other finished circuit boards. They were arrayed in order, numbered in her mind. She just needed the casing. That thing that would link them all together and make it do what it was supposed to do.

Half a day. A joke. Even with all the knowledge at my disposal I can only move so fast. Some things are going to be left out. Some things are not going to be ready.

"I should probably go round up the airmen. Get ready for an assault." Weiz said quietly beside her.

"Harvey and Kristin are already taking care of that side of things." She didn't mean for it to be salt in the wound, but the Commander flinched back at the words. "And I need you here if I am to finish anything in time."

Weiz looked defeated. She did not try and argue the point, she just slumped to lean against the wall, and watched Deidra at her work.

~

They were at the foot of the mountain. Or close enough to it. Above, and somewhat to his right, he could just make out the ship the others had taken.

Greenway turned to Gordon. "It will take everyone some doing to get up there, I would think."

"Depends on the angle of ascent," she replied. "I see a scree slope up there that would be useful. But it's all a moot point if we don't know where to go once we get up there."

Greenway closed his eyes for a moment.

They'd gotten this far, and they would make it to that ledge where the ship was. But that could not be the end of the story. There had to be some way for them to find them inside the mountain. Assuming they hadn't just taken up residence in a cave. And assuming whatever was in the mountain wasn't easily navigable.

He felt outward with the earth. Let it tell him what it felt. *Whose footfalls do you feel? What is natural and what is not? Give to me your secrets, for they are mine now.* He wasn't sure it this would work, or if he'd be able to correctly interpret what he felt. But he reached out and felt something.

"There are others on this mountain side," he told her, eyes still shut. "They can lead the way for you."

"And where shall we find these others?"

"Go to the ledge, you will not be far behind them. In their panic, they will run toward what they presume is safety, and they'll have led you to the others. The important ones."

He opened his eyes. Gordon was frowning, her chest heaving. He hadn't noticed before.

"And you?" she asked him.

"I'll be around. You'll need to be able to see what you're doing when you're in there." That was as much as he cared to explain for the moment.

A drop of rain landed on his left cheek. He wiped it off with the back of a hand and looked up to the sky. Lightning arched down on the other side of the mountain, the accompanying thunder almost deafening.

Behind him there was a clatter of falling weapons as townspeople put their hands to their ears. Greenway looked back at them but said nothing. The airmen would make sure they picked them up before they continued on.

More rain drops. Thick and heavy. Then a deluge. Getting up that slope had just gotten a lot harder for his people. *But there is nothing I can do to make it easier, is there? A ramp with surer footing, perhaps?* He glanced back, then shook himself with a sigh, and forced the mountain to build a steep ramp for them. It would get muddy and difficult, but it would be safer than scree.

"You're in charge of these ones now," he told Gordon. "You get them up there, and inside that mountain. You find out where those others a holing up and you get them to come out. I don't want them dead, you understand? I want to give them a chance to surrender."

She gave him a single nod, then turned back to the townspeople. She began shouting orders.

Greenway watched for just a few moments before he turned his attention to the top of the mountain. He was going to want a decent position. He didn't want to be in easy view, but he also needed to be able to see the bulk of one side. Better off from a distance than up close. Having Harvey's power at that moment would have been advantageous.

He chose his direction and set out.

It was strange, in his own mind. To think of that time before the Day of the Giant Killers. To remember that person he had been — huddled, scared, convinced he was in some kind of hell or purgatory with demons following his every move — and compare it the person he was now. The change was... immense. *I think I was insane.* An unsettling thought fallowed; *perhaps I still am.*

He struggled through the foliage, the rain falling heavily, obscuring his view. He could barely see a few feet in front of him. He wasn't sure how he was going to be able to see the mountain in this.

Then it was like a voice whispered to him. Perhaps the earth itself. That he didn't need to see. Just feel.

He stopped.

~

Gordon watched as Greenway disappeared into the downpour. She could no longer make out the ship on the mountain. The rain was a grey sheet two feet from her face.

She turned to Winch and Ainsley. She knew that they'd made an attempt, though neither one spoke of it. Ainsley had not approached her again about killing the man. That in itself was enough.

"He wants us to get them all up there. Says we'll find someone to follow once we're there."

Ainsley grunted, spat, then turned to the townspeople. He gestured with an arm, and the exhausted group followed as he set them a trail.

Gordon was torn. She'd had a few opportunities. But every time she'd taken too long to decide. Had let what the man was saying get into her head and make her doubt her cause. She had that choice to make once again. Right now.

Follow the group into the mountain? Or follow Greenway and get her shot off?

The townspeople were streaming past her. Shadowed figures in the gloom of forest and rain. But she could see them. She did not know where Greenway had gone.

A cowards answer then, she told herself, disappointed.

She followed the townspeople. Maybe she could prevent some bloodshed. Maybe.

~

Harvey paced in front of the building entrance. The space was dark except for the torch Kristin held as she leant against the door frame.

They were waiting for the airmen to arrive.

"You know all their names, right?" he asked. He was worried, she could tell. If these ones died, someone had to know their names to mark their gravestones.

She nodded. "Xavier, Rich, Zim, Hadley, Fyord, Ellis, Constance, Bridges, Walt, Dames, East and Duntz."

Harvey paced a little further up the street. "Surely they should be on their way back by now?"

Kristin breathed a sigh. *Like a mother hen.* Strange that she'd not seen this side of him before. "They probably are. But Lance also said that the rain had started. So, they'll take a little longer than they should."

"I should have just taken all the antennas."

"They needed to get out of this place for a while, Harvey. It was their choice. Now stop your pacing, it's not helping anyone."

"I could just go out and get them."

"No. You can't. We need to stay here."

"*Why?*" There was a note of such anguish and frustration in his tone.

"Why are you acting so whiny all of a sudden?" She pushed herself off the door frame and settled the brand against the wall. It didn't look like it would burn. It was stone, after all.

Harvey threw up his hands. "I don't know!" His voice came out somewhere between a hysterical laugh and a grunt.

Kristin slapped him.

"God fuck it, woman! What is with you and hitting people? You need some fucking help, you know that?" He held a hand to his left cheek where her palm print was coming up in a red welt.

She stood, hands on her hips, head cocked to the side. "Well, when I punch people, I suppose," she mumbled. A hard admission, but she didn't want to put him offside. "But a slap is a proven cure for hysteria."

"Hysteria?"

"You looked like you were panicking."

He took his hand away from his cheek and she winced at the bruise already starting to rise.

Harvey looked like he was about to say something, but instead turned at the sound of boots. Lots of boots. Slapping down hard on the streets and avenues. Echoes in the cavernous city. Voices, both strangled and clear, rising in crescendo as the owners drew closer.

The ground beneath them began to rumble, and Kristin caught Harvey by a sleeve before he could fall.

That damned army of Greenway's had found them. Somehow, some way, they'd found them.

"We need to get back inside!" she shouted at Harvey above the roar. He didn't argue.

~

She slipped on the mud slope and found herself sliding down to collide with a hapless townsman. The hoe he'd been carrying landed first, and his head hit it hard enough that the blade bit and buried deep inside his skull.

This was not the first death on the slope, but it was the one that halted Gordon and allowed her to get back up. That man, his eyes wide in surprise, his cheeks gaunt with hunger, eyes red rimmed from exhaustion, would stay with her. The man's death had saved her from her own, and she didn't even know his name.

She clambered on.

On the ledge, the airmen and townspeople were filing into a hole in the mountainside, their pace slowed due to the width of the opening. She pushed her way along until she was at the front of the row.

Winch stood to one side, watching.

"Was it like he said?" she asked him, out of breath. "You found someone to follow?"

He gave her a nod. The place was dark, the opening barely enough to shed enough light for them to see the ground in front of them.

She tapped the man on the shoulder and moved on.

The streets were dark and smelled of dust, and she groped blindly for a moment before she realised she could follow the sound. The sound of *hundreds* of boots cracking down on to the hard stone road.

That isn't right, she thought, worried. Though she kept moving, following that thunderous roar. *There isn't even a hundred of us. Not even with all the townspeople who made it this far. Where are those other sounds coming from?*

~

It wasn't an illusion she was creating. Just like those nights by the river, she made the whole thing *real.* Those airmen deserved another chance. A chance to make things right. They had to fight. But this time, not a giant. This time, it was Greenway and his army.

They cannot die again. They're already dead. And when those people reach them, they'll find nought but vicious warriors who don't see them. Though that will not diminish the effectiveness of their strike.

Perhaps she was torturing herself with their memory. But it was one that she had not played out since the second last day on the plains. They still haunted her, and she could not let them go.

She'd seen Kristin and Harvey come running in, and Deidra had given her leave to go do something to slow the coming hoards. It was all she could think of.

From the doorway where she stood, looking out into the darkness of the city, she saw flashes of light here and there where one of their airmen was running with a torch in hand.

They would make it, or they would not. They could not afford to wait much longer. As soon as the ship was ready, they would leave.

Weiz turned and made her way back to the ship. She had to help Deidra with the finishing touches. *It's too late. I am not worth the blood they would spill for me, and yet, like a coward I cringe in the depths. We are not gods. We're too flawed for that. Too insecure. Too human.*

Already, there were footsteps close behind.

~

Greenway kept his eyes closed. It was easier to visualise that way. The mountain. What might be in its depths.

He tensed his shoulders, arms held wide. He gripped at the air with one hand and twisted with his hips, making a flinging motion. Then did the same with the other.

Chunks of stone and dirt were torn from the mountainside. Trees were flung into the air, to land, skidding in the mud. Whatever creatures this forest held fled with the destruction of their home.

Inwardly, Greenway smiled. *And god said, let there be light.*

~

Kristin felt the ground shift beneath her. The logs still burning in the cook fire, scattered and rolled across the concrete floor.

This is it, she realised. The moment from her vision. Greenway had begun his decimation of the mountain.

None of the airmen had yet arrived back. Weiz had gone to the streets, though what she planned to do was anyone's guess.

Lance was out there somewhere. *Lance, with hand outstretched...* But she'd seen no more. She didn't know what it meant. The image flickered in her mind like photographic stills in a flick book.

She saw Weiz, in a hurry, heading toward the ship.

Harvey looked torn between going to her and staying with Kristin. He glanced at her, eyes pleading. "Do what you have to," she told him.

She watched him walk away, and understood in that moment.

He's not going to save her. But it wasn't because he wouldn't try. He'd just be too late. There was something else he had to do, and Weiz was going to make him do it.

Her attention was drawn back to the entrance by the sound of people. The first person to come into view was Rich, and she was running. Behind her Xavier lurched forward, dived into a roll, and came up ready to fight. A few more of the airmen came in, Lance among them. Then there were faces she didn't recognise.

It was time then. Fight or die. The ship wasn't ready, and they had to give Deidra time to get it done.

~

Deidra snapped the last of the circuits into place and buried the board beneath the floor panel in the passenger's section. She glanced up to see Heinrich working furiously on the calculations.

Weiz had conjured up a blow torch and was welding some transmitters in place. They were important. Deidra had placed them herself. Power conduits.

She made her way back to the bridge of the ship and pressed a finger down on the comms console. "Half an hour," she informed those who were still outside the ship. Hopefully they could give her enough time to get the minimum finished. She could already hear the masses entering their building.

She noted Harvey waltz up to Weiz, a short conversation with few words, the situation tense. Then Harvey disappeared mid-step as he turned on a heel.

Deidra sat down at the drive console and switched it on. According to the trajectory that Heinrich had laid out for them, she noted that they'd travelled just over four-hundred and eighty-two light years. A lot closer then she'd have guessed given just how different the stars looked. As this was not the original equipment, and the power generation would be comparatively small, she wasn't sure that she could get them back to the *time* where they'd started.

Place, yes, time, no. But only because I don't have the original calculations. And Heinrich did not have his original notes. She got to work.

~

Gordon entered the building just ahead of Ainsley. It was lit by electric lights in some places, though they were strangely dim. But, for the most part, it was scattered brands and logs that might have originally been from a single fire.

Townspeople were engaging the airmen at will. The scientists were nowhere in sight. Those were the ones that Greenway instructed they go for first. Without them, Weiz and the others would be stuck here.

But that was not what she wanted. Her plan to get to Greenway might have failed, but she still had her bullet.

It was clear that the odd-looking ship in the centre of the cavernous building was the focus of this company, and so she made for it with all speed.

"I can still do the right thing," she told herself.

Her feet struck the ramp and it flexed beneath her. A face in the doorway, but she could not stop her momentum. She collided, knocking the figure down. She winced.

Someone came at her from behind. She fell, her chin hitting the metal deck. She tasted blood in her mouth and rolled onto her side to see Ainsley, a smile on his face as he looked down on her, knife in hand.

"This one is mine," he told her, and walked over her into the ship.

~

He saw Greenway at the bottom of the mountain, as his visions overlapped, from where he was to where he'd be. He took a step, and hammered the man in the face with a fist. The bastard staggered back only a single step before righting himself. He wasn't even bleeding.

Greenway laughed at him. "We can't kill each other, Harvey. It's against the rules!" Then he lunged, tackling him to the ground.

The earth stopped shaking, though debris still rained down.

Harvey was on his back, trying to get out from underneath the gaunt man. He tried to get his knees between them and lever Greenway off, but he was slippery, moving first one way then another, each time landing a blow on Harvey's midriff that made him want to curl into a ball.

The rain hit like pebbles against the skin, numbing his face and hands. He was frustrated, tired and angry. Why wouldn't this man just let them go?

"We have the right to go home!" he yelled between breaths.

Greenway backed away, breathing hard and looking insane. "You don't have the right. Not anymore. You gave it up the day we became what we are. *You* made a choice, even before then, to stay here! You didn't ask any of us. So why should I ask you?"

Harvey managed to get a good grip on something beside him. He heaved it into the side of Greenway's head, and the man slid off him.

"This is not about *me!*" he yelled as he got to his feet.

Greenway was already on hands and knees, shaking his head clear of the blow. Watered blood ran a fast river down the side of his head. He swung his head to face Harvey. "It *is* about *you! All* of you."

Harvey stepped forward with the intention of smacking the man again with the rock in his hand, but Greenway tripped him up with his legs.

Once again, he was on his back, the breath knocked out of him. But Greenway didn't follow it up with more blows, this time. He just stood over Harvey.

"You cannot abandon this world, Harvey. It will not let you. *I* will not let you. And if you choose to leave, then someone else needs to take your place. For that to happen, you must die. So take your pick, *Captain*."

Rain pelted his face and he had to hold a hand over his eyes to see the other man clearly. He rolled onto his side, gripped the other man by an ankle, and smiled.

Harvey rolled, and with his movement, the scenery changed.

He let go of a gaping and indignant Greenway at the edge of the village. "Enjoy your temple," he grunted, even as he rolled once more. And landed on a burning log inside the building where he could now hear fighting. The last thing he heard from Greenway, was a muffled curse.

~

Heinrich held the knife in front of him. He'd made a mistake the last time, though he'd not known it until now. He'd dodged a bullet, so to speak, and for that he was grateful. *Deidra can have her failing memories; it just means I won't have to kill her.* The mistake he had made, was that he'd chosen the wrong power.

For the weeks they'd been in this tomb, he had tried to change himself, inside. Tried to be a helpful member of the crew. But he knew it wasn't in him. He required recognition. Validation. He was the master of new science, not an errand boy. Not a second-rate scientist working on other people's projects. This was *his* project. Everything that had happened to these people had happened because of *him*. And he deserved a share of that power. Demanded it.

Weiz. She had a power he could put to use. Not just a benign power, but something that could do damage if he chose. Or *create*. And he liked that idea more than any other.

She was different to Fields. She would see it coming. But he knew what he had to do.

He glanced through the passenger section doors at where Weiz was now in combat with an airman from Greenway's forces. She might see it coming, but she might just be too busy to do something about it.

~

Lance ducked his head behind the desk of his office as a shard of rock hurled toward him. The ground no longer shook, and he suspected that Harvey was keeping Greenway occupied, even as his dedicated minions attacked. As much as he'd have liked to unleash his Weatherman powers, doing so inside the mountain would probably cause more problems than it solved.

Deidra had assured him that the natives would not be able to harm him, as long as the airmen with them hadn't given them anything from Earth. He wasn't about to take that chance. He was a combat pilot, not a marine.

More projectiles were aimed in his direction, slamming into the desk. One of them had been big enough to make a large dent in the metal.

He'd heard Deidra, not too long ago now, over the speakers outside the ship. Half an hour, she'd said. He didn't have a watch, couldn't keep track of time. But he didn't want to be late.

He turned his head this way and that in an effort to draw inspiration from his surroundings. The projectiles no longer flew in his direction, but that didn't mean much.

Fuck. I am going to have to fight eventually if I want to get to the damned ship. He surged up from his position, ready to unleash bursts of wind in the direction of anyone who attacked. But they'd already moved on. He was alone.

Somehow that fact was disappointing.

Lance strode out of the office and looked both ways. The ground was littered with the dead, dying and unconscious. The smell was worse than a latrine pit. Shit, piss, blood, sweat, bile, burning flesh. He'd always witnessed such things from a distance.

Someone came at him from the right. He ducked under the

expected blow, only for a fist to connect with his jaw and send him spinning sideways. He blinked and saw a fist coming for his face. His arm came up in time to block it.

It was an airman, he noted now. His face a contortion of rage. And while he didn't have time to contemplate the plight of the man as he joined the fight, he did see that there weren't many of the opposition left standing. And those were mostly airmen. Those natives had wasted their lives. For what? So Greenway could play out his tantrum?

The airman he faced now looked familiar, but he couldn't put a name to him. They circled. The man held a knife in one hand, but continually feinted at him with the other.

Lance stepped sideways, and instead of aiming at the man with a punch, he imagined the blow extended, past his normal capabilities, to smack the man square in the face and send him tumbling. He didn't get up.

The Pilot raced toward the ship.

~

Deidra fell forward, solar plexus slamming into a lever, her chin into the console, as an airman careened into her back. Her breath exploded from her lungs, and for a second, she thought she might vomit.

What she was doing was important. She held to that. They had to get home, though she now only vaguely remembered what that was like. Bits and pieces, pictures in her head, but no associated feelings. The price.

The airman was pulled off her by Weiz, who continued her battle while the Scientist ignored her. She had to continue her work.

Time was running out, and the calculations were almost done. They'd be missing things — things she was sure ships were usually built with — but as soon as she finished what she was doing, she planned to take off. The only person she absolutely *had* to wait for was Lance.

~

Weiz felt the knife as it entered her thigh, but instead of letting it drop her, or be yanked out to allow the blood through, she twisted savagely. The knife was drawn from the grip of the airman, but the manoeuvre made her stagger a step to the side.

The airman lunged at her. Shoulder collided with midriff. She was driven to the deck and her head bounced on the hard metal.

A face loomed over her. A name, just on the edge of memory. The knife twisted in her thigh. Came out. Blood gushed.

Someone behind her kicked out and connected with the airman's jaw. He sprawled off to the side, and she was surprised to see Heinrich walk over her to finish the man off with a knife in the throat. Quick, efficient, he went straight for the carotid.

But then he turned his gaze toward her.

She returned his cool regard.

He took a step closer.

Everything was in slow motion. The sounds of fighting. The way Heinrich bent over her and grabbed the collar of her coveralls. The knife as it first swept back, and then started forward, only to stop. The arm falling away. The grip on her coveralls loosened, and again her head smacked the deck.

Heinrich fell on top of her, and it was like time had sped up again. She pushed him off and squirmed out from under him to sit up against the bridge door frame.

A hand waved in front of her face. "Are you going to be alright?"

Weiz didn't remember this person. At all. She squinted at the woman, then at the apparition that appeared behind her. Harvey. A smile crept onto her lips.

She reached a hand out to him, even as she toppled sideways. She couldn't move.

Everything was going to be fine. *He came for me, Papa. He came for me.*

~

Liza Gordon looked behind her at the Commanders smiling gesture. She knew Captain Harvey's face, of course, but she doubted he'd recognise hers, and so promptly got out of his way.

"I tried," she said lamely.

Harvey had his hands on the wound in Weiz's thigh. His expression was one of strain and fear. He murmured to the woman in soothing tones.

They were positioned just inside the door to the bridge, and she could see Ainsley was dead, a savage wound in the throat. Heinrich, equally as dead, with her last bullet in his head. There'd been no time for thought. And Greenway wanted them alive.

Since when do I care what Greenway wants? She shook her head. She felt she might have been in shock.

Someone bumped into her on their way to the bridge, and she glanced at them to see tattoos in the back of a bald head. Viatri, she thought his name might be. Or was it Sinatra? She wasn't sure. Either way, a Giant Killer.

No one seemed to notice her presence, or maybe they just didn't care.

~

Kristin twisted away from the grip of the airman and slammed him in the face with an elbow. His head cracked back with a satisfactory snap, and he fell to the ground unmoving.

Faster, stronger, heal faster, true. But getting hit in the face still darn well hurts. Motherfucker. She spat blood on the ground next to the prone form, rage seething barely beneath the surface. The punch had split her lip, and cracked a tooth. She hoped her regenerative powers would include righting that tooth. Otherwise, it would be a trip to the dentist, a prospect she did not enjoy.

She turned, expecting to face another townsperson, or perhaps an airman. But there was no one. She saw a few furtive figures running into the ship, but aside from the occasional rock fall, that was the only movement.

Looking up she saw that the roof of the building had contracted. Strange, that she had never wondered how they might get the ship out of the mountain. How the previous occupants of this city might have gotten it out.

She ran toward the ship.

A hand snapped out from the ground, and she tried to kick it off, but fell hard on her hip.

"For fuck's sake!" she yelled in frustration. So close, now.

The hand pulled at her ankle. She gazed down and tried to locate the head that belonged to the arm, but it was difficult in the gloom. The fires had mostly gone out. Rain was getting into the building.

She kicked out indiscriminately until her boot connected with something solid and the hand let go.

On hands and knees, she forced herself to her feet and limped for the ramp.

There was no way she was going to miss this ride.

EPILOGUE

He pulled the throttle lever up and began his ascent. The collapsing cavern had already destroyed half of the buried city, and the rubble still fell. It was going to be a risky ride, but Deidra assured him that they *had* to be in space before they could use the frequency generator, because the field was too wide, they'd take some of the villagers with them.

Behind him, Harvey was crouched over Weiz's limp body. Kristin sat at the controls for the light speed propulsion device, while Deidra had taken position next to him, ready to flip the switch on the generator as soon as they broke atmosphere. Xavier, as always, took his station at the Nav console.

Lance dodged out of the way of a large boulder, but debris still showered over the ship, a hail of chips and dust that clouded his view port. The engines whined — something had caught in them — then spluttered back to a roar, and they shot out of the cavern with room to spare.

Behind them, the mountain dwindled, the pressure of ascent

pushing the Pilot back in his chair. "No inertial dampening?" he yelled over the noise. He was becoming lightheaded.

"No time!" Deidra screamed back, though he barely heard her.

Within a few minutes, they broke atmosphere, and suddenly became weightless.

Lance eased off the acceleration and let them drift into orbit. He turned to Kristin and nodded.

She pressed a button, and the interior speakers came on. "All crew members in the rear cabin, we apologise for the unexpected turbulence and current zero-grav situation, but we should be shortly arriving at our chosen destination." She nodded at Deidra.

The Scientist pulled on a lever, and the engines took on a note of panic. "Three," she intoned. Then she pulled the next lever in the line. "Two." For the last she pushed a sequence of buttons. "Here we go."

It didn't feel like anything had happened. No great shuddering, no snaps or crackles, not even the slight EMP effect that they'd felt when they'd popped up in that other solar system.

"Are you sure that worked?" he asked.

Deidra spread her hands wide. "See for yourself."

Through the view port, at first a tiny spec no bigger than another star in the sky, Earth began to emerge. The familiar oceans and landmasses no more than smudges through cloud cover, were never-the-less the most welcome sight he'd seen in months.

We're home, he thought. It was so hard to believe. After the incident with the Giants, he'd been so sure he never would never see it again. And yet here they were.

There was cheering coming from the aft section as Kristin told them the good news. A grand total of seventeen, including themselves.

But as they drifted closer, fast approaching, something did not sit right in his gut. "There's something…" he said, but wasn't sure how to finish.

"Missing." Kristin nodded, a confused expression on her face.

"Perisus Station, Ultimus Station and The Docker Rack should all be visible by now," Xavier told them.

Harvey had gotten to his feet, tear-streaked face impassive as he looked upon his home world. "I can see my son," he said softly. It was difficult for Lance to look at him.

What can I say to that? I missed my music collection. I am looking forward to sleeping in my own damned bed. My parents might have missed me, but I rarely see them, and I like it that way. Harvey had just lost the love of his life and was replacing it with this need for family. A son he'd hardly ever mentioned. *Doesn't mean he wasn't thinking of the boy.*

"But we have this problem, sir," Kristin ventured.

Earth was so close now that it took up the entire view port, and the European Continent filled their vision. He'd have to take controls back up again soon and control their entry. But it was just that — they *had* to land. That shouldn't have happened. They were supposed to land on The Docker Rack.

The situation was giving him a little deja vu.

"I don't mean to be a party pooper here, Deidra, but what the hell is going on?" He braced them for a very bumpy re-entry sequence, aiming for a thirty-degree descent into atmosphere. He'd have to land them at ATF headquarters in Nevada.

"I can't say for certain," the Scientist told him. "But from the look of the satellite we just passed, I'd say we're not when we're supposed to be."

"When?" he queried. He wanted to make the eye tattoos dance, but somehow that didn't seem appropriate to the situation.

"Well, I had to make adjustments considering how we'd ended up where we did in the first place." She defended without heat. Pure logic. There was something cold in the way she spoke now.

"So," Kristin ventured. "*When* are we? And *how do we get back?*" Lance thought the tone of her voice told enough of the story for everyone.

Why the fuck is this shit happening to us? A single tour of Jupiter that should have taken six months, and instead... Even silently, in his own mind, he didn't know how to finish the thought.

Deidra shrugged as if it meant very little. "Somewhere between mid to late 1957," she told them.

Lance almost let go of the controls. *Doomed,* he thought. *We're never going to get* home.

ABOUT THE AUTHOR

Lee was born and raised in Sydney Australia. Prefers cats over dogs, coffee over tea, and cars over bikes. She also thinks the biography section of the book is a little strange.